LOVER'S
PARABLE

The LOVER'S PARABLE

Through
A Seven-World
Journey

BRADY MILLERSON

To my wife and children...
what a journey our lives have been.

CHAPTER ONE

Waves of fire glisten and spread across the surface of the fiery globe of the sky that the ancients of Planet Blue had once called the Savior. But through countless ages the meaning behind its name and its glorious history had become lost, relegated first to myth, then to random, natural motions. Although its primitive appellation would continue to be carried on through childhood dreams and stories of fantasy, the men of the world, growing ignorant and throwing aside the ways of their ancestors, would believe themselves to be nearing an age of matured reason. They began putting away their puerile past. Following in the footsteps of the masters of the age, the Savior would simply become an object known merely as the Great Star.

Like the wings of an infant bird, the Savior's arms spread out and sway across the expanse of space. In due time, just as the bird matures and attains to flight, so too do the arms of the Savior lift from their roots to reach out towards the heavens beyond.

The illusion of this molten plasma, twisting and flowing, spreading out into the blackness of the void, conceals the true wonder in its bosom, the fantastical assumption that it is a single entity, yet it is composed of many: the beauty of a single particle of energy. In the Savior's arms, they are more numerous than all the stars of the heavens. And each one has been destined for someplace, for somewhere and for someone.

Six spheres exist in a perpetual run upon their elliptical tracks within the Savior's realm. Since the beginning of time these planets have orbited this most brilliant star. Behaving as the vultures of death skating across a desert sky, they ever gaze solemnly at their sustenance below. They must, for this age, continue to be pressed along by an invisible force, encircling continually around that fiery object of which some believe to be a dying beast.

Of the six, there is one peculiar in its own right, as it appears to be illuminated with the radiance of the sapphire, bright and warm. But once again, the illusion has been granted, as nothing could be so beautiful without the illumination of the Savior to enlighten by way of reflection. And as it so happens, on this particular day, and at this particular moment in time, the Savior's arms have, as it has done for so many eons past, reached out to lay the tip of His finger upon Planet Blue.

A stream of heat and light blanket the shimmering world, filtering its luminescent particles through the dense layers of mist and smoke. Downward they flow, cutting through the thick atmosphere, dispersing the soft, pink warmth of morning upon the cold, gray covering of the City of Labor. Concrete pillars belch out their steam, rectangular structures decorated with dull, gray columns upon their faces that stretch up to the layers of pinkish-blue hues above. The Savior has extended his daily salutation.

Towering, concrete walls, *the Corral*, twist and turn upon the perimeter of the City. Even the buildings tall enough to peek over it have not been granted the windows necessary to provide a view of the surrounding countryside. It is a most well thought-out metropolis. So tightly packed together are these abodes of man, so ominously designed that never does the gift of light reach into their inhabitants' domains. The highest buildings stand closest to the city walls, then the next highest are layered within, then the next highest, then the next and so on. Each building's rooftop extends across and over-reaches the building before it, acting as an awning for its shorter counterpart, preventing the natural light above from creeping in.

For generations of workers, refraining from the glory of the Savior was the law, at first obeyed, and then embraced. He is not welcome to settle in the City, yet no one can recall why. As most inhabitants of Labor have never seen the world beyond their Corral, neither do they care about what is out there. This is what they have been trained into and conditioned to become. It is their duty to block Him out. So, buildings upon buildings are stacked in such a manner, shading all eyes from His glorious light.

Labor: the City of Work, the City of Drones, the City of Shadows and Perpetual Darkness. Ever moving, despite His unwanted presence, the Savior continues to paint the surfaces of all the City's towering peaks with His brightness.

The streets are crowded with a population of strong, hearty men and women. They move along the dimly lit sidewalks carrying materials and goods. Manually operated transporters of various sizes are in abundance: white, sterile automobiles with low powered, pumpkin-orange headlights roll through the streets, owned by the masters of the planet, men of which no citizen has ever seen. All the vehicles, of which the public has free access to, are at their disposal so long as they are used for the assistance of helping to keep the City functioning in its perfect order. The hum of the engines never cease as the automated production lines pump out various products for the consumption of the inhabitants of the City proper, the mysterious others fighting in distant lands and those living at the end of the mysteriously enclosed road known simply as *the Highway*.

High above the human automatons animating in procession and unquestioningly performing their duties, a youthful couple is perched at the lip of a rooftop. Their clothing colored with a deep contrast to the sterile whiteness of their surroundings. They sit with a warm and secure closeness. They are in a world of their own.

A gentle heat blows across Labor's concrete covering. The destination of the particles of light has finally been reached thousands upon thousands of kilometers from whence they came. They fall like a warm rain, caressing the tender cheek of Sofia and settling upon the face of John.

Sofia peered down at her feet dangling off the towering structure, a death-falling distance above the edge of the Corral. Somewhere in the eerie dimness beneath her, the men and women of the City continued about with their daily business, unappreciative and willfully unaware of nature's morning dance. They work.

That is all they do, she thought. It is what has always been done, will always be done, and no one will ever question as to what the end result is that they are trying to achieve.

"That Savior-rise was beautiful, wasn't it?" Sofia spoke in her still, soft voice.

John held her hand gently. For a moment he did not say a word. Then, as if a sudden joy had overcome him, he exclaimed, "Look! A wishing star!"

Sofia's eyes barely caught a glimpse of the hair-thin slash of light that split across a patch of deep blue. It was a wishing star: an unusual morning phenomena witnessed only by the free of heart and those willing to turn their backs on their economic captures. Neither she nor John knew anything about the cause of these rays of light that would appear and then suddenly vanish away. They were a most rare occasion so early in the morning, but quite frequent during the darkest moments of the night. And, although very few inhabitants (if any, as far as they knew) were aware of such a common occasion when the stars were lighting up the sky, she and John had kept it as their little secret that there is a time, when most of the city lies in slumber, that the wishing stars fill the firmament with a dance second in beauty only to the rise of the Savior.

As the dim slit faded into obscurity, Sofia leaned back on the cool, white surface of their Labor Apartment: Building 1A. With a sigh, her soft, blue eyes gazed upward into the sky. She was only fifteen, quaintly dressed in a plaid ribbon-topped dress with a white undershirt. Oddly enough, she wore cotton pants beneath her skirt. For despite her feminine appearance, she was clearly a tomboy at heart. But nevertheless, climbing up the pipes and cables that decorated and interconnected all the buildings in order to reach the differing levels of Labor's rooftops in only a dress, she believed, was still quite unladylike.

Her eyes were colored as the heavens themselves and John often commented that looking into them was like looking through her and seeing the sky beyond... but he meant it in a polite and endearing fashion. Although she understood what he meant, she quite often played the fool and pretended it offended her.

John shielded his face from the Savior as half of its body arose above the distant hills. It was now too bright to look into, and burning red eyes would be a dead-giveaway that he had been Savior watching... and with Sofia, no doubt. Carefulness was de jure when exposure was occasioned, as sun-baked skin was all the evidence needed to prove their disobedience.

John was just as soft spoken as Sofia. At sixteen years of age, the features of change, of which all boys must bear, had not made the appearance in even the slightest of hints. His dark hair was cut short, a *military cut* they called it. It was the style of which all the men wore. There was no other way. He was appareled in his usual dark, school-dress pants with a button up shirt. His black leather boots were tightly laced-up, ankle-wrapped and bow-tied... again, it is what all the men wore.

He glanced at his watch and said, "We'd better be getting to school."

"Already?" Sofia asked.

By the disappointment in her tone, John knew within his heart that she was just as desirous as he to stay on that rooftop all day. Going to the Education Building day in and day out was not how he wanted to spend his youth. Thousands of children crammed into the cold, sterile rooms to hear lecture after lecture. The exhaling of coldness, the lack of emotion and the fear instilled by their instructors: it was a process of breaking down and building up. John often pondered as to why it was that they were the only two beings in existence with feelings of uneasiness about all of it.

Although it was quite out of place considering his strict, regimented upbringing, at such a young and tender age the concepts of youthfulness and aging were very real processes for John's contemplation. How scary was the idea that there was to him an obvious, conscious effort being forced upon all children, so that the boys and girls of Labor would grow up to become like his own parents: the Monster and his wife. John shuddered at the thought of lying in his bed at night: the screaming, the cursing. How often he would slip out the front door without drawing anyone's attention, meet up with Sofia and lead the way silently down the hall to the Forbidden Room which housed the stairwell that would lead them to the rooftop. There they would breathe sighs of relief. Nobody would miss them, neither would anyone be checking in on either of their empty beds. What joy would fill their hearts as they freed themselves from those corridors of hatred: so many unhappy couples shouting and slamming, crying out in despair.

John's parents, like most adults in the City of Labor, were spiteful, always bickering and gnashing their teeth at one another. But the Monster was different than most of the other male adults. Perhaps it was John's close proximity to him by relation that made him feel this way, or even his direct dealings with the man that gave him that impression. Whatever was the cause for his consternation it did not matter, as he was a most frightful sight to behold. Having spent a considerable amount of time on the Red Plant, the Monster was notorious for his outbursts of violence. Whatever the Red Plant was, it had given him a remarkable temper of which he was unable to contain.

John had never inquired about the arena in which his father conducted his business. It was only by a sheer mishap that he had overheard his mother speaking to a neighbor about it, and even then he could not make out much detail. All he could gather was that his father had some direct hand in the ongoing wars taking place somewhere in the distant lands, somewhere at the end of the tunneled road that interconnected the City with this mysterious place.

The Monster was one of the several Labor inhabitants with access to that Highway: the heavily patrolled, asphalt road, which stretched from the edge of the City entrance to the distant unknown beyond the hills. Its entire length was covered over with concrete walls and ceilings, preventing anyone traveling it from seeing the grass and the trees of the surrounding world. The transporters that exited the City were filled with finished products that had been designed and assembled at one of Labor's many production facilities. The vehicles entering into Labor were loaded with raw materials gathered from unknown lands.

Permission was required to enter the Highway at all times. And every destination upon it was the same: a place where there was some apparent involvement with the Red Plant.

There was a guarded, red, brick passage, *the Gate*, which stood between the City and the Highway. It was a striking contrast to the sterile, grayish-white Corral that enclosed the City due to its crimson color, and also due to the fact that it was the only break in the entirety of the continuity of the wall. It had several aisles through which the workers would drive their transporters after being retinal scanned and positively identified.

Most of the work force, those individuals with authorization to perform their duties outside of the city, is similar in demeanor to the Monster, cruel and mean. For most of the populace, the Red Plant was a mystery of which the ignorant did not inquire about, a mystery of which John had no interest in discovering its truth.

Oftentimes, when they were alone on the rooftop, John would sit silently staring at the open, free land. These were the most serene moments of his life, and the most conducive times for pondering its deeper meaning. He wondered what his destination in life was and what was to happen when his education was complete. Would he become just another slave in an isolated cubicle, designing (as was his occupational appointment) machines for a cause of which he knew nothing about, for a war that had spanned further back in time than his historical knowledge possessed, even generations.

The war seemed to exist only on the tele-monitors, the news-prints and announcements during the Education lectures. A vague enemy existed somewhere. There were soldiers fighting. But these soldiers, they were not from Labor City. He had seen many pictures of them and motion captures of their hard fought battles. The thought of where they might be from was too perplexing. As far as he knew, neither he nor Sofia had ever met one. They were not related to anyone in the military, either. Although John did inwardly harbor a bit of envy with regards to their heroic exploits, it was a relief to know that he would not become one.

John knew that his life was prearranged: what type of position he would hold, where he would live, how he would live. It was *all* preplanned. At the end of the workday he would probably have to return to some pathetic grovel, like his parents' apartment, with nary any room to stretch out his legs and actually call *home*. Just as every married male in the building, he would probably bicker with an over-stressed wife that rapidly grew too old and ugly to have any desirable qualities. He would struggle to pay his rent, to pay for food, to pay for clothes. He would always *just make it* at the end of every paycheck. Most of his economic loss would go to the powers that be. Where the money went from there was as much of a mystery as the Red Plant, considering Labor seemed to require little maintenance to sustain it. These were the deeper thoughts of John.

But today there was a peculiar energy in the air. It seemed so different than all the past moments of their rooftop time together. There was a springing forth of inner light, like the grasping of an idea after spending many nights trying to comprehend some difficult concept. It filled up John's heart the moment that light from the dark void of space had fallen upon him. Even though his thoughts of the future were, at the same time, causing him to feel that familiar emptiness, he knew today was the day that he needed to do something about it. With a quick glance at the stair-step, concrete buildings, that bizarre pattern of gray, white sterility that marched out to the center of the city, John knew something was different. An acute desire to change his course in life was pressing upon him.

"Why don't we leave Labor forever," he asked, "and never come back?"

"John," Sofia's voice broke, as she sat up, pulling out a few strands of hair that had snagged on the uneven texture of the porous rooftop.

Her hand slipped out from under John's grasp as she attempted to rub the pain out.

"Leave? Leave to where?" she asked.

The rich green of the hills, rolling to the horizon, settled upon a bluish-white sky. It was the direction from which the Savior was traveling. Perhaps all this time it was a sign: the way to freedom. Was it their destiny to find their way up here? Was the direction of the rising light actually a path that was beckoning them to follow it to a land where they could be free to be together, to escape? Although nobody ever spoke to him of that which existed beyond the City's walls, John knew deep within his heart that there was a calling from something... or someone.

"How about out there?" he said, pointing towards the east.

Sofia did not answer him. She was just sitting, staring: a rational, existing being, visually consuming the environment. Although she was silent, he knew that she was actually considering the proposition, contemplating making that final run with him.

As the shedding of an article of clothing drops gently to the floor, so she let her hand fall back onto his. Sofia left her matted patch of hair untouched. The great beyond was before her: that immense mystery of their world. What could be out there, she thought. Was John just being silly, or was he onto something with that suggestion?

The flowering fields and grassy abundance were tempting her desires. What an adventure they would have.

Chapter Two

The metallic door creaked to a close. A single ray of Savior settled upon John's eye as he eased it shut. Sofia caught a glimpse of the thin, honey colored stream that narrowed to the width of a hair before fading away completely. The corridor was so dark that, had she not already known, she could not make out the slightest hint that John was in the room. At long last the blooming of the sickly red glow from the retinal scanner illuminated the Forbidden Area.

The Savior gazing ended in such a strange fashion, John thought. The two of them had never spoken like that before. It was a crime to speak of the outside world. How much more when conspiring with another person about an escape? They had already broken so many laws by leaving their colorless existence below, engaging with the illuminated world above. Planning an escape could not be any worse. Since they had found their rooftop paradise they had ipso facto made themselves enemies of the state. It was a fearful thought at what the punishment would be. But those few, fleeting moments of time together in their little slice of paradise was well worth anything that could be thrown at them, if they happened to be caught.

Time is such a strange concept. It goes by without notice. And the moment one notices the particular time of which one is thinking, that piece of time has already passed away. That moment of time is gone forever. These thoughts stirred in John's consciousness as the two of them bathed in the red light of the Forbidden Room. Where had the time gone and where would it lead?

It had been a couple of years since John and Sofia first happened upon the defunct scanner of the Forbidden Room. Passing through the ocean of people that commonly tread upon the sidewalks everyday as they were returning home from the Education, there was nothing in particular about the day that would lead them to believe that their lives would be changed, or that there was going to be an alteration in the way they would view their entire world.

For some odd reason, of which she had no previous inclination, Sofia passed her gaze upward just in time to see an object fall from their apartment's rooftop overhang onto the next building below. She beckoned to John to cast his eyes upward as well. But the object was already out of sight, as it could have only been seen for a fraction of a second due to the limited amount of space that was visible.

With a tight grip, Sofia wrapped her fingers around John's hand and pulled him closer to the curbside and out into the street. She wanted to move faster without being further hindered by the crowds.

"Come on. Let's go see what that was," she said with a laugh.

Although John momentarily considered holding Sofia back from her desire, deep down inside he was just as curious as she was to solve the mystery of what it was that she had seen.

After a great deal of maneuvering, it was not long before they made their way to the entrance of their apartment building. The swinging, glass doors slammed into the walls as they rushed through with the urgent intent of reaching their destination.

Arriving at the computer terminal mounted on the wall first, without hesitation Sofia peered into the camera of the retinal scanner. There was the familiar sound of the mechanical drive system stirring behind the two sliding, metallic doors of the elevator. The glowing red screen of the monitor was replaced by a green *approval* hue as the doors slid open, revealing the white-tiled compartment inside. They stepped in with haste, their bags dropping to the floor as they settled in for the ride.

Of the two of them, Sofia was the more adventurous. John was fond of adventure as well, but not nearly as fond as she, for it was Sofia who had always initiated the fun. And, although they really had not been on a *true* adventure before, they both felt that rapid beating of the heart, believing that this was the closest thing as they could possibly get to a genuine venture.

The metal railing was a familiar feeling pressing into their shoulder blades as they rested back against the walls of the upward moving vehicle. Living, as they both did, on the top floor, the ride always felt rather drawn out and slow. But today, that time-sticky feeling was even more pronounced. They were giddy with wonder at what they would find once they reached the Red Room that housed the Forbidden Door that opened to the rooftop.

With a ringing of the muffled, digital bells, the doors creaked aside, and John and Sofia hurried one another out. The hall, like the rest of the city, was cold and uninviting. It was partially lit by the low intensity, orange lights that were scattered across the ceiling, leaving patches of blackness along its eerie corridors. As they made their way down its poorly illuminated path, Sofia startled at the sound of a slamming door that echoed from around the corner and down one of the long, blackened walkways. She felt John pulling her back into the shadows as footsteps could be heard making their way from the same direction as the curious slamming.

It seemed as if many minutes of silence had passed, when suddenly, a silhouette appeared to round the corner several doors down. Whoever it was, he limped with a gait that neither of them recognized. One footstep was hard, making the clackity-clack sound of a shoe upon linoleum, while the other was soft and almost completely silent. The stranger slowly made his way to the threshold of apartment eleven-ten. His head looked this way and that way with an air of caution before bending over the apartment's door scanner.

The red light was glowing brightly as his eyes neared the cups. That is when the face of Mr. Sanders was momentarily exposed. The scanner had not only given away his identity, but it also grossly exaggerated the features of his already worn and wrinkled face, giving him the appearance of someone to fear.

Although John lived in the apartment directly in front of room eleven-ten, and Sofia's parents were housed just a little further down the hall, neither of them had very much contact with the man. He was a unique character in the building, readily recognized by the pair as the old loner with an oddly hunched back and a balding top with a horseshoe-shaped tuft of hair that wrapped around his head from ear to ear. He hardly ever spoke with anybody (especially after the Labor Security reassigned his wife to Restful Haven nearly two years ago). He was also the last of the aged engineers of his generation to live, or rather pass the time, outside of Restful Haven, the final destination where a worker was sent to expire.

Mr. Sanders gazed into the scanner's eyecups, accessing the security identification network. His face morphed from a blood, red tone to a sickly green as the *approval* screen appeared on the scanner's monitor. The door's lock released, then he disappeared into his abode. He closed the door with such gentleness that there was no sound until the automated-lock initiated.

John eased forward, careful to stay within the shadows. With his hand held tightly to Sofia's, he led the way forward. As they passed along the wall, just opposite Mr. Sanders' peephole, a muffled noise of mournful wailing filled the emptiness around them. Sofia's attempt to move into the light and press her ear against the door for a clearer sound was met with a silent waving of John's hand. He pressed his finger against her lips, motioning with his eyes toward the winding corridor that led to their original terminus.

They continued to move past several abodes, silently making their way through the apartment halls. It was quite the contrast with regards to the noise level when compared to the evenings when all the grown-ups had returned home from work and the cursing and screaming began.

At long last the Forbidden Room was in sight. It was a much more narrow access to the rooftop than either of them could have imagined. Having never entered into the Forbidden Area's glowing arena before, but only gazing upon it from a distance, there was an unexpected, liberating feeling that entered into both of their hearts upon seeing it so close.

With all the novelty that The Room had brought to them as they stepped their feet into it, there was one item of which they were both very familiar with, and it was quite apparent to them that something was askew. The retinal scanner, which allowed access through the Door, was intermittently flashing, something neither John nor Sofia had ever seen before.

Crouching down to get a closer look, John could see that the underside cover was missing. Upon further inspection, he noticed that a few wires had been cut from the circuit board and were pushed back into the body of the scanner, as if to be hidden from sight.

"Someone's been messing with this," he said with a curious look. "Maybe we should leave... before we get blamed. What do you think?"

Sofia thought for a moment before shaking her head in agreement. Reaching up and grasping the topside of the unit, John hoisted himself up. But an accidental depression of his finger across the retinal-sensor plate initiated a metallic click that emitted from the door jam, just beside the knob. The Red Room suddenly filled with that same sickly, green glow that had painted Mr. Sanders' face just moments earlier: *the glow of approval*. A mischievous smile formed at the corner of Sofia's mouth as her eyes passed a quick glance towards the doorknob and then back again at John.

"Oh, no, young lady. We're not going up there," John quietly protested.

"Oh, yes we are," she whispered. "Don't you want to see what that strange man was up to?"

"No. It's none of our business."

John began to walk toward the hall from which they had first presented. He had not taken but three steps before there came an interruption of his gait made by an abrupt tightness from around his neck. He was suddenly pulled backward by the collar.

"What are you doing? Stop that," he growled, pulling at his shirt.

"Please go up with me," Sofia giggled.

The curling of John's lip was a sure sign that he was thinking, thinking hard. Sofia walked up the small flight of steps to the roof-top entrance.

"Come on, we haven't got all day," she laughed.

"Alright," John spoke with a stutter. "But if we get caught up there, I'm never talking to you again."

With a triumphant smile Sofia slowly turned the knob to the Forbidden Door. A blinding gust of golden light filled their faces as it drew open, causing them to momentarily look away. Through squinted eyelids, their burning, watery view allowed only a glimpse of the blurry imagery of what there was before them, but it was beautiful. It was pure and fresh.

Their eyes quickly adjusted to their alien surroundings as they ascended the flight of stairs just beyond the doorway. Finding themselves standing high above the City, with a panoramic view unlike anything they had ever experienced in the past, neither John nor Sofia was able to say a word.

The expanse above them was so deep and blue, decorated with puffs and waves of all sorts of curious cloud formations. There were creatures of various feathered species flying in circular patterns. There was the Great Light burning in the sky of which no one spoke openly, but only that of which children handed down to children over many generations in their silly, mythical stories.

The walk to the rooftop's edge was exhilarating. They were, for the first time, able to openly see the rolling hills and thick green trees that spanned for an incomprehensible distance before disappearing over the horizon. It was obvious that there was nobody else with them. They were alone, but together.

Sofia peered into John's eyes with that irresponsibly playful smile again and slowly moved away from him. Her sly demeanor was letting him know she was gearing up for something adventurous.

"What are you up to, girl?" he questioned with a pseudo-authoritative tone.

Holding John's hand as she moved away, her steps were rhythmical, proceeding with a suspicious purpose. As their arms stretched out she suddenly dropped his hands and began sprinting across the concrete structure, leaping and laughing like a captured creature finally set free. John watched with delight for a moment. He was hesitant. But, upon seeing the stairs that would lead him back into his gloomy existence below, he knew that it would be foolish of him not to join in on the fun. Racing around, hopping over the pipes and cables that stretched here and there, it was the most incredible, and least expected, event of the day... in their lives.

Being the cautious person that he was, John's running area was further from any of the drop-off points at the edges of the roof than Sofia's. But as the calming comfort of being far from the misery of daily living was settling in, he began to make wider his playful perimeter. It was not long before he realized that he was at the edge of the apartment that faced inward into the city. He was gazing out over the same place from which the mysterious body was seen falling from the street below. He slowly dropped to his knees, guardedly creeping towards the edge, overlooking the rooftop of the next building. There was an object, brown and shiny, propped up against a lattice of gray and white pipes and cables. It looked terribly out of place.

"Sofia, come. Look," John yelled pointing towards his discovery.

Sprinting from the other side of the building, leaping and howling, Sofia strode up beside him, panting and out of breath. Holding onto his arm, she peered over the side.

Glancing at each other with heartfelt smiles, it was hard for them not to laugh at the thought of the *limping man* in the hallway. The mystery was solved, and the outside world was unmasked for their pleasure... all because of Mr. Sanders, whom, having left a personal item of his as evidence that he was up on that rooftop earlier, would now be one shoe short of a pair. Sofia's face was aglow. And John knew that henceforth, nothing would ever be the same again.

The most beautiful things in the world had been hidden from them: the warm rays of light, the gentle, blue sky, the rustling leaves of the trees outside the wall. The breeze of life sifted through the short bangs of John's hair. A new world had been waiting for them. A new world was found.

Peering around the corner, John was surprised to find the glow of artificial light emanating from under the door of his parent's apartment. They never left the lights on if they were not home. With the morning having become quite worn, they should have been gone by now. But the shadowy beams that broke through it made him question whether or not they had, for some odd reason, not left for their work quarters for the day.

"Why are the lights on?" whispered Sofia.

"I'm not sure," John said, as a puzzled expression smeared across his face. "Maybe they left without turning them off."

Although the words fell from his mouth, he knew it was not true. Something was not quite right.

"Wait here," he whispered.

As he edged forward, each step seemed to increase the volume of the thumping of his heart, causing an intense pressure to build in his head. When he finally reached the door, he pressed his ear against its cold, white metal. There were voices inside! He quickly glanced at his watch. At this time of the morning nobody should be home!

The loose, metallic release of the door's security lock caused John to step back. He looked down the hall at Sofia.

"Find a way to get to the hills, girl. I'll meet you there," he called out.

Sofia's hair fluttered about her face by the force of rushing air that rippled throughout the hallway as the door was torn open.

"There you are!"

It was *he*... the Monster!

"Where have you been, John? Star gazing again, no doubt," he roared, "Do you think we're that stupid? Do you really think we don't know? You've been up there-on the rooftops- with that... that girl, haven't you?"

Sofia pressed herself against the wall trying to stay still and hidden in the darkness. John's white shirt crinkled between the fingers of his father's hand. His head snapped back under the violent convulsion of the Monster yanking and dragging him into the apartment. The floor beneath her trembled in synch with a heavy, dull report that echoed in her ears, like the sound of John's body dropping to the floor.

The Monster stepped back out into the hallway. He was burly and cold. By the faint light of the apartment he appeared to be split in two: half black, half revealed by the dull glow. His thick arms protruded out from his broad shoulders, hung high off the ground by his unusually long, thin legs. His eyes seemed to be scanning the cross cut shadows, moving back and forth... back and forth. He was patient and calculating. Then suddenly he stopped and stared straight ahead. It appeared that he had caught sight of something that needed his attention... something at the corner where Sofia lay huddled in terror. He took one step forward, paused, then took another.

A tear drizzled down Sofia's cheek. The creature was closing in on her. The hallway suddenly filled with screams and cursing, issuing out of the walls where John had been taken, and yet, the cautious, clacking sound of the Monster's shoes on the linoleum floor kept their pace. Like drum beats playing to the tune of the shattering glass and John's cries, closer and closer they moved.

Sofia wanted desperately to go to John, but there was no way. She had to get out of there before it was too late. She was not supposed to be there. She was supposed to be sitting at her desk in the Education right now. And the worst part of all: the Monster knew of their paradise on the roof! She had to move. She needed to move! Pulling herself up to her feet and preparing for her escape was absolute. John would find her if she fled to the hills by herself... he had to! Whatever was beyond the walls, she thought, had to be better than this place. What could possibly be worse?

The only way to escape was down the elevator or through the fire escape. There was no other way to get away from the approaching beast. Due to its location alone, the elevator was out of the question. The fire escape, on the other hand, was down the corridor near the Forbidden Room. Opening it would certainly set off the alarms. She could make for the rooftop. Over the years she and John had figured out ways to reach all of the buildings with little effort. With no one to see them they had become quite adept at using the system of cables and pipes that connected all the structures in the city. That was her only recourse, her best chance to make it away safely. Getting down to the streets and then finding a way out of the Corral would be the most difficult task of all, but it was not something she could let herself be concerned with at the moment.

By the sound of it, the steps appeared to be within an arm's reach around the corner. It was now or never. With that thought, she turned to make her way back to the Forbidden Room, but found herself face to face with Mr. Sanders. The old man quickly pressed the palm of his hand against her mouth.

"Say nothing," he whispered.

His large fingers firmly coiled around Sofia's upper arm. He quickly, but quietly, guided her along the hallway into the crimson glowing of the Forbidden Area. Pulling her out of the doorway he pressed her against the wall.

Sofia did not fight him. She obeyed, not out of fear of the old man, but out of fear of the approaching Monster. Mr. Sanders peered around the corner. Deep wrinkles protruded from his face, giving him a terribly contradictory appearance relative to the assistance that he was providing at the moment.

From Sofia's position, the hall appeared to be alive as the shadows of the Monster swayed to and fro, seemingly reaching out to them. As the echoing, methodical tapping of his footsteps suddenly stopped, Mr. Sanders reared back, pressing himself heavy into the wall, as if he were trying to become one with its material being. As the beads of sweat began to form around her helper's temples, Sofia could smell the mildew-like perspiration spilling from his pores. The Monster was near. He was coming for them.

The glaring eyes of madness had made their way to the opposite end of the hallway leading up to the Forbidden Room, squinting with a suspicious aura. As the tone of John's screams intensified, the Monster, looking back from whence he came, hesitated.

Then, returning towards the direction of his abode, he retreated. The tap, tap, tapping of his footsteps faded away until they were heard no more.

CHAPTER THREE

Mr. Sanders' apartment was similar to the one Sofia's parents lived in, maybe a little more decorated, but none-the-less similar in all other aspects. She sat on a dark wooden, four-legged, flower patterned sofa set against a lime-green wall. There were old pictures hanging about the room of what appeared to be Mr. Sanders and his wife when they were much younger. With a hint of suspicion she watched the old man gathering some teacups and small, porcelain plates from the cupboard as he slowly prepared something for the two of them to snack on.

There was a light rising of steam twirling up to the ceiling from a shiny, stainless steel kettle that whistled from the stovetop. He placed a couple of teabags into the cups and, as he began to pour the water from the kettle, his hand revealed a tremor that, under most circumstances, was otherwise unnoticeable.

Henry Eugene Sanders was his full name. He was as equally well known in the city of Labor as John's father, the Monster. He was the oldest person in the complex, perhaps even the oldest person in the history of Labor to not get sent to Restful Haven upon reaching such a late term in life. He was a rather plump man with a peculiar, horseshoe-shaped mustache that tapered inwards at the edges of the lips, giving him a rather somber demeanor, even if he was not actually feeling sad. His nose was somewhat round and large, supporting a pair of circular spectacles near its tip. He walked with a slow, steady gait, as if he were sore somewhere on his body that he was not complaining about. And although he was not short in stature, his suspenders held his pants a little higher than the waist, giving the illusion that he was lacking in the height department. He also had a distinct way of speaking, using exaggerated gestures with his arms and hands.

"I've been watching you two," he said.

The corners of his mouth pulled back, creating ripples upon his pale cheeks, an odd half-smile spread across the left side of his face. It was a discomforting statement, to say the least. How long had he been *watching* them, she wondered, fearfully drawing the conclusion that he was going to turn them in to the Labor Security. The revelatory declaration was quite unnerving. As she was now unable to maintain eye contact with the man, Sofia nervously looked around the room.

"I know that the two of you are thinking of running," he said, turning and pointing toward the wall, in the direction of which the Savior set. "To the hills, right... out there?"

For a brief moment the desire to lie began to build up within her, but Sofia refrained, choosing to remain silent instead. He seemed so sincere, in a foreign sort-of-way, as if he wanted to help, but, what his actual motivations were she could not discern.

The cushions of the sofa were beginning to show their thinness as she fidgeted about in the seat, trying to get comfortable. Having both the physical and mental uneasiness at such a disconcerting time was nearly all Sofia felt she could endure. Her head was beginning to throb as she fought back the urge to let herself go, to completely and emotionally let her mind break down.

Mr. Sanders began to open his mouth, as if to complete his thoughts, but he was caught unawares, interrupted by the muffled yelling and screaming emanating from John's parent's apartment across the way. It was beginning again, trickling through the door, instilling a fresh assault on the auditory senses. Casting his gaze in the direction of the voices on the other side, Mr. Sanders' expression of concern revealed somewhat more to Sofia that his motives were other than malicious.

"That boy's getting a good lickin' about now, yes indeed," he mused before glancing back at Sofia. "But, I don't want you to worry about that right now."

Placing the cups and porcelain plates, served with slices of bread, onto a two-handled tray, he gathered up their late morning refreshments. Steadily walking over to Sofia, he set the tray on the coffee table situated in front of her. Pulling up a chair with a matching, flowery-patterned seat, he sat down, simultaneously scooping up one of the teacups.

His eyes disappeared behind his steam-fogged glasses as he lifted the cup to his mouth and took a sip, giving him the appearance of some kind of bizarre android with digitized visual organs.

"Go on, now. Help yourself," he said.

Hesitating for a moment, Sofia politely gathered up her teacup and began to take a drink. Another muffled scream brought her to a pause. With a quivering lip, she eased the teacup away from her lips, forcing herself to swallow what sweet liquid had made itself into her mouth.

"I was about your age when the misses and I met," Mr. Sanders began again, picking up a tarnished picture frame from off of the coffee table. "We were so in love, Helen and I."

He turned the picture toward Sofia.

"This was Helen, my wife", he said, gently handing the picture frame to her, as if it were a newborn child.

It was not an unfamiliar face Sofia was looking at in the photograph. She remembered seeing Helen Sanders many times as they passed one another in the hallways and on the busy sidewalks, sometimes even riding up the elevator with her.

She had been a secretary down the street before being taken. And although, in the past, she and Sofia had several close physical encounters, Sofia had never once spoken with the woman. With the exception of John, Sofia gave little mind to the other citizens of Labor. They just existed.

Yet, something about the black-and-white image was quite odd to her. The picture was not exactly the same Helen she had the occasion of seeing. The photograph before her was different and more composed: it was the picture of a Helen that was young and lively. She generally looked the same, of course, except that the thin, gray hair that Sofia remembered her to be adorned with was flowing so vibrant and healthy, her skin was so smooth and her eyes so bright. This was a woman from a different era, a different time altogether. This was the woman that Mr. Sanders was in love with.

From above his steam-coated lenses, Sofia could make out what appeared to be the formation of tears at the inner corners of Mr. Sanders' eyes. A flushing sensation spread across her cheeks as she noticed that he was staring at her with a protective affection. As she handed Helen's memorial back to him, Mr. Sanders received it with earnest, grasping her by the hand. Leaning forward, his voice was soft, almost private in tone.

"We often spoke of running, too," he said.

Slipping her hand away from his, Sofia could feel that recently experienced, startling uneasiness beginning to fill up within her heart once again. Although it had been waning while staring into the comforting eyes of Helen that appeared to gaze back at her from the photograph, it was now a mixture of fear and curiosity, a dreadful denouement that was exposing to her that someone had somehow heard her speaking with John today on the rooftop. That had become one of their most intimate secrets, as equally secret as the Savior watching and wishing stars. And yet, this complete stranger had somehow become privy to their dreams.

"What do you mean?" Sofia stuttered.

Sinking back into the chair, accompanied by the creaking of its old wooden frame, Mr. Sanders smiled.

"Oh, come now, I've seen you two up there," he said, pointing to the ceiling. "You can see right over the Corral, can't you? The hills are covered with trees. Trees are everywhere, as far as the eye can see."

With an accusing smirk on his face he leaned forward and said, "They're quite inviting, too, aren't they?"

Sofia did not answer the question. Her nervously wandering eyes were speaking for her. Mr. Sanders reclined back once more and said, "Yes, indeed. I've been watching you two for quite some time: roof hopping, swinging around the cables, walking across those structural, connecting beams. The smiles on your faces and..."

He hesitated and took another look at his Helen in the picture, "...and the way you two would hold hands."

He cast a glance to Sofia from above his spectacles and said, "I've been there, too."

Standing up, he took a deep breath before walking to another picture hanging within a rustic frame upon the opposing wall.

"We were just too old and unfit to survive out there," he said, turning around. "But, we did have a plan. We had everything planned."

He strolled over to an old wooden, roll-top desk. The tremble of his hands appeared to increase in intensity as he slid open a small, hidden drawer nestled within its side. Black as coal was the aged box that he exposed to Sofia's eyes. With a queer expression of determination, he picked it up, placed it against his chest and brought it over to her, setting it upon her lap.

"Go ahead. Open it," the old man gestured with his hands, as if he were the one opening the ebony colored package.

The top of the box slid off with ease. Inside, wrapped within a thin, white paper, Sofia found a peculiar knife with a blade that folded into its own handle, a brass compass, a monocular instrument and a black leather notebook.

Lifting the book out of the box first and fanning through all the pages, the familiar aroma of fresh air and green trees filled the air. The leather of the book was worn and limp from, what appeared to be, extensive use. Upon closer examination it was some type of homemade, field manual. There were drawings of edible plants, maps for locating water sources, shelter designs and other relevant items for such a book as this. But, what caught Sofia's eye as the strangest wonder was a sketching that spanned the entire last page and onto a piece of matching paper glued to the inside of the back cover. It was a bird's eye view of Labor City, but it was scaled to about one centimeter. Surrounding it was an extensive, hand-drawn, topographical map of a single landmass upon, what had to have been, their tiny planet: the hills, the mountains, the streams and rivers. There were places noted with question marks. Some were drawn with skulls and crossbones surrounded by square perimeters made up of Xs done up in red ink. A thin, black line, which apparently represented The Highway, extended northeasterly out of Labor. It was long and winding, continuing for quite a relative distance before heading due east and finally terminating at a picture of some type of flying apparatus that was surrounded by more red Xs.

To the west of Labor, nearly equidistant to the city as the image of the flying machine was to the northeast, there was drawn another rather peculiar object, a sketch of another flying machine. But this one was different. It was broken in half and entangled among the trees. It had the words *food and shelter* scribbled next to it in large print, bold and underlined.

Sofia placed her finger on the picture of the northeasterly compound. "What's this?" she asked.

With lowering brows, Mr. Sanders began to take on a more serious demeanor.

"That's a place I do not want either of you to ever go near... ever! Do you understand me? It's..."

A sudden crash, accompanied by the creaking of the opening of a door outside, caused him to stop mid-sentence. Quickly, but silently, Mr. Sanders made his way to the front door, placing his ear heavy against it. Holding out his arm with a hushing sound towards Sofia, she realized that she had made a rustling of the wrapping paper that was held in her hand beneath the leather book. Ceasing her activity, she would only move at his command.

Chapter Four

The warmth of the blood smeared across John's forearm as he wiped the oozing liquid from his mouth. He did not want to open his eyes... he did not want to look again into the stinging glare of the Monster standing before him. The throbbing of his temples caused the tears to trickle down his cheeks, tinged in crimson as they passed through the cuts and abrasions that painted his face. Winded and panting, a nauseated feeling engulfed his stomach as the saltiness of the tears ended their journeys, filtering through his lips and onto his swollen tongue.

John had found himself in similar positions to this in the past, but something more sinister was bearing down on him this time. Beatings were not an uncommon event. Not for him or for any child of Labor, for that matter. The linoleum floor, cool and lonely, a familiar site from the perspective of which he now existed, was just another reminder of the wastefulness of life within the Corral. But, the pounding of his head, coupled with the reeling of his mind, was much worse than he had ever experienced. He felt as if Death himself was looking over his shoulder. John, for the first time in his life, believed that the Monster's abuse was clothed with a hatred that could only end in his own demise.

"Get off the floor," the Monster growled.

The searing pain in his body made it difficult to move, let alone any thoughts to bearing his own weight. But, he knew the game: if he disobeyed the miserably, sadistic creature standing before him, he would be soon to suffer a worse fate under the further release of the man's anger.

Forcing himself to roll over in an attempt to push his body up off the floor, John could feel a rib, maybe two, rubbing their cracked edges together. Pulling in a deep breath while splinting his side with his arm, his lungs filled with the stale air of the apartment. He was, at a minimum, thankful that they were not punctured.

As the lids of eyes drew back, he could make out the immense violence that he had endured: there were streaks and sprays of blood on the wall next to him, and puddles that were scattered across the room, even forming beneath his partially lifted body. But from where it was dripping he could not determine, as his whole essence at the moment was a mass of agony.

"You're going to the Academy today, John. You're going to learn how to be a productive citizen of Labor. And you're going to love it," the Monster yelled in his ear.

In the pooling, liquid life that was falling from his wounds, John could see the Monster's distorted reflection staring back at him. Like the reflection from some macabre mirror as described in the old children's fairy stories of many years gone by, it was a terrifying site to behold. It was as if the Monster's reflection was his own and he was actually looking at himself. Perhaps it was a sign of why today he *should* die: because that reflection was his future. Maybe this was the end: no more Sophia, no more roof-top adventures, no more light of the Savior to settle upon him. If the Monster was not bluffing, then everything worth living for was gone.

John knew in his heart that, if he were going to the Academy, he would be going to the grave, yet living. The incinerators of Restful Haven seemed so inviting: a flash of light, perhaps even a fraction of a second of pain, and the blackness of death would cover him forever. But he was, unfortunately for this moment in time, not elderly. He was a youth. And he understood that he was about to be sent to a place of which, if he should survive its paces, his return to Labor would be in the state of suspension of all reality. He would continue to exist, not as John, but as the engineer, the worker, the drone, the obedient. Whatever they wanted him to be, that he would be.

Like all the tales of ghosts and goblins and other such stories that children mature out of, the Academy was similarly held in the same mythical status by all the school-aged persons of Labor. It was a common term found in an idiom expressed whenever a child was disobedient: *the Academy walls must have your name written upon them.*

Although there was always the insubstantial threat of being dragged away to its dungeons, John had never known of any of his classmates, or anybody from the past few graduating classes for that matter, to be so dysfunctional that they needed to be sent there. There were stories of torture and deprivation, various abuses and even death to those that entered its iron doors. It supposedly existed in a cold and sterile, brick and mortar building that was erected somewhere just outside Labor's Corral. It was not known whether it truly existed or not, but most of the youth believed that there was something out there, something to fear should they ever get too far out of line.

Struggling to pull his knees in closer, there was a sudden tightening of his shirt from around his ribs. Taking in even the shallowest of breaths became next to impossible. The crimson, mirrored image was falling away, and the ugly reflective surface was coagulating into a plastic-like dullness lacking any luster. The Monster's grunting and panting was a sign of the strain his muscles were enduring as he lifted John to his feet.

"Time to stop playing games now, son. We need to be going," he said.

The vise-like grip he held upon John's shirt eased up as the Monster was seemingly satisfied that John was able to maintain his balance without any assistance. As the strain around his torso relaxed, John was finally able to take in that much needed air in order to gather his senses.

From the corner of his eye he noticed a figure standing behind the beastly man. Realizing that it was his mother brought him no comfort whatsoever, as the moment he made eye contact with her, he could see that she was staring at him with that same mask of insanity that the Monster wore.

Strangely, at such a miserable time, there were details of the woman of which John was able to absorb. Her blouse was an impressive sight: a common, gray-white secretary shirt that had the appearance of being sloppily decorated with a can of red spray paint. The underside of her chin and several areas of her skirt exhibited the same splattered pattern. From which wound of his she had ostensibly received this ghastly adornment John could not be certain. Was it from his head, his arms, or his back? It could have been from any one of these... but for now it didn't really matter.

Her open hand lifted up high above her head, as if she was about to give a pledge. Without warning, it was brought down upon the side of John's face with such an intense force that it sent salivated projectiles exiting from his nose and mouth, splashing upon the Monster's shoes.

"You're finished here," she grumbled.

John's underarms burned, as if hot coals were being forced into them, as his two tormentors took hold of him and dragged him to his room. When they released him he dropped to the floor, limp and pale. He could hear the Monster leaving, walking away, his footsteps audibly waning down the hall.

The sounds of someone rummaging through the closet outside echoed throughout the apartment as articles of clothing and stored items were being thrown around, crashing to the floor and walls. The man then returned, panting and enraged. With one final blow, a suitcase was thrown upon John's abdomen causing him to curl up writhing in pain, coughing and sobbing.

"Pack your things. We're leaving in 10 minutes," the Monster spoke before exiting the room once again, followed by his sneering wife.

As she passed through the doorway, he could hear the steps of his mother pause as she turned back with an evil eye. The blackness of the world was closing in on him as she closed the door, saying, "Whatever you've not placed in the luggage will be thrown out."

The loneliness that had blanketed his being when he awoke on the floor after an unknown period of unconsciousness was now more than he could bear. He wanted to let himself drift off to the long sleep of death. But as strong as his will was to make a final exit from the world, he knew that, just as in birth, it was not his to command.

As the frigidness of the hard floor began to seep through his shirt, stealing the precious heat of his being, he began the endeavor to move forward, to live, not for his own gain, but for Sophia.

His body could be broken and shattered, but there was something that existed within him that he knew could never be destroyed. With all the strength he could muster he took to his knees, resting his head upon his bed and weeping. He ran his hands across the familiar smoothness of his sheets with the full realization that it would be the last time he would feel the soft warmth of cotton for a very long time, perhaps, ever again.

"There must be someone who could help," he sobbed. "Anyone. This couldn't be all there is. There must be something more. Help me please, Great Savior... or You, the Great Unknown beyond my understanding! Please, help me. Please, help Sophia."

The tension of John's muscles began to settle. For some odd reason he gained a peculiar feeling of freedom that was suddenly overcoming his entire inner universe.

He was contemplating for a moment about the peace that had entered into his soul, when an acutely strange awakening brought him back into the sensual world. Within his palm he felt a hard, squared object. He had unknowingly moved his hand under his mattress, sliding it above the surface of the box spring. Pulling his arm out, he realized that he had happened upon an old, yellowed, folded letter from Sophia that he had hidden several years ago. Spreading out the note, he lifted it to his eyes and read:

John,

Should our Savior cease to shine, or to the Haven I must go to rest my body and mind, my love for you will never die. You will live with me beyond death itself. You will always be a part of me.

Yours forever,

Sofia

A tickling drizzle fell across his cheeks, as John's tears dripped from the edge of his jaw line, falling upon his legs. He was joyful and terrified in his heart, neither feeling being more dominant. Folding up the letter he placed it into his pocket. The journey ahead was not going to be easy, but he knew he would survive no matter what was about happen to him.

CHAPTER FIVE

Fighting to keep the pace that his parents were dictating, John's limped gait made his escort to the elevator one more torturous event that he had to endure.

Keeping watch from his peephole, Mr. Sanders knew from the fact that John's parents, having not gone to work this morning, as well the severity of the beatings they had been giving to the boy, would make the Academy the most likely of places where the young man's journey would end.

"This isn't good. No, indeed," he said.

Sofia's eyes lifted with concern, "What's not good? What do you see?"

"No good at all," he repeated.

Attempting to gain Mr. Sanders' attention seemed a futile task. He continued to stare at the floor, mumbling under his breath. He was too caught up in his thoughts to pay Sofia any mind. He glanced about the room as if searching for something. His eyes appeared wide and frantic as if he were trying to figure out a solution to John's predicament.

Pacing about the room, the leather of his shoes creaked upon the hard floor with each step. In the still silence the sound was almost deafening. Mr. Sanders walked over to the sink and turned on the faucet. He splashed some water on his face. Picking up a towel and drying himself off, he immediately turned back towards Sofia. With a smile and a snap of his fingers, he said, "Wait here. I'll be right back."

As he proceeded out into the hallway, from down the corridor Sofia could hear the elevator door closing and the Monster's voice, deep and muffled, was cut off in the process. The apartment door was beginning to shut when Mr. Sanders peeked his head back inside saying, "Don't go anywhere, okay. Just wait here for now."

He began to close the door once again, but hesitated, saying, "And, um... be ready to move fast when I return."

And with those words he winked his eye and walked away, shutting Sofia inside his apartment.

Gathering up the black box and all of its belongings, Sofia set it upon her lap, folding her hands over it. She knew that she had to patiently wait for him, to trust the old man.

The threshold leading to the hallway, worn and dreary, reminded her of the horrors of the reality of her situation. She could envision the Labor Security forces crashing through it, weapons drawn, the splintering metal and wood tearing through the space between her and them. Reminding herself that it was only a potential reality did not bring any consolation. It actually only existed in her head. Nowhere else, she thought, trying, to no effect, to assuage her fears.

Alone in the dimly lit apartment, Sofia's silhouette was a flat, black substance cradled on a piece of old, wooden furniture with a lime green backdrop.

CHAPTER SIX

The sterile, white car sat parked under a dim, orange light, just one amongst a scattered dozen of the identical vehicle in the underground parking structure. Seeing it was a relief to John, as his legs could scarcely carry him much further. The Monster was trying to get as much anguish out of him as possible. This was verified all the more in John's thoughts, as his captor had chosen the furthest vehicle he could find from the elevator.

"It's going to be a rough ride from here on out," the Monster commented with his head held high. "No more fun and games for you."

Glaring down out of the corner of his eye, he gave a snide smirk of success as he witnessed John moaning and grimacing in pain.

With only three cars to go before he could finally get some rest, there arose a familiar voice that prompted the three of them to put a halt to their trek. The voice reverberated off of the concrete walls and ceilings, disguising the direction from which it came.

"It's about time you teach that boy a solid lesson," said Mr. Sanders. "He's been asking for a sound beating for quite some time, has he not?"

Turning back towards the elevator lobby, the Monster grasped John by the shirt collar keeping him from falling over. John's mother smiled and said, "Hello, Mr. Sanders."

Her eyes then cast upon John to whom she scowled and said, "Mr. Sanders is one of the finest men in the City. You could only wish to grow to be half the man he is. He's given his whole life to the work we do here, never complaining, always busy."

Mr. Sanders belched out a laugh, saying, "We are all great men when we work for the cause."

Like the blind patriot that he was, the Monster took comfort in the words, and John could clearly see it written upon his face.

"Our boy has been caught performing some of the most heinous acts today," the Monster said. "Would you believe that he's been on the rooftops watching the Great Star rise and set?"

Mr. Sanders' feet fidgeted in discomfort.

"You don't say. On the rooftops, eh?" he asked, clearing his throat. "What, in Labor, could you be doing up there, son? You, um, shouldn't be doing that. That's not good. No, indeed."

John caught a glimpse of the suspicious glance that shot from the Monster towards Mr. Sanders, but, it was obviously only meant to be seen by his mother. The odd lowering of his brow coupled with the peculiar squint was quite queer, as if he thought the old man was acting strangely.

The Monster spoke, "We've had enough of his rebelliousness. We've tried our best. But, he's going to the Academy today where he'll be straightened out for good."

By the puzzled expression that Mr. Sanders face was exhibiting, John was unable to discern the meaning of the bizarre communication transpiring among the adults. He had never actually seen them talking together in the past, nor had he ever seen them interact in any manner other than dropping passing salutations to one another. They were at odds with each other, yet they were not.

"Oh, my," Mr. Sanders said. "The Academy! You have been bad. Yes, indeed. Very bad, I must say."

Gesturing with his hand to the Monster to step a little closer, Mr. Sanders took him by the arm, moving the man a few feet away from John and his mother. Huddling together, the two of them began to discourse in mumbles and whispers.

The audible murmurings taking place between them were mostly of a softer nature, but it was intermingled with several moments of course verbal encountering. Unable to comprehend any of their words, John could see that the conversation flowed back and forth equally between the two participants.

The old man's hand gestures were subtle, refusing to give away any hints as to their topic of discussion. Suddenly the Monster burst out in laughter, patting his elder on the back. They both turned to John.

As he approached with a smile, Mr. Sanders said, "Come with me, son. I want to talk with you for a moment."

Placing an arm around the young man, as if he were an old friend, Mr. Sanders led him back down the path from which he had come. Out of sight from his parents, he had brought the suffering boy back into the elevator hall.

A cloudy and disorienting effect was beginning to settle within John's head as the pain began to wear deeper into his body. Feeling the weight of Mr. Sanders' arm pressing upon his shoulder caused his stomach to churn. The old man, recognizing John's frail condition, assisted him as best he could as he moved them towards the elevator's retinal scanner. Looking back, making sure they were not being followed, Mr. Sanders peered into the security lenses.

It took a few minutes, but in a moment the door opened and John's elder, anxiously looking over his shoulder, ushered John in to the elevator car. Nervously pressing the button to get the elevator moving to the top floor, Mr. Sanders began to grumble and curse under his breath as the doors refused to shut and the Monster's voice, inquiring from around the corner, resounded with concern and distrust.

"Is everything alright Mr. Sanders?" the Monster called out.

The old man's head protruded out of the threshold of the elevator, saying, "We're doing fine. I'm just about finished talking with him."

His shaking, wrinkled finger tapped upon the button once again, but there was no response. The doors continued to remain wide open.

With a frantic look in his eye, he pressed it several more times. But still the doors would not close.

"Alright, Mr. Sanders," the Monster said with an obvious irritation in his voice, "we need to be leaving now."

"Yes, thank you, Mr. Sanders," John's mother called out. "But we really must be going. It's getting quite late."

The brisk hustle of footsteps from within the garage began with a tone that meant business. Mr. Sanders moved John further back into the elevator, as if to shield him from an approaching storm. By the increased volume of the tapping of the shoes it appeared that his parents would be rounding the corner at any moment. The old man closed his eyes and began to speak in an eerie whisper to someone, yet no one else, besides he and John, was present. By the expression on his face and the tremble in his voice, it appeared that he was pleading for help. Unable to control his legs, John held on to the familiar, cold railing and slid to the floor.

The voice of the Monster was beginning to rise just beyond the entrance to the lobby when the vibration of the doors and the humming of the motors began. At the moment of the first motion towards closure, the Monster's shadow became clearly visible, stretching forth with a ghastly display of elongated limbs protruding off of a thin trunk. The footsteps were now just within reach of the elevator car and closing in fast. The doors finally met, sealing the two parties one from another. Opening his eyes with a sigh of relief, Mr. Sanders looked down upon the broken young man, sickly and limp, at his feet.

"Okay, my little friend," he said. "There's no turning back now."

With a pious lifting of the head, facing upward towards a sky of which he could not see, Mr. Sanders closed his eyes and said, "Yes, my dear, today I'll be coming home."

The screeching sound of the elevator doors opening from down the hall brought Sofia to an unnerving attention. Standing up and listening intently, she could make out the sounds as of an animal panting and struggling, which was fast approaching.

"Sofia," came a soft, but strained, whisper.

Cautiously moving to the door, she pressed her ear firmly upon it, discerning the distinct groaning just outside.

"Sofia, open the door, it's me," the whisperer repeated.

Hesitating for a moment and thinking that, perhaps, maybe it was a trap, she refrained, not even daring to peer through the peephole for fear that the dimming light that was passing through it would give away the fact that she was actually inside.

"Sofia, please hurry. There isn't much time," the unfamiliar voice spoke with urgency.

With a trembling lip she closed her eyes, knowing that the Monster could be standing on the other side. Her mind began to wander as if she had lost control of her thoughts. Hovering above what appeared to be her body, she could see herself sitting upon the edge of a building, feet dangling above the streets below. The light of the Savior was caressing her face. And, although she was merely a spectator in this vision, there was a soothing blanket of heat passing through her on its journey towards her likeness. As a queer calmness began to grow deep within her, she settled her heart to accept whatever the consequences of opening the door were.

The lock's bolt was cold to the touch. As she began to turn it, Sofia heard a distinct thud. Something heavy had fallen to the floor just outside. She placed a firm grip on the dial, turning it clockwise. The door suddenly opened. Stepping back and nearly losing her balance, Mr. Sanders fell into the apartment, stumbling over John's body and catching his arm on Sofia's shoulder.

"What took you so long?" he asked, irritably out of breath.

"I wasn't sure if..." she began to say.

But her eyes fell upon the horror of John, nearly limp and dripping with blood from his head. Sofia instinctively let the black box drop from her hands. Falling to her knees beside him, she took hold of her dear friend.

"Oh, John," she cried, looking franticly to the old man. "What happened to him? What are we going to do?"

"We haven't much time," Mr. Sanders said, trying to catch his breath. "They're right behind us."

Gesturing with his hands to Sofia, he continued, "Quickly, pick up the box and help me move him to the fire escape. We need to get to a transporter and get out of here!"

CHAPTER SEVEN

With the virtual dead weight of John upon their shoulders, Sofia and Mr. Sanders stumbled awkwardly down the hall. With one of his arms dangling around each of their necks, the two of them were able to assist him by taking up just enough of John's body mass so as to allow him to keep up a steady motion. The fire escape ahead was their only hope for making a getaway. They determined to press forward, knowing that there was not much time before the Monster would be catching up.

The screaming of the alarm tore through the hallway, drowning out all the ambient sounds of the City outside as they opened the apartment's emergency retreat. Sofia's eyes dripped with tears as the shrill sound cut into her ears, creating a tension throughout the muscles of her skull that throbbed and burned. Easing John through the threshold, she and Mr. Sanders worked together to make the transition as smooth as possible despite their worn and weak legs. As they proceeded to descend the skeletal frame of the fire escape, maintaining their balance with each step required an intensely focused concentration on their part.

Spotting a single, white vehicle parked at the end of the alleyway below, Mr. Sanders, wheezing and coughing, motioned with his eyes to Sofia that reaching it was now their primary objective.

"That one over there," he yelled, his voice barely audible above the wailing alarms. "Come on, we can do it. Just a little further."

Sofia's spirit was beginning to feel the crushing blow of defeat. The numbness of her torso and extremities were assaulting her from every angle. Although she wanted to give in to the desire of her body, which pressed her to lie down and give up, she turned her back to such foolishness, closing the thought behind her veiling curtain of devotion to John.

Afraid to look back for fear that the Monster would be standing directly behind her, Sofia kept telling herself that everything would soon be over. The several flights of stairs from which they had already descended were an incredibly conquered feat. The final stretch was now before them.

By the heavy perspiration dripping from Mr. Sanders' forehead and chin, the moist stains on the armpits of his shirt and the gasping breaths, Sofia was certain that he was as equally burdened as she. But with the hardship of her current discomfort, she continued to hold on to the hope that there could, perhaps, come some good from all of it.

Upon reaching the bottom plank, the three of them stepped onto the asphalt. John's legs buckled under the strain, causing him to collapse to the ground, inadvertently bringing Sofia and Mr. Sanders to the pavement with him. Lifting her head to the shadowy alley, poorly illuminated by the dim glow of orange colored, overhead lamps, Sofia's mind was spinning and reeling from the exhausting experience that she had endured just moments earlier.

Pulling herself alongside John, she raised up to a sitting position. Leaning back against a rusty, garbage dumpster. It took a few seconds, but she was able to reorient herself to their current position. The transporter was a mere stones throw away. Feeling physically and emotionally overwhelmed, she knew that, without John's help, dragging him that final distance would be more than she and the old man would be able to accomplish.

"John, we need to keep moving," Sofia pleaded. "We're too close to give up now."

Grabbing onto the side of the dumpster, Mr. Sanders pulled himself up to his feet, dusting off his shirt. Scooping up the black box that had slipped out of Sofia's arms during the fall, he began to push ahead, leaving the two of them behind.

"Wait," Sofia called out. "Where are you going?"

"I'm getting the transporter for us. Just stay there," he yelled without looking back, painfully limping and audibly wheezing and hacking.

With his hand cool and dry upon her knee, Sofia wiped the red smears from John's cheeks and lips with the sleeve of her shirt. The rise and fall of his chest was slow and deep. His eyes were half open, but he was, to her consoling, making eye contact with her, although he was not talking. As she ran her fingers through the blood soaked hair that covered his forehead she said, "I can't believe we're doing this. I just want us to be together, always."

Her voice was completely inaudible due to the high-pitched wail around them, but the communication of the message was all too apparent as a smile formed at the corners of John's mouth. She could see by his demeanor that he understood every word that she said. As the muscles of his forehead and cheeks relaxed, his eyelids fell shut. Having always been of a strong spirit, she knew that these wounds would not be the death of him.

A soft thunder, like a distant storm, appeared to be fast approaching. Its sound was rather course and artificial as it mingled with the fire alarm. Sofia's mind was too caught up in the moment. The rainwater could shower upon them from off the overhanging rooftop without any notice.

The chaotic clamor stifling the usual noise of the City around them was like being in an enclosed structure. It was providing Sofia with an imaginary sphere of safety. She was unaware that the rumble of the vehicle that had driven up alongside her and John was the source of the new disturbance and not some distant formation of clouds unseen. Nor did she hear the driver's side door open, from which appeared Mr. Sanders who had opened the rear passenger door as well. He was already leaning over John, awaiting her assistance with getting him into the transporter.

As she began to return to her senses, Sofia felt an unnerving feeling come over her, as she could hardly believe that she could be so captivated by the images formed by her own imagination that so little care of the present world could be noticeable. The voice of Mr. Sanders, struggling, and in need of help, was bringing her back into the present reality, and, along with it, the urgency to move!

Grabbing John under the armpits, Mr. Sanders had made an attempt with all of his strength to pull him towards the backseat of the vehicle, but he was too exhausted to complete the task alone. "Take his back and help me lift him up," he yelled, shifting his body around and wrapping his arms about John's legs.

Sofia took the old man's former place, slipping her arms under John's shoulders. Hoisting his limp body up to his knees, the two of them dragged him beside the opened, rear door. With a single motion, they simultaneously pushed and pulled, but the backward motion was unmanageably unsustainable and Sofia stumbled into the backseat with John's upper body lying dead weight upon her. Leaving the young man's legs drooping on the ground outside, Mr. Sanders ran around to the opposite side of the transporter. Opening the door, he took hold of John's shirt, making one final attempt to achieve his goal. The body moved with ease, and he was relieved to see the ordeal coming to a closure. As he completed the task of dragging him entirely within the vehicle's confines, he could see that his little couple was safe and secure.

Closing the doors behind them, Mr. Sanders missed the shoe that had slipped from John's foot during the scuffle. It had landed upon the pavement and was kicked around as they struggled with John's body. Eventually it found its way under the cover of the wheeled machine, out of sight and out of mind.

The old man sat down in the driver's seat. Depressing the accelerator with his foot, they were at last set in motion. He did not bother turning the lights on just yet, so as not to be seen from above. But instead he chose to drive, hidden among the shadows of the alley in order to keep out of sight should the Monster, or anyone else for that matter, catch a glimpse of them making their escape. The alarm was sufficient enough for their purpose. It would definitely hide the noise of the transporter. Everything else was clean. Their tracks were concealed for now.

"Sit on the floor," Mr. Sanders directed Sofia, as he pulled a safety harness over his shoulders. "We don't want to be seen together."

Squeezing her body down onto the cold, rubber-matted space behind the front passenger seat, there was a sense of comfort being so enclosed and encapsulated from the outside world. The rumbling of the motor, the sensation of movement, these gave the affirmation to her that they were leaving the apartment behind and were now moving ahead into the uncharted territory of absolute non-conformity to their culture and all its laws.

With the temptation looming over her, Sofia took one last glance out the back window at the emergency stairwell high above. It was from there, the lofty structure that they had just descended, that he became visible, obscure in the dimness, but observable none-the-less: that evil man from whom they were running.

The Monster was rushing down the initial flurry of steps on the winding labyrinth of the fire escape, moving with speed and determination. Shrinking back down to the floor, Sofia tried to convince herself that it was too far for him to see them. Repeating over and over in her mind that they were safe, she mentally replayed the image of his descent. She was looking for any clues that could reassure her that he had not seen them fleeing in the transporter. But after a moment's attempt, whether he had seen them or not, it did not matter. The fear began to crawl in. Sofia could not imagine how they could ever escape from their current predicament.

As they reached the long end of the alley, the screeching of the alarm began to fade away. Looking into the rearview mirror, Mr. Sanders could barely make out a figure, a person perhaps, standing at the approximate area of the rusty dumpster. It appeared to be picking something up from off the ground. Seeing the black box on the front seat beside him was a relief, as he *knew* that they had left no evidence behind as to how they had escaped, and to which direction they were headed.

Mr. Sanders' forehead was decorated with beads of cool sweat that seemed to melt down his face and spread into a thin film that made his neck reflective and shimmering. His shirt was darkened at the collar from the moisture, and his eyes were pacing back and forth as the transporter exited the alleyway, turning onto the bustling streets of Labor.

Never-ending crowds of people moved along the sidewalks like a gentle, meandering stream, completely oblivious to the occupants of their automobile. Slowly, but steadily, their machine merged with the traffic. The apartment was now far behind, and there were no signs, as of yet, that the Security Forces were on the prowl.

From Sofia's vantage point on the floor, she was able to lay back and look upward at the progressively decreasing heights of the buildings. At this distance from the Inner Square, the buildings were still too high to see the overhanging rooftops. But on account of her rooftop escapades with John, she was able to tell by the various designs of the pipes and cables that were strung between them that the structures were decreasing in size. It appeared that they were heading towards Main Street, the only road in the City that led directly to the Highway.

Recognizing many of the generic store names and street signs that were passing by at a consistent pace, it was easy to create a mental map of the order of their path. If they were, somehow, able to leave the city and actually obtain access to the Highway, Sofia had no idea how, exactly, they were going to succeed in getting through the surrounding walls to make their escape to the woods. It was all in the hands of Providence, now. There was no way to douse the fires they had started.

The drive felt slow and dully mundane as the transporter crept along with the traffic. Sofia had never paid any attention to the multitude of crated products that left the city on the larger transporters. With so much time on her hands, she read to herself the stenciling on the sides of the various units that passed by: *Golden World Crystals, Red M-15, Golden World Dresses, Raw Uniform: Women, Golden World Men's Garments, Red Uniform: Men, Golden World Automobiles, Golden World Deluxe, Raw Mining, Red Uniform: Women, Golden World Appliance,* etcetera.

The names of *Golden World, Red* and *Raw* were such a common site throughout her entire life that she had never given her mind over to the thought of what exactly they were. Although a curious itching was growing within her as to what items were to be found inside the crates, she knew there was really no way to gain access to them from her current place. So, continuing on with her time-wasting activity, she read off in her head the next title that appeared.

CHAPTER EIGHT

It had taken a few hours, but Sofia was certain that they were finally within a few blocks from the first critical destination point, as the overhanging rooftops were now coming into view. The lights at the center of the City, brighter and more distinct than those of the rest of Labor, once in her line of sight, would be the landmarks by which she could determine that they were halfway to the red, brick Gate. Mr. Sanders had not spoken to her since their retreat from the apartment, and she was startled to find his face looking down upon her.

Leaning his head back over the seat, he spoke to her in a reassuring voice, "We're almost there. Just be calm and stay down, okay?"

"Yes, sir," Sofia acknowledged.

Unsure of where exactly they were headed to, or what they would do if they ever made it there, Sofia rolled onto her side, reaching her arm up to John. She felt around until her hand had settled upon his, and closed her eyes.

Among the thousands of transporting vehicles that traveled the streets of Labor, Mr. Sanders felt certain that nobody would be able to follow them. And, even if the Security Forces had been notified, they would be hard pressed to find them within the densely populated City. As long as they could get through the checkpoint, he thought, Sofia and John would be free.

The time was moving by at an abnormally fast rate where minutes felt like seconds, and the hours were like minutes. They seemed to be rapidly approaching the Highway Security Gate, yet they were barely crawling along upon the heavily impacted road. To Mr. Sanders, it only seemed like a short moment ago that they had left the apartment, when in fact, it had been several hours since they departed. The flashing red lights mounted on the automated rails could be seen in the distance. Swipe the hand and look into the scanner. That's all it would take and they'd be on their way, he thought.

"Please, let these children live," he mumbled under his breath. "They're so innocent. Please, help them."

As the day was wearing on, curiosity got the best of Sofia. Peering over the front seat and out the window, she was able to see the lines of vehicles slowly approaching the Gate. Some were filled with multiple crates with only a single operator, while others were strictly designed as people movers and were full of workers heading towards the Red Plant. All of them were waiting to pass through one of the several stalls that separated the City proper from the Highway. Making her observation as brief as she could, her curiosity was relieved, and she let her body fall back onto the floor

They were now at an uncomfortably rhythmic, stop-and-go pace, as each of the transporters had to come to a complete halt in order to let the drivers scan their vehicles out of the City. The lights of the Gate were beginning to illuminate the interior of their vehicle. They were unnatural and unsatisfying, unlike the Savior's light. Sofia covered her face, as the rays streaming through the windows seemed like the eyes of the masters of Labor watching over them.

In her mind everything was now a frightful mystery. She had never been outside of the City, had never experienced the drive of the Highway. She had never been so scared. As the vehicle pulled alongside the scanner, Sofia's hair feathered back from the breeze that followed the opening of Mr. Sanders' window.

The same eerie, red glow that filled the Forbidden Room was now flooding the interior of the transporter. With a glance towards John, his eyes closed and resting soundly, she wondered if in his dreams the world had suddenly been bathed in the same crimson hue that had settled upon his face.

For a moment there was no movement from the front seat as a mechanical hum from the scanner wafted through the air. The Gate did not immediately grant permission to enter into its world. As it appeared to be taking more time than reasonably necessary, Sofia began to wonder if they were about to be caught. Were they being purposely held back from the Highway? Was the arrival of the Security an immanent event? The anxiety that gripped her was bringing with it that awful, cold sweat, as she felt compelled to lift herself up to see what was restraining them.

Grasping at the vinyl seat, the cool moisture of her palm made it slippery and wet, too difficult to get a firm grip on. Instead, pulling herself up by John's shirt, she was able to adjust her body to a more plausible position from which to see.

As she was about to peer over Mr. Sanders' shoulder, there was a sudden change in the illuminated features of the transporter's interior. From the blood-red tones grew the sickly green coloring. The rumbling motors of the gate began to grind. The security rail was lifting! With the vehicle lunging forward, Sofia fell back to the floor with a mild thump of her head on the side door. The craziness of the day's events was taking hold. As the fearful anxiety began to morph into an anxiety of wonder, Sofia's whole view of the world she once thought she knew was now taking on a whole new perspective.

The sensation of the rapidly accelerating speed with which all transporters traveled along the Highway was a novel feeling. A strange tickling in Sofia's stomach was just one of the events of the moment that was assisting in building up the excitement inside of her. Where they were headed was one of the many pieces of data that she still had not been given. But she figured Mr. Sanders' plan up to this point had been skillfully executed. He seemed to know what he was doing.

Pondering on the events of the day, it became apparent to Sofia that her life seemed as equally sustained in its entirety as it was in the secluded moment of the here and now. It was as if some unknown Force had masterfully planned it. Was everything happening under such determined conditions that attributing it to coincidence would be out of the question? Could it be that there was nothing happening that was not part of some teleological function, an actual, meaningful end to all of it?

With John sleeping next to her, she placed her hand upon his cheek saying, "Rest, my dear friend. I believe our time is coming."

Closing her eyes once again, she was able to drift away to that wonderful world of dreams.

The intense beating of Mr. Sanders' heart was causing his chest to tighten. Clenching his left breast, he struggled to keep his breath. His eyes were fastened to the Highway. It was all too familiar: the multitudes of empty vehicles littering its edges, the deep blackness and contrasting dim canopies of orange haze emitting from the ceiling-mounted lights. He had to keep his mind on these commonly seen objects in order to ease himself of the rising anxiety that was creeping in, as every few minutes he would pass by a Security vehicle driving down one of the lanes of opposing traffic.

Unlike the city, the velocity of the vehicles was of a relatively rapid rate of speed. The feeling of racing along the smooth, black road of the Highway was much more relaxing and free spirited, giving a sense of separation from the cramped quarters of Labor.

There were many miles between them and the end of the road. Mr. Sanders, cognizant of the necessity for a plan of action in order to get the children into the green hills that existed beyond the Highway's walls, pondered considerably between several possibilities. There was only going to be one opportunity in the matter. He wanted to choose the option with the best possible chance for success.

It seemed so strange to him that, in their days, he and Helen found it so easy to visit the world outside. Their frequent excursions to their hidden place of solitude and peace were always filled with moments of joy, a joy that, sadly, on every occasion, ended with the disheartening return to the doldrums of their humble abode in the dreary apartment complex.

Why did they not stay in their home in the forest? Why did they always return? These were questions that the old man kicked himself with every day of his life. Perhaps it was the fear of being caught that kept them from permanently fleeing. Or, maybe, it was all part of a universal scheme of which he was not privy to. He did not know the answer to his own questions. But, as their once-in-a-lifetime chance to disappear from Labor was so close, and committing to the change was so difficult, in the end, just as they were about to wipe off the dust of their feet to the City, they were thwarted by a stroke of bad luck.

Discovering that the tunneled, drainage complex, that was so readily accessible to them at the time, had been suddenly sealed off, replaced by a more compact system, too narrow for any human to pass through, was a devastating blow to Helen. They would never return to their little paradise. Gripped by an endless bout of depression for the remaining years of her life, Helen existed in bodily form only. The old man could do nothing for her. He just watched as she withered like an autumn leaf, before being taken to the Haven. There must be a way to get the children out here, he thought. There has to be.

Tilting the rearview mirror downward, Mr. Sanders could just barely make out Sofia's arm spread across John's chest. As her hand moved to his head, and her fingers filtered through his hair, an idea came to his mind: the walls of the Highway were relatively thin and fragile at certain areas. If he timed everything just right, he thought, he just might be able to collide the vehicle into it with just enough force to create an opening for them to escape through. He could then commandeer another vehicle while the impact site was in chaos. That would allow him to easily make it back to the apartment for, what he believed to be, his final return home.

With a strong feeling that Helen was watching over him, he began to set the plan into motion. They once had a dream that could not be fulfilled, but he believed that through John and Sofia that dream was about to be realized.

Glancing into the mirror once more, seeing the two children so tranquil, so in love, he understood that his entire life had been destined for this moment. This youthful couple would live in that physical paradise of which no other person of Labor had ever seen or could ever imagine, he thought. And before nightfall, he and Helen would be in their own paradise, together at last.

"The young man's been sleeping for quite some time. Another hour's drive will give him the rest he needs to help the two of you with the journey ahead," he said.

There was no response from Sofia this time. Assuming she was asleep, he continued the drive without saying another word.

CHAPTER NINE

Atugging sensation at Sofia's shoulder accompanied a faint calling from the old man, bringing her out of the deep sleep and into that semi-conscious state between reality and the fantastic. In her dreamy state of awareness, she could hear John and Mr. Sanders speaking to one another, as friends converse openly and frankly among themselves. Rubbing the crusty build-up from the corners of her eyes, she expected the voices to fade away into oblivion as she began to fully awaken upon the bed of her room, but the rumbling of the motor beneath her head, and the white-gray metallic roof staring her in the face from above, reminded her that the events of the day were more than a mere game of the mind.

"Wake up, girl. It's time to get up," John's voice grumbled as she felt him shaking her shoulder.

"Is she awake yet?" Mr. Sanders asked with a tone mixed in anxiety and frustration.

"Yes, sir."

The haziness of Sofia's awareness made it difficult to fully comprehend what exactly was taking place around her.

John sat up, clutching his ribs. "Mr. Sanders said we're almost there."

"Almost there? Where are we going?"

The old man looked back over the front seat and said, "*Your final destination.*"

Pointing at the cargo straps situated beside the seatbelts, the old man was wide-eyed and, for the first time, showing his fears openly through the tones of his voice.

"You need to secure yourselves in tightly. I'm really not sure how hard of an impact we're going to have," he commanded nervously.

"An impact?" John questioned, "What impact?"

"Are we going to crash?" Sofia asked, sitting up.

"Trust me, please, children," Mr. Sanders interrupted, "Everything's going to be alright. You're about to receive the gift of freedom... something of which neither of you have ever really had. The rooftop was only a small sampling of what's in store for the two of you. You just need to trust me, okay?"

Sofia did not respond. She looked to John as if she wanted him to make the call as to whether or not they were going to go along with the old man's scheme. With the blueness of her eyes staring back at him, the contrasting red streaks strung around her eyelids indicating the heavy exhaustion hanging over her, John hesitated to answer. Brushing back the long strands of hair dangling in front of her face, Sofia tucked them behind her ear and whipped her eyes towards Mr. Sanders and then back to her companion, as if to say "*Well, aren't you going to answer him?*"

John was at a crossroad: his agreement to participate in Mr. Sanders' plan, if everything worked out as the old man wanted it to, meant that there would be no small cubicle waiting for him in some near-future, adult life, no small grovel to live in. His wife would not lose the luster of her hair, or the fair complexion of her youthful skin to the life of a slave for a master of which neither he nor she would ever see. In essence, things would be the way he always wanted them to be. But, to refuse his help would mean that all these terrible things would be the reality of his future. It seemed too obvious as to which direction he should set his feet to walk. But, the choice was his. And each path had to have its own moral consequence. The causal nexus of each one was too expansive to comprehend the differing outcomes, and John was feeling too inadequate to carry the responsibility that was being placed upon his shoulders. Which type of life did he want to live? An opportunity was being granted to him, to actualize the potential of anything he chose within the realm of what is humanly possible under the given circumstances. Sofia's eyes were still in the waiting. John had to act fast. He could not delay any longer. Mr. Sanders needed an answer.

"Okay, then," he said. "What do you want us to do?"

"Leave it to me for now, John," the old man responded with a nervous smile, "You'll have plenty more decisions to deal with in the coming days. Just quickly buckle in. Secure yourselves well. We're getting close."

Lying down and squeezing himself into the back of the seat, John reached down, helping Sofia to climb up from the floor beside him. Cuddling as close together as they could press their bodies, beginning at their legs, they tightened the cargo straps and the seatbelts around themselves. They were nearly complete with the securing detail up to their mid-torsos when a strange vibration from the engine compartment began rattling the vehicle.

The sense of speed that Sofia first experienced at the outset of their Highway commute was far less intense than what she was feeling at the present moment.

"Are you two almost finished?" Mr. Sanders yelled over the roar of the engine.

The vehicle shifted into another gear, and the acceleration of the transporter began to cause a strange, almost nauseating, sensation in their stomachs.

"We're almost done," John fired back.

Pulling Sofia's head down into his chest, he gave a firm yank on the final strap that provided the security over their shoulders.

"We're ready."

Weaving in and out of the traffic, Mr. Sanders focused all his attention on his end target. It would all fall upon the timing. He needed the vehicle to accelerate faster. He needed an opening, a clear and direct path, unhindered by the other machines on the Highway. With only a few minutes left, he had to think his plan through, to get everything in order. There could be no mistakes. This was probably the last chance for anyone on the planet to experience the joy of freedom.

As his heart began to race and his senses became keener, the awareness of Mr. Sanders' surroundings intensified. He knew what the most important detail was that the proposal needed to succeed: a divine intervention.

The appropriate time to veer off course, to squeeze into the unoccupied space between the empty vehicles lining the Highway, to collide with the walls at the proper angle, was fast approaching. Whatever the fastest obtainable speed their transporter was capable of, he thought, it would probably be the minimum needed to penetrate the concrete upon impact.

"Everybody hold on tight," he yelled, checking the straps that secured his own body to the seat.

Holding her hands to her ears as the high-pitched grinding of the engine became almost deafening, Sofia pressed her head tighter into John's chest. His eyes were tightly shut. And, with Sofia held so close to him, if Death itself were to find them on this day, he knew there would be no regrets.

Metallic components of the vehicle's exterior were stripping away, crashing into the passing vehicles, throwing trails of sparks off the road and walls of the Highway, as the vibration of the wobbling tires began to cause the transporter to self destruct and fall apart.

"We're getting closer," Mr. Sanders mumbled as the area ahead, where there was just enough of a bend in the road, a slight curve where they could make a nearly direct impact with the wall, came into view.

With the accelerator forced to the floor, the vehicle bore forward, smoking and fragile. There were now only a few hundred meters to impact. A transporter ahead suddenly jumped into his lane, causing the old man to gasp at the fact that the driver had unknowingly situated himself in a hazardously oriented position. Mr. Sanders had only seconds to decide: decelerate, and get behind the new obstacle, or else make an attempt to pass it.

With a deceleration being completely out of the question, knowing that he had to have the maximum force behind him when he collided with the wall, he pushed ahead, despite the fact that he would be cutting close to missing the bend altogether.

As he began gaining on the vehicle, it became immediately apparent that once he pulled in front of it, the driver would not be able to brake fast enough. He would be forced to pile head-long into their transporter's tail end: a benefit to them by giving more than enough energy to break through the Highway's wall, but the collision would probably kill the innocent man, as Mr. Sanders could clearly see that the poor sod was not wearing his safety harness.

"Fifty meters," he said, grumbling through his clenched teeth.

Upon hearing the words, John tightened his grip around his girl for the last time. There was nothing more he could do to pre-pare for the coming destruction.

This was the consummation of Mr. Sanders' venture, the end of all things in his life of which he could have a direct, rational influence. As he passed the final transporter, there came a single, fraction of a second, when eye contact was made between him and the other vehicle's operator. It was at this moment, as if he entered into the domain of the infinite, where there is no end and no beginning, and all the motions in the world that are encap-sulated in the realm of time come to a stand still, that a mental snap-shot of the final, sedate expression of the stranger's face was captured in his mind. Knowing that this man was not going to survive through to the end of the day, Mr. Sanders wondered if the operator would have even cared had he been given that piece of knowledge before leaving for work this morning.

Before the thought had been given the opportunity to make its entrance into that great expanse of the brain, the memory vault which stores the experiences of the days of living within the world, the old man cut the steering wheel sharply, throwing the trans-porter aside, making the desperate attempt to cast a straight path to the wall. The front bumper of the stranger's vehicle caught onto their rear section in a violent contorted motion. Metal to metal, the two vehicles fused into one uncontrolled, speeding mass.

Thrown back across their lane of origin and skidding perpendicular to the direction of the flow of traffic, there was another impact by an unseen vehicle whose single passenger's screams were momentarily heard, before being suddenly cut short.

The overhead lights, flashing in strobe-like sequence, passed through the windows, revealing in one fleeting second, the impact site passing by... they had missed their mark!

"Hold on," Mr. Sanders screamed, as he gave up control of the vehicle to the laws of nature.

The rubber of their tires shredded under the shearing force exerted against their machine, scraping its rims across the asphalt in a show of glowing sparks, as they slammed into the empty vehicles parked at the edge of the outer lane. Hurtled into the opposing traffic, they impacted another transporter headlong, sending their vehicle into a wild spin.

The sounds of tearing metal and shattering glass, accompanied by muffled screams and splintering crates, filled the Highway as they rebounded off another transporter, whose occupant crashed through his own windshield, splattering on their front hood before disappearing into the smoke and mayhem.

Piling upon one another, the automobiles of the Highway were crumpling and spinning among the ensuing chaos, their drivers blinded by the dark, cloudy debris filling the tunnel. Tumbling end over end, their transporter came to an abrupt stop. With the smoky air and blood smeared upon the windows obscuring visibility, John and Sofia still had that odd sensation that they were moving, even though they were not. Their equilibrium was askew: there was no way to discern as to whether they were upside down or right-side up. Another sudden blow to the front of the vehicle sent them into an erratic spin accompanied by more crushing and twisting of metal. The rotational motion suddenly stalled, all movement of their transporter finally ceased as it butted up against a mass of steel and glass.

Oddly bright, yet familiar, bars of light that became visible through the back window accompanied the sounds of rocks and gravel falling upon the roof above them.

After a moment of disbelief at the unforeseen turmoil that he had initiated, Mr. Sanders, taking in the sounds of sirens and yelling, screaming men and women hidden among the black smoke-filled Highway, the screeching tires and accompanying grinding metal and shattering glass, knew that the devastation that he had caused was still an ongoing phenomena in the distance.

"Is everyone okay back there?" he panted and coughed.

Silence was the only answer. The transporter was dark and lifeless. The old man unbuckled himself, rotating his neck around in an attempt to stretch away the stiffness that had settled in. Leaning back against the headrest, he struggled to take in a breath of air through the thick, polluted atmosphere.

The silence of the children was finally broken by the sound of the bits of gravel and glass, which had slowly seeped in through the shattered windows, being brushed aside. A movement from behind him, buckles unhinging, gave him the relief he was looking for.

"John? Sofia? Is everything alright?" he questioned.

"We're fine," John spoke coughing and spitting.

"What are we going to do, now?" Sofia inquired fearfully, with the same hacking that had overcome her companion.

Climbing into the back seat, Mr. Sanders followed after the brightness emanating from behind them, leading him to its source between the thick puffs of smoke. Squinting tightly as a heavy breeze cleared the blackness away for a brief moment, he was suddenly flooded with the light of the Savior. There it was, just out of reach, visible through the series of twisted, metallic partitions and shards of glass: the trees! The rear end of the stranger's transporter had penetrated through the wall.

"Help me to carefully break out the rest of the window. We have to work quickly," he commanded them. " It's the only way out."

As the glass was already shattered, very little effort was required to kick their way through it. Removing pieces of the torn uphol-stery, they covered up the remaining sharp edges that protruded from the pane. Squeezing his way through, John could feel the heat of the Savior as intermittent beams of light fell upon him. Reaching back for another large piece of fabric, he assisted Sophia out of their wrecked vehicle and onto the hood of the stranger's transporter. Seeing the dead man inside, bloody and torn, in brief glimpses as the light passed through the smoke, John dropped a large piece of fabric covering over him, cautiously concealing the corpse from Sofia's sight.

Blindly feeling about on the floor, Mr. Sanders eventually hap-pened upon the black box that he was searching for. Scooping it up, he placed it under his arm and held it securely. Crawling par-tially out the back window, he handed it to John.

"Take this. You're going to need it," he said.

John looked suspiciously at it and asked, "What is it?"

"Ask Sofia. She'll tell you," he answered and then began to climb back in, moving towards the front seat again. Hitting at the front windshield, he hollered back, "Now go. Get into the woods and stay far away from here, you hear me? Never return to Labor as long as you live."

"Wait. Mr. Sanders, come with us," John cried out.

"I can't," he said, kicking out the shards of glass from the wind-shield. "I'm going to be with Helen now, John. The people that know us believe she's dead, but we're the only ones that are alive, boy: the four of us. I don't want you to say anything more about it. Now go on. Go and live!"

With his eyes burning from the smoke, acting as a camouflage to the true reason for the tears that he was shedding, John crawled through the windshield of the stranger's vehicle, and assisted Sofia inside.

As much as he desired to see that the old man was safely escaping to some other part of the planet, John felt an intense anguish in his heart, as he knew that they had to leave him behind. They had to keep moving.

As Sofia crawled in behind him, John looked back, wondering why the old man had gone through so much for them. He had broken all the laws of the City. He had sacrificed everything he had for their safety.

Pulling his legs out through the frame of his windshield, Mr. Sanders sat on the hood of the transporter. Looking back through the series of windows, he shouted, "Go now, John. Take Sofia away from here. Liberty awaits you! But, mind yourselves, children: stay away from the red Xs. Sofia knows what I'm talking about. Heed the warning young ones! Stay far away!"

"Mr. Sanders," returned the cries of the youth from the smoky veil. "Thank you!"

Sliding down from the rear of the stranger's vehicle, John fell on to the grass, soft at his feet, just outside the gaping wound of the Highway. The air was cool and fresh. Taking Sofia by the hand, John helped pad her fall as she dropped down beside him, taken aback by the beauty of the land. Freedom was so close, but they did not have the time to savor its sweetness. They began running towards the thicket ahead, making haste to leave the world of Labor forever behind them.

A strong breeze blew through the opening of the wall, clearing out the smoke and allowing for an instance of clear visualization. The glimpse was brief. One final picture of life was captured in the old man's mind. It was of a young couple, pure and alone. It looked like Helen Mae and Henry Eugene Sanders. They were sprinting into the woods, never to return. They took a moment to look back over their shoulders: their last view of Labor and all its horrors. They were frightened, and yet determined.

Entering into the dangling vines and thick brush at the edge of the tree line, the Savior glistened off the tears that were flowing down their cheeks, and then, like magic, they disappeared.

CHAPTER TEN

Wading through the rubble and debris of the local devastation, searching through the blackness of the smoke and dust, Mr. Sanders sought out a vehicle that would get him back to the apartment.

With the increasing multitude of rescue worker units and Security Force members trying to control the scene, he attempted to creep within the darkened areas along the edge of the Highway. Perhaps, he thought, commandeering a vehicle when he was further away from the crash site would be more conducive to maintaining an air of anonymity.

Looking back, the distance that he had already traveled was difficult to determine, especially with all the flashing lights and piercing sirens making an onslaught on his senses. The old man knew that he had to be patient if he was going to make it through this to the end. Placing his hands in his pant pockets, he continued the long stroll home.

The smoke began to thin. Although still hazy and mildly suffocating, the screeching and flashing was quite a ways behind. The old man now felt safe enough to secure for himself a transporter without looking suspicious in the least.

Stepping into one of the empty machines from the dark side of the walkway, he slid into the driver's seat. Starting up the engine, he pulled out onto the asphalt road and continued towards his end goal: the long-awaited meeting with Helen.

The apartment lobby was cold and dim as Mr. Sanders walked through the glass doors. Scanning his eyes at the terminal, as he had done several thousands of times in the past, he looked upon the color-changing screen. The elevator car appeared, the doors slid open and he entered in.

The air felt still. Much more stale than it usually did. He was quite surprised that there was no Security Force detail waiting to arrest him. Upon reaching the top floor, Mr. Sanders stepped out into the dimly lit hallway, all the more perplexed that he was free to make his way unmolested to his own little pad. But, before heading to his place of communion with Helen, he had one more task to complete before everything would be finalized. Kneeling down beside the elevator's retinal scanner, he pulled off the underside covering. Tinkering with the wires inside, the red glow upon its face turned green. The doors would remain permanently open, putting the elevator permanently out of commission. As he walked away from the sabotaged terminal, he chuckled to himself with an anticipatory giggle.

Once inside his familiar abode, he found everything exactly as he had left it earlier in the day. There was no ransacking of the rooms, no law enforcement officials waiting to place him in handcuffs. There was not even a message left for him in the mail-shoot.

Although no one was yet present to perform the operation, he knew that he was about to be taken from the world of the living. At the moment it was merely a game of torment, but he was not going to be playing along. He knew that the Security Forces would soon be coming, tearing through the door with their weapons drawn. They knew very well that he had taken the children. But what he had done with them he would never divulge. They would not be getting any information from this old man, he thought to himself. The plan was already set in motion, and Helen was waiting for him.

The teakettle had just begun whistling, and the steam floated skyward from its spout. Mr. Sanders took it up in his hand, pouring himself one final cup of his favorite drink. A dab of sweetener dribbled into the liquid as he stirred the mixture with a fine, silver spoon.

After placing the cup on a small porcelain plate, he pulled out one of the kitchen drawers, placing it on the countertop. Reaching his hand inside the empty recess, he withdrew a matte black, L-shaped object, which he immediately dropped into his pant pocket without giving it a second look.

Setting the cup and plate down upon a finish-worn area of the dining room table, he sat down to the tune of creaking and cracking of the old chair. It had long been nearing the end of its tenure. To his surprise, set upon the placemat where Helen used to sit, was a pair of shoes: one belonging to him, the other, a smaller sized, black boot that appeared to be the type of foot-covering worn by the school-aged youths.

Downstairs, the darkness of the apartment entrance lit up with flashing lights and the sounds of screeching cars, as several units of militarized Security personnel burst through the doors, making their way up to the elevator entrance. The retinal scanner was filling the room with its flashing crimson strobe of light. Realizing that it would be a futile effort to try to fix the system, the Commander rerouted his unit to the Security Stairwell. Taking up tactical positions outside the building, dozens of similar units surrounded the apartment complex. Every possible exit was monitored. There would be no escape for their prey.

Lifting the teacup to his lips, Mr. Sanders closed his eyes, allowing his taste sensation to go unhindered. The liquid was warm and sweet as it went down his throat. With the young couple away, as far as he was concerned, it was the last good thing in the city with any worth.

The weapons' metallic chatter, clanging against the belts and harnessed gear strapped across the chests of the State's agents, moved with a rhythmical chime as they ascended the steps in their orderly fashion. Opening the door of the top floor, the lead man stepped out of the way, allowing the rest of the unit to enter into the hall. Gracefully moving in formation along the dark side of their pathway they took up their appointed positions, stacked man-on-man alongside the walls outside of apartment eleven-ten.

With the familiar red flashing of the retinal screen, the Commander knew that the only way to get to the old man on the other side was to destroy the door. Gesturing towards it with a quick hand signal, another agent untied the straps on the back of the agent standing before him. Removing a steel-black, cylinder with two circular handles, he made his way towards the apartment entrance. Bracing his feet on the floor, the agent cocked his arms back and prepared to breach the room. The Commander took a step back, giving a soft knock on the entry door to the apartment directly across from Mr. Sanders', at which point the light streaming through its peephole blacked out.

Setting the cup down upon the table, Mr. Sanders sensed that he was not alone. Removing the black object from his pocket, he pointed it in the direction of the hallway entrance. There was nothing more to fear. He would soon be going on a permanent trip... with his dear wife.

"Watch over them, Savior. They're just children," he whispered.

Splintering wood and metal debris exploded into the apartment as the black suited men outside poured into the living room. The cracking of the weapons sent multitudes of projectiles hurtling through the smoke-filled air, embedding hot metal into the walls around the old man as his body fell limp to the floor.

The Security Force agents' shouting echoed throughout the hallway as they seemingly filled every corner, room and orifice of the apartment, securing its premises.

Particles of drywall and wood crumbled under the thick, rubber soles of the boots of the Force Commander as he made his entrance into the room. Lifting up the visor of his helmet, he knelt down beside the battle-torn corpse. The pooling blood around Mr. Sander's head and torso was well advanced, and had created a tiny river that flowed towards his stretched out arm and the cold, blued, unloaded pistol that he held in his hand.

Drops of crimson life dripped from the handle as the Commander lifted the weapon up, admiring the detailing.

"Have you ever seen one like this before?" he asked one of the agents standing at his side.

"Nothing like that, sir."

Opening up a plastic bag, the Commander dropped the handgun inside. A smeared trail followed along its path as the firearm slid down its clear walls. Wrapping up the opening and placing it into a security pouch dangling from a thick, black strap at his waist, an expression of ponder lighted upon his face.

"I wonder where he secured a weapon like this?"

CHAPTER ELEVEN

The dense, green brush and thick trees decorated with dangling, leafy vines that surrounded Sofia and John had created an atmosphere of disillusionment, causing them to lose track of the amount of time that had passed by. They did not have to travel far before becoming lost within the woods.

Reaching up to the sky, with a natural pleasure unlike those unbefitting concrete structures of Labor that basked in the same light, the towering trunks held their authoritative position, even blotting out from view the smoke that had been billowing up from the recent destruction to the east. With their hands held together tightly, they slowed the pace and began the ascent of the first of many hills that would need to be conquered before achieving a comfortable distance away from the City.

The steep climb of the first hill that they had to endure required much assistance from the large boulders and rope like vine that, protruding intermittently from the ground, necessitated the use of muscles of which they had used only during those occasions when they would be roof hopping. John struggled to overcome the sharp pains at his side as he grasped and pulled, strained and lifted. His one bare, tender foot, sore and blistered, was unaccustomed to being exposed for such a long period of time, and it hindered his natural, athletic abilities.

Purple flowers, tiny and fragile, peeked out of the green grass in abundant patches, quilted into the fabric of the beautiful tapestry that, at long last, was their own, the paradise they had always wanted to be a part of. There was a faint self awareness of their soiled clothing, thick with the smell of burning rubber and sweat, faces smeared in black soot and dried tears, that appeared so out of place amongst the fresh and pure atmosphere of the new world.

Assisting as best she could, Sofia began the climb ahead of John. Clinging onto the thick vines streaming along the hill's side, she held out her hand to him, encouraging him to struggle against the pain.

With the apex of the rocky mound in sight, and their initial steps to freedom long behind them, the first comforting rest that they were hoping for appeared to be soon approaching.

Decorated in gorgeously, towering trees covered over with thick leafy ropes, green moss growing from their trunks' sides, shimmering leaves and colorful winged creatures of various types, the hill, leveling off and flattening out, brought them an easing of the journey, allowing them, once again, to hold one another's hand out of pleasure and not by mere necessity.

With the westerly view of the landscape spreading out before them, John and Sofia found it difficult to express the feelings that were flourishing inside. There was a spectacular wave of thick clouds washing over the distant, rolling, green swells of land. Its beauty was unhindered by the dull presence of Labor's buildings that were the essence of a suffocating, claustrophobic environment. They were able, for the first time, to fully appreciate the magical wonder of the world beyond the walls without being constrained by the evils of the City.

The first rest of this new life's adventure was enjoyed upon the soil's bed of soft, green blades. Shade was provided by the umbrella-like covering of the tallest of trees that had overlooked this enchanting scenery for a time spanning an unknown multitude of generations.

The opening of the black box was an intense moment for Sofia, as she knew of the importance that Mr. Sanders had placed upon it. John had not had the pleasure of viewing its contents before now. Leaning back against the tree, he began examining them, finding a particular interest in its little black book.

Intently studying the details of each page, he would occasionally make an examination of the compass in conjunction with the directions being described on its proper use.

"This is amazing," he said, "Come here and have a look at this."

As Sofia scooted beside him, he held the apparatus on the flat of his palm and remained still, allowing the needle to come to a rest.

"It always points in the same direction. It says here," he paused, scanning for a particular, handwritten passage before pressing his finger upon it and reading aloud.

"When used as a tool in the experienced hand, the map in the back of the book will allow the possessor of said tool to navigate the entire world without limit."

"That is amazing. So we can go anywhere we want?" Sofia asked, scanning the horizon.

"Anywhere, apparently."

"But, we need to stay away from the red Xs. That was what Mr. Sanders said, right?"

"The red Xs? Oh, that's right."

Turning to the last page and placing his finger on the area far to the northeast of Labor, he said, "These Xs here. Did he tell you something about this place?"

"Well," Sofia began, "we were interrupted before he was able to give me any detail. He just made it clear that it was a place that we should never go to, that's all."

With an inquisitive complexion, John brought the book down to his lap. Seemingly perplexed in thought, he opened his mouth as if to speak, but no words came forth. Giving him the space he needed to think, Sofia did not interrupt. Instead, she sat in quiet patience and waited. After a few moments he spoke up.

"You know what's different about this?"

"Different about what?" she asked.

"This whole escape from Labor. It's just different than I had imagined it would be like."

Sofia thought for a moment, and asked, "Does that bother you?"

"Well, not too much really. I was just thinking, though: this morning when we were on the rooftop, when the Savior lifted over the horizon... it was different, unique, as if a sign was being sent from someone... or, something. It was telling us that we needed to travel towards it, not away from it, to the east: the direction of the rising."

Taking the book from his hand, Sofia opened the back cover. Flipping it around, with her finger stationed upon the sketch of the flying machine, she shook her head in disagreement.

"I don't ever want to go there. Ever. Mr. Sanders would not have warned us about it if it wasn't a bad place."

"I won't take us there," John said with a short tone. "I know it's the place of the Red Plant. But it..."

He paused with an air of concern, leaving Sofia hanging on his word.

"What?" Sofia inquired.

"It just felt like," he hesitated again, placing his fist over his heart, "someone was calling to me, almost pressuring me to get us to leave the City, to show us something... and then all of this: Mr. Sanders and his plans. It seems far beyond mere coincidence, don't you think?"

The idea did have an almost queer, even alien, feel to it when the events of the day were placed into the category of *mere coincidence*. But attributing every detail to some conscious, self-aware intelligence was far beyond her comprehension. Was it possible that each event, each step of the day for that matter, was effected by a cause that was directing them in the way they should go? Unable to follow this train of thought into a deeper, more comprehensive series of musings, Sofia stepped off its philosophical path. She felt that, if the causal connections of the events of the day could be traced back to someone or something guiding them along this mysterious journey, then fighting it would be no more fruitful than living the life of a dweller in the tents of Labor. Someone had to make the choice for the two of them. Either she or John would have to take the lead.

Placing her hand upon his, she consented to him all the responsibility of decision-making. The words were difficult to verbalize at first, but exonerating herself of this duty, she believed, would allow her a greater freedom to be the friend and companion that John needed, allowing him to grow into the resourceful leader they would both require to survive.

"Wherever you go, John, I'll always be there with you, following close behind," she professed. "I may not always agree with you. And, sometimes I'll express my dissatisfactions. But our little tribe, you and me, needs a chief."

She touched her finger to the tip of his nose, and said, "Tag, you're it."

The day was wearing on, and the Savior, looking down from the sky above, was a necessary object for traveling the path ahead. As long as they had the light, the landmarks cataloged by Mr. Sanders would be visible. After many days, they would finally reach the sight on the map marked *Food and Shelter*.

The first night's sleep was difficult, requiring John and Sofia to secure a temporary dwelling in the back of an outcropping of boulders, of which they were able to locate at the midpoint of one of the hills. There was a small stream nearby that flowed gently through the valley below from which they refreshed themselves, washing off the scrapes and abrasions that they had accumulated during the day's events. The drips and splashes colliding with the stones and soil along the water's edge could be heard throughout the night, intermittently interrupted by the howling of distant animals, and the flapping of unseen wings. The snapping of twigs and rustling of leaves consistently startled the young couple out of what minimal sleep they were able to procure, so that by the Savior's first light they awoke blood-shot in the eyes, too weary to continue at the same pace that they had traveled the previous afternoon.

The brightly colored berries dangling from a nearby patch of green, leafy bushes helped to sustain their appetites on this tolerably cool morning. As neither John nor Sofia had ever had such fresh and sweet edibles before, they laughed and giggled with delight as they ate of the fruit of the land. With an overabundant supply at their disposal, the two of them consumed the treats with such reckless abandon that it did not take long for a sour nausea to settle into their stomachs.

As mid-morning was upon them, the sugar rushing through their blood had awakened their minds, allowing them to think more clearly. Despite the weariness of their bodies, they finally descended the hill and entered into the valley.

Following the stream that had eventually widened out by approximately three meters, the thickness of the brush was considerably denser than the hills above, forcing them to move at a slower pace than they already were. But unlike their travels upon the hilly terrain, they now had an unlimited source of water that would keep them hydrated and cool as the intensity of the Savior's heat increased throughout the day.

It was mid-afternoon. By the indication of the compass' needle, and the strangely contorted dead tree that they discovered through the use of the map, John determined that they were nearing the halfway point in their excursion. Although it appeared that there were many more kilometers ahead before the end of the journey, a great deal of that distance would be covered by way of the valley and not in the uphill and downhill trudge that had marked the initial path.

By late afternoon, the coolness of the water was relieving them of the hot, sweaty enclosure of their leather shoes, or in John's case, shoe. As neither of them had ever had the opportunity to walk with their feet unprotected for any prolonged periods of time, the small stones and decaying branches and bark of the trees, were a minor impediment upon their path due to the tenderness of their soles. The mid-point to their final destination would not be met as planned, as they had once again significantly reduced the rate at which they were traversing the land. And, although neither John nor Sofia had any care about it, many more hours would now be added to the overall trek to reach their goal.

Entering into the second night, John realized that they had fallen far short of their purposed point of rest: a place marked on the map where they could sleep in the protection of a grove of dead trees and large boulders. Flipping through the pages of the book, to a section marked *Shelter Procurement*, he quickly scanned the sketches and tiny notes left behind by Mr. Sanders.

"Apparently a shelter could be erected *anywhere*, if needed," he read aloud. And, being that they were *somewhere*, he felt that it was quite within the realm of possibility for them to set up a sleeping quarters right where they were standing.

As the darkness of the night was beginning to bear down upon them, the two of them worked together under his direction as efficiently as they could. Gathering together as many of the large, dead branches that they were able to find, they followed the directions to the best of John's ability to comprehend the engineer's constructing guide. Finding a suitable starting point between a relatively large boulder and a nearby tree situated at the edge of the stream, they began to set up their temporary housing.

Raising a thick branch here, leaning one there, tying together corners with newly cut vine: the image of a basic safe house was beginning to take form. With the final glow of light about to fade away, the outermost layer of dead leaves was spread upon the "roof" of their home. John held his hand out, assisting Sofia down from the boulder to stand beside him, to admire their work of art.

"We did it. Can you actually believe we finished it?" John asked with a tone of accomplishment. "And so quickly, too."

"With just the two of us, I think we could do almost anything," Sofia replied.

Standing before them was the completion of the first project that they had ever created together. Lopsided and disproportioned, dangling tree limbs and drying mud, it was hardly a thing of beauty.

John placed his arm around Sofia's shoulders.

"Yes, Dear, I think we can," he said.

Their final view of the shelter was melting away before their eyes as the blackness of night gained control, when suddenly, from out the darkness, the creaking, crumbling sounds of wood and falling leaves, snapping and fractured, the crushing annihilation of their project was proverbially crashing down around them. A lesson of Life was, although unwelcome, necessarily received. Due to the earlier waning light, John had been given little time to read the fine print in the manual regarding ground conditions when building a shelter. In his haste he had overlooked the warning: *Build on dry, solid ground.*

"At least the roof will make for a nice, soft bed," Sofia whispered. With muscles aching, and a hunger greater than mere berries and leaves could alleviate, the exhausted couple began their third day of freedom anew scratching at the raised bumps on their skin, an irritation received from the rash-inducing leaves used for their bedding. It was another one of Life's lessons duly received.

Bathing in the cold water of the stream gave a mild, if not temporary, relief from the itching. Another delay in the journey had found them. As the newly unearthed, hindering event was out of their control once again, they attempted to ignore it, reminding themselves that their present predicament was merely an uncomfortable inconvenience when compared to the misery that they had left behind. It would be just like the day when they walked away from the City, its oppressive walls and darkened heart had disappeared into the past. So too would the current discomfort fade away. By the end of the day it would exist merely as a memory, nothing more.

The morning's light brought forth beams of golden rods that broke through the leaves and reflected off the dust of the forest. The terrain, stable and flat, made for a relatively simple excursion. John and Sofia, despite the burning skin that they were both in possession of, were now feeling the euphoric effects of their liberation from the confines of the City of Labor.

With the ease of walking of which the valley's floor allowed, John held the book in front of his face, taking in more of its data necessary to their livelihood, while Sofia held his other hand and led the way.

"We won't be doing this now," he spoke, without removing his face from the book, "but, we'll be needing to start fires on our own... to cook food."

"What kind of food?" Sofia asked, as she had never considered where meat and vegetables actually came from.

Shrugging his shoulders, John replied, "I don't know. I haven't reached that part of the book yet."

"Well, I hope it's good food, because I'm starving," she said, kicking at the passing rocks.

"Mr. Sanders was a resourceful fellow. I'm sure he thought of how to get tasty food, too."

As the trees of the valley began to thin out, John and Sofia eventually found themselves knee-high in a grassy clearing. Taking cover beside a group of large stones set beside a rotting trunk, they spotted a herd of four-legged creatures, antlers rising off of their heads like trees without leaves, dancing and playing with one another in the open land.

It was a beautiful sight to see the creatures so lively and free as they methodically glided about in a choreographed display of jubilation. The fur covering their skin was short and silky, speckled with small, brownish patches of darker areas that gave the appearance of eyes covering their bodies. Their torsos were suspended about a meter above the tips of the herbage by their thick legs. Contracting muscles cast waves of shadows across their thighs as the creatures pushed against each other, butting their heads together and entangling the branch-like structures between them.

"Let's try to get a closer look," Sofia said, beginning to sneak forward.

Holding on to the hem of her dress, John followed close behind. Keeping low in the grass, the hair of their heads visible to only the most keen of observers, they moved along with cautious curiosity.

The melodic, ostentatious display became more vibrant as another herd appeared out of the small thicket behind the two adventurers. Through the rustling leaves and moist soil, the rhythmical, steady gait of the approaching group of animals seemed to be dictated by the prancing creatures of the field. In the herd's hypnotic trance, Sofia and John did not appear to be residents to their reality. Their uniform, almost robotic, movements by which they conveyed themselves toward their kindred soul mates, a testament to the bonding force between the male and female subset of any species, was a splendid presentation beneath the lights of the Savior.

Passing within mere centimeters of the two wanderers, the towering bodies and muscular features of the creatures were made more distinct due to their close proximity. Sofia held her hand out, her curiosity overpowering her reason. Before John could put a stop to her folly, she let the smooth hairs of one of the creatures' forelegs brush against her fingers. Looking back at John with a joyful smile, she could see he was not impressed.

With the animal continuing onward with its forward pace, she paid little mind to her friend's prudish expressions. Refusing to retract her arm, her fingertips came into contact with the animal's hind leg. As if it suddenly became aware of its surroundings, it immediately suspended its movement, rearing up and standing upon its hind legs in an erect fashion, stiff and controlled. With its breathing heavy and forceful, it seemingly held the others at bay. It appeared that Sofia's touch had broken the spell under which the creature's mind had been held captive.

The tugging at her skirt by John was all that was needed to convince her to scurry back beside him into the safety of the grass. With its nose to the sky, the herd's leader began sniffing into the air, its ears pricked up and attentive.

"What are they doing?" Sofia whispered inquiringly.

"I'm not sure. Just don't move."

Following suit, the rest of the herd, one-by-one, took up a similar posture as their point guard. Ceasing with their jubilant exhibition, the other party in the open field began posturing up in the same fashion until the two opposing groups were a mirrored image of one another.

A mild disturbance emanated from a yellowed patch of grass, equidistant from a stony cluster in the field to the conjoining parties, sending a panic response throughout the clearing. Multitudes of small winged creatures fled to the sky, violently rustling the leaves of the outlying trees and the field's heavy blades.

As the heavens began to darken under the clouds of flapping, screeching fowl encircling above, the two herds, their members dropping back to their four-legged stances, heads looking about with overpowering fright, dispersed in a disorganized manner in an apparent attempt to become as equally scarce removed from the open land as the feathered creatures now suspended between soil and Savior.

A blur of Reddish-brown fur began filtering through the grassland from whence the original disturbance had its beginning. With innumerable directions, it split up, like particles of light sifting through the clouds, scattering at various angles. Although difficult to see in detail, these newly arrived beasts traversed the field with the greatest of speed, plowing forth in the several directions by which their antlered victims hastened to escape.

Unsure of which way to flee, John helped Sofia to her feet. Keeping a low profile in the grass, he desperately scanned their surroundings for a path to a secure refuge.

The antlered beasts began toppling over and disappearing into the grass, leafless branches rising and falling in the struggle to survive. Their horrific screams and agonizing cries joined with the fluttering of the winged flocks.

"Come on," John yelled, his hand grasping Sofia under the armpit.

Forcing her to run towards the nearest hillside, where the security of the woods awaited, she could scarcely maintain his pace. Tripping over her own feet and the small stones hidden among the foliage, John bored Sofia ahead in spite of the fear that was consuming her.

"What's happening, John?" Sofia cried.

"It doesn't matter... just keep running," he panted.

Behind them, the screaming, tearing flesh and the snarling of a multitude of beasts, was instilling a terror in Sofia with such intensity that her heart began beating with a force that made her vision a disorderly spin. Her mind, cast into a surreal world of blackness and gloom, was so overcome, that she slipped on an unseen stone and fell to the ground.

Sobbing uncontrollably she wailed, "I'm so scared. I'm so scared."

Dropping to her side and placing his arms around her, his mouth beside her ear, laboring with exhaustion, he spoke, "Sofia, we need to keep moving. We don't have the time, girl. There's something bad out there. Get up, let's go."

She was lost in her own world of horror. She had become another irrational creature waiting her turn to leave the land of the living, along with all the other beasts in this arena of death. He had to think for her... he had to *make* her listen!

Placing her arm around his neck, John stood Sofia up and began the slow and steady trudge towards the tree line ahead. With the weight of his overwhelmed companion upon him, the soft, stony soil added to the difficulty of each step. The macabre screams of a murderous rampage were continuing to feed their ears with a symphony of destruction. He was afraid, too, but he was equally, if not more so, determined not to let all that Mr. Sanders had worked for come to nothing. The muscles of his thighs scorched with the planting of each foot. His lungs burned with each breath he grasped at, causing a sheering of his already wounded ribs. But this was not their end. Whatever it was that was killing those poor creatures it was not getting them. He would see to that.

The first trees of the woods were just within reach, and the screams were beginning to fade in the distance. John felt the relief of seeing the cover of green leaves and the thick trunks so near.

"We made it girl," he said. "Everything's going to be..."

Before he was able to complete the sentence, a flash of blurred fur and a sharp blow sent him tumbling forward. Finding himself face down in the damp soil, he lifted his head to catch his breath, but found himself face-to-face with Death. Snarling through the bloodstained fur at the edges of its mouth, a creature crouched, hideous and cruel, staring him in the eyes. It strafed to the side slowly and methodically, as if it was uncertain as to what the new threat was that was standing before it.

Lifting himself slowly, so as not to startle his predator, John raised himself up. Grasping onto a fist-size stone, he motioned with his other hand to Sofia, who was frozen in fear behind him, to slowly back away.

The crimson tinted saliva dripped from the mouth of the wild animal while it circled about, growling, gnashing and displaying its jagged teeth. As John lifted his hand in preparation to throw the stone, the creature lunged at him with open jaws. Falling backward John instinctively thrust his weapon into the animals face, sending shattered remnants of teeth and flesh into its throat. The beast's long snout, crumpled inward by the force of the blow, blew streams of blood and tinted excretions across the stone and along John's hand and arm.

Blindly stumbling about and clawing at its head, the beast snorted and gasped under the bubbling of blood that was filling its lungs. Spinning around in circles it finally crashed to the soil in violent convulsions less than half a meter from John's feet. It was dead, but the threat was not.

There could be no delays now. John pulled Sofia up by the arm.

"We have to keep going," he commanded her. "There could be more of them."

She held his hand as he led the way. The sticky coagulated serum, the evidence of John's heroic action, was oozing through his fingers and onto her palm, emitting a nauseating stench into the air around them.

"We need to get back to the water," he said. "The way that animal was sniffing the air before they attacked, they must be able to smell this mess."

There was a lone howling in the distance followed by several beasts chiming in. At first it was disorderly and at various distances, but after a time it became uniform and singular in location.

Looking over her shoulder, Sofia felt the eyes of many unseen foes lurking in the trees around them, watching them. As she and John neared the water's edge, they were once again in the shadows of the woods.

John knelt beside the water and began vigorously rubbing his hands across his arms while dipping them into the cool stream. Cleansing himself of the creature's bodily fluid reduced the heavy stench that came with it, but only to the degree that, he believed, would not be detectable by their pursuers, if they existed at all.

The rotting smell still remained in his nose, but it would not be a giveaway to their whereabouts.

Sofia stayed a few meters away, standing upon the shore, quivering and tearful.

"You need to wash up too, girl. Come on down here and get cleaned up."

Turning about with every movement of the forest, and scanning each area for any signs of an impending threat, she walked down, standing close beside him. John could see in her eyes the toll that the beast's presence had taken upon her soul. Her innocence was now awash in the dreadful reality of the new world of which they were now citizens.

"Sofia. You need to wash up right now," John said, looking up at her.

She hesitated. Looking down at the dried stickiness that coated her fingers she spoke with a stuttering voice, "Oh, okay. I am. I will."

Her hands were trembling as she settled beside him and began rubbing the blood into the drifting waters. Teary-eyed and sniffling, drops fell from her chin and the tip of her nose, plopping onto her distorted reflection below. She leaned her body against him and continued rubbing until there were no more signs of the creature's life upon her.

"As beautiful as the world looked from the top of Labor, I never imagined that we would find it so harsh," she sobbed.

"Don't worry, Sofia. You are all that I have in this world. I won't let anything happen to you. I promise."

Another uniform howling of the bestial pack echoed throughout the forest. Grabbing Sofia by the hand, John led the two of them deeper into the thickness of the woods. Due to the severity of the situation, direction mattered not, and it was not long before they had lost their bearings. The evening was now falling fast upon them, and the pursuing creatures had not been heard for a comfortable period of time. Finding a suitable place to spend the night would not be easy, but it had to be done.

The third night brought with it a new item into its reality: fear. Not having been able to locate their position on the map, the young couple bunkered down between a series of boulders that they found protruding from the side of one of the hills that they happened upon.

Every snap and every flutter brought with it a startled awakening into the blackness of night: clouds above disallowing even the faintest of starlight to seep in. Distant howls heard during the previous times of darkness now possessed faces. Hideous and cruel, they would forever be etched upon the minds of John and Sofia.

The Savior's light would return in the morning, but with all the disturbing events of the day, sleep would be near impossible to come by.

CHAPTER TWELVE

Sofia's blue eyes were like drops of liquid sky upon the green grass that grew out of the moist dirt beneath her head, burning with the sensitivity brought about by a night of restlessness. Rolling over to greet John, she found an empty, flattened patch of emerald blades in the place where she had last felt him lying during the night.

"John," she sat up, calling out. "John, where are you?"

"It's alright," John called out, his voice rather faint, but within close proximity. "I'm right up here."

His head peeked over the rocky formation above her, the compass dangling from a string about his neck.

"I'm just trying to figure out where exactly we are on the map. I'm pretty sure that we didn't go too far off course, though. I'm thinking," he said, pointing out across the valley, "we just angled off a little from the direction to the crash site. If I'm right, we should be there by tomorrow."

The late-morning trek had gone by without incident. Moving at a relatively brisk pace, they traversed a greater distance than John had anticipated, partially motivated by the fear of the creatures of the valley, partially by the desire to reach a place that they could call *home*.

From the top of a steep hill they witnessed the patchy, cumulus clouds sailing across the blue expanse, casting their roving shadows upon the flowing land. From their newly acquired vantage point, they took a small rest, snacking on the berries and other edibles that they had collected along the way.

The warm breeze filtering through the leaves and grass flowed in beautiful patterns of rippling green waves along the hill's westerly side. Far from the previous day's harrowing experience, John and Sofia were both feeling the internal relief of having not heard or seen another creature like the ones they experienced in the valley behind them.

Knowing that the time was quick to get away if he let them get too caught up in the beauty of the moment, John put an end to their rest. As there were many more kilometers to cover before they were to reach the crash site, he did not delay in resetting their course. Taking Sofia by the hand, he led her down the hill.

Talking with one another about what possibilities the site held regarding, as it was labeled in the little, leather book, *Food and*

Shelter, was a good way for them to pass the time. It was difficult to refrain from letting their imaginations get the best of them. After all, creating the mental images of comforting home sites in the mind was such an easy thing to do when the desire for it was so close to the heart.

The hours had passed by without notice. Taking another momentary stop at a nearby tree allowed John to pick up a new waypoint in the distance that would help them to keep moving in a uniform direction. Small, fury creatures scurried about, playing in the branches. As the couple took to their feet, moving onward once again, larger, long-eared animals appeared to follow them down the hill.

Reading aloud from the little, black book, John detailed for Sofia the method Mr. Sanders described as to how they could make a fire with a stick and a piece of dry wood. It sounded simple enough to him. After all, placing the tip of a long, thin branch into a woodchip-filled, notched out portion of a thick piece of timber, and spinning it between the palms of his hands until the friction of the two surfaces had generated enough heat to see smoke, could not be that hard. After a small discussion on the topic, they both decided to attempt the activity once they reached their campsite later that evening.

As the morning had been, so became the rest of the afternoon. The time together was not without appreciation, and a great deal of it was spent in the discussions of the wonders around them. There was not a moment that passed by that seemed wasteful or monotonous.

Finding a watering hole that was pre-marked on the map was an immense self-accomplishment to John. With a great deal of the day well past, he charged Sofia with the task of finding some berries and edible leaves for their meal, while he scrounged around for the building materials and the perfect pieces of wood necessary to start the night's fire.

After an hour's time, all the resources were gathered. Before beginning the arduous task of constructing their shelter, John chose the task of fire starting as their first duty at the site.

Sitting upon a rotting, fallen log, he placed a large portion of wood between his legs as diagramed in the book. John's knife easily broke through the outer, bark surface as he cut a relatively deep depression into it. Dropping in some bits of crumbled chips into the notch, he then inserted a long, pointy branch. The stick was a perfect fit, sliding into the groove without rubbing too tightly against the inner diameter of the hole.

Sandwiching the branch between his palms, he began rolling it back and forth, as directed by Mr. Sanders' instructions. The motion naturally pulled his hands downward proximally to the tip, forcing him to stop the action in order to bring his hands back up to the top of the stick. Every few seconds he needed to repeat the operation and, after a minute or two, his hands began to feel hot and painful.

"This isn't quite as easy as it ought to be," he said, as he strained under the work of the primitive tools. "Will you give me a hand?"

The task did not look too difficult from where Sofia was sitting. Standing up from the rock that she had been using as her seat, she walked over and climbed upon the log, kneeling down beside him. Attempting to copy John's example, she made an effort to roll the branch in unison with him. Unable to get the rhythm down properly, after several attempts, she ceased in the struggle.

"I don't think this is working correctly. Are you sure you're doing it right?" she inquired, striving for a tone that would not offend.

"No. I'm doing it right," he barked.

Several blisters, and a few painful minutes later, John picked up his wood burning project and, turning towards the dense forest behind him, he threw it as far as he could.

"It's too warm for a fire right now, anyway," he said, flushed and discouraged. "Maybe we'll try again some other time."

With his fire-making enterprise now behind him, he and Sofia set about with the building of their shelter.

It wasn't long before they were settling down for the evening under a semi-structurally safe lean-to. Lying on their backs, partially under the cover, they stared into the light-fading sky above. Clouds marched by in formation, dressed in dark-pink-ish hues of glowing light set against a deepening blue stretch of space. This was the first time since escaping from Labor that they had been able to gaze into the night air. As the purple and blue swirls of the last light, the final remnants of the Savior-less world, faded into obscurity, the lights of the first stars of the heavens began to appear... and with them the multitude of wishing stars.

At first they were a comfort for John to see. But, as the darkness seeped in, and the wishing stars became more pronounced, there was something out of sorts with their movements that he did not recall seeing all those nights on the rooftops of Labor.

"Do the wishing stars look the same to you?" he inquired.

Sofia concentrated on a few streams of light gliding through the sky.

"Pretty much. I don't really see anything out of the ordinary. Why do you ask? Do they look different to you?"

Tracing his finger along a single light moving along its trajectory in space, he followed it until it disappeared over the horizon. Moving his hand back to the star's place of origin, he found another one that had suddenly appeared in the exact place as the former. Performing the same tracing movement upon it, his hand slid across the sky in an identical arc.

"Doesn't that seem rather odd to you?" he asked with his hand suspended above them.

"I didn't see anything," she responded rather abruptly.

"Here, let me do it again," he said with a hint of frustration. "Now, watch closely."

It wasn't long before another identical light appeared overhead. Tracing it once again with his hand, it seemed to follow the identical path as the previous ones, with a single exception: at the end of the arc, just above the distant hills, it made an unnatural change in its path before disappearing from sight over the planet's horizon.

"What was so different about that?" she remarked.

"That wasn't the oddest thing you've ever seen? It was following the exact same path as all the stars before it, but just as it reached the hills over there, it suddenly changed course."

"I'll try to pay closer attention to the next one," she said, holding her arm out and pointing to a wishing star that had just appeared to the North.

For the next hour or so, they continued to trace out the paths of several wishing stars with their fingers. It appeared that all of them followed the same four sets of initial arcs in the sky before veering off into one of six different directions over the curved edge of the planet.

"I wonder if the smoke and fumes that came out of the factories of Labor kept the sky too polluted and obscured for us to see this," John mused.

"That could be why we didn't notice it before," Sofia replied. "Isn't it amazing what the stars can do?"

Looking away from the heavens above, there was a clearly discerned disappointment in John's demeanor, and he replied with a somber tone, "Yeah... amazing."

Sofia's smooth, youthful skin reflected against the dim lights falling from the illuminating bodies of the night. Watching her out of the corner of his eye he was saddened by the fact that she either did not recognize that there was something askew in that parade of beams that etched themselves across the blackness of the night, or else she was willfully ignoring it in order to keep alive the hope that all those wishes she had made in Labor would one day come true.

As the night was further upon them, John decided that it was best to get into the shelter and get some rest for the coming morning. Cuddling close together, the warmth of their bodies made the cool ground beneath them a tolerable temperature. Falling into a deep sleep, their fourth night was soon to be over.

Chapter Thirteen

The new day's journey brought with it a spirited flight down the hill as the intrepid explorers returned back into the valley. Because the previous night's sleep was spent in deep slumber, both John and Sofia had become so refreshed by the rest that they had acquired that they spent some moments playfully jogging through the grass. Purple flowers, petals spread wide open and leaning into the Savior's rays, grew in great patches along the path, helping to create an atmosphere of newness and purity once again.

By mid-day John redirected them to the top of an approaching hill from where, he thought, there existed the possibility that they would be able to see their objective. The climb seemed rather mild in contrast to the previous day's steep hills. Without exerting much of their energy, they arrived at the lookout point ahead of schedule.

Placing his hands above his brow, shielding his eyes from the glare of the Savior, John scanned the rolling hills in the distance.

"I know it's on one of those two mounds over there," he said, pointing westward.

Looking intently in the same direction, Sofia followed his lead, but came up equally short in identifying the correct location. Everything looked the same: green trees, green grass, protruding boulders, rolling hills. There was nothing to suggest that the planet had a great, open wound torn from its side, impaled by a crashed machine.

"I'm not seeing anything that looks like a wrecked vehicle," she said.

"Strange," John replied, with a perplexed tone. "It has to be over there."

Pulling the black book out from under his arm and turning to the back cover, he scanned over the details of Mr. Sander's sketch before returning his eyes to the distant hills.

"I think it's on the other side of that ridge. Let's try to circle around it. Maybe we can see it from a different angle."

Descending back into the valley with a new waypoint waiting at the top of the next hill before them, Sofia asked, "Why don't we just go straight over there?"

With the interruption to his reading, he replaced the book back under his arm and said, "I don't know what we're going to find there. It just seems best if we observe the place from a distance first, just to be sure it's safe."

The answer was a reasonable one as far as Sofia was concerned. Resting content with it she allowed herself to be captivated in the moment, observing the feathered creatures of the sky chirping and playing, swooping between the branches of the trees.

As they walked through the knee-high grass in a single file line with John leading the way, John's nose was, once again, stuck in the little, black book. To pass the time, Sofia began plucking a few flowers from their stems while they brushed against her legs. She slid one behind her ear fully appreciating the fresh, sweet aroma in the air surrounding her as the delicate, purple flora released its fragrance to the wind. With a gentle rub upon her arm of the pistils from the bundle she had gathered, the aromatic splendor had now become an article of clothing: a part of her person.

Upon reaching the base of the final hillside Sofia could see that the flowers were thinning out upon its face, completely fading away into non-existence a few meters below the summit. Uprooting several more clusters, she placed them into the side pockets of her dress. She wanted to continue to smell pretty long after the patches of beauty had passed her by.

The climb to the top was lightly challenging at best. But, as the pinnacle of the hill was now within reach, John could feel his heart beginning to beat with that anxious rhythm that he had experienced several times past on their journey. What would happen if the safe house had been removed without Mr. Sanders' knowledge of it, perhaps picked up by a Security Force clean-up crew or some other agency of Labor, he thought to himself. Or worse, maybe it was set up as a trap, and they were falling right into it.

With each step his distress was intensified until the solicitude ultimately deteriorated into an incontestable fear. The waypoint was finally reached. As they overlooked the lateral aspects of the two hills diagramed on the map, John came to the conclusion that his apprehensions may have been unfounded.

The sketched image was rather faded due to its age, and John was unsure as to how accurately the crash site had been portrayed by it. Going on the details Mr. Sanders had penciled in, it appeared that the fractured, cylindrical vehicle, having scraped away an extensive, narrow path for itself, was imbedded deep into the hill's soil, separated at the mid-section, the aft portion resting at its side in an L-shape. At the time that the drawing was crafted, the local vicinity surrounding the unnaturally, freakish structure appeared to have been scorched and exfoliated. The hill, injuriously affected, would have been an extreme contrast to the surrounding landscape. But, from his and Sofia's current perspective, it became quite apparent that the wounded incline had long been healed over, and was now painted green with the grass and vines, and decorated with the young, narrow saplings that had sprouted up with time.

Concealing away its scars, and along with it the lifeless intruder, it was instantly made obvious and relieving to John's soul, knowing that the site could only be immediately discernable to those persons pre-possessed with the knowledge of the traumatic past of the planet.

"So, this is where we find the *Food and Shelter*," John said with a touch of uncertainty and a dash of doubt. "What do you think of it?"

Looking out across the small valley leading up to the one hill that they had spent so many days searching for, Sofia could see that it was not the castle-like structure with golden arches and inviting aura that she had hoped would be awaiting their arrival. In fact, it did not even appear to be accessible without a bit of work on their behalf. From what she was able to gather from their lofty center of observation, it seemed as if the whole arrangement had been blanketed over by the hill itself in an attempt to disguise its hideous lesion from the Savior above. But, she concluded, this was their final place of rest. They were being granted a permanency that they never could have thought possible before today.

"It's…" she said hesitantly, "… different."

As they reached the base of their lookout hill, John and Sofia entered into the thicker trees of the valley. The realization that they were finally reaching the end of their pilgrimage made it difficult for them to cease with their giddy laughter.

What began as John's earnest desire to travel eastward, to seek the land of the rising Savior, was detoured by the Unseen Forces that govern the events of the ages. Leading them instead towards the place where the Savior settles at the end of His daily march across the sky, Providence had given John an odd, but comforting, message, informing him that he did not have quite as much control over his and Sofia's destinies as he once thought he had.

The events of the past week seemed but years ago. The world that they had left behind was as equally far, if not farther, from their minds as they were in distance to that terrible City. Moving his hands through a drape of dangling vines, John proceeded to push them aside, allowing Sofia to squeeze through the narrow opening between the trunks of the trees.

"Oh, John. Look," she said, pointing towards something just out of his view on the other side of the tree line.

Hurrying through the natural threshold, John desired to see what had caught Sofia's fancy so intensely. The world beyond was quite different than the lush green forest that they had been traversing. The grass was somewhat darker in color, almost emerald in appearance, and much shorter in length, while the trees, stubbier and relatively narrow in diameter when compared to the thick trunks of their older brethren, were thinly spread and far from maturity. Completely passing through, John let the curtain of vine fall back into place behind them.

Finding themselves standing in the center of the monumental channel that the flying craft had carved into the land before skidding to a halt upon the hillside, there was a sense of minuteness and inadequacy that befell the two of them that not even the tallest of hills, nor the expansive views of land that they had witnessed spreading across the planet, had been able to achieve.

Expanding for hundreds of meters ahead lay the unnaturally widened path leading up to the two portions of the vine and moss covered vehicle. Two mounds of soil protruded from the edges of the trench, forming fantastic walls of grass decorated with various colors of flowers, as if to form a majestic walkway for two weary travelers. The two halves of the air machine were massive in height and breadth, even at such a far distance. Their diameters were of relative length comparable to the medium sized buildings of Labor.

Pieces of metal debris, great and small, littered the landscape, creating an entirely novel world-within-a-world feel. Walking with a reduced pace in order to gather in the oddly formed environment by way of the many senses upon which it was affecting, they noticed that even the sounds emitting from the local area had a unique aural impression. The chirping of the tiny, grass-dwelling creatures was of a high intensity, whereas there had been only minor sounds generated by them in all the land of which the two had journeyed over. There were unique and colorful flying creatures, which appeared to sing among the trees. The flowers were of a deeper purple, almost to the point of blackness, and held a slight bend towards the Savior's direction. Glowing, flying insects buzzed above the grass with illuminated bodies that sparked in intermittent flashes.

They had been directed to this magical place by a merciful hand. And the desire to give thanks to someone, perhaps Mr. Sanders himself, seemed in order. But, neither Mr. Sanders, nor anyone else for that matter, was available to receive their gratitude. It was just Sofia and John, alone but happy.

The towering cylinders, cloaked in vines and thick green overgrowth which had seeped interiorly from between its cracks and punctured skin, dripped light-reflected dust from high above as John made the first step inside. The heavy creaking of the metallic floor shifting under his weight reverberated off the walls and into the inner chambers beyond his visual realm. A partition, designed to block further exploration into the deeper aspects of the vehicle's body, was thwarted in its plan by its damaged, metal door that had apparently broken off during the catastrophic event. It was now solidly lying flat upon the floor, allowing access into the blackened room before him.

Stacked in an orderly fashion against the craft's rounded walls, just outside the doorway were several small crates with the words *Golden World Foodstuffs* and *Red Lights, Battle*. The lids, previously broken off, had been lightly reset to allow for the ease of removal. Motioning to Sofia, who was peering in through the drapery of vine behind him, to continue to remain outside the vehicle, John lifted the lid off of one of the boxes. Reaching inside, he pulled out a cardboard case. It had the words *Candy Bars* written over it in a wide, bold font.

Tearing it open and revealing its contents, John found a food item of which he had never seen before. While most of the food products of Labor were generically labeled with blue writing on white paper composed in simplistic terminology, these were individually wrapped bars with colorful designs on the packaging, overwritten with dainty words regarding the nutritional value of the snack that was encased inside.

"I think I found some of the tasty food you were hoping for," he whispered as he threw a single bar towards Sofia's direction.

Clasping both hands around it as it sailed through the air, she immediately tore off the wrapper revealing a small, brown, rectangular edible. It gave off a sweet scent that was most inviting.

"Should I eat it?" she questioned.

John read the packaging to himself, "*Choctacular Delight.*" He then said to Sofia, "I have no idea what that means. I'm not even sure if that sounds good. But, it says here, '*It's a sensation to the taste buds*.'"

Taking another sniff off the wavy top of the bar, Sofia said, "Oh, it smells wonderful, though."

"I don't know, girl. I guess you might as well try it. Mr. Sanders didn't say anything about there being food we should avoid."

With her eyes closed, Sofia's teeth sank into the creamy chocolate, biting off a portion of the bar's corner. Allowing the succulent richness to fill her mouth, she hesitated to chew it at first.

"Well," John inquired, "is it any good?"

Nodding her head in the affirmative, she continued to savor the moment, moaning with delight.

"So, what's it taste like?" John asked with an expressed annoyance.

Opening her eyes, she took another bite.

"It's so incredible. You just have to try it," she spoke through a full mouth.

Pulling out another bar and simultaneously ripping the wrapper off and tossing it to the floor, John chomped off half of the treat in a single bite. With a grimacing brow, he chewed on the confectionary for a moment before suddenly opening his eyes wide and declaring, "This is so good."

As the berries had affected them earlier in their escape, so now the sugary meal was accomplishing an awakening in their minds. With their feet dangling off the edge of the fractured structure, they sat together, just as they had often perched so many times on the edge of the rooftops of Labor. Holding onto the partially eaten candy in one hand and their other hands clasped one to another, they held off from further exploration in order to better the enjoyment of their newly found edibles.

"This is so strange," John said. "I have this weird pressure around my head."

"I wonder if it's made of the same thing that's inside the berries we've been eating," Sofia responded.

"I think so, but these must be much more concentrated. I only felt like this after the first time we ate them."

With four bars each eventually consumed, the accompanying nausea of overindulgence began to set in. Placing the case back inside its crate, John was more than glad to get the sweet bars out of his sight.

"I don't think I'll ever eat another one of those things as long as I live," he said, holding his stomach.

Feeling a bit more comfortable regarding the safety of the vehicle, Sofia entered through the vine. The shifting of the metallic floor caused a lightly audible, vibratory sensation to roll through the vessel.

"I don't think I'll ever eat another one, either," Sofia belched in agreement.

Placing the lid of the crate back onto its former place, John pulled the top off of the next wooden box beside it. Lifting out one of the small, brown boxes inside, he read aloud from the cover, "*Red Lens Battle Light.*"

"Battle light? Is that one of those lamps that the soldiers in the pictures are sometimes using?" Sofia asked.

"I believe it is," he said opening its carton.

Pulling out an olive drab, cylindrical casing with a red lens-containing head that bent at a ninety-degree angle from the longer body, he turned it around in his hands inspecting its plastic construction. Depressing the black switch at its side caused the lamp to awaken. The interior of the vine-draped room suddenly lit up with a similar red glow to that which illuminated from the scanners outside the apartments of labor.

Shining the light into the doorway, John peeked his head in and looked around.

"What do you see?" Sofia asked with anxious curiosity.

Stacked from the floor to the rounded ceiling, and spread throughout the entire area, were crates of various sizes. There was a path that appeared to have been deliberately left opened between them, where a walkway had been left, leading around a corner and into the darkness.

"It looks like a storage room of some type," he said, pulling her by the hand.

With the red lamplight casting bizarre shadows from their moving bodies, and the vine and roots of grass dangling overhead, Sofia couldn't help but startle at the appearance of movement all around them.

Inspecting the labeling of the crates against a piece of paper on a clipboard hanging from the wall, John figured that the Sanders must have been organizing and cataloging the entire inventory of, what must have once been, a cargo ship.

To one area they had separated men and women's clothing, out of which John found himself a new pair of shoes, along with various items, such as cases of books, appliances and medicinal elements from antibiotics, to creams and lotions from *Golden World*. While in another area there were stacks of boxes labeled *Red* and *Raw* that contained uniforms, boots, various crates of small arms and ammunition, mining tools and machines. The largest of the groupings was in the food department, where the crates were densely stacked to the ceiling.

Following along the labyrinth-like path among the wooden containers leading them to another doorway, of which they found the door having been previously removed and propped up against the wall, they entered in. Finding themselves in another room of nearly the same dimensions as the previous one, John and Sofia stood in awe at the sights before them. From floor to ceiling, with minimal space to move about, crates of food were so bountiful that there must have been enough to feed an entire army of men for many years. As the room was filled to capacitance, there was no way for them to continue further into the inner chambers of the vessel.

"It looks like they were using this place exclusively as a warehouse," John said, moving the light from label to label. "There's enough food here to last our entire lives."

"More than enough," Sofia interjected.

"But, if this is the storage place," he looked inquisitively at her, "then the other half of this vehicle must be the place where they were planning on living."

"You mean where we'll be living? Let's go see it."

Snapping the lamp out from John's hand, Sofia let out a taunting howl before quickly disappearing through the doorway, entering into the maze of crates leading back to their point of origin. Caught off guard by the suddenness of her folly, John was left standing momentarily dazed in the blackness with only a faint glow of light and her giddy laughter leading him out.

"Sofia," he yelled, desperately running towards the faint glimmer of the lamp. "That's not funny, you bad girl!"

Trying to keep within a suitable distance so as not to lose sight of the illumination completely, at every turn John bumped into the walls of the crates, occasionally tripping over the rope-like vine scrawled across the floor.

The corridors made by the stacks of boxes were not as easy to maneuver between with such a dim light illuminating his path. As the fear of falling too far behind was growing stronger with an inverse proportion to the strength of the glow of the lamplight, he suddenly found himself alone within the darkness of the vessel.

"Sofia! Get back here," he screamed at her, but she was long gone from his presence.

With the last glimmer of the precious light cut off, along with her girlish squeals, groping blindly with his hands and feet, feeling his way along the walls, slow and steady, was his only option. Racing around with the youthful, imaginative thoughts of his mind, the frightful expectation of one of the forest's hairy creatures grabbing him by the shoulder seemed inevitable. As the cool beads of sweat began to well upon his brow, the anxious stuffiness of the thick blackness engulfed his entire being. He felt the familiar, dull pain behind his eyes as he tried to hold back his tears. Against his resistance to do so, he succumbed to the childish urge to cry.

Minutes passed by, and, feeling his way around a sharp corner of crates, he finally caught site of that familiar glow of the lamp as it filtered through the doorway a few meters ahead.

Exiting from the darkness, he emerged into the red-lit room

where he found the lamp standing on its end, propped up on the open lid of the candy crate.

"Sofia," John whispered. "Where are you, you naughty girl?"

Pulling back the drapery of vine, Sofia peeked her head in, chocolate stained lips and all.

"Is everything alright?" she asked with an air of indifference.

"That wasn't funny," he said to her delightful giggling. "And, besides, I thought you weren't going to eat anymore of those things."

She licked her lips then, one-by-one, she sucked the sugary smears from her fingertips.

"I wasn't. But, hearing you cry made me work up an appetite."

"Very funny," he said, wiping the moisture from his cheeks, "I wasn't crying. I was just concerned about you."

CHAPTER FOURTEEN

L ifting his legs over the twisted, metal edge of the vessel, John held on tightly to a vine with one hand, and with the other he assisted Sofia with the climb. The lower half of the machine had been fractured off from the unexplored upper portion, and was situated perpendicularly to it, lying at the base of the hill.

Appearing similar to the storage half, the vine and thick moss and grass, overlaid the semi-embedded metallic hull with a cloak of living green. A peculiar tunnel of organically overgrown crates and scraps of torn metal had been previously arranged at the center of the rounded wall of what had once been the middle room of the vehicle when it was in its original state. Depressing the switches on the lamps that each of them now carried, John and Sofia cast their lights upon the entrance. A reflection returned back to them, bouncing off of the peculiarly set chrome décor dangling off of the steel hatch nestled at the distal end of the manmade cave.

Arm-in-arm the two adventurers cautiously moved in, pushing aside the sticky webs, blowing at the dust and flying insects that manifested in the lamplight. Carefully stepping over the contorted trails of vine that spread like thick, green veins upon the floor, they finally reached the decorated, hinged plate that hindered their further progression. Handing his lamp to Sofia, John grasped at the metallic, spoked wheel situated in the middle of the door, cranking it in a counter-clockwise fashion, grunting under the exertion.

After an intense, high-pitched grind poured forth from the lock's hidden mechanism, the wheel began to turn with minimal effort, completely unbolting from the wall, allowing the door to swing wide open. Retrieving his lamp from Sofia, John peered inside, carefully sweeping his light back and forth about the room. Various orange-yellow reflections littered the walls from the mirrorlike golden-brass ornaments adorning the long hidden abode.

"What do you see?" Sofia asked.

Stepping over the threshold and into their new home, John held his hand out to her.

"It looks safe enough," he said. "Come, take a look."

Taking a firm hold of John's arm, Sofia stepped over the lip of the threshold and moved inside, flashing the cone of light from her lamp in various directions in an attempt to better orient herself to the new environment. Although the monochrome, crimson spectrum that her lamplight emitted was not favorable to the appreciation of that afforded by the natural light of the Savior, Sofia perceived by the flowery designs of the rug-covered flooring and the beautifully embellished living arrangements, that the layout of their new quarters could only have been chosen by Mrs. Sanders herself. Considering all of the Golden World furnishings crated in the warehouse vessel, the Sanders certainly had a variety of choices with regards to the enrichment of their place of residence.

Following the beam of his light around the room, John happened upon a thick, golden, satin rope dangling beside the entrance like a gilded vine. Shining his light upward, towards its attachment point high above, he could see that it extended through a series of pulleys, terminating at a junction box attached to a metallic plate out of which wires of various colors trafficked across the ceiling and walls. Concluding from his minimal experience at the Education that it was essentially the actuator of an electrical circuit, he gave it a firm tug. In the blink of an eye the room was filled with a soft, white light that dropped its illumination from the brass fixtures attached to the bracing that crisscrossed overhead. The gentleness of the atmosphere was accompanied by a melody of brass horns with a woodwind instrumental backdrop that began streaming out from an ornamentally carved, wooden box. The beautiful sound machine was wired to another apparatus that housed a strange black, plastic disk spinning within it at a steady revolution. Beside it there were stacks of other licorice colored disks leaning against the wall.

Panning his light across the ceiling, following the traffic of wires, John traced them to their point of origin. The Sanders, through their incredible engineering prowess, had somehow wired the entire arrangement to the wrecked vessel's power system, seemingly giving them a virtual supply of unlimited electricity.

With the comforting brilliance of the lamps, and the warm rain of auditory loveliness blanketing their senses, the gorgeously adorned room, now visible in its entire kaleidoscopic splendor, was a unique universe in itself. The wood flooring, deep and rich, that spanned from wall to wall, continued its spread into the adjoining rooms, an incredible witness to the constructive abilities that the Sanders had once possessed. The broad, flowery rugs displayed upon the floor were varicolored in hues in similitude to the natural world outside. By the way the furniture was situated, it was quite obvious to both John and Sofia that they were standing just inside the entrance to their newly acquired living room.

Off in the corner, a richly decorated, low profile table was placed in the center of a squared series of high-legged couches. A bookshelf carved with ornamental patterns, matching that of the wooden outer shells of the couches, rested against the arch of the wall, filled with a multitude of reading material. The trim that was fastened to the walls was of a carved floral arrangement, not unlike that of the rest of the finely crafted artistry of the rest of their *palace*. Waist high tables topped with brass works of art, completed the adornment, along with several paintings and a rather peculiar statue of a youthful male with a soothing ambience of expression, humbly walking with his eyes lifted to the sky.

"I wonder who this is supposed to be," Sofia commented.

"I have no idea," John said, looking closer at the detailing of the face. "He does look quite familiar, though, doesn't he?"

"Strangely familiar, I'd say."

As John continued to ponder on the identity of the stony image, Sofia passed through the next threshold. Pulling on the room's golden rope, she opened it up to the same illuminating beauty and melodic symphony of the former parlor.

Standing in what appeared to be the home's bedroom, the enormity of the sleeping quarters was oddly overwhelming. The cylindrical chamber was of equal size to that of the largest compartments of the *warehouse* vessel. But instead of housing a multitude of various sized crates, there existed but a single bed and a few makeshift rooms with only the interior hull of the ship, several meters above, substituting as the ceiling.

With much assumed difficulty, the Sanders had somehow managed to mount a steel railing across the diameter of the hull, situated between the ceiling and the floor. Energy transfer occurred from another junction box straddling the wall besides the railing. From this box, a rainbow of wires streamed along their pathways, with some terminating at a series of brass ceiling lamps just overhead.

Partitions of richly decorated wood, constructed at the far end of the sleeping quarters, housed a lady's room and a separate men's room, each adorned with a mirror of extraordinary reflective clarity and a bath of eggshell porcelain, pure and bright. There also existed a complex reservoir and drainage system designed using the plastic and metal pipes and clamps intertwined among the various fluid containers that were once part of the ship itself: another testament to the ingenuity of the creators of the project.

Taking into consideration the amount of work that had been performed at their home site, Sofia figured that the crash must have happened many years ago, perhaps long before she and John had even been born. It brought tears to her eyes to think of the happiness that Mr. Sanders and his wife had once experienced together while they were preparing this very room in anticipation of one day escaping from Labor. She felt as if she and John were too undeserving of becoming the recipients of another couple's hard work.

Stepping through the threshold and into the bedroom, John could see that Sofia was deep in thought. Remaining silent so as not to disturb her moment of reflection, he watched as she walked alongside a wood framed bed that was ornamentally carved at the headboard and footboard, and matched to the artistic motions of the floral arrangements of the wooden furnishings of the previous room.

She was running her hand across the soft, satin-like sheet with its silvery sheen and colorful embroidery that was spread across the mattress. Although he was unaware of it, there was a soothing of her emotions in the action, as when one relaxes in the warmth of a bath. Picking up a pillow stuffed with a material so light and comforting that it was like holding a cloud in her arms, Sofia closed her eyes allowing her mind to come to terms with the reality of the events that had taken place over the past week.

Her radiance reflected off of his eyes like the brilliant reflection of the Savior off the mirrored stillness of a pond of water. Sofia's beauty was not merely in her youthful skin, soft and smooth, nor in her hair, thickly flowing and yellowish-white. It was in the way she wore her heart on the outside, revealing the innocent, but discerning, young lady that was concealed inside the body of a petite girl.

She was glowing under a golden reflective aura, saturated with the gentle mist of musical splendor. The image, like a black and white photograph, was captured forever in his mind. Incited by the portrait before him, the impassionate sensations within his own thoughts began tearing at his heart. Although their current situation was a reality, it felt more like a wonderful dream. One from which they could never awaken.

The emotional trauma of the past few days had caught up to Sofia and was now laying siege to John's consciousness as well. Grasping and rending him in an incomprehensible number of directions, he could not find any way to pinpoint from where it began or where it ended.

Volatile and kindled, he was like an overloaded circuit, ready to burst into flames at any moment. But, he now understood why

Sofia was so lost in her own world: Mr. Sanders was a friend, the shortest of which duration had no factor. It was eternal. They had only known him for a fraction of time within this world. He was there one moment and then he was gone. But in some ways he seemed to be continually keeping watch over them. He was the father that each of them had always wanted, the only caring soul within a city devoid of feeling.

He and his wife had attempted to create for themselves a paradise within a paradise, far from the suffocating enclosure of the City of Labor. Their self-sufficient home, with all the supplies that would be needed for several generations to survive, seemed to be an impossible episode within an environment where chance reigned supreme. Could they have just wandered upon it by accident, or was it essentially handed directly to them by way of a determined, causal series of unimaginable proportions?

The material items of which their home was furnished, and of which were crafted, crated and stacked in their warehouse, were neither destined from their originators for the City of Labor, nor were they meant for the Sanders themselves. Certainly they were not for him and Sofia. They were pre-labeled for Golden World and Red, wherever they may be found. But, in this time-space continuum as a whole, as can be seen by the fates of these inanimate objects, by the occurrences of all the events that had transpired over the past week, what appears to be one's destiny in life can be altered within this causal nexus by sheer will, as well as by forces unseen, by a ripple effect initiated through a causal series set in motion by an action committed too long ago for anyone to remember. A simple, random throw of a rock, a left turn when one should have gone to the right, the seemingly minuscule actions in the lives of all people had profound effects in the world causing untold harm or benefit to innumerable others.

Whether he and Sofia were brought to this point by accident or purposeful design, John was not absolutely certain. But there existed that suspicion in the back of his mind that attributing everything, if not anything at all, to accidental phenomena was merely a baseless cop-out, a reason not to reason. Could there possibly be a valid framework to begin with chance interactions as the basis for the initiation of all causal events? Would their own hands now be required to carve their paths, or was there an Overseer of sorts, leading them onward? Were all the recent events merely a series of means pushing them towards a greater end, or was there truly an end at all?

As John stepped back into the material world, leaving behind that black-and-white, inner realm where self evaluates self and the cogs and gears of the mind attempt to keep a consistent perspective on all things, he found Sofia positioned upon the bed, curled up like a fragile infant. The slow, deep breaths by which her chest was rising and falling indicated that the exhaustion had finally overtaken her.

With the end of the musical score, a sliver of silence entered into the room, patiently awaiting the start of the next orchestral piece. As he made his way towards the bed, the creaking of the floor beneath his feet, which was previously inaudible, seemed out of sorts, adding an imperfection to the room's comeliness, making a deduction from its overall beauty.

Approaching the bedside, John sat down beside her, brushing the thin strands of hair from off of her face. Sofia was his only friend, his lover and companion on their journey into the unknown. He would protect her with his life, for she was all he had… and the soft hum of brass instruments accompanied by the symphonic, smooth layers of a wood blown instrumental backdrop fell once again, like warm rain, upon them.

CHAPTER FIFTEEN

The celerity by which the couple acclimated to the new environment was of no surprise, as the Sanders had taken great care in creating an ambience fit for the nourishment of the soul. From the smallest pieces of glassy, decorative articles, to the largest of paintings that adorned the walls and the auditory streams of music that accompanied all the visual assemblage, everything was fitted just right for encouraging an inner peace.

The first few weeks were an adjustment period, as John and Sofia found it quite awkward adapting to the new environment without considering from whence they came. Achieving the mindset to live immediately and completely in fearlessness and harmony after years of forced structure and policing, was difficult at best, and the days, nevertheless, went by in such a fleeting manner that even a retrospective consideration of any particular event during the present interval was nearly impossible. This was the only period when the tormenting entity, of which only time could do away with, maintained a presence in their minds. Wherever they were and whatever they were doing, it was always shouting out about that one frightful possibility: that at any moment someone could happen upon them and they would once again find themselves returning to the prison-like confines of Labor.

After several months without any contact from the Security Forces, or from any other persons of the City for that matter, the two of them began to feel less vulnerable regarding the potential loss of the permanency in their lives, and they quietly settled into their daily routines. They had organized each day to allow time for meal preparation and eating, the taking of several walks throughout the local lands and to the enjoyment of hobbies. The living conditions were remarkably well tailored to their spiritual and physical growth, and with each day that passed them by, they felt the strength of mind that comes with a confidence in one's own ability to cope with stressful situations. Looking to the future, there was only the light of the Savior, as the entire world seemed to be illuminated at their feet.

Chapter Sixteen

It had now been nearly two years since the great escape, or, nineteen months, to be exact, and Sofia had finally found the happiness and stability that she had always wished for. But, as John had pointed out long ago, he still had that pressing desire to follow the path leading to the Savior's rise. Although, curiosity and adventure were untamed creatures within both of their hearts, Mr. Sanders' warnings still rang loudly in Sofia's ears, and she continued to refrain from discussing any matter related to their journeying to the northeasterly lands.

In the days of living in Labor, John never seemed to have the time, nor the resources, for learning anything other than what he was forced to at the Education. But, with all the time that was available from this moment until the day in which he would pass away, he figured that there was more than he could ever hope for. Taking on the challenge of reading all the books at his disposal, he first began the task with the writings available in their library.

After several months, his knowledge began to increase with regards to the various topics with which the Sanders had stocked the shelves. There were novels of, what he assumed to be, strangely fictitious lands and peoples, field guides related to unique animals, plants and flying creatures of which he had never had the occasion of seeing with his own eyes. The military guides dispensed their information to him with experienced precision related to firearms use and many outdoor skills, of which he would put into practice during their several wanderings in the southern and western spheres. The warehouse crate log, of which the Sanders had used in their cataloging process, had revealed to him that there were more books available with a quantity so vast that he knew he would not be able to read them all during his lifetime.

Sofia had also taken up a newly found hobby for herself. During the earlier days of living in the crash site, they had spent much of their time rummaging through the warehouse. They were wholly fascinated by the novelty in the wealth of material goods available to them. But there were several crates, loaded full with various fabrics of assorted colors, stitching materials in abundance and stacks of patterns that caught her attention. As the crates were organized in close proximity to another grouping of wooden boxes, she figured that there had to be a relation between them, and so she had John pry them open. Nestled inside within a cocoon of straw, she discovered several stitching machines and their instructional manuals detailing the techniques for their use. It was the beginning of a new and wonderful enterprise for Sofia to express herself artistically.

After several weeks of practice with the simpler projects, she hastily advanced herself to the production of the more basic garments. She spent many hours of the day with her hands, actively taking part in her newly found craft. After many months, she had become quite proficient, although not perfect.

Night after night she would put on a display of the gorgeously streaming costumes for John to admire. As she was still, relatively speaking, a novice in the fabrication of the more fanciful apparel, John often had to bite his tongue to keep from smiling too hard, revealing the laughing that was hidden within him as she would prance about, spinning and dancing, not realizing that her lengths were uneven, or that the hems were sometimes undoing themselves.

During the cool of the mornings, before the Savior had poked His head above the horizon, John, having taken up a secondary hobby in the art of rifle shooting, would use these hours to the improving of his skills. Although Sofia would sometimes accompany him during these practice sessions, even taking the time to learn the art for herself, she eventually lost her interest in weapon utilization, desiring to spend more time with her hands in the fabrication of clothing.

Finding several crates of weapons and ammunitions of various sizes and calibers that had been destined, some for Red and some for Raw, John chose a medium length, shoulder mounted machine with iron sights to train with. Just as the books and fabrics, foods and other odds and ends, the ammunition was in such abundance that he was able to get in all the practice he needed to eventually become a superior marksman.

An empty tin can exploded from off the top of a rock approximately three hundred-fifty meters down in the valley below. From the prone position, John lifted his head from his weapon's stock and smiled with delight, as it had been the furthest distance that he had been able to hit a target with any degree of accuracy. Outfitted with a military uniform and hip pack, and adorned with the grass and branches methodically detailed in the books for blending into the environment's greenery and brown rocky terrain, he was camouflaged within the natural world, completely eliminating his bodily silhouette.

Sitting up, he placed the rifle across his lap and pulled out a binocular, looking-glass apparatus from the pouch hanging at his side. The panoramic view from his vantage point allowed him to see for many kilometers in all directions.

He and Sofia had, through their daily walks, established a circumferential boundary of safety from which they had ventured from on only a handful of excursions to the south and west since their arrival at the crash site. They had set up markers denoting nearby hidden supplies, which were helpful at first in keeping their minds in a positional perspective when roaming about. But after several weeks the guideposts were of little use, as the two of them had become so intimately acquainted with every nook, every tree, every outcropping of rock, that there were no natural entities within their confines that were unknown to them.

After scanning the perimeter around the hill, John looked to the sky. As the Savior had not made its presence known just yet, he could make out the last few wishing stars taking flight across the open expanse of purple and blue.

Of peculiar interest to him during this general time of the morning was not so much in the increasing of his weapons skills as it was in the careful observation of the *stars*, which were to him obviously not naturally occurring phenomena. John's morning shoots allowed him to monitor that perfect moment when the planet was angled just right to the Savior's rays, allowing him to study the transient vapor trails that dispersed the early light as the vehicles retreated from the northern territory before disappearing into the vastness of space. Where, he wondered, were they traveling from, and where were they heading?

The flying warehouse with which they were now using as their home, he concluded, had to have been a *wishing star* at some point in time before it met its untimely end. Like one of the small, wheeled transporters used in the City, but of a greater caliber and capacity, these airships appeared to be used for transporting goods to other citizens of the planet in far away lands. That was the only explanation he could think of as to how to reasonably apply the names *Red*, *Golden World* and *Raw* to the scant information that was available to him.

Sofia was just finishing up with the final touches of her skirt when John entered through the door. Setting his weapon down beside the bookcase, he passed her by. Without saying a word, he vanished into the bedroom.

"How did the shooting go today?" she inquired, clipping some thread and resetting her needle.

"It was alright," John called from the bedroom closet.

Entering back into the room dressed in a fresh shirt and clean pants, he walked over to the bookshelf, carefully scanning through the rows of titles. Looking over the top of her stitching machine, Sofia watched him with a cautious, but curious eye. He was acting rather odd. Pulling out several books, John flipped through the pages of each one rather haphazardly before returning them back into their rightful slots. She could see that he was not actually reading any of the material inside.

"What are you doing?" she asked uncomfortably.

"Just looking for something," he said, in a mildly harsh tone.

He was rather annoyed by her inquisitiveness, as he knew that bringing up the pretentious *wishing stars* would cause a contention to arise between them.

"What are you looking for?" she asked.

Placing another book back into the empty space from where he had originally pulled it out, John turned around with a frustrated sigh, sitting down on the sofa chair beside him. He closed his eyes, leaning his head back

"I was just looking for some pictures, that's all."

Flipping off the light on her machine, Sofia strode over, taking a seat on the short-legged table in front of him. Desiring to say something she would not regret, the distress in her face was apparent. By the demeanor that John would often return home with after each morning's session, it was more than obvious to her that his behavior had something to do with the those terrible northeasterly lands. She was well aware that, over the past few weeks at the least, he had been up to something other than shooting.

"You really want to travel up there don't you?" she said.

Letting out another sigh, John moved his lips around as if contemplating his next words. She was on to him, and perhaps, he thought to himself, there had been a subconscious effort behind his actions with the hopes of bringing the avoided topic to a head.

"I don't know what it is, girl. There's been this... I don't know how to explain it... pressure, I guess."

"Like a headache?" she asked.

"No. No, more like I need to do something, but I'm fighting against it."

"It has to do with the *wishing stars*, doesn't it?" she said with a sullen tone.

"That... and other things," he said, mumbling under his breath.

"What other things?"

"*Golden World, Raw*. What are they? Where are they?"

"I don't know."

"I know you don't. Neither do I. But I feel so compelled to find out, as if there were answers there."

"Answers to what?" Sofia's voice was a mixture of amazement and sadness.

Sitting up and leaning forward, he met her eyes. After pausing for a moment he looked around the room. Then, waving his arms in the air, he said, "To *this*. To everything around us. Why did that old man help us? What is this broken down machine we live in? Why do we call that glowing ball in the air *the Savior* but our parents just call it a Great Star? I just want answers. Maybe then I'll be fulfilled and I won't have this nagging sensation pulling at me all the time."

Excusing herself from the room, Sofia was speechless as she walked down the hall behind him, disappearing into the kitchen area. The conversation was ending as it always did when the *wishing star* topic was brought up. John could hear her opening a cupboard. By the sound it, she was gathering a cup from one of the cabinets and pouring herself something to drink.

As she had not returned for several minutes he leaned his head back once again, closing his eyes. But the sound of her returning footsteps brought him back to an upright position. Taking up her recently vacated seat, Sofia held a cup out for him.

"Here, it's fruit juice," she said with a half smile.

Taking the cup from her hand, John pressed its rim against his lips. The sweet sensation filled his mouth as he savored the first sip. Although they had an easy access to all the new and exotic foods, neither of them had grown too accustomed to any particular item yet so as to begin taking them for granted.

"I've been thinking a lot about what you've said in the past, about searching to the east and to the north. Whatever Red is, I really don't want to know. Mr. Sanders strictly warned us not to ever go up there. Wherever the Highway leads, it's not good. We have it so nice here, John. During all those nights on the roof-tops of Labor," she said, as her lip began to tremble and the watery pools began to form at the corners of her eyes, "this is what I had wished for... nothing more. I have no desire to find out what Red is, or what Golden World's people are like. But I promised you that I would follow your lead, no matter where it was you were taking us. If to the north or to the east is where you are going, then fine, I'll go. But, please, promise me this: after you find what you're looking for, you'll bring us back here to live out our days in peace. And you'll never speak another word about going up there ever again."

It was difficult for him to see her so afflicted. Her reddened, tearing eyes were the result of his doing. He did not want to commit to the journey at this time knowing that it grieved her so. But on the same note, he could not let it go, leaving that gaping hole in his heart, that yearning for closure before going on with his life.

As they sat together among the twinkling brass of the orna-ments of the room, John finally made up his mind.

CHAPTER SEVENTEEN

Caught between light and darkness, the sky was a tapestry of blue and purplish layers of paint, as the stars appeared to be rolling up inside the Savior's canvas, disappearing along the easterly expanse. The land was still dim and layered in the misty, low lying clouds, rolling with the sounds of the chirping and humming insects and the scurrying about of the nocturnal beasts. Silhouetted against the early morning display, John and Sofia climbed up to the top of the first of many hills that would be standing in their path as the two of them began the journey into the dreaded northeasterly lands.

Taking every extra precaution that he could think of, they began their tour with a more northwesterly traversal, with John leading them in the direction of the darker skies. As far to the side towards which the Savior would set as they could keep path with before necessitating an easterly run, the safer they felt. They would travel to the last northwesterly point on the map that the Sanders had documented. Then they would cut eastward, heading into uncharted territory.

Clothed in the attire of the soldiers pictured on the walls of the Education, they were equally armed with a single shoulder-fired weapon held across their chests. While they each had one hand on the rifle, remaining on stand-by with a finger resting outside their trigger guards, the handheld firearms strapped to their thighs waited at the ready for the other. Unlike the original journey to their home, they were now well suited to the environment of which they were traversing. The oft repeated walks and southerly excursions that they had made in the past prepared them well for the long trek ahead, as they were both saddled with the burden of carrying sufficient supplies to sustain them for several days.

On paper, the plan was simple, if everything went according to John's expectations: they would carry just enough food necessary for their well being, sustaining them just long enough to get them to their destination. Once there, they would either resupply their stock, or, if the situation was found to be incompatible with his scheme, they would abandon their backpacks and ammunition satchels, returning to the safety of their home with only their weapons in hand and as much of the load as they could carry within their pockets. The return trip would be a relatively quick and easy one, as the burden would be much lighter.

Considering that they were prepared to such a greater extent than any previous venture, John was feeling an over-confidence of which both he and Sofia were well aware. It was a presumptuousness which was causing a growing consternation and a trickle of doubt in Sofia's mind about their abilities to survive for an extended period of time within the unknown dangers of the northeasterly wilderness.

The misty exhalations were an uncommon sight for Sofia, as she was mostly accustomed to her indoor activities at such an early hour of the morning. The grass was wet with dew, softened upon its top layer by the settled moisture. With each step, she felt her feet sink a few centimeters under her weight. It was no wonder why John would often return home after his morning sessions covered with patches of mud.

They had only been traveling for approximately thirty minutes. Having never carried such a heavy load upon her person before, Sofia was already beginning to feel the warm wetness of perspiration dribbling down her chest and building up in the pits of her arms. With such a long road ahead, she settled it in her mind that the discomfort was going to be the norm for quite some time.

John had Mr. Sanders' sketch book in front of his face, lit up by a miner's light that was strapped across his forehead. The miner's device was one of the more useful items of which their warehouse rummaging had uncovered. Using the book in conjunction with the compass, he was planning the course that they would make once the Savior's light manifested in the east.

The still dimness upon the land caused him to unwittingly whisper when he spoke.

"It's strange how the details of the map suddenly cut off once it passes a certain area to our north," he said, "even though it's rather far from the forbidden area."

"Maybe they didn't want to take any chances, either. By getting too near to those places, I mean," Sofia remarked with purposeful implication.

"You're probably right. When we get to the last checkpoint in a few days, we'll slow ourselves and be a little more careful."

Sofia knew John understood what she was implying by her comment, but he was not going to take the bait.

Climbing to the top of a steep grassy mound as the Savior's edge peered over the easterly horizon, awakening the world with its presence, John and Sofia could see that the western landscape was similar in spirit to that of the southerly area from which they had ascended. The hills were thick with tall grass, and as green as emeralds, with patches of trees spreading for kilometers, running throughout the valleys.

Looking over his map once again, John could see that there was not much that was scaled with accuracy from this point forward. In fact, it appeared that there were many visible peculiarities that should have been jotted down as structural waypoints that were purposefully left omitted. Much of what they were now encountering was officially left in John's hands to fill in the details, as Mr. Sanders did indeed warn them against entering the northern region. And, by the lack of specifics drawn upon the map, the old man had been quite serious.

There was an almost nostalgic feeling during their first few days of journeying, as the world seemed so expansive and endless. The skies above were so blue and inviting. Unlike their first encounter with the wilderness, they had all the provisions they needed to ensure their safety, and with that simple crutch to ease their burden, it gave them a greater freedom to enjoy the beauty of the world visually and audibly. But, the uneasiness of which John felt inside about keeping Sofia in the dark, so to speak, regarding the lack of details in the map as concerned the northern territory, was a burden of which he alone knew he had to bear if he wanted to prevent any sort of mutiny on her part. He wanted to tell her the truth. He wanted her to know that they had been traversing an uncharted region, that he was no longer a map-reader, but had become the mapmaker. But he knew that she would demand that they return home, and so he kept it to himself.

The Savior's rise on the forth day brought with it the soothing heat of the morning. Taking a rest at a nearby watering hole, the sojourners removed their long-sleeve shirts, hanging them over the tops of their backpacks and relieving themselves in the privacy of the bushes.

As the soil began to dry and harden, the work that they required of their legs eased up. The trek through the grassy hills became more conducive to their intended brisk pace.

The feathered creatures of the sky were joyfully playing in the rays of light, racing from tree to tree. They joyfully sang below the soft clouds of cotton-like puffs that strolled across the blue expanse, bringing John and Sofia's memories back in time to their first encounter with the delicate country.

As the brightness of the day had removed the fear of which each night's darkness brought, John and Sofia took advantage of the utility of their slings, dropping their protective guard and allowing their weapons to hang over their shoulders. With their hands becoming free from their battle ready posturing, climbing the hills and rocks, and walking together in general, became much more pleasant.

The air was so fresh and invigorating, encouraging that child-like, exuberant feeling of adventure that had become stifled by the complacency that arose over the past several months of living so luxuriously.

But, the time of the morning for the *wishing stars* to make their appearance by way of their thin, white tails was, once again, at hand. Sofia, seeing John looking up to the sky, made every attempt to ignore him. As much as she was enjoying the thrill of their walk together, she did not want to discuss the potential reality of the artificialness of her beloved celestial objects.

From the top of a grassy knoll on which they found themselves, Sofia and John could see the misty fog of the north rising above the land before dissipating under the heat of the Savior. As far as their eyes could see, the terrain rippled for kilometers in waves of beautifully rolling, green hills and patches of blooming trees. To the far north there appeared steep, peaked highlands that arose from the soft green of the valley below it, white tipped and black-ened at their bases, forming a wall of nature's own design. It would have been an intimidating sight to behold under most circum-stances, but it was of little consequence at this point in time, and merely another opportunity of adventure due to the rejuvenated hearts of the youthful couple.

John, looking over the area of the map of which Mr. Sanders had decorated with the red Xs, could see that their destination was situated at the base of one the mounts hidden among the cor-dillera. As his old friend had neglected to add in the details as to which mountain in particular it was that he was referring to, John figured that their own investigation would eventually bring about its true location.

Finding a shade tree along the same outlook, the two of them dropped their gear and settled into its coolness. The sweet sensation of the moist cake, of which they retrieved from out of their packs to snack upon, enlightened their senses, satisfying the hunger that the past several hours of walking had induced.

"Somewhere over there at the edge of the forest, we'll find whatever it is that this red area is referring to," John said, pointing towards one of the snow-covered peaks.

Hearing him speak of the area of which Mr. Sanders strictly warned them against caused a sudden nausea to build within Sofia's stomach. Wrapping the last half of her pastry in its aluminum shell, she placed it back into her sack.

"How long do you think before we get there?" she asked, wiping the sugary crumbs from her lips.

As John was about to open his mouth to answer, an eruption, as of a low, distant rumbling from the direction of the mountain range cut him off mid-sentence. Filling the valley with its deep voice, it brought about a panic amongst the animal population as flocks of winged creatures fluttered into the air to escape it.

"Maybe we should bypass that area," Sofia said, cupping her ears.

Scooting himself beside her, John placed his arm around her shoulders as she tucked her head against his chest.

"I'm really scared, dear. I know this is what you want to do, but I'm worried something bad is going to come out of this," she said.

John did not want to make any promises. The guilt upon his shoulders regarding the map was punishing enough. Instead of giving her empty words with a lack of wisdom, he settled his head upon hers. Closing his eyes, the two of them sat in silence until the roaring overhead had passed them by.

The darkness of the fourth night entered into the world as the Savior laid Himself to rest over the westerly horizon. The tentlike, wooden, sleep structure was erected long before the first stars began to make their appearances. The sleeping sacks were in order. The evening meal was well past.

From the manuals that John had read, he had gained an understanding of the fact that during the blackness of the night the shimmering of even the dimmest of lights could be seen from many kilometers away. As they drew nearer to the mountains, he made certain that their campfires were well doused long before the darkness fell.

The temperature of the air was growing steadily toward the cooler side. Carefully gathering up the hot stones from the fire pit, John and Sofia placed them under the dirt inside their shelter, creating a comfortable, warm floor upon which to sleep.

As the night was now heavily upon them, the two of them found it difficult to fade away into the world of dreams: the rumbling from the forbidden zone was continuously in their ears.

Leaving the warmth of his sleeping sack, John blindly rummaged through his backpack. Finding the spectacles that he was looking for, he crawled to the entrance of their abode.

Rising up in the distance, he could see with his naked eyes the cause of the rumblings that they were experiencing during their afternoon rests. They were pinpoint in size, like tiny stars. Strange, fiery objects arose in a direct line straight from the planet's surface before veering off to the southwest. Although he said nothing of the sort, John had his suspicion that they were vessels not unlike the one of which they called *home*.

Raising the binocular up, the flames reflecting off the cornea of his eyes were exceptionally bright. Shaped like upside down water droplets, whitish-orange in color, they ascended in great numbers, but at varying rates.

"What do you see?" Sofia inquired from her sleeping bag.

"It's amazing, girl," he said, "You need to see this."

Although she truly wanted to fight against the desire to see what John was looking at, after a moment of stubbornness, her curiosity got the best of her. Crawling beside him, Sofia grabbed the glasses from John's hands, placing them against her face. Taking in her first look at the true nature of the mysterious *wishing stars*, she was astonished at the fact that their flames were the only things visible, while its source was completely unseen.

"It's just like the fire that comes out of the missiles that the soldiers use on the battlefield," she whispered.

"Only much bigger," John added, "I'm pretty sure that our home at the crash site was one of those at one time."

Sofia dropped the binoculars to her lap.

"Now that I think about it, I think you're right. Who would have thought... all this time we've been living in a *wishing star*."

John let out a slight giggle. He had not really thought about the flying craft from that perspective.

"It is funny when you think about it like that," he said.

They continued their *star* gazing for only a brief moment longer. John did not want to delay their early morning journey by sleeping in too late. Pulling the binocular back from Sofia's hands, he returned them to his backpack, saying, "We need to get to sleep. We still have a long way to travel."

Slipping back into her sleeping sack, Sofia leaned over and kissed John on the cheek before rolling back and closing her eyes. She wanted to fade away into her regular nocturnal slumber, but the excitement of finding out the truth of their homely vehicle, once a machine capable of flying through the air, was almost too much for her wandering mind.

Chapter Eighteen

As John and Sofia stepped out from a grove of trees off the northern slope of a wide hill, the Savior was beaming down from his throne on high. The afternoon of the fifth day was now upon them.

Trudging through the grassy, soft soil, they kept a pace that was in rhythm to the beat of the tune that they were humming together. It was an instrumental piece of which they were both fond of that they often played on the music machine back home, a tempo that allowed both time and distance to pass by with an unnoticed rapidity. Music had become an integral part of their lives ever since the great encounter with the crash site. It was a tool that adjusted the soul, eased the mind and helped to create an ambience that rejected loneliness. It was, in essence, an entity with its own unique voice. Like another companion on their long trek to the mountainous regions, the music would help them keep their minds off the more monotonous aspects of the journey.

It had been an uneventful day. Skirting by unawares, another night was already falling upon them. The place of origin for their *wishing stars* was becoming ever so close.

Although John was partial to the idea of star gazing, he did not want to waste their precious sleep time on his and Sofia's night watching, even refusing her request to stay up late into the night staring through the binocular. He wanted to get up before the Savior's rise, taking advantage of the cool of the morning, using that extra travel time to make up for those prolonged rests that they had taken during the earlier days of their journey.

With their heads upon their pillows, the rumbling of the north was a moderate irritation, lightly vibrating the soil beneath them, rattling in their ears and teeth. Although it seemed as if they were never going to fall asleep, the strenuous marching of the day eventually caught up to the both of them. Within a few minutes, they had each entered into their individual worlds of restful tranquility.

In the darkness of the early morning trek, the beasts of the forest seemed less at ease than they had been on the previous day. The fluttering amongst the trees, the high pitched cackles intermittently raining down from the sky, and in the distance the howls of the black-haired creatures of the valley urging one another with their terrifying screams could be heard. The atmosphere reeked with tension.

Nineteen months away from Labor had made John and Sofia's crash site home feel so secure and pleasant, making it a place of relative peace and harmony. Although it was far from perfect, neither of them could have ever dreamed up anything more realistically possible with regards to their well-being. The experiences that they had lived through had given them a concrete understanding regarding death and decay within a world with such a contrary aesthetic flair. With the drapes of mist hanging so heavily upon them, Sofia was feeling the claustrophobic menace of wandering so far from what had become such a familiar comfort.

Scanning about with a disorganized rhythm to her eyes that seemed to dance to the beat of the fear that was drumming up inside of her, an extra amount of effort was required on Sofia's part to maintain a sense of composure. The miner's light strapped to her head had little effect under the circumstances of the current environment. The light was reflecting too proximally off of the fog, allowing the illumination to reach only the closest of objects. Under the suffocating encapsulation of the dense, cold canopy of moisture that was hanging over the forest and clinging to its soft, wet floor, she made a conscious resolve to slow her rate of breathing.

With a visibility that consisted of mere silhouettes and varying shades of blacks and grays, she had little to work with as regards to the imagery surrounding her. Perhaps a meter or less beyond the rear sight of her rifle was all that could be discerned with even a crude sense of accuracy.

The movement of the mist seemed to flow like streams of oil falling into a gently agitated pool of water with random, wavy patterns deceptively crawling about, as if they were actually living, breathing beings. They were creating within themselves shadows and shapes of hideous forms. They were borne along by the terrible, distant howls, and Sofia's own rampantly running memories of that frightful day in the valley not so long ago.

With his compass held in front of him, John kept his headlamp fixated upon the needle, permitting him to keep a relatively straight path northward. Due to the weather conditions, there was no allowance for him to plot out the necessary, distant waypoints that would keep them on an accurate track. As no other choice was available, a generally attained, northern path would need to suffice for the time being.

The heaviness upon the rustling leaves, periodically piercing their restless surroundings, caused Sofia to keep a vigilant posture with her weapon at the ready. Her trembling hands felt out of sync with her wildly receptive senses. She felt numb and disconnected from her physical body, as if it were a foreign object. Only her mind and its perceptible abilities seemed to be a single entity existing as one with the environment. Another crack of a branch sent her spinning toward its direction behind them, the beam of light from her forehead showing the way to her point of concentration.

"Did you hear something?" she whispered.

"Nothing unusual."

"I think something's out there," she said with more volume.

"It's probably just the animals in the trees waking up," John said, trying to comfort her obvious expression of anxiety.

"No, I think it's something else," she fired back, cautiously walking backwards, keeping a close eye to their rear while clumsily trying to keep up with him.

After proceeding a few more meters, an almost unworldly silence settled upon the local vicinity. Only the sounds of their gentle footsteps treading through the spongy, dew-covered soil emitted any hint of proximal life.

"What just happened?" Sofia inquired nervously.

"I'm not sure, really," he said, trying to maintain a tone of control, although he was beginning to feel the tendrils of fear crawling over him.

Another cracking of a branch, accompanied by the scurrying of a heavily bodied entity, resounded from the same direction as the original commotion that had been causing Sofia such concern. John immediately came to an abrupt halt.

Scanning his ears about, he attempted to grasp at the true direction of the clamorous activity that had suddenly brought them such angst and dismay. Intent on staying motionless until he was able to hear the sound once again without the distracting noise of their footsteps, he motioned to Sofia to stand still, to wait patiently. He knew that whatever it was that was hiding behind the veil of fog would instinctively make its move sooner rather than later.

"See, I told you," Sofia began to say before being cut off by John's hand, as it was placed over her mouth.

As the rustling proceeded once again, it appeared that there was something encircling them, moving about just outside the visible spectrum of their perimeter. Due to the methods by which the creature was operating, coupled with the disorienting thickness of the mist surrounding them, John found that it was difficult to gauge whether he was hearing the stirring of the leaves under the wings of the flying creatures as they moved through the trees, or if it was truly originating under the feet of a ground dwelling beast sadistically motivated with the intent of doing them harm.

Bringing his rifle to bear, he peered over his sights. The reflection of his light upon the mist was like a great, white wall blocking his view. He held his breath, waiting for another breach in the silence. There was a long moment of emptiness, an almost hollow, sublime feeling of disconnection from reality as they stood their ground, anticipating the worst.

With the sound of a rustling bush entering from the darkness at his side, John turned his hips and, in a single, continuous motion, blindingly fired off a single round toward its direction. The brass casing ejected from the port of his rifle, arching through the air, and impacting the soil a few feet away. The report of the weapon echoed throughout the forest beyond their gray covering. Bouncing off a pile of dead leaves, the metallic cylinder found its resting place in a puddle of water hidden amongst the tall grass. Several screeching, winged beasts aroused from their slumber. Taking flight, the rustling of their wings created an eerie backlash as falling leaves and dust reflected off of the vague bloom of dispersed morning haze that was dimly filtering through the trees and fog. The animals were seeking their safety in the hidden expanse above.

For a moment it appeared that the invisible threat was nothing more than the sounds of those harmless creatures of the sky. John, feeling secure with the idea, lifted his compass to his eye and reacquired their previous course.

"See, there's nothing to be afraid of," he said, rubbing her shoulders, "Let's go."

Sofia continued looking back down the path behind them, discontent with thought that the tree dwelling creatures were the cause of her concerns. The gloominess of the unknown was unnerving. As John was now at least a meter ahead of her, she left off her surveilling, running to catch up to him. She was unable to hear over the noise of the crushing leaves under her feet the guttural hissing of the hidden threat.

As the two adventurers had once again settled back into the routine of their hike, it was not long before they determined that a sudden increase in the frequency of snapping branches and crushing leaves was becoming quite consistent. Something was dreadfully amiss with John's simple explanation of what exactly it was that they could not see lurking within the shadows. It now appeared that they were being stalked.

Raising the flat of his hand up, signaling for Sofia to hold her position, the two of them ceased all movement.

"Don't move," John whispered.

Remaining motionless once again, they both began to slowly dig their feet in, with John guarding the rear and Sofia taking point. With their weapons held tightly to their shoulders, they anxiously pulled aim in every direction from which a crack or rustle, movement or sound, presented itself.

Pulling the compass' lanyard from around his neck while continuing to keep a steady picture through his sights, John handed it behind him to Sofia.

"Here, take this and keep it pointed to the north. We need to keep moving."

Grasping the shiny object from over her shoulder, Sofia held it as still as her trembling hands would allow, waiting for the glow of the needle to settle into her view. Adjusting her body so that she would be facing the determined northerly direction, she whispered, "Okay, I'm moving."

With his cheek resting upon his weapon's stock, and his right hand held tightly to its pistol grip, he grasped onto Sofia's backpack. Walking backward, he continued to cover their rearward sector.

"Be ready for anything, girl," he said. "We're going to get out of this, I promise."

Pulling her weapon's stock under her armpit, Sofia held it in place while wrapping the compass around the fore grip, securing it with the lanyard. This allowed her to keep her rifle at the ready while still being able to keep their course.

A terrifying howling from the mist several meters to Sofia's rear sent shivers up her arms. The yelping creature was causing several more animals of the valley to awaken to her and John's presence. The beasts were lifting up their voices in random inflections of shrieking and barking in the southerly distance, followed by rippling waves of tumultuous cries rolling closer with the passing of each second.

Sofia attempted to turn around, feeling more secure if she was facing the incoming menace. John tugged at her shoulder strap, reminding her sternly, "You need to be the front, the lead. I'm the better shot. Just let me control our backs."

As the tide of bestial cries reached the outskirts of their present domain, Sofia began to see herself as an alien wandering into a territory of which the indigenous creatures had no predilection for hospitality. She and John were, without a doubt, becoming the prey of the huntsmen.

A single entity had been tracking their every movement. At first the deep, guttural gnarling of the beast was low and barely audible. Hidden amongst the gloom, it seemed to know that it was alone, weak and outnumbered, content not to show itself in the open. But, as Sofia led her companion deeper into the beast's territory, the temporary safety of her and John's own numbers was beginning to diminish: the intensity of their unseen foe's salivating snarl began to crescendo in proportion to the confidence it was gaining as the members of its pack gathered beside it.

"John," Sofia cried out, making another attempt to look behind her, "there's more of them. What are we going to do?"

"Just keep moving," he said with a panicking tremble.

The uselessness of the miner's light was becoming more determinate, as it was hindering John's ability to see beyond its hazy partition. Reaching up and flipping the switch off, his action was immediately followed by Sofia's mirrored response. Hidden within the dim grayness of the world, he pushed her forward, forcing her to pick up the pace. Aimlessly drawing his rifle towards what sounded like a concentrated host of creatures gnashing to his side, he squeezed off several bursts, sending hot projectiles into the fog. The flash of the muzzle lit up the dim surroundings, allowing him a fraction of time to catch a glimpse of the horrific black-haired faces, teeth long and pointed, staring back at him. He fired off another burst towards their hideous eyes to the reception of the sounds of yelping and thrashing, sending their pursuers into a chaotic commotion.

High-pitched screams and barking madness had rolled through the forest following his wild shots. And it appeared that the wounded among them were beginning to spontaneously attack the others in their party. Leaning into Sofia's back while continuing to keep watch behind them, John forced her to keep moving at as brisk of a pace as he could maintain without entangling their legs together.

The pounding of the beasts' heavy feet were gathering around them once again. The perimeter of safety was lessening. It seemed as if the entire pack was preparing to simultaneously rush in.

"Where are we going?" Sofia cried out.

"Just stay close-," John said, as he suddenly caught sight of a shadowy figure at his flank.

A single beast lunged from its cover, salivating streams spewing from its open mouth mere centimeters from John's face. Reflexively bringing his rifle up to meet it, he fell backward to the ground, bringing Sofia down with him. With his finger clenched around the trigger, a burst of fire wildly flourished from under the belly of the animal. Scorching and tearing its fur, multiple projectiles passed through it, boring a gaping exit wound across its back and sending flesh and bone spraying into the air.

The dead weight of the corpse crashed to the soil beside them, pooling blackened blood around its torso and involuntarily convulsing. John scrambled to his feet wiping the blood splatter from his eyes.

"Let's go! On your feet," he yelled as he pulled at Sofia, "We need to move!"

Grabbing her by the arm and hoisting her up, John pushed her to action. Tripping over the hidden obstacles and struggling against their own blindness, he forced her to run into the blackness of the forest.

Panting and gasping under the strain of the backpack's weight, each step was a fight. Pulling against the heavy suction gripping her boots, Sofia's feet were sinking deeper into the progressively softening soil.

The trampling of the creatures' paws was not far behind, and they were gaining fast. With his rifle held behind him, John let loose with his weapon's blast, firing frantically in the general direction of the tumult. By the sound of clamor, the concentrated steps of the beasts were disorganizing, scattering about the periphery.

The eminency of the Savior's rise was finally upon them. The visual draw was beginning to increase just beyond a single meter, giving John and Sofia the time they needed in order to react more quickly to the fallen trees and large rocks that intermittently made their sudden appearances from out of the gloom.

The moisture beneath their feet had taken on a sudden transformation. John and Sofia were no longer simply running through muddy soil. At first they began splashing through several small puddles. But before long, the water level was over the toes of their boots.

As if stepping through a curtain, the young couple exited the fog and found themselves standing at the edge of a great body of water, the opposite side of which was too distant and mist layered to visualize. John fired off a few more bursts of his rifle into the air, allowing him to gain more time in order to decide what their next move should be.

Sofia was bent over, propped against her knees, overstrained and vomiting.

"I don't want to do this anymore. I *can't* do this anymore."

The howling from the deep of the forest signified to him that their foes were regrouping. If they stayed too close to the land, it was only a matter of time before he and Sofia would be found.

"Get into the water," he commanded.

"What? No, I can't swim," she resisted.

"Neither can I, but we can't go back that way," he said, pointing towards the barking commotion.

Moving into the shallow of the lake, John grabbed Sofia by the front strap of her backpack.

"If we have to, we'll dump our packs and figure out what to do later. They're getting closer, Sofia, come on."

The initial coolness was soothing to their legs, giving the both of them a renewed vitality as the water was, at first, only deep enough to spill over the tops of their boots. The terrible cries from behind were becoming more distant. It appeared that the enraged beasts had finally lost their scent. With the barking and yelping of the creatures dying out, through the splashes the two of them were making as they lightly waded through the water, the low rumbling of the unseen wishing stars could be heard once again, rising in the skies above.

As John and Sofia moved further out into the lake, the thinly risen layer of fog above them had almost completely dissipated, revealing the starless, deep blue hue of the sky, pastel pink and whitewashed to the east, signifying the nearness of the precious daylight.

The watery depth was gradually deepening. It was now up to Sofia's breast line, and the muscles of her arms were burning under the strain of keeping her rifle from dipping into it. Exhausted and overwhelmed, she lost all care for keeping the weapon in prime condition. Letting her arms drop down, she chose rather to walk with her firearm under the water's surface.

John continued to keep a tight grip on the strap of her backpack, paying close attention to every step he was taking for fear of stepping off of an underwater cliff or slipping on an unstable stone.

The liquid was blue and dark. The further out towards the center of the lake they traveled, the colder it became. After a few hours, they had progressed quite a distance from the southwesterly shoreline. With the Savior burning down upon them, the chilliness was of little concern.

Bumping his knee into the side of a solid structure, John realized that they were standing beside a rather large underwater boulder. With his hands feeling their way to its top, he was surprised to find that it was situated just a few centimeters below the lake's surface. Assisting Sofia with her waterlogged backpack, they climbed to the top of the rock and sat down, giving their feet the much needed rest.

"Will you hand me the compass?" John asked, pulling out

the little black book from his shirt pocket and surveying the surroundings against the available data of the map.

Lifting her rifle out of the water, Sofia could see that her weapon's foregrip was empty. The compass was nowhere to be seen.

Chapter Nineteen

It was not something that John had planned for when he was attempting to consider all of the potential situations that they could encounter with such a venture. The firearms, the food, the quick-start fire sticks, clothing items of various sorts. He thought that he had planned so well. The compass was the only item of which he never would have guessed they would find themselves without.

They had been trudging through the immense body of water for quite some time while the Savior stared down at them from his perch in the heavens, having burned away the entire blanket of mist long ago. The water was still at the level just below

John's breast line, and it had been that way since long after they had distanced themselves from even the faintest of howls. It appeared that this was as deep as the lake was going to get, and they would most likely be safely crossing the entire reservoir without much difficulty.

Being somewhat shorter than he, Sofia was trying as best that she could under the circumstances to enjoy the coolness of the water as it reached up just under the neck collar of her shirt. Although they were moving much slower due to the density of the liquid, some of the items in her pack apparently had some buoyancy to them, causing her burden to feel much lighter on her shoulders.

The rippling fluid splashing against Sofia's face relieved the burning redness of her skin. Considering that she and John had little to say to each other since her loss of the compass, she did her best to ignore his active silent treatment, knowing that she had already apologized more than once. Although his frustration with her was apparent, she knew that he would soon forgive her.

With the visibility finally having become fit for point-setting, John had chosen an oddly shaped cluster of trees situated at the far, north end of the lake, approximately a thousand meters towards the direction of the towering, white peaks. They would need to suffice as their guides, at least for now. By the time they would be reaching the other side, he knew that most of the day would have been already well spent. Darkness would be nearing. And he and Sofia would be rushing to procure everything necessary to the building of their nightly structure before the blackness set in.

The expanse above had become, once again, that soothing baby-blue layer that contrasted deeply against the surrounding greenery of the shoreline and the hills beyond. The deep blue tones of the water seemed so fresh and inviting.

"It's too bad that we won't be able to go all the way there like this," Sofia commented on their water traversal, breaking the long silence between them. "This is actually quite fun."

"It's alright," John replied rather sternly. "But we need to stick to the trees. By nightfall, when the cold settles in, you won't want to be here."

Finding another boulder upon which they could rest, they took one last break from their travels through the lake, eating some dried fruit and enjoying the warm breeze. It was another special experience that the two of them were able to enjoy together.

The lake's surface was lightly rippled and blessed with serenity not unlike the quietude of resting in the shadows of the trees at the tops of the hills. The only unnatural detail capable of ruining the quietude of the moment came in the form of the pollutive noise filling the skies like an endless rolling thunder of a distant storm.

The low roaring of the flying ships of the sky would continue to be heard throughout the remainder of the afternoon. For Sofia, having wandered upon another paradisiacal world hidden among the trees, would yet be the accompaniment of that solemn reminder that always lingered about: John's mission to bring in some type of closure for himself. All of the so-called idyllic locations that they were finding were merely pseudo-paradises. As long as there existed within him that tenacious longing for the missing puzzle piece that he seemed to believe would allow him a completion of his being, the mysterious unknown that he so desired would continue to be a partition between them.

CHAPTER TWENTY

The Savior was just beginning to touch the peaks of the hills that decorated the westerly horizon as John and Sofia walked out of the water and onto the rocky shore. The end of their long day was at hand, the compass was gone and the Burning Star, with assistance from the mountains of the north, would now be their chief navigator.

They had much work to do while the light was still present. Emptying their backpacks and spreading out their contents on the large boulders scattered about, they began the late afternoon's duties by letting their gear and clothes dry out in what little heat remained of the day. They then took up the arduous task of gathering the necessary materials for building their shelter.

Many of the chores at hand had become quite a routine over the past several months since leaving Labor behind. The simple things, like fire starting and acquiring a shelter, did not add to their burden in any way.

By nightfall their fire was doused, and they had settled in for a good night's sleep, neither of them having the energy for sky watching. As the last bit of fading light retreated over the westerly hills, Sofia cuddled up close to John, placing her arm across his chest. She intended to quickly fall into a deep slumber. The silence of the forest, the unusual absence of the chirping insects and the croaking of the web footed creatures, allowed the night's sky to roar with a passion.

It was difficult to fall asleep. The deep hum of the flying ships caused a vibration in their cloth covering, rattling the sticks that formed the framework of their shelter.

"I'm afraid the closer we get, the louder it's going to be," John said with frustration.

Sitting up, Sofia pulled her backpack alongside her and began rummaging through it. Pulling out her first aid kit, she removed two cotton balls.

"Tear these in half and stuff them in your ears," she said. "It might help a little."

Following her lead, John pressed the soft material into his ears and closed his eyes. Although it did dampen the sound a bit, it was of no use in limiting the abuse upon his tactile sensation. Sofia did not seem to be as ill affected by the strange vibrations as he. And it was not long before John could feel her rhythmical breathing against his back as she fell asleep beside him. It was only the exhaustion of which she had been enduring that could have brought her so easily to such a restful state, he thought.

The oscillating clamor continued to rattle throughout his skull. But, it was not enough of a nuisance to ward off his own wearied mind. After a period of deep thought, he joined her in slumber.

The mid-afternoon heat of the Savior was held at bay by the dense leaves of the valley trees that they had been journeying under for the majority of the morning's trek. Following a stream that ran a course to the northeast, John attempted to make an addendum to Mr. Sanders' map. To the best of his poorly artistic abilities he added his own notes and detailed sketches.

Paying particular attention to Sofia's whereabouts whenever he was looking through the little black book, he gave extra precautions to keeping secret the fact that he essentially had no idea as to what dangers were potentially lying in wait for them around each corner.

Splashes of water had moistened the rolled up pant legs that were pulled up around Sofia's knees as she waded barefoot through the cool stream. The thick, old branch she held in her hand assisted her balance, as the smooth, slimy rocks beneath her were rather unstable.

Unaware that John was no longer plotting their course based on the Sanders' previously observed milestones, Sofia paid little attention to what he was writing and where she was being led. It never occurred to her to question him as to which paths were safe and which areas were not. She was confident that John was in control of their current situation.

"As soon as we reach the end of this valley, we'll finish the day on the top of one of the hills," he said with an authoritative tone. But which hill in particular, he had no idea.

"Wherever you think is best," she said, regaining her balance as she slipped on a stone. "I'm in no hurry."

The rest of the afternoon was rather undiversified and monotonous: Trees and water, water and trees. It was dim, and rather humid, but non-oppressing to the soul. Every so often the Savior would peek through a tiny clearing between the branches, splitting the air with his comforting beams of light. It was quite a beautiful site. And Sofia and John would take the time to let the rays settle upon their hands whenever the opportunity arose. The comfort of the trek was made all the more enjoyable by the fact that their load was far less of a burden to them now than it had been at the beginning of the journey. They had consumed most of their rations, and were nearing the end of what little food they had left.

There was one thing that did stand out as rather strange to them, though: the further north they traveled, the quieter it became with regards to the ambience of the forest. There seemed to be fewer animals and buzzing insects within earshot than there had been in the forested areas behind them. Even the fowl of the air had, for some time now, ceased with their squabbling.

With the odd sensation of being watched hanging over them, due to their all-too recent run-in on the other side of the lake, they began taking frequent rests from their travels, attempting to listen for the sounds of any creatures that may have been stalking them. After several undertakings over the course of a handful of hours, they had concluded that there was nothing of concern with regards to their safety. Perhaps, as most of the clatter seemed to be caused by the flying machines rumbling in the sky above, the beasts of the forest may have been wearied of, even threatened by, the unnaturally thunderous engines of the *wishing stars*, migrating to less unnerving locations.

The early, evening breeze began churning the leaves of the sparsely growing trees as it made its way towards the south. Sofia and John had just taken the first few steps that marked the descent from the top of the hill, finally releasing them from the densely forested area, eventually placing them into the grassy plain beyond.

Moving aside the last of the leaved branches blocking their way, John held a bough up high allowing Sofia to pass through. As she ducked her head under it and made her way out into the open, the westerly Savior was bright and warm. Looking across the distant plain, she exclaimed incredulously, "John, look! It's *the Highway*!"

The thick branch swung back in place as John let it fall back into its original state. As he approached her, he could now see from over her shoulder the serpentine path of the Highway slithering between the hills and through the valleys. It ascended towards the mountains hidden behind the hills on the other side of the plain. It was now quite apparent from John's perspective which mountain it was that the concrete structure would be terminating at. Quickly pulling out the little black book, he jotted down some notes, making a rough sketch before tucking it back into his pocket.

The intensity of the rumbling overhead was presently accompanied by an unaided visualization of the tiny, teardrop shaped flames of the airships as they lifted off from their launch sites several kilometers away. With the ability to see them due to their relatively close proximity, John and Sofia were also able to note the incoming vehicles, of which they had not noticed before, appearing out of the sky, just over the mountains. They seemed to be traveling at a rather slower rate of speed compared to their rising counterparts, descending upon the same general location.

To John, the sight of the airships was terrifying, yet exhilarating at the same time. They were also a relieving addition to his well-being, knowing that he would possibly have some answers soon as to whom the vehicles were being sent, perhaps even gathering enough information as to where the northerly descending vehicles were coming from. He could not help but feel as if an empty hole in his soul was about to be filled. But to Sofia, it was all too dreadful, as Mr. Sanders' warnings had never been lost to her.

"There's our new guide," John said, motioning towards the Highway. "It'll lead us exactly where we need to go."

His tone was not reassuring. He seemed less confident than he had been in the recent past, as if he was not sure if the answers he desired were going to be worth the risks. Sofia was not quite sure as to how to reply to him.

"Do we really *need* to go there?" she asked, hearing the words slip lightly from her mouth, but unable to actually let them reach a volume in which John could hear. "Will the answers we're about to receive provide the satisfaction you're looking for?"

With all her heart she spoke the words, but they never made it to John's ears. The words fell upon the particles of light, sticking to them like pollen sticks to the bodies of the bees. It rolled through the air and through the leaves of the trees, climbing through the thin moisture of the heavens, where it was given over to the Savior.

Taking hold of his hand as he began to move down the hill, Sofia was no longer feeling the desire for adventure. The Forbidden Zone was now within reach. She reasoned within herself that, unlike the Forbidden Room of Labor, this area was considered off-limits according to the word of a trustworthy father figure. Perhaps now was the time to heed his words.

Having the ability to reason between various choices is such an odd characteristic of the human species, she mused in her reflective thought as they descended further down the hill. There are some actions in this age that are right and some that are wrong. Sometimes obedience is necessary to keep a man from delineating into moral ambiguity, and in the process losing his own person to a world without limits. Sometimes obedience, if nothing more, merely functions as a mode of survival.

John, Sofia questioned, was not blindly walking into a trap of his own devising, was he? Certainly he had some concern, some inner light revealing to him the foolishness of traversing without a compass to guide them. He, Sofia concluded with some reservation, would never do anything to hurt her. He was her best friend, all of his secrets belonged to her. She had to keep placing her trust in him.

Following the path of Labor's tail, the Highway, was essentially to be guided by a dubious leader: the path would end where that which is good desires not to be. By using its services, Providence, or Luck, or whatever it was that had brought them to this point so safe and secure, would have the provisions that they would no longer be requiring. To John, the concrete serpent was the path to his enlightenment. To Sofia the future was becoming dull and obscure. Nothing seemed clear now. And although she wanted to say something against their new course of action, she was hesitant to speak her mind. She wanted nothing more than to turn back and go home.

CHAPTER TWENTY-ONE

The full body of the Savior was sitting above the hill covered horizon to the east on this cool, clear morning, as John and Sofia reached the edge of the tree line that was separated from the concrete wall of the Highway by approximately ten meters of grass covered field. After much time away from their crash site abode, through the experiences that they had gained by walking amongst the towering, thick trunks of the westerly trees, and climbing the massive boulders and hills that existed throughout the land around their home, the walls of the Highway now appeared much shorter in stature and less intimidating than they had remembered them to be.

Cautiously hidden in the thick of the forest, they roamed in a parallel direction with the concrete structure, always maintaining the distance that they felt was comfortable enough to feel secure from those traveling within.

"Do you think there's any way for someone to know we're here?" Sofia questioned with a whisper.

"I don't think so," John replied. "I'm sure no one can hear us, but I don't want to take any chances."

As the day progressed and remained unchanged with regards to the wall and its gray washed face, ceaselessly staring back at them, curiosity was beginning to take hold of John. Due to its silence, he began to wonder if the transportation tunnel had been abandoned. It was an odd conclusion to come to. But, he was having difficulty comprehending the absence of the sounds of the vehicles emanating from within contrasting with the high volume of traffic that he had known to usually flow at a constant rate through it. The desire to see if the Highway was still in use was more than he could endure, and he became determined to find out.

Allowing his hand to relax, he released Sofia's fingers from his grip. Looking her in the eyes, knowing she would object to his plan, he anticipated her prudence. From the canted posturing of her head, she was onto him, giving him a look of annoyance that said, "Now what are you up to?" Holding up the palm of his hand, preventing her from getting the first words in, he said to her, "I know you don't want me to go out there. I just want to see if I can hear anything in the tunnel."

"Why?" she began to question. "What difference would it...?"

"I'm just going to go see," he interrupted, trying to reassure her fears. "Nothing's going to happen. Just wait here."

As he stepped out of the woods and into the open, just beyond the last, green tuft of brush at the forest's edge, the warmth of the

Savior fell upon him. With the exception of the sounds made by the roaring of the flying machines overhead, the world seemed so still and sparsely teeming with life. The air was calm, almost motionless. The sight of the Highway, as it was so near in proximity to his person, caused his heart to race, bringing back so many terrible memories and feelings of their life under the City's shadow.

Silently crouching down, he inched his way across the waist-high grass towards the brightly reflecting gray-white partition standing before him. Dropping to a prone position at the halfway point, he disappeared among the tall blades, waiting and listening.

A stinging sensation pulsated from Sofia's hand. In anxious anticipation for John's return, she had unwittingly torn a piece of skin from one of her fingers. She did not realize that she had been nervously biting at her nails. The blood dripped from her wound as she squeezed it out, falling onto the soil and dead leaves at her knees. Placing a band-aid over it and maintaining the pressure, she resumed her watch over John, who had by now started again with his slow and steady advancement.

It was not long before he finally reached the wall. He hesitated before walking directly up to it, feeling the convective warmth circulating off of its surface. With the palms of his hands reaching out, John took one more step, making his first physical contact with Labor in nearly two years.

With an ear pressed against its surface he could sense the vibration of the transporters zipping through the tunnel on the other side. Giving a quick glance over his shoulder, he was unable to find Sofia. She was invisible to him, camouflaged amongst the green growth. But she was there watching, and he knew she was just as curious as he had been to know whether or not the tunnel had been abandoned. Waving his hand about, he began motioning to her that everything was secure. It was safe to come out.

Sofia could clearly see him urging her to come to him. As hesitating as John had been during his approach to the wall, Sofia was far more unresolved in her decision to leave the safety of the forest, or to make any type of contact with the treacherous City. The whole idea lingered in her mind like the olfactive pungency of a decaying animal lingering in the nose long after its fetidness has disappeared. She wanted nothing to do with it. Feeling the cool of the dirt under her hands, she sat down, uncompromising in the matter, waiting for him to return back to her.

After several more attempts to persuade her, John realized that she was not going to budge from her position. In order to avoid wasting anymore time, he returned back to the forest. It was enough that she had gone along with all of his outlandish plans up to this point. He could not reasonably have everything his way.

As the night began to settle in, the cold northerly wind was beginning to fall upon them with a chilling effect that even their sleeping sacks were unable to fend off. The two of them found it difficult to get the rest that they so desired. The dirt beneath was losing heat fast, while the airships above ceaselessly roared out like a beast in its anger. Sandwiched between the two disturbances, John and Sofia curled up under their lean-to structure, heads pulsating and toes numb. Leaving his sleeping quarters, John slipped himself inside of Sofia's sack, pressing up beside her. Huddling together under the covers of a single bag, the warmth of their bodies made the night's rest much more tolerable.

"We may have another night or two before we get there," he said. "I'm sure it's only going to get colder."

Sofia tightened her arms around him. She was quite satisfied with their new arrangement.

"I don't mind," she said. "This works out just fine."

Nearing the northern, mountainous region, Sofia and John began to feel the nakedness of the thinning trees. The forest's leaves were becoming more and more scarce. The timberline had been receding away from the Highway for quite some time and was now distanced from it by a little more than two hundred meters. Desiring to stay hidden among whatever was left of their dying protection, they left off from following the tunnel. As they skirted the thicket's edge, they kept watch over its slithering body as it rolled over the treeless hills and into the distance before disappearing completely.

After traversing a few more kilometers, the land had become barren and completely devoid of foliage. A light, flaky substance was beginning to fall like that of snow. Observing the behavior of the newly found material, Sofia took note of the thin, floating flakes as they settled upon the soil, melting into a fine powder. Occasionally, one of the whitish scales would land upon her shoulders or chest. Any attempt to wipe it off would cause it to disintegrate, smearing across the fabric of her clothes.

The cold, lifeless northern valley was the final crossing in their long journey. They were nearing the end. With the long, cylindrical transporters overhead, loud and keenly visible without requiring any visual aid, the couple descended the downward slope into the dried, yellow, dreary plains. It appeared that the eroded hills ahead, steep and lacking the integrity to make climbing safe, would require them to remain in the lowlands for a long time to come.

The crisp wind howled through the canyon as they rounded a steep bluff, finally leaving the lowlands behind. John and Sofia had finally reached the area of which Mr. Sanders had marked with the Xs: red, rusted fencing, broken down and mangled, long ago fallen into disarray. A few standing walls, crumbling and wasted, were all that remained of the skeletal framework related to a compound that no longer had a functional capacity in the order of Labor's governing structure.

Another towering, missile-shaped object burned into the skies overhead, filling the air around them with more flakes of ash and dimly falling, smoldering debris. Aglow like tiny, orange fireflies, it settled upon the thick soot that covered over the natural soil.

Pulling a shirt from Sofia's backpack, John used his knife to cut it into two long strips. Handing one to her, he began wrapping it around the lower part of his face.

"Put this on," he said. "My lungs are burning. We shouldn't be breathing this stuff in."

Sofia followed suit. Tying the strip of fabric in a knot behind her head, she was able to breathe much easier. The burning sensation, that she really did not notice until John mentioned the quality of the air, was beginning to subside. With the environment so polluted, Sofia figured she would not be seeing John's face for quite some time.

The roar of the engines was frightfully resounding throughout the canyon. Sofia and John had to be constantly plugging their ears as the vehicles entered and exited the base consistently at least a dozen or more times every thirty minutes.

For some time now they had been able to see the rocketing machines unaided by their binocular apparatus. It was quite clear now that their home had indeed, at one time in the past, been a transporter of the skies.

As another airship propelled itself further into the heavens above, its terrible thunder fading away as another incoming vessel was making its approach, Sofia and John continued through the entrance of the ruins. Stepping upon a long, metallic, hinged apparatus covered under a thick layer of ash and dust, John knelt down, lifting it out of its ashen heap. He immediately recognized that it was an old-fashioned, manually operated barrier arm, similar to the electronically controlled versions used at the red brick gate from which the Labor Security controlled the entrance to and from the City.

"I wonder if this area was the checkpoint center that all the people that had constructed the Highway had to pass through to get to work," he said, kicking up a cloud of white powder from off of a rusted beam.

"It could have been," Sofia responded, looking around the abandoned station. "I guess when they completed it, they had no use for this place anymore."

"Nope. They just left it to waste away."

The soil, deep beneath the ash of the long-forgotten hub, was dry and crumbly. Its fine-ash covering kicked up into clouds with each breath of the wind. Like walking through wet sand, the tracks of John and Sofia's feet trailed behind them, deep and defined. The ruins of the old center were an eerie reminder of the control that the powers-that-be had over the citizens. John now understood why Mr. Sanders would not want them to enter into the present domain, if, and only if, it had been a currently functioning base of operation. But, the Highway no longer terminated at this junction. It continued further north, perhaps just over the chain of hills at the base of which direction they were headed.

"I wonder what was here that Mr. Sanders wanted us to avoid," John commented, without an immediate word from Sofia.

Pulling a rectangular, metal sign out from under a heavy layer of dust, Sofia glanced over its face. A few stenciled characters were still amazingly recognizable after so many years of neglect.

"I don't know. But I'm sure he had his reasons," she said, dropping the sign back to the ground with another cloud of dust added to the already polluted air.

Burning under the assault of the airborne particulate, John's eyes were beginning to blur and water. Sofia's frequent coughs and guttural clearings of her throat was a sure sign that she was feeling rather miserable as well.

As John began to lead Sofia out of the northern area of the compound, heading towards the final chain of hills separating them from their long-awaited destination, the hollow echoing of what sounded like the voices of men could be heard in the distance just around the edge of the steep bluff. Although, at this point, the strangers were too far away for either of them to discern the specifics of what they were actually saying, their utterances were consistently increasing in volume, evidence that the men were heading towards their current position.

"They must know we're here! What are we going to do," Sofia's voice began with a tremble.

Looking for somewhere to hide, John could see that there was very little they could do to conceal themselves in such a wide-open and desolate expanse. With little time to waste, he turned back towards the ruinous station with Sofia close behind.

"Follow me," he said, running into the shadows of the crumbling walls.

Dropping his backpack from his shoulders, John buried it under a mound of powdery ash, commanding Sofia to do the same. Rubbing the fine dust into the fabric of his clothes and upon his exposed skin, he said to her, "Cover every part of your body, they're almost here."

Gray and thick, they were an image of ghostliness as they dumped handfuls of the powder upon each other. The backpacks beside them, buried and hidden, had now blended into the world, appearing as nothing more than soot-covered rock. As they placed the finishing touches upon the skin of their faces, it was within a few minutes time that they were both completely free of their natural aspects. The voices of the men, clear and distinct, were now just around the corner of the wall. Pulling Sofia to the ground, John kept her close by, showing her how to burrow her arms and legs deeper into the soot. Placing a heavy grip upon her arm, he silently forced her to stop moving. The men had entered the compound.

CHAPTER TWENTY-TWO

The newly arrived group made its way into the center of the abandoned station. John and Sofia could see that they were a party of nearly a dozen men. Mostly of middle age, burly and decorated with the same angry expressions that the Monster always had on his face, they were the type people of which neither he nor she had any desire to make their acquaintances with.

Dressed in orange jump suits with heavily equipped tool belts slung around their waists, their thick black boots and white hardhats gave them a bulky and intimidating presence. They had strapped under their jaws, and covering up to their noses, breath-

ing masks, with hoses that connected to the filtering devices attached to the their belts at the smalls of the their backs.

"The ash probably triggered 'em. But, who turned it on in the
first place?" one of the men growled at his companions as they
entered the compound.

"I hate coming to this area. I turned those things off months
ago. Absolutely no need for them anymore: false readings, animals tripping them. Absolutely no need at all," said a shorter,
more mature and slender worker.

"Must be that new guy. Who else would turn the blasted things
back on? I'll have a talk with him. He needs to stop following pro-
tocol all the time," another worker grumbled with a laugh that
brought chuckles to the rest of the clan.

The two trespassers were as still as hand drawn objects upon an
artist's canvas. Covered over with the same substance that blanketed the rest of the area around them John and Sofia remained
motionless, watching as the men split up into two parties.

Across from each other, set into the corners of the concrete
foundation of one of the former buildings, were two metallic
structures. Opening them up, the two teams worked together,
simultaneously performing the same tasks. Grunting under the
strain of the weight, they removed the outer shells of the units,
lifting them up and revealing the rather large and noisily humming computer mainframes contained within each one. While
one person from each team knelt down beside the exposed screens
inside, the others sat down and rested, talking among themselves.

Although he and Sofia were quite a few meters away from the
nearest group, John could see that the individuals kneeling down
were holding handheld computers that they had plugged directly
into the main frames of the once protected systems. As the technicians began inputting data onto the screens of their portable units,

the humming ceased, and the other men, without being ordered to do so, began lifting the heavy shells and replacing them back to their former states.

"That'll take care of it," one of the computer techs said, lifting his hard hat and wiping the sweat from his brow.

"Hey, why don't we just relax here for a little while? They sent us here, and I'm in no hurry to go back," said another worker.

"And what are we going to do, let ourselves get buried alive? No thanks," said another, kicking up a cloud of dust.

"Well," said one of the men in a low, deceitful tone, "I'd been loading for the prissy folks at Golden World all day, and you'd never guess what I'd found."

With those words, all the men began to gather around, questioning the man and begging to be let in on his secret.

"Take a look at this," he said to the gawking wonder plastered on his comrade's faces as he removed a few bottles of dark, straw colored liquid from the sack hanging on his thigh.

"And this too," he said pulling out a long rectangular box, which he proceeded to open, revealing the smaller, cellophane covered boxes inside.

One of the men walked over to him and placed his arm around his shoulders, announcing to the cheering of the party, "Jimmy here's one of the best. Always looking out for his mates."

With those words they began passing out the smaller boxes, of which everyone tore open with a savage hunger. Removing the long, brown, cylindrical items from inside, each man placed the cigar between his lips, while the thief among them walked around, assisting them by providing a flame with his stolen matches. Exhaling small plumes of smoke from their noses and mouths, they were like giddy children during a celebratory gathering, noisy and jovial.

Opening up the bottles to the delight of all the men present for the occasion, they began passing them around, sharing the alcoholic contents with laughter and cursing. It did not appear to John and Sofia that the men would be leaving anytime soon.

As the afternoon wore on, the soreness in Sofia's hips were becoming less and less tolerable. The two of them had remained motionless under their blankets of dust for several hours. The bottles of the inebriated workers were emptied some time ago. The men, drunk with overindulgence, stumbled about slurred in speech and half laughing in their confused states of mind.

One of them declared, "We need to return to the warehouse before someone notices we're missing."

Unknowingly abandoning most of their equipment, they began making their way towards the end of the compound. They were nothing more than a disheveled moving mass of idiocy heading back to their base of operation.

As they disappeared around the edge of the bluff, John and Sofia sat up, their ashen coating falling from their bodies like thick icing melting from a cake in the heat of the day. The team's merry, but disjointed singing was partially silenced by the distant sound of another flying transportation vehicle in the north that was making preparations for landing. The voice of the men, playfully voluminous, slowly but steadily faded, indicating that they were just outside of the compound returning from whence they came. As the engines of the sky drew closer, the workers became less and less audible until only the roar of the vehicle overhead was all that could be heard.

It would have been too dangerous for them to be out in the open during the day's light, especially with the Labor work-

ers roaming about so freely. But, with the amount of time that
the men had just spent working their way into their drunken
stupor, the dim ambience of the dusk was beginning to settle
in. The time of day most conducive to wandering about was almost present.

Pulling themselves up to their feet, John and Sofia began slap-
ping at their clothing, removing the fine powder coating.

"Let's leave everything here buried in the ash. If we hurry we
can follow those men to see where they're headed to," John said.

"Let's not get too close to them," Sofia added with a concerned tone.

"We won't. I just want to see where they're going."

Moving their feet gently and silently upon the canyon floor
they made their way to the edge of the bluff, peering over the rocky
fringe. The workers, in their rambling conditions, had not gone
very far. Struggling to maintain their composures, the drunkards
were unsuccessfully attempting to feign sobriety.

The downward slope of the ash-covered path that they were
making their return on was undoubtedly giving them a challenge
with regards to their balance. Frustratingly stumbling over their
own feet, they were cursing and mumbling incoherently.

As the incoming transporter made its landing somewhere on
the other side of the hill to the north, its engines cut out. The dull
ringing of the ears and the distant ramblings of the inebriated
workers were the only audible sounds.

Moving slowly and quietly at the bottom of a towering cliff, John
and Sofia made their way to a sloping edge. As he was about to take
a look around it, John realized Sofia was no longer tailing him and
holding onto his shirt. Looking back over his shoulder, he could see
that she was holding herself back, hiding a short distance behind
him. Content with her safety, he continued with his former action.

The workers were exiting out of the canyon, walking on a path that rounded the base of the final hill. John held his hand up, keeping Sofia at bay. After several minutes had passed by he eventually lost sight of the men. Turning back and taking Sofia by the hand, he led her towards the canyon's outlet, continuing on the same path as their drunken guides. Keeping her near every ash-covered boulder that he could find, just in case they needed a quick cover, a place to hide, John began rubbing the fine dust into his clothing and onto his skin once again, encouraging Sofia to do the same. He was taking every extra precaution he could think of to ensure his and Sofia's safety before moving across the barren, open land between them and the final mound.

Upon reaching the base of the hill, they left off following the workers. Moving up the steep face, John was hoping to continue tracking them from a higher and much more inconspicuous position.

The rocky mound was wider and taller than he had anticipated. Instead of continuing with the pursuit, John chose to leave off their current objective, having them work their way to the top first. Hoping that the advantage gained from the higher ground would allow for a better understanding of what it was that he was actually getting them into, John laid out his plan for Sofia. It seemed like a reasonable decision to her. Anything that would keep her from delving further into the inner recesses of the Forbidden Zone would be more than acceptable.

As they began nearing the summit, they could scarcely hear the sounds of several engines faintly idling somewhere to the north.

"We're almost there," he said, scaling ahead of her.

Sofia was struggling behind, clinging to the protruding rocks that were functioning as their steps and grip-points. She was well aware of her own mixed feelings of fear and excitement of finally reaching the end. But, the wonder of the unknown was helping to make the difficult climb seem all the less unmanageable.

Pulling Sofia up and over the final edge of a short cliff, John made certain she was safely with him before continuing onward. The land mass had flattened out. They were now able to walk the rest of the way unhindered by further acclivitous areas.

The hill's apex was well within sight. And a calamitous event, that had already been apparently unfolding somewhere on the other side, was causing a raucous activity of incomprehensible shouts and muffled speech. Tones of men, caught in the throes of anger and fear, boisterous and cruel, were followed by several echoing cracks, like the distant sound of gunfire.

"Wait here, girl," John said, attempting to sit Sofia on the ground. "Let me go make sure it's safe."

"But, I want to..." Sofia began to object.

"No, I don't want anything to happen to you. Just stay put and I'll be right back," he demanded, pushing her down by the shoulders, forcing her to sit upon the ash covered surface.

"John, wait," she began to say, but he was not listening to her. Within a few seconds of time, he disappeared over the hilltop.

The lip of the downward slope was unstable and slippery under his feet due to the thick powder that had built up over the years. John settled beside a layer of ash-covered stones, using them to secure his body to the hillside. He suddenly found himself overlooking the installation of their destination, and he could hardly believe his eyes. Burnt, blackened concrete launch pads spread out in rows and columns, loaded with missile-shaped transporters docked and ready. Scaffolding butted against them with technicians and inspectors moving about like ants scurrying about.

Multitudes of high-volume, metallic warehouses organized in the same manner: rows and columns that spread across the land for several kilometers set him in a momentary awe. He was an alien witness to the compound's breadth from such a high vantage point. Had he finally found the Red Plant?

Below, on the road at the northerly base of the hill, the continuing commotion brought him out of the amazement of his discovery. He watched in horror the annihilation of the men he and Sofia had been spying on all afternoon. Several Security members, clad in black and masked with similar breathing systems as the workers, but fitted with eye protection that gave them the appearances of walking insects, had surrounded the group, apparently executing most of them, as several men lay, some face down in pools of blood, others thrown back in various contorted positions, bleeding profusely from their heads and chests.

"I don't want to die," one of the last surviving men stuttered before a bullet was fired into his skull, bone and matter following the exiting slug. The other Security members turned their weapons on the two remaining workers. With a single shot each, the men fell in the same manner.

The gunshots coincided too perfectly with John's disappearance from her view. As he had not returned for several minutes, Sofia was certain that a terrible event had befallen him. Although he expressly forbade her from following him, she needed to know that everything was well and that he was still with her. She put it in her mind that he would probably be walking over the hill at any moment. But if he did not return to her soon, she would go against his wishes, and seek him out on her own.

The tension gripping the muscles of Sofia's chest with each minute that passed by was more than she could bear. It had been five, maybe even ten minutes since John walked over the ridge, but it felt like hours. Finally ignoring his demands, Sofia stood up and began to cautiously make her way up the remainder of the slope.

Nearing the hilltop, she could hear the voices of men, although indiscernible, talking amongst themselves in a non-threatening manner. John was sitting at the edge of a cliff-like formation on a northward drop. Covered in ash and nearly invisible to her visual sense, Sofia nearly walked by him, as he blended almost too perfectly into the environment.

She was hardly quiet as she closed the gap between them. John turned to her holding his hand out, signaling for her to stand still. By John's reaction, it was quite apparent that the two of them were close to danger. Crouching down and proceeding to cover her body in the same fashion as he had done, Sofia was soon just another natural formation buried within the powdery gray world.

Leaving the blood-bathed bodies where they fell, the Labor Security officials boarded their vehicles. The lead official removed his mask before taking his seat. John was able to catch a glimpse of the man, who did not look dissimilarly to the Monster from such a distant view. As the door closed, the Security transporters turned back towards the direction of the launch area and warehouses. The dense clouds left in their wake followed them in plumes of billowing smoke.

The day was well spent, and nighttime was soon to be upon them. The automated lights of the fenced-off installation were beginning to pop on, dimly at first, and slowly brightening.

John was suspicious of his familiarity with the agent he had just seen. Could that have been his father? The man was equally heartless, taking the lives of the workers without hesitation. Perhaps, he thought, he could find the answer to that question as well, once they infiltrated the compound below.

By the time the setting of the Savior over the westerly hills was upon them, an innumerable series of transporters had come and gone. John and Sofia's lengthy wait in the darkening land was rewarded with another inconspicuous capture of the behind-the-scenes workings of Labor's authoritarian structure. The cone-shaped illumination of the headlights of another wheeled vehicle appeared from the direction from which the Security personnel had earlier disappeared. With a rectangular bedded trailer in tow, it was heading towards the site of the massacre. The bloody area had been long covered over with a thick layer of ash. Prepared for what it was that was awaiting them, the men that exited the newly arrived transporter, orange suited with full-face masks that connected to a case hanging upon their thighs, blew the gray, powdery layer off of the corpses with the motorized blowers that were strapped to their backs.

Dragging the bodies beside the trailer, they were soon stacked up like the warehoused crates, mere objects without any significance as human beings. It was nauseating for John to watch: working in teams to hoist them into the bed, the men held the corpses by the hands and ankles. Swinging them back and forth in a pendulum manner until there was enough momentum, the orange suited agents released their grips, throwing the dead into the awaiting container.

With a strong metallic thud echoing in its hollow, the first few bodies made contact with the floor of the trailer. After the first layer was piled in, the remaining cadavers were landing with a grotesquely spongy bounce.

By nightfall the deceased were gone. The area around the execution site was now strictly lit up by the towering poled-lights situated throughout the compound and lining its entire perimeter. As equally bright as the noontime daylight, the brightness was reflecting off the whitened surface of the surrounding environment and the metallic warehouse structures, casting a strange aura upon the land. The beams dispersing through the dust carried a winter like glow across the base and the outlying vicinity.

Leading them back to the ruins, John was in deep thought about what exactly it was he was hoping to obtain once inside the compound. The workers, their deaths forever seared into his mind, had mentioned Golden World. Someone had to know something regarding that area. And, perhaps, some answers regarding the Red Plant would manifest if they found the time to do some in-depth investigating.

Sofia did not ask what John had seen on the other side, or what fate had befallen the drunken men. By John's demeanor she was aware that something awful had come to them, and she was in no mood to hear the details.

The ruinous station was now their temporary base of operations. John figured that they would need to further reconnoiter the area before making a decision as to how to proceed. If time did not permit them a sufficient span, enough to accomplish all the things he wanted, they could always return back to the ruins and wait until the following night.

Sofia refrained from speaking a single word during their return. It did not feel appropriate under the circumstances. Answers to her questions would be forthcoming soon enough, whether she liked it or not.

Chapter Twenty-Three

The northerly sky was aglow over the distant hilltop as they reached the abandoned station. Recovering their packs was found to be quite the chore, as the layers of ash had built up to a significant degree since they last saw them. Finding their gear hidden in the dimness of the night was not going to be an easy task.

Locating the general area where they had left off in pursuit of the drunkards, they crawled upon their hands and knees, pushing aside the powder until they found their belongings.

"I know you're not going to like this," John began to say.

Sofia was beginning to hate those words. Nothing good ever

followed them. Before he had the chance to lift his hand, rudely interrupting her, she cut him off mid-sentence.

"I know what you're about to say, and if you're thinking of leaving me here while you go in there, you'd better think again," she boldly announced. "If something were to happen to you, what would become of me? You're all I have. Please, don't leave me behind like that again."

Her words were piercingly convicting. And John was beginning to realize how selfish he was becoming. All along he had been neglecting Sofia's feelings for the sake of his own curiosity and self-fulfillment. She was quite correct in her words, but John was so sure that they were close to the answers he so desired. They were so close he could almost taste them. He had brought her this far, but he knew that it was being effectuated through a terrible form of deceit on his part. If he went into the base alone he would not need to keep watching her back, too. It was all about him, now. He was no longer thinking as if the two of them were one, and it frightened him.

As John reorganized his thoughts and removed the single, objective motivator in his whole excursion from the equation, Sofia was all that was left: his best friend and companion. Her security and happiness needed to be his greatest concern, even if his desires said otherwise.

"Okay," he said. "I won't do that to you again."

Crawling beside him, she wrapped her arms around his shoulders, saying, "Thank-you."

The final meals from their packs were little more than morsels of left over items that they had rationed off during the past few days. As this was hopefully to be the last night that they would need their gear, they emptied their packs of most of the necessary contents, ammunition and fire starters, and folded up and buried everything else.

The Savior had, several hours ago, fallen over the horizon when John and Sofia finally prepared themselves mentally, as well as physically, to the abandonment of the ruins, making the final journey into the launch base. Placing their rifles across their backs, they began taking their first steps towards the true unknown.

"Before we head that way, maybe we could gather up the tools that those men left behind," John whispered. "We might find something of use."

"That's a good idea," Sofia agreed.

Their hands were groping through the thick powder, feeling around for the pile of equipment that they had seen the workers leave behind earlier in the day during their alcoholic bingeing. But it was difficult to locate with any precision the whereabouts of the gear within the dark, ash-blanketed environment.

After a minute of digging around, John was ready to give up when Sofia suddenly exclaimed, "Here. Look what I found."

Pulling up a leather utility belt, she handed it over to him. It was quite heavy and burdened with tools. While John held it in the dimness of his cupped lamplight, inspecting its contents through what little illumination filtered from between his fingers, Sofia pulled up another item. It was a rather small, rectangular object with a dangling cable protruding from one end. Pocketing a screwdriver, John could see that Sofia had found something of potentially great importance.

"What do you have there?" he asked.

"A machine of some type, I think," she said, holding it out for him to take.

Examining it under the light, John could see that it was the computer apparatus that the technicians had used when they were working on the mainframe security systems. Finding a switch on the side, John brought the screen to life in a blazing blue aura that he immediately covered up with his hand before powering it down to the state that they had found it in.

Placing it in his shirt pocket he said, "I think I'll hold onto this. We might actually have some use for it later."

"Do you know how it works?" Sofia asked in amazement.

"Well, no," he answered. "But I'm sure we can figure it out if we need to."

Just outside the fenced perimeter of the launch area, John and Sofia remained prone positioned and motionless, camouflaged under their ashen cloaks, their faces masked by the cloth coverings John had fashioned for them. The chain link fence, less than a meter out of their reach, appeared somewhat flimsy and poorly constructed. John was not able to recognize its quality while he was stationed on the hilltop earlier in the evening, but it was still the only thing separating them from accessing the base. Several hundred meters to the northeast, they could see that the Highway terminated at, what was probably, a heavily guarded gateway.

The compound was teeming with activity. Men and women, clad in orange suits, with hard hats, goggles and sound deadening blue ear protectors, worked like robots on an assembly line, objective and cold.

Manned, forked transporters loaded and unloaded the erectly standing, missile shaped vehicles stationed on the launch pads with incredible efficiency. Lifting and unloading the uniformly shaped, wooden boxes with effortless motions, the crate-filled forklifts were driven to one of several warehouse terminals. Their boxes, peculiarly stencil-marked *Blue*, were scanned by a technician with a handheld apparatus reminiscent of the retinal scanners from the apartments of Labor. Afterwards they were sent on their ways to various other areas of the base.

Working in opposition to the off-loading teams, other crews simultaneously reloaded the air-transporters with various sized crates, stenciled upon their sides with their respective destinations. Upon the scaffolding that was wheeled alongside the airships' hulls, men were hastily inspecting and documenting the integrities of the fuselages, while the technicians were laboring with the welding and wiring of the internal and external systems.

With the same handheld computer of which John hid in his pocket, he and Sofia observed a technician plugging his machine into the access port just outside of the loading bay doors of the nearest pre-launch vehicle. As the man moved his gloved fingers across the screen, the metallic grind of the gears began to roll, the massive steel door began its slow descent and the engines of the airship fired-up, churning in unison with the flashing yellow lights and blaring horns that surrounded the launch pad.

As the scaffoldings were wheeled away by unseen operators, the doors and panels of the airship were sealed shut, and the roaring of the vehicle elevated, reaching an intensity that caused Sofia and John to cover their ears. The launch area was cleared. And in a flash of flames and smoke, it took to the air, riding upon its southwesterly trajectory.

For at least an hour, the couple watched dozens of launches and landings, each one identically executed as the first. As one vehicle distanced itself to a comfortable degree for them to remove their hands from their ears, another began to make its descent onto the unoccupied pad. As it touched down on the concrete slab, concealed within a billowing cloud of smoke and agitated, airborne ash, another vehicle, from the distal side of the base to the north, began its fiery ascension closely followed by a transporter that was descending to take its place.

The cloud of dust formed by the vehicle that just touched down was starting to settle out, and the grounded ship was becoming faintly visible. The bay door, already opened long before it was in view, was an important piece of data with which John was using to construct his plan. The forked vehicles were just starting to move into it: approximately sixty seconds of time from the moment the transporter made contact with the landing zone.

After several dozen exchanges with ground control and the night sky, the pattern was beginning to become quite evident as to how the base operators were organizing the ships' landings and launches. John began to see the opportunity at hand for them to infiltrate the base.

"If we time it just right," he whispered, "we'll be able to climb the fence, hiding in the dust cloud. It looks like the airship's door opens right when it lands. We have about sixty seconds before those forked transporters start moving into it. I think we can sneak in and hide inside one of the out-going crates."

"And then what?" she asked, incredulously, overtly displaying with her tone her thoughts on the foolishness of his plan.

"Well, I don't know just yet. We can figure it out when the time comes."

Sofia stared at him in disbelief. She didn't blink. She just stared.

"Do you have a better idea?" he asked.

"Sure. I was thinking we could-," she began to say.

"We're not going home yet," John interrupted.

Looking back at the launch pad, Sofia was beginning to wonder what the purpose was. What was it that John was hoping to obtain from any of this ridiculousness, she thought.

"Alright," she said with a sigh. "Let's get this over with."

As the nearest vehicle had just landed, placing it in the back of the line for lift-off, John knew it would be a few minutes before it would be prepped and ready for launch. Moving up the line of concrete pads in a northerly fashion, the missile-like structures were synchronously arriving and departing from the base with uniform precision.

As the last rocket arose to the sky, John began to crawl closer to the fence with Sofia in tow.

"Are you ready? It's almost our turn," he said looking back at her.

"Just give me the word," she responded unenthusiastically.

Walking up to the bay-door, terminal port, the technician plugged his computer in and waited for the forked transporter to make its final exit.

"Get ready, girl," he whispered.

Even in the cold, drops of sweat were trailing down John's forehead, dripping off of his brow. The perspiration darkened the edge of the cloth, facial covering at the folded rim that crossed his cheekbones. The bizarre creation of exposed flesh, blackened with moist soot that was partially washed away by the streaming liquid, and the staggered, ashen stripes, gave John the appearance of being scarred by a claw that had once torn his face.

"I'm ready, John. Just don't lose me in that smoke," she said.

Making its way out the bay door, the forked vehicle rolled down the ramp and into the nearest warehouse. With the transporter cleared, the technician moved his fingers across the computer's screen.

"As soon as I get over, I'll wait for you. We need to keep our bearings in that smoke. Otherwise, we're sure to get caught when the dust settles."

The engines began to churn. The bay door was closing, its gears grinding and wailing. Feeling the grip of Sofia's hand at the tail of his shirt, John reached back and touched her one last time before the lift off. With the vessel set to take flight, those who had been working to load and unload it began dispersing to meet the needs of the next vehicle in line.

"Are you sure you want to go through with this, John," Sofia yelled, but her voice was drowned out by the intensity of the engine's screams.

Covering their ears, the flames began to glow with a beautiful white-blue brilliance. Bursting forth from its thrusters, there was a sudden flash of blinding light. The missile took to the sky, trailed by a plume of smoke, leaving in its wake falling ash and smoldering residue.

It was with clockwork precision that the roar of the vehicle had finally made it outside the of the audible discomfort level, when the incoming vessel began to make its approach.

"There it is, girl," John said as they watched it drawing nearer.

As the reverse thrusters began to scream, slowing its descent, Sofia could feel her heart pounding heavily within her chest. In a moment, its cloud would cover them. There was no turning back. John had set his mind to this course of operation. The responsibility would fall on him, but ultimately, the currently unseen effects, upon *them*.

Chapter Twenty-Four

The ash covering of the soil gave little, if any, cushion to the impact as Sofia hit the ground, tumbling to floor on the other side of the fence. With a loss of her awareness of the objects within her surroundings, her bearings of the physical world were wholly distorted. She stood up, blindly reaching out to John to no avail.

The bright lights of the base dispersed in the chaotic swirl of fine particles and heat. Through her squinted eyes she found it impossible to discern the direction of the fence from which she had fallen, let alone the transporter that she needed to find her way to, hidden somewhere in the dense shroud.

"John?" Sofia began to scream. Under the thundering power of the vessel's engines her voice was inaudible, even to her own ears.

"Where are you?" she continued to shout.

The time allowance was falling away fast. Sixty seconds: that was all John said they had before the engines would cut out and the dust would start to settle. Sixty seconds, and she knew that at least thirty of them had already fallen to the past. Aimlessly taking a few steps ahead, her fingers pierced through the familiar metal links. She had found herself once again at the fence. She had gone the wrong way, and John was nowhere to be found! Twenty seconds.

The squall of the engines had not died yet. There was still time. She had to think. The ship should be in the opposite direction of her current location. She needed to run. Ten seconds.

Releasing her grip, she pushed herself forward. The transporter was out there somewhere. John must be waiting for her. Five seconds.

Several steps into the run, stumbling over John, she met up with him as he fell to his back with the full force of her weight upon his chest. He may have been talking, but she could not hear his voice. Then, suddenly, the engines cut.

"Where were you," he said.

"Me? Where were you?" she asked incredulously.

Rolling over and climbing to their feet, John grabbed Sofia's hand, "I can't believe this. We need to hurry."

The dust was beginning to settle out. The transporter was faintly visible in silhouette form against the burning exterior lights of the base. The bay-door gears were grinding. The door was still opening.

As they reached the concrete pad, they could just barely make out the ramp as it unfolded from below the ship's hull. The dispersed light from its interior illuminated their path.

"We're almost there," John panted.

Ascending the ramp, they entered into the storage bay coughing and exhausted. Cool and clear, the air was fresh in comparison to that from which they had just come, but there was little time to enjoy its refreshment.

A ladder on the wall leading to a small, circular door on the ceiling indicated that there was another area above them. With little time left before their dusty cloak of concealment was gone, John ordered Sofia to climb.

"Go faster, girl. They're going to be here any minute," he ordered.

"I'm moving as fast as I can," she said nearly losing her grasp.

The vertical ascension was vertigo inducing as the narrow rungs and handles gave Sofia an insecure feeling at best. With no time to lose, she moved, hand over hand, foot over foot, as fast as she could, with John's head keeping close to her heels.

From over his shoulder John was able to get a good visualization of the outside environment through the airship's threshold. The clarity in the features of the terrain was quite high. The dust had completely settled. By the sputtering of the engines of the forked machines John knew the workers were drawing near.

As they reached the final rung John climbed up beside Sofia, securing her to the ladder.

"Quickly, open the door," he said with a panic.

With her hands able to break free without fear of falling she let go, releasing her grip and further entrusting John with her safety. Grasping the handles of the door's central locking mechanism overhead, Sofia rotated it around, swinging the door upward. Climbing into the blackness of the room above, she rolled out of the way making room for her companion.

The first of the utility vehicles had just entered into the bay as John climbed inside. Quietly letting the door close and securing its lock, he felt around until he found Sofia standing beside him. The light of the lower compartment was drowned out. They were all alone in the dark.

The miner's light strapped around John's head lit up the interior of the empty room with a brightness that was aided in large part by the reflective, sterile surface of the white walls of the transporter's hull.

"I believe this is the first storage room back home," his voice echoed off the metal walls as he moved his light across another ladder, following its path to the ceiling.

"Then the area below us is our home?" Sofia asked.

"I think so."

"So, what are we going to do now?"

John was not sure as to what the next move was that they should make. He had not anticipated how easily they could be spotted from within the light flooded storage area below. Knowing that they still had some time before their airship was scheduled for launch, he said, "I think we should see what's at the top of this thing. By that time they'll be finished reloading below. We should be able to sneak out and find a way further into the base."

"Maybe," she retorted. "But we'd better hurry. I don't want to be stuck in here when it takes off."

John knew by the muffled vibration against the wall that outside the scaffolding had just butted up against the transporter. They would have plenty of time to make it to the top and back down before lift-off, he thought.

The climb to the next threshold was equally high, but not nearly as frightful as the previous ascension from the bay below. They were free to take each step with more caution, considering there was no one that they were attempting to flee from.

Opening the door above, they found themselves inside of another room with the same dimensions as the former, and containing the same sterility, as well. Back home, in the southerly forest, this was their second storage unit.

After ascending another nearby ladder, the two of them found themselves in yet another identically sterile room with another ladder leading upward.

"How many of these are there?" Sofia asked rhetorically.

"This is so crazy," John murmured. "What do they need all these storage compartments for if they're not going to use them?"

The illuminated circle emitting from his flashlight moved across the floor and ceiling revealing nothing that would hint at the purpose for the three empty sections of the airship.

"We should probably keep moving," Sofia encouraged him.

John was certain that he would find *something* if only he had the time to search. He stopped his exploring long enough to comprehend the immediacy of her statement.

"You're right. We should probably hurry. Let's see what's in the next room."

Climbing through the door's opening, they were finally presented with a smaller, but equivalently empty area. Approximately half the size of the former three compartments, its only other dissimilarity was found in the single, white table in the middle of the room, bolted to the floor at the base of its four legs. Another ladder on the opposite end of the wall led up to a short walkway that terminated at yet another metal door. Unlike the others below it contained a circular window above the wheel of its locking mechanism.

"If there's going to be any answers, we'll probably find them in there," John said.

Not desiring to delay any longer, Sofia made the first move to the ladder and began the climb, followed closely behind by John. Pulling herself over the final rung, she ran to the door. Standing on the tips of her toes, the glass opening allowed her to see the individual chairs mounted to the walls, facing upward towards the ceiling. Beyond the fact that they were empty, there was nothing else of significance that she could determine from the limited view that the tiny window, and her short stature, would allow.

Creaking on its partially rusted hinges, the door swung open under John's command, and he proceeded to enter first into the brightly lit compartment. A small ladder was mounted between the upward facing chairs, allowing for easier access to the oddly arranged seats. Organized in such a way so as to allow for manual control of the vessel, the chairs were situated before a down-powered, computerized control station: an array of switches, lights, screens and other mechanisms. The "ceiling" was merely the apex of the ship, composed of a single, cone-shaped, window unit that spanned the diameter of the cockpit, allowing a view to the multitudes of twinkling stars shining down from the heavens outside. There were several terminals mounted on the side of the control station, similar to the ones that the workers were accessing at the ruins, and the technicians were channeling on the exterior of the hulls.

"To think, that all this time this is what was buried in the hillside back home," Sofia commented.

Removing the miniature computer from his pocket John knelt beside the terminals, taking a closer look at his handheld's dangling cable.

"If everything we were looking for is stored in this little machine, I'm going to feel pretty foolish bringing us all the way over here for nothing," he said, lining up the connectors.

The monitor in his hand lit up blue and bright as the cable made contact with its compatible slot. The control system began to power on, and John's monitor booted up to a menu screen with six nonsensically labeled icons decorating the interface.

"What are all those?" Sofia asked, her face lit up as blue as her eyes.

"I'm not sure," he said.

Labeled with the word *RawMat*, the first icon on the screen resembled a pickaxe with a tall plant crossing over its handle, forming the shape of an X.

"What do you think? Should I press it?" John asked.

"I don't have the faintest clue what that's referring to. Try it, I guess," she said, motioning to him to be more aware of the urgency of their situation.

Tapping his finger upon the image, the screen began to fill with streams of data, scrolling through a series of numbers with no discernable relation to anything that he was aware of.

"What is all that?" Sofia asked.

"It's just nonsense to me," John answered.

Swiping his fingers across the *Back* button, he was brought to the main screen once again.

"Try the one that says *RePla*," Sofia requested, pointing to an image where two rifles crossed like Xs at the barrels.

As he tapped his finger upon the icon, the same result appeared on the screen: scrolling numbers without discernable value. Returning to the main screen once again, he realized that there were two paging arrows located at the bottom corner.

"I wonder what these are for," he said, depressing the right facing icon. As the former icons disappeared, a single image appeared in their places. It was a flame, with the word *ManLa* written below it.

"It's probably the same thing," Sofia said, looking back towards the door. "We really should be going now, don't you think?"

Sofia was right. As much as he wanted to stay, John understood the immediacy of the moment. His hand grasped at the cable. He was ready to yank it out of the terminal. His hopes of finding just one piece of useful information hidden somewhere in the vessel's computer system was about to come to an end. With that agonizing thought bearing down upon him, the sixth sense that he was about to miss something important, John released the connector, and depressed the icon.

Sofia had already walked to the entrance of the control room. Looking back, she could see by the flashing screen that John had found something of interest.

"What do you see?" she asked.

Lifting his eyes to her, he said, "I tapped the *ManLa* button. Now it just keeps flashing the words, *Stand-By*."

With a single step in his direction, Sofia paused as the lights of their cabin suddenly died off. The pilot's screen above John began to blink for a brief moment, until it solidified into a single blue screen.

"John. What's happening?" Sofia asked, nervously looking around the cabin.

John was unaware of the power being supplied to the airship's main system, as he was too involved with the changes taking place on his own screen.

"It says, *Access Override: Permission Granted*. I think we've got something here, girl."

His face was aglow with a joyful glee as Sofia walked up to him. But a deep rumble from below, and the disengaging sounds of the scaffolding unhinging from the hull, immediately brought him to his feet.

"Oh, no," Sofia stammered. "John?"

"I know. I hear it! We need to get out of here. Let's go," John yelled, tearing the cable from the terminal and pulling her towards the door.

A mechanical, female voice bursting out from the cockpit speakers brought them to a halt as the rumbling under their feet began to escalate.

"Initiating manual launch in t-minus twenty seconds."

"What did she say?" John shouted above the roar of the engines, looking about, confused and panicked, "Did she say, "*Manual Launch*"?"

"That must've been what *ManLa* was. Oh, no. I can't believe this is happening," Sofia cried.

"This can't be real. This just cannot be real," John repeated to himself.

"T-minus ten seconds and counting," the feminine voice announced, monotone and cold.

"We need to strap in," he yelled, pulling her back towards the pilot's chairs, "We're about to take off."

Climbing the short ladder, they rolled onto their backs and into the seats, crossing the restraining belts over their chests and across their laps. Thousands of pinpoint stars stared back at them through the window from the blackness of space. The pilot's control panel was awash with needles moving across gauges and blinking lights. By the sound of it, the engines were reaching their maximum intensity, but the interior of the cabin was apparently insulated well enough to dampen the noise to a tolerable level.

John could see Sofia staring at him from the corner of his eye. As he turned his head towards her he said, "I can't believe I got us into this."

"It's okay," she said with a half smile. "I just hope you don't have to drive it, too."

And with those final words, the thrust lifting the transporter into the sky pinned them to the backs of their chairs. Sofia's high-pitched moans were all that she could express under the heaviness of the force being exerted upon her.

CHAPTER TWENTY-FIVE

The spherical bulbs of vomit that hovered a meter above Sofia's head slowly made their way to the nearest wall, attaching
themselves to its surface. She and John had released their safety
harnesses several hours ago. Beginning their egress from the pilot's
chairs, they floated down to the lower cabin where they found a
little respite beside the bolted-down table that they used as their
place of security.

Abandoning the pilots cabin had been their chief priority
ever since the transporter had left the outer atmosphere of
their home planet. After picking up a pre-programmed trajectory leading them along a path towards a distant sphere, the

engines automatically cut power. The vessel continued upon its course, rotating along its lengthwise axis at a relatively high rate of speed. With the distant stars spinning uncontrollably around them, neither John nor Sofia was able to hold down the contents of their stomachs. The low gravity of space travel had never been a part of the plan.

Their target planet was probably several thousand kilometers away, maybe more. But before they had left the cockpit, it was visible as a floating, dim orb reflecting off the Savior's light in the shape of a half circle. Centered directly to the nose of the vessel's conical head, it was the only object visible through the window that did not appear to be revolving around them.

John could not talk. The disgusting taste in his mouth was making it difficult to ignore the nauseating feeling rumbling around in his gut. Holding on to the table's leg he attempted to keep his mind in a neutral state, avoiding the connection of his thoughts with the current state of his body. Sofia was in no better shape than he. She had wrapped the sleeves of her shirt around another one of the table's legs before tying it off at her ankle. Floating about with the muscles of her body as relaxed as she could possibly get them, she was kept in her current position suspended in the center of the room by her improvised tether. She did not dare to open her eyes for fear that the dry heaves would start up once again.

For the next few hours they remained in their meditative frames of mind. Weary and physically broken down, they were like human shaped helium balloons, peacefully floating free.

Acclimating slowly to the novel environment after several hours of misery, John and Sofia were finally able to work their way down to the lowest storage area. There they were able to secure for themselves some juice and salt crackers from one of the many hundreds of crates, mostly marked with the words *Golden World*, with a few *Raw* and *Red* boxes at the distal areas from the bay door. After overcoming the initial queasiness under their encounter with zero gravity, the feelings of weightlessness had become something quite satisfying. With the ability to move from the lowest deck to the "table-room" with minimal effort on their part, they began playfully floating around, making a game out of their current circumstance despite the severity of their present situation. Tossing balls of juice from their straws towards one another was just one among several other forms of silliness that they were exhibiting. Killing time was not going to be a difficult objective to complete.

Periodically checking in on their relative position to the approaching planet, it appeared that they were making significant progress towards their unintended destination. Although it was still quite a ways off, it no longer appeared as just an insignificant ball floating in space. Their proximity to the strange new world allowed them to see that is was brown in color for the most part, with swathes of green covering approximately ten to twenty percent of the exposed portion of its visible face.

The pilot's screen had not changed in appearance since they had left home. It still continued to display the countdown time to landing, which currently read, *47 hours 33 minutes 15 seconds*, and flashed in the upper corner, *Auto Pilot Engaged*. John had attempted on more than one occasion to obtain some usable data through the use of the handheld computer, but was unsuccessful in his endeavors. Tucking away the handheld into his pocket, he finally gave up trying.

With nearly two more days of travel left, it appeared that, overall, the entire course of their journey would not be ending anytime soon. The control of the situation was out their hands. Spinning a cracker in Sofia's direction from across the room, John watched it as it whirled around like a falling leaf. The time would go by much too fast, he thought.

CHAPTER TWENTY-SIX

John could hardly believe that their arrival at the new planet was already upon them. As he slid into the pilot's chair he gave a glance to Sofia. She was in the same mental boat as he. The past couple of days had been so incredible that she hated to see them coming to an end.

Turned about on its central axis, the nose of the airship was now facing the direction from which they had launched nearly three days prior. The pilot's screen was counting down from twelve minutes to destination. Entering into the planets atmosphere, the vibration of the vessel was intensifying under the returning friction.

Buckling themselves in, the two of them could feel the reverse thrust of the vehicle as, once again, their bodies were crushed into the chairs, making it difficult, if not impossible, to verbalize their discomfort. Having to endure the strenuous pressure being exerted upon them made the short duration of the landing process feel much longer than it actually was.

As the color pallet outside began morphing from the deep blackness of space and starlight to the soft, baby blue of a familiar sky, the vehicle began to settle into a steady decline. The pressures upon their bodies assuaged. The cruel discomfort began to resolve.

The pilot's screen now read *3 minutes 48 seconds* to landing. An entirely new world was just within reach. As they looked upon each other, John stretched his hand over the ladder between them, to which Sofia responded in like fashion. Taking each other by the hand, the uncertainty of the next few minutes were building up an anxious anticipation within their bowels as regards to what was in store for them when they made their exit from the airship.

The steadiness by which the transporter was falling felt slow and controlled. The vibratory response upon entering the new atmosphere had now completely ceased. The remaining time spent between heaven and soil culminated in a consistent, almost wave-like, liquid feeling that caused their stomachs to tingle.

Jarred back against the shock absorbing springs of the chairs, they could feel their vehicle touching down on the concrete pad. Unbuckling his harness as the engines began powering down, John lifted himself out of the chair and climbed down the ladder.

"Listen," he said.

With her eyes moving about the cabin, Sofia tried to grasp at the sounds he was hearing, but everything was silent. Released from the restraints of the chair, she sat up, turning to the side and allowing her legs to hang over the edge of the seat.

"I don't hear anything. What do you hear?" she whispered.

As the engines completely cut power, the pilot's computer station went cold. The lights in the cabin blinked off. The Savior's rays of light were filtering through the darkly tinted window, casting simple shadows along the walls.

"I don't hear anything either. It seems too quiet," he said in a low, soft voice.

After being assisted down from the chair, Sofia followed John to the doorway, where they opened it with cautious care. Making their way down the walkway and descending the ladder, the eerie silence was causing John to become more than mildly concerned.

Opening the first of the three storage bay doors, they began to progress down the ladder. With normal gravity having been restored, both John and Sofia were feeling a bit unsteady due to the vertigo inducing height of the descent. The cabin was empty just as they expected, but there was still nothing but silence from the outside world.

Descending the second and third storage areas resulted in the same soundless phenomena. Listening intently with their ears pressed against the final door, there were no vibrations pulsating throughout its metal composition, there were no screeches from the hydraulic systems of the forked vehicles unloading and loading the airship, everything was the same: silence. Carefully pulling back the door, John let it creep up just enough for Sofia to peek inside.

"Do you see anything?" he asked.

"Open it just a little more."

The space widened as John made just enough room for her to drop her upper torso through. With a cursory glance, she could see that the bay was untouched. There were no signs that anyone had entered in.

"There's nobody here," she said, drawing her head back out of the threshold.

"You're kidding," John retorted.

"No. I'm serious. Take a look."

Retracting the door all the way back, John knelt down, peering through in amazement.

"They haven't even opened the bay door yet," he said.

Sitting back against the wall, he thought for a moment. The bay doors always seemed to open upon landing. Why was this any different?

"This doesn't seem right, does it?" he whispered.

"It is rather strange, I think," Sofia responded, not really sure of what to make of the situation.

Standing up and positioning himself behind the door, he said, "Stand back for a moment."

Closing them off from the lower bay, John rotated the locking handle. Sitting back down once again, he placed his hand over Sofia's.

"Let's just wait a little bit. I'm sure nobody knows we're in here. But I just want to see what happens before we do anything else."

"This is getting scary, John," Sofia said, moving closer to his side.

"We'll be alright. Don't worry yourself over this," he responded.

John kept his composure resolute in order to help Sofia remain calm, even though, he figured, he was probably more afraid than she, due the fact that he really did not have any control over their predicament.

It had been, perhaps, an hour or more since they had sealed themselves off from the deck below. With her head snuggled against John's abdomen, Sofia had fallen into a restless sleep, intermittently twitching and mumbling, while using him as her pillow. Other than their movement, there had been no activity inside the airship. As far as John was able to discern, the outside seemed to be equally composed. He did not want to wake Sofia, but they could not remain in the transporter forever.

"Sofia," John whispered, nudging her arm.

Readjusting her head, she rolled onto her side, continuing with her heavy breathing.

"Sofia, it's time to wake up, girl," he said a little louder.

With a light shaking of her shoulder, she sat up with a startle, speaking in a frightful, disoriented tone.

"What is it? Is someone coming?"

"No. No, it's nothing," he said, attempting to calm her fears while rubbing her back. "I was just trying to wake you up. It's been quite a while now. I think we should go down there and see if we could find a way out."

"You mean, go outside?" Her words were veiled in disbelief.

"Yes, why do you say it like that? There hasn't been a single sound since we landed. I don't think anybody's out there," he commented.

"I don't know about that, John. How do you know they're not waiting for us? Maybe they want us to open the door and walk out so that they don't have to take any chances of coming after us in here. We are armed, you know."

"I know that. But, listen-"

"John," Sofia interrupted him, "this whole thing's getting too crazy. I don't want to-," she began to say, the corners of her eyes filling with tears.

"Sofia, it's okay. Listen, dear. Just-"

"I don't want to be here anymore. Really, I don't."

"Sofia, I think we're the only ones here. There hasn't been a single sound from outside."

"You're not listening to me again," Sofia interrupted. "Will you please-"

"Look, Sofia, we've made it this far-"

"Take me home. I really want to go home, now. Just take me home."

"Sofia, you need to listen to me. There's no-"

"There's no what?"

"No sound," John repeated.

"What do you mean no sound? Of course there's no sound. The Labor Security... they're probably waiting outside for us. They never seem to make noise. They just sneak up on people."

"No, girl. They're not waiting for us. Just calm down and-"

"How do you expect me to be calm when-?"

"There hasn't been a single transporter that's taken off or-"

"A single what?"

"Transporter. There are no transporters taking off or landing. Just listen, okay. I think we're the only ones here."

As she buried her head into his chest, tearful and frightened, John ceased in his efforts to convince her of their safety. She needed the release. Their adventure was getting far beyond what he had promised her, and stepping out into the alien world, he feared, would throw her over the edge of the boundary of her own sanity. For all the troubles he brought to bear upon her, stepping aside while she vented her emotions was the least he could do.

Sofia had wept, stating her frustrations and anxieties, for, what felt to be, another hour before calming down. She had become apologetic for her outburst, and afterward she looked emotionally drained. John hated hearing the penitent words that fell from her mouth. He was the one that needed to be apologizing, not her, and he was well aware of that fact. But for some selfish reason, of which he could not comprehend at the time, he was unable, or more to the fact, unwilling, to ask for her forgiveness.

With the spiritually traumatic moment behind them, they finally left the upper storage bay behind, descending the ladder into the vessel's crate-filled compartment below.

Placing a few bottles of water and some salt cracker packages into his thigh pocket, John led Sofia to the control panel. As they were not about to get into a firefight with the Labor Security, should they find themselves face to face with them once the door opened, they slid their rifles over their shoulders by the slings, hanging them across their backs.

The handheld computer's connectors fit directly into the ports at the side of the airship's towering metal door, bringing the menu screen upon its display. Unlike the vessel's Pilot Control System, the icons were straightforward and obvious in their implication. Swiping his finger across the words *Panel Open*, the gears above them began to grind. Within seconds the wall of the transporter began to rise.

The thick, triangulated locking hubs that protruded from the bottom of the rising, bay door, like the teeth of a metallic beast, lifted from their sockets, giving way to hot gusts of swirling debris and dry, dirty air that reeked of rotting flesh. Gagging under the control of the stench, Sofia and John wrapped their face coverings around their noses and mouths. Although it did stifle the odor to some extent, it did little to remove the taste of death that had coated their tongues. Unlike the ash filled base that they had left behind, the dust passing through the threshold was brown and heavy, completely devoid of the gray-white soot that they should have been exposed to had the area been a base of heavy transporter activity.

The rising barrier of the hull had opened to an area approximately leveled with their knees. Kneeling down, they were able to gather in the first view of the mysterious world.

The light outside was quite dim despite the high position of the Savior in the sky, as it dispersed in a yellowish-beige glow, blanketing the parched, wind-swept station. The few warehouses that were visible from their point of view were similar to the metal structures back home, but they were completely unmanned and devoid of the stacks of crates that John and Sofia had expected to see.

Cautious to avoid stepping into a trap, they peeked around the edge of the opened bay with a controlled curiosity. The base was much smaller than they had expected it to be. And just as their first glance had suggested, there was not a soul to be seen. Unlike the busy system that they had experienced within Labor's base, there were only a half dozen empty landing pads and sealed-off warehouses that made up the entire station. The thick bars of the surrounding fence created the relatively small arena in which they were enclosed.

As John and Sofia stepped out of the transporter and onto the ramp, they both felt an odd sense of being free, yet trapped. And although they both experienced the same emotions simultaneously, neither was aware of the others thoughts, as they had not the desires to share them with one another.

John's hand was tightly wrapped about Sofia's palm as they hopped off the ramp and onto the crumbling, dry surface of the planet. The hot wind kept a steady cloud of dust permanently floating in the air, polluting the blueness of the sky above with its thin, blanketing veil.

Because it was only lightly obscured, it appeared to them that the heavens above were quite overt in displaying the contrails so difficult to see back on Labor's planet. The white lines of the airships trailed and crossed over each other, sailing to and fro from a far off base, whose view, they believed, was only obstructed by the heavily barred fencing around them.

Lifting the binocular to his eyes, the white lines of hundreds of transporters suddenly became visible contrasting against the blue face of the sky. They were joined every few seconds by freshly added streaks.

"There's hundreds of them up there, girl. Where are they all going?" John questioned. But he received no answer from Sofia.

There was something quite concerning with regards to the high volume of flights taking place above them, but what it was that caused that feeling was shackled to John's unconsciousness. There was no way for him to discern what it was that caused him to feel so uneasy.

As the young couple reached the fence, they were surprised to find, a few thousand meters below on the down slope, a densely populated city. Through his binocular apparatus, John was able to make out tens of thousands of people, like tiny ants due to their proximity, moving about through the streets, and entering into and exiting out of the surrounding farmlands, baking under the heat of the Savior's rays. The buildings, although lacking in visual clarity, appeared to be constructed close together, squared off by the natural layout of the cross-system of roads that ran throughout the urban complex.

Further out on the distal side of the metropolis, beginning at the edge of its limits, John could see the flatlands, expansive and green. Perfectly squared upon its visible sides and surrounded by the deathly world of desert sand and sparse, brown vegetation, it rolled out for an innumerable distance before disappearing over the horizon.

Children and women seemed to be more abundant than all the citizens of Labor combined. John could clearly see that the larger bodied population was covered with colorful, rippling dresses that waved about under the command of the wind, while the smaller framed citizens were running about with a disordered chaos.

The road leading to the city was, to his horror, littered with the rotting carcasses of what were perhaps the village's deceased. The dead were varied in shapes and sizes, surrounded by clouds of buzzing insects and partially covered over with blankets made from the same flapping fabric of the women's attire. Smaller plots of land bordering the highway were being farmed by groups of women who were indifferent to the decaying bodies that were lying nearby. They continued with their business, as if the corpses were as common an entity as the sand and the rocks.

With the closer proximity of the fields below the abandoned base, John could make out more details of the common populace. They were all female, completely emaciated, existing as nothing more than skin and bone. The exposed flesh of their bodies was mostly tan, some nearly blackened, under the light of the Savior. They appeared to be, for the most part, in various stages of pregnancy, with their bellies protruding out from under their colorful tops. Many of the women held infants in swaddling bundles that wrapped over their shoulders, allowing them to continue to work, even while breastfeeding.

Handing the spectacles to Sofia, John said, "Here, take a look. It's terrible: all those poor people down there. I've never seen such poverty."

As the binocular's eyecups pressed upon the sweat-drenched sockets of her eyes, Sofia could see why John was struck with such awe at the sight. The city seemed to her to eclipse the breadth and width of Labor, but with one distinct exception: there were no walls.

"How strange. It seems like they're free to leave their homes and wander where ever they wish," she said.

"Look around, though. Where would they go? It's all dead land. There probably isn't a single water source for kilometers in any direction. Maybe none at all on such a dry planet."

"But look at how green the land is over there," she retorted, pointing towards the flatlands. "There *must* be water on the planet."

"But, that might be the only place where it springs up."

John then directed Sofia to turn the binocular downward, so as to allow her to see the source of the stench. She only glanced at the dead for a moment before handing the binocular back to him.

"I don't want to see anymore," she said, looking back towards their transporter. "Are we going home now?"

"It sounds bad," John began. "But we should probably go down there. Maybe we could try to talk to some of them. They had to have seen us land. And they certainly don't seem to be hostile."

"But, why would you want to go down there? Those are dead people on that road," Sofia protested.

"That city probably has some answers."

"Answers to what?"

"I don't know. To anything, I guess."

It had not been an easy task convincing Sofia to leave the station, but John eventually won out in the end. As they followed along the fence line, Sofia kept a close watch on the people below, anticipating some kind of response from the planet's inhabitants regarding their presence. But, after several passing minutes of insignificant action, it appeared that there was not going to be an incoming investigation.

The entryway to the compound was just a few hundred meters ahead of them. It was built with an identical layout to the Security gate constructed at the City of Labor. Approaching it created an almost dreamlike state within John's mind, as it was such a familiar site.

Rounding the corner of the gate's booth, John tugged at its door as they walked by, but it was locked. Through its glass partitions, the interior looked clean and orderly, but lacking in life, as its control panel had been completely powered down.

Ducking under the vehicle-security arm, he and Sofia found themselves on the dirt road that led directly to the city below. Unlike infiltrating Labor's base, there was nowhere for them to hide. Considering that John might, perhaps, be the only male present once they were within the city's boundary, and the fact that they were dressed in military garb, there was no possible way for them to blend in, either.

For the first few hundred meters following the path, the soil was similar to the dry ground that they had first encountered at the landing base at the top of the slope: completely barren and devoid of anything other than rock and dirt. But, as they descended further, green plots of land, in approximately one-acre, fenced lots, began to manifest... along with the dead.

Sofia was aghast at the site of the decomposing shells of women and children. Holding onto John's arm and smothering her face into his shoulder, she refused to watch where they were walking.

Working with their archaic farming tools, the colorfully clothed laborers plowed and dug, picked and hoed, without paying any attention to John and Sofia's existence. As if to purposefully ignore them, the women appeared to consciously avoid making any form of eye contact.

A particular plot of land, its rich, dark soil set in columns of long, thin mounds, butted up against the dry, dusty road. Busily tossing about handfuls of seed, two women, emaciated and blackened of skin, were working it, inching along a path that neared the roadside edge of their garden.

"Hello. Could you tell me-," John began to say, pulling Sofia's arm, so as to sidestep a maggot-covered corpse of a young boy, but the women turned their backs to him and began to walk away.

"That was odd, wasn't that," John asked, glancing down at Sofia, then back at the women.

Swatting at the flies that were buzzing around her head, Sofia made no reply.

"Do you think it's the rifle that frightened them?" he asked. But again Sofia would not answer him.

Neither of the women looked back. They just continued walking to the far end of the parcel, oblivious to the couple's presence. Before they could reach it, in bewilderment John turned Sofia away from them, continuing their walk towards the metropolis.

After what felt to her to be a relatively short span of time, Sofia took a moment to peel her face away from John's arm, looking back up the slope. The tip of their airship was visible over the wall of the landing facility, appearing as a small structure mounted upon a low-lying hill. It was, to her surprise, quite the distance behind them. The city before them, on the other hand, was growing terribly nearer. And she now could see that it was not a robust economic metropolis by any sense of the words. The distant view, coupled with the dusty haze floating about the air, had obscured what was actually a massive, economically oppressed environment. It was now within a reasonable distance for her to gather its minute details without the use of any visual aids.

John was equally amazed at the oppressiveness of the land. He could hardly believe that it made Labor City actually look quite comfortable. As there were no threatening entities presently near, John, knowing he was moving entirely contrary to Sofia's wishes, continued to lead them onward.

The disparaged city's features were in full view. There were no apartments or buildings as their first glimpses had indicated, or in the sense that they had understood them through their experiences on Labor. All the structures were mere huts, makeshift in design and rather asymmetrical in form. Roofed over with layers of cardboard, they did not appear to be endowed with any structural integrity. The housing proper was constructed of randomly placed, stained and weathered scraps of the same plywood crates that John and Sofia had seen on the airships and warehouses back home. They could even make out the areas where the stenciled letters had once been, denoting which places the crates had been destined for, but were now faded or else sprayed over with black paint, defacing them to the point of complete illegibility.

As Sofia and John closed in on the masses at the edge of the city, as far as they could tell, there were still no men present. The women, dressed in tattered, torn skirts of various colors and patterns, their skin tones generally like those of the others they had seen on the outskirts of the city, nearly black as night, were busy transporting raw cotton and produce in wicker baskets that they carried, balanced upon their heads. Their drop off seemed to exist somewhere on the other side of the town, as their lines meandered towards the direction where the flatlands began.

The unsupervised male children were equally tanned, and poorly dressed to the same degree of poverty as the women. Some were attired in torn filthy shirts, others were wearing nothing but underpants, barefoot and covered with blood-splattered layers of dried mud. They wildly ran amok through the crowds in various sized parties, violently playing a game under which it appeared that the rules required the use of heavy wooden sticks. Hitting one another, scrapes and abrasions appeared immediately upon contact, often drawing blood that dried in thick streams that dribbled down their necks and backs, rolling down their chests and arms. Chasing one another with their high-pitched shrills and laughter, they skillfully weaved in and out of the lines of their laboring mothers, hopping over the fly-infested bodies of the dead that littered the dirt streets. The weaker of the youths stood alone, crying with no one to find comfort from.

The female children were sedate in comparison to their male counterparts. Huddling together in smaller groups, they appeared to be learning various skills that were being taught to them by the older girls. They worked diligently and silently with their hands, keeping their heads lowered and focused on the tasks at hand.

As John and Sofia entered deeper into the periphery of the town, they soon found themselves walking amongst the throng, terribly out of fashion and alien to the culture, yet not a single person paid them any attention. The poverty they were experiencing would have been unimaginable up to this point in their lives. Their only economic experiences were on Labor, where the word *oppression* seemed a rather over-reaching term to describe their former place of living after seeing what true oppression actually consisted of.

With each step further into the city, the smell of death grew more intense. Dry-heaving under the stench, Sofia could do little to keep her gag reflex under control and the tears from continuously pouring from her eyes. Filled with the decaying pieces of flesh and bone, the streets' edges were scenes of carnage. Dried blood had soaked into the surrounding dirt and rock, giving a bizarre crimson color to the city's pathways.

Having created an invisible bubble around the two travelers, the women of the town were purposefully keeping their distance: everywhere John and Sofia moved, the throng would simultaneously shift equidistant away, keeping an arm's length between them at all times.

Contrary to the behavior of the women, the male youth were star struck by their presence. They trailed closely behind the two strangers, enviously eyeing the weapons slung across their backs. The children pointed at them and smiled. And on several occasions a few of them nearly ventured into the invisible sphere only to be hindered by the nearest apathetic adult. None of the boys spoke a single word to them. They just watched and followed with an almost eerie reverence that bordered on worship.

Free to wander wherever they desired, it wasn't long in their journeying through the congested streets before Sofia and John realized that they had become completely lost. Isolated from the indigenous population, separated as outcasts, there was no way to tell if they could be understood through verbal communication, as none of the adults exhibited the slightest hint of recognizing their existence.

Approaching another crowded intersection, and perplexed by the circumstances at hand, they made their way to one of the street's corners where a cardboard overhang looked to provide some shade. Stepping up a crumbling, concrete slab underneath it, they leaned back against the plywood dwelling that faced into the throng. In accordance with the treatment that they had been receiving, the occupiers of the structure immediately separated themselves from the two sojourners, covering the nearby windows with old, stained cloths.

As the two of them began to take their rest in the cool of the building's shadow, the rumbling of a wheeled transporter, its horn rhythmically belching out to a continual series of faint screams and cries, could be heard somewhere in the distance making its way towards their position.

"Do you hear that?" Sofia asked. "That doesn't sound good. Maybe we should find a place to hide."

"Let's see what it is first," John said, standing upon his tiptoes, attempting to catch a glimpse of the vehicle over the heads of the masses.

From his perspective, the source of the commotion was causing a dispersion of the crowds. Basket-burdened heads were moving aside in rapid succession within a cloud of wailing children and distorted banter.

Climbing up a rusty pole that protruded from the dry soil supporting the wall of the nearby building, John could see the women parting ways around a speeding military transporter. Scurrying out of its path, the throng was behaving as water does, separating before and reuniting behind, just as when a man moves his hand through a pond's glassy surface.

The blaring of the machine's horn was putting the fear into the populace as the masses unhesitatingly gave the right-of-way to the vehicle that was rumbling through it. Intermittently making contact with some of the women, the driver appeared to have little regards for the lives of the citizenry. Bouncing off the thick metal of the vehicle's front end like rag dolls, lifelessly hurtling to the ground in puffs of dust, the bodies fell twisted and tortuous on the hard, dirt road. The contents of their baskets were left in the vehicle's wake, a temporary memorial to the insignificant existences of the fallen women. As the machine moved past, the crowds unflinchingly regrouped, continuing on with their former business.

The vehicle was drawing within a distance for clear sight, and John could see that the transporter was identical to the Security vehicles of Labor, with the exception of its purplish-red stained grill and headlamps, and the manned, long-barreled, automatic weapon mounted on its rooftop. It was fast making its way towards the intersection below him. Scanning about for a place for him and Sofia to run, John could see that there was nowhere to hide, especially due to the fact that the women would not allow them to blend in with their company.

"It looks like the Security's heading our way," he said, hopping down and taking Sofia by the arm, escorting her back into the throng.

"What? The Security? Here?" she questioned.

Ignoring her words, John led Sofia into the middle of the crossroads where the concentration of the citizenry was the heaviest. The vehicle was closing in, and he was at a loss as to what he should do next.

"What are we going to do?" Sofia called out to him.

"Just follow me," he unintentionally snapped at her under the duress of the moment.

As the vehicle entered the intersection, the women began pushing against one another in order to remove themselves from its destructive path. Rushing Sofia into the masses, John was hoping to buy them a little more time before the women realized that the couple had delineated from their demeaning *bubble*.

For the moment they were concealed within the hordes of panicking women as the armored body of the vehicle rushed by with its trail of death left in its wake. Continuing on its straight course, the crowds rapidly recovered from the trauma, swallowing the vehicle up at the rear. As the *bubble* suddenly began forming around the two foreigners, the rooftop gunner, disappearing behind the closing wall of baskets, turned around, and for one fleeting moment he met John eye-to-eye.

As the transporter exited the intersection John could hear its tires grinding to a halt, tearing into the thick crumbling dirt, straining under the burdening weight of its metallic shell. The idling vehicle was engulfed in the growing dust cloud that it had stirred up. Spreading out like a blanket over the basket-covered heads of the women that surrounded it, the dispersed light of the Savior gave the appearance of elongated spokes of a golden wheel reflecting its image off the surface of a shimmering pool.

Attempting to remain anonymous, John began to steer Sofia out of the intersection. But his plan was shuttered by the sudden, thundering burst of gunfire that sent the peoples scrambling to clear the streets. Falling to their knees at the edges of the road, the women covered their heads, shielding themselves with their arms. The broken baskets and produce littering the street, brought fruit and other raw items rolling at the feet of John and Sofia, who now stood alone, staring up the barrel of the transporter's gun.

Crying children and weeping, whimpering women huddled close together against the walls of the street's buildings, while John and Sofia woefully held their position, desperately trying to maintain a neutral stance. They were hoping to avoid provoking the men of Security to violence.

"Drop your weapons," a voice boomed through the vehicle's side-mounted speakers, echoing throughout the walls of the city.

Slowly reaching over their shoulders, the young couple slid the rifle slings over their heads, dropping their weapons upon the ground, followed by the side arms that hugged their thighs. Cautiously reaching into his pocket, John removed his knife, letting it fall to the dust at his feet.

"Empty the rest of your pockets into a single pile in front of you. Then, turn your pockets inside out," the voice burst out.

Following the official's orders, they were soon standing before a small heap of items. These were the few belongings that they had reserved for, what should have been, the final leg of their journey back on Labor: ammunition, food, the handheld computer, the little black book and a few odds and ends. There would be nothing left in their possession now were it not for the clothes that they wore.

"Take two steps back and drop to your knees, placing your hands on top of your heads," the voice commanded.

Distancing themselves from their last few remnants, John and Sofia eased down to the ground, the hot soil under their knees painfully pressing into their skin. Clouds of dust kicked up into the air by the wind as the door of the transporter drew open. A group of heavily armored men descended from the rear compartment, guns drawn, heads helmeted, eyes glassed over by their reflective goggles. They were calculating and cold, only moving under the hand-initiated queues of their lead officer.

As the agents were closing in on them, John knew that soon he and Sofia would be separated. He hung his head low, ashamed and defeated in spirit.

"Sofia," he whispered.

But she did not answer. Eyes closed and silent as death, the tears dripping off the ends of her cheeks were speaking for her.

With the barrels of the Security's carbines pointed at their heads, the two wanderers were forced to lie face down upon the street, the taste of the soil's dust strong and bitter in their mouths. The metal cuffs ratcheted firmly around their wrists, securing their hands behind their backs, leaving them helplessly at the mercy of their captors as they lay under the burning eye of the Savior above.

John was nearly a half-meter away from the pile of their belongings. He watched a Security agent tossing the items, one-by-one, into a black canvas sack. Curiously eyeing the handheld computer before dropping it into the bag, the agent turned his masked face toward John. Fearful for their lives John immediately removed eye contact from the man.

From one of the side streets that crossed the intersection, the rumbling commotion of another approaching transporter was making its way towards their position. Distant gunfire, followed by women wailing and screaming, began to rise throughout the distal parts of the city.

"We've captured two of them. Deserters from Red, I'm assuming by their uniforms," the Commander spoke into the mouthpiece that wrapped around the side of his head, attaching at the helmet's orifice beside his ear. "Yes, sir... Affirmative... That's affirmative. No, sir, we're processing some of them on the north end. ETA: one hundred twenty minutes. Roger that. Out."

Sofia was still shutting the external world out of her mind. John could see that she was mentally distancing herself from the horrors of their captivity by removing all traces of reality. It was the only thing she could do to cope with their terrible predicament. With his face to the ground, he too closed his eyes, hoping to walk with Sofia in their forested home on Labor, throwing away all the evils that he had brought upon them. The whispering of the Security officials amongst themselves was an incomprehensible wind blowing about the canals of his ears. What it was they were communicating between one another was of no consequence to him. John knew that he and Sofia were going to be sent back to the City, back to their home planet. They would never see each other again.

The crunching of dirt under the feet of several men brought John's eyes to a meeting with their black boots as he and Sofia were hoisted up to their feet.

"Two detainees. Captain wants them separated during trans-
port," one of the agents said into his microphone.

Motioning to the Commander, the Security official that had
just finished bagging their property reopened the sack. Extracting
out the handheld machine, he handed it over to his superior. The
Commander looked it over and made a quick glance towards John
and Sofia before dropping it back into the bag. Leaning his head
beside the agent, he made an inaudible verbalization to which
both men immediately cast their sights back at the young couple
before departing from one another.

Speeding into the middle of the intersection, the second armored transporter arrived in a trail of dust. Its freshly adorned grill
was covered over with crimson splashes and hair-tangled flesh.

Exiting the vehicle, several agents approached the young couple. Assuming their duties from the Commanding Officer, they
set about forcing John and Sofia upon two separate paths. Escorted to the first vehicle, John watched with heartfelt suffering
as Sofia, her chin upon her chest, willingly obeyed their orders.
Struggling to make the climb with her hands bound to her back,
the steep ramp at the rear of the machine was a challenge for her
petite frame. Disappearing into the blackness of the transporter's
personnel compartment, she was followed closely by her captors.

With his prisoner quarters idling just ahead, John conspicu-
ously gazed around at the cowering women and children as he
stepped over the bloodied body of one of the transporter's victims.
Passing by the closing doors of Sofia's wheeled cell, the men of Security behaved mysteriously, communicating sometimes through
their microphones, but mostly in hand gestures and whispers.

Nearing the vehicle ahead, John watched as its steel ramp extended from its underside by the influence of a hidden motor and
its grinding gears. The rear door simultaneously opened upwards,

revealing the dark mouth to which he would soon be subjected.

Behind him, Sofia's transporter was turning itself about in the middle of the intersection. John attempted to look back, but was hindered by a gloved hand that grabbed him by the face, preventing him from engaging in even that simple act.

With the light of the Savior reflecting off the soil and into the fully open cabin of the transporter, the interior of the vehicle was dimly illuminated. Its walls were lined with a single, metal bench seat that extended along its entirety. He could see that it was padded over with a thin layer of plastic-covered foam that protruded through the cracks and tears created under its years of abuse. The floor was stained in a brownish-red hue that was putrid in odor, releasing an iron taste upon the tongue that intensified with each breath.

Entering in, and compelled under threat to take a seat in the middle of one of the benches, John could see the dark, splattered liquid along the ceiling and walls that had dried in variously sized patterns and drippings, like bizarre tears running down a rusted face. He was cognizant of the fact that he was not the first prisoner to enter into the vehicle's belly.

As the Security agents took their seats beside him, the door began to close. John felt the dusty breeze of air that entered into the cabin as the men turned back, pulling open the metal sliders, revealing the slits in the walls of the cell that performed the actions of ventilating windows.

The vehicle began to vibrate as the motor revved up. And soon they were in motion. Through the openings that were ventilating the interior, John could see the passing buildings and basket-carrying women speeding by. The horn of the transporter was loud and overbearing. The sensation of motivity was heightening. They were only a mere seconds into the drive when the screams began, and the knocking of bodies off the transporter's front side could be felt, heavy and cruel.

The agent in front of him was either sleeping, or staring down at him through his reflective goggles. It was difficult to tell which it was. Already anxiety stricken, John was made all the more uncomfortable by the presence of his faceless escorts.

The ride to their destination was, he assumed, to be at least two hours away, if he understood the Commander's words correctly. It had been years since he and Sofia had truly been apart. His companion was nowhere to be seen. He wanted to plead for help, not for himself, but for her safety and consoling. Could he ask it of the Savior? Was He listening? A being that actually watched over all the events of the material world, and had an actual hand in its destiny and functions, seemed remotely untenable under the circumstances. How could such hardships be a reality under the hand of such Benevolence, John thought. But there was no other choice. All his options were depleted the moment that the gunner spotted them. Closing his eyes, he began the inner search of desperation.

"I'm such a weak man," he said within himself. "If You exist, as it appears You do through our many ventures and their outcomes, please, look upon us once again and help us."

His words were silent, but sincere. Deep into the pleasure of communing with the Unknown, John subconsciously let his final words break forth from his tongue, "More than myself, please, help Sofia, my love. And let her know that I'm so sorry for what I've done to her."

The particles upon which the vibrations of those words were carried, released from his lips, sailing through the powdery air, wrapping around the dust of the cabin. The turbulent draft threw it wildly about the walls and ceiling, tossing it through a slit-window, where it was captured and borne along by the atmosphere's fluid matter. Retreating from the transporter, falling under the determinate control of the Savior's light, it hasted through the streets, filtering through the weavings of the baskets, passing through the throngs of women. It sailed above the blood stained dirt of the roadways and passed through the nostrils of a recently deceased woman, who, to the astonishment of the basket carrying crowds, sat up with a sudden gasp. Piercing through the hairs of their heads and along their children's exposed skin as they playfully ran through the crowds, it shuttled down the alleys and across the rooftops, over the buildings and through the doorways. Out one window it entered another. Swirling through the many rooms of the makeshift hut, it passed over a stillborn infant held in its weeping mother's arms, giving a burst of life to the child, who awoke with a sudden cry. Out the door it fled, over the railing, freefalling towards the busy street below, swiftly gliding along the swarming, dirt walkways, causing a glorious uproar as several more women and children awoke in the streets from the slumber of death. It fled from the village, riding upon the waves of the breeze that crossed the green of the flatlands where hundreds of thousands of women were working the fields. It whistled through their veils and the handkerchiefs that wrapped about their heads like a song of joy. It shuttled across their dresses and through the vines. It crossed amongst the leaves and around the dangling branches of the trees, ushering a bursting forth of fruit from the orchard. It wafted across the water-filled channels that brought its life saving fluid to the rich farmlands, streaming towards the dirt road that ran along the flatland's periphery, chasing the billowing dust that followed a lone vehicle. It raced through its tire driven cloud and around its spinning wheels. Upward it climbed, catching a ride on its armored hull. It sneaked in through its windowed slit, leaping across the shoulder of a Security agent that swatted at an unseen pest. It hopped upon the waving hair and bobbing head of a meditative young woman whose body moved under the influence of the jostling ride. Upon entering into the canal of her ear, Sofia opened her eyes to the voice of John.

Chapter Twenty-Seven

The perpetual dripping by an unseen water source kept Sofia in a state of mental numbness, captivated by its hypnotically consistent tapping. Rhythmically persistent, it was like a torturous metronome: precise and unforgiving.

Aglow in the murky flood of a dim, pumpkin-orange light mounted directly above her, the interrogation room was chilled and damp. Its cold, concrete floor sucked the heat from her body through the thin, tender skin of her bare feet.

Stained with the appearance of splattered rust, the drain fitted beneath her metal chair released the same odor that engulfed her earlier in the day when she had entered into the vehicle that had transferred her to her current place of terror. The room was ominously familiar. It held to the same atmosphere that consumed the hallways and classrooms of the Education: isolating and indifferent to the sufferings of its captives.

Attempting to rub away the clear nasal excretions streaming down her nose and dripping off of her upper lip caused her wrist to be met with another painful tug. Sofia was once again reminded of the chains that held her at bay. Bolted to the floor, the frigid chair was unyielding to her struggle against the leather straps that kept her confined tightly against its back.

The walls of the cell were covered over with mirror-like panels that dimly reflected her ghastly figure. The room's corners were like the blackness of a dark cave, uninviting and terrible. The fearful expression scrawled across her thin face, the hollow skull-like shadows cast upon her eyes, repeated itself over and over again in its layers of reflections. It was a disorienting effect that was partially alleviated by staring at the scant, gray areas of the floor.

Sofia's back faced the only entrance into the cell: a steel door with a slider that covered a small rectangular window. It was only faintly visible to her in the image on the wall due to the pre-knowledge she had of its existence.

Sofia recalled being led into the room and restrained to the chair. It had been perhaps an hour ago... or, maybe it was two hours... or three. She had lost her sense of time under the degrading treatment that she was being forced to endure. It could have been four or five hours for all she knew.

As she sat alone wondering what was to become of her, the sudden manipulation of the locking mechanism to her back caused her to startle. A metallic rattling echoed throughout the room, as if the lock's system had been designed with a chain-like structure. Within a few seconds the rust splattered door creaked open.

By the sounds of the footsteps, Sofia knew that she was no longer alone. Several persons had entered in together.

Unable to turn about, coupled with the inability of the faint lamp above her head to illuminate the corners of the room with any facilitative degree, she frighteningly called out, "Is someone there?" But there was no response, only the sound of the dripping of water.

The silhouettes of a small group were faintly visible through their mirrored reflections. Standing in the shadows, the agents had no details to discern of. Even their outlines were quite obscured.

A twinkling, orange light blinked on and off around her image in the mirror, intermittently revealing an empty chair facing at a ninety-degree angle to her left. It was fixed to the floor over a similarly stained drain as hers. The strange apparition was directly in front of her. Yet, it appeared to manifest momentarily, directly through her faint reflection as if her image was superimposed upon it. One moment it was there, and then it was gone.

The empty chair had ceased to be. Then, without further disappearances of its object, the light flickered on once again, and firmly settled: there was another room hidden behind the mirrors!

Two Security agents entered into its cone of light escorting a third man. Chained about the wrists and ankles, a black, canvas bag covering his head, he was walking between them. The thickness of the walls had apparently prevented any noise from escaping the room, as there was no sound heard coming from the other side.

Forced to the chair, the man sat down while the agents proceeded to secure his wrists and ankles to the chains that linked to the eyebolts protruding from the concrete floor. After securing the belts around his waist and chest, one of the agents disappeared into the darkness. With the last remaining agent removing the hood from off of the man's head before vanishing from sight, it was John that was sitting before her, distressed and isolated!

Reaching out, as if to stand up and take hold of him, Sofia was again reminded of the painful recourse of her actions. Her chains drew her back to her place of confinement.

By the direction he was facing, John was oblivious to her presence. She could see that he was frightened, and thankfully unharmed. But his relative safety did not help with the nauseating feeling of helplessness that was overshadowing her.

An agent, dressed in a blue-black uniform similar to, but slightly different in fashion of that seen on Labor, stepped into Sofia's light. His reflection behind her was cold and stiff.

"How do you know this man?" he asked through a soft, but deep voice.

"He's my friend," she nervously responded, attempting to look back over her shoulders.

"Red is quite far away. How did you get here?" he asked.

"I don't know what *Red* is," she said with a sniffle. "We came from Labor."

Stepping out of the light, the agent began to converse with the other men in the room. The name seemed to cast a murmuring disbelief throughout their discourse as they spoke with one another and whispered into the microphones that telescoped from their earpieces. After a moment of what seemed to be a tense debate among the men, an agent from John's room stepped into his cone of illumination, standing directly in front of him. Grasping John under the chin and around his cheeks, the man forced his head around, bringing John's eyes in contact with Sofia. Upon releasing him, the agent disappeared into the gloom, leaving the two of them to do nothing but look longingly towards each other.

Although his eyes were hidden in the black, hollowness of the shadows that were cast down from his brow, Sofia knew that John was looking directly at her. His lips uttered her name. There was no sound, but in all familiarity, she could hear him.

"John," she whispered back.

Entering into her cone of light, a heavily armed man unlocked the restraints from around her arms, letting the chain-tailed cuffs crumble to the floor. As she rubbed at the reddened, circumferential abrasions that had formed around her wrists, the reflected agent in the mirror behind her stepped back into his darkened world.

"Can you point to the young man you say traveled with you from... what did you call it? *Labor*?" the deep voice asked.

Lifting her finger towards John, Sofia innocently obeyed. The agent was pleasant and calm as he thanked her for her cooperation. John tilted his head in bewilderment at her gesture. Through her reflection he appeared to be confused by the fact that she had directed her attention to him in such a manner.

The sweat was beginning to drip down his forehead as she brought her arm back to her side. John had no idea why Sofia had just pointed at him, but something about her action did not feel quite right: as if she was accusing him for his foolishness.

"She said that you kidnapped her, and brought her here against her will," a voice growled from the darkness lingering in front of him.

"What? Why would she say-?" John began to say.

"I don't know. Why don't you tell us?" the grumbling voice asked.

"I already told you," John responded," I'm from Lab-."

"Labor, Labor, Labor. That's what you keep saying, but there's no planet called *Labor*."

"It's not a planet, it's a-."

Cut off mid-sentence by the heavy strike of a gloved hand against his mouth, John's ears began ringing the moment his teeth were slammed together. As his head was swung violently away from Sofia's view, from over his shoulder, he knew that she had witnessed the blow. Silently calling out within his mind to the Great Unknown to spare her from having to endure the same treatment, John once again hung his head in shame for being the cause of all her troubles.

Terrified at the sight of his abuse, Sofia cried out, "Why are you doing that to him?"

"He said that *you* stole a computer and used it to hijack a transporter back to this base," an agent answered as he walked up beside her, revealing the handheld that they had taken from among the abandoned equipment on Labor.

"Hijack a what? I never-" Sofia began to say.

The laughter that burst forth from the men was demeaning and sadistically playful, as if her turmoil was par for their enjoyment. John was sucking on his swollen lip as another agent entered into view from the darkness around him. Releasing the cuffs from around his wrists, they dropped to floor, allowing John to wipe the blood from his mouth.

"Don't worry, sweetheart, we don't believe him. We're sure that he stole it, just like he stole you," another deep voice mocked Sofia from the dark.

"We're not stupid," the agent standing beside her said. "Your uniforms prove that you were trained here at some point in the past. We've checked all the records. There's been no report of any-one escaping from Planet Blue or Golden World, let alone here. But we're going to find out sooner or later who you are."

Turning around, the agent began to leave the cone of light, saying, "It really would be better for you if you were more truthful to us."

"Tell me," one of the men whispered, moving his face into the light, running his hands through the wavy strands of hair that hung beside Sofia's ear, "did you two return here to break your comrades free? Was this the *Great Uprising* we've been hearing about?"

Pulling her shoulder away from him she stuttered, "I don't know anything about that."

"Oh, but you do know. That man there," he said, pointing to John, "is a criminal: a deserter and a terrorist."

"No, he's-," Sofia interrupted.

"The two of you keep insisting that you're from a place you call *Labor*. Then I guess you two know how to work. You're going to find out what *labor* really is."

"But he's not a criminal, he's my friend, my love," Sofia said, as she began to cry.

Sofia was tearful and tormented, and John could do nothing to help her.

"You've really done a number on that girl, haven't you?" the agent standing before him said.

"I didn't do anything to her," John whispered.

"Look at her crying, she's telling them everything. We know who you are and what you did... we know you better than you know yourself," he laughed.

Unable to contain herself, Sofia buried her face in her hands. The wicked elation and mocking from the darkness was a torture worse than death. The men began to cruelly detail the savagery that they wished to act upon her and John. Heartless and evil, they ridiculed and taunted, threatened and railed.

"Who's your lover, little girl?" a laughing voice called out. "Point to him or we'll kill him."

She raised a finger towards John, but she refused to lift her eyes, afraid of seeing him so distraught. The room was engrossed with wickedness, and all she could do was obey... obey for *his* safety.

Sofia's hand was leveled at him once again. Her finger had a rhythmical bounce that coincided with her intense weeping.

"They just informed us that you attacked her... a young innocent girl like that."

"I never attacked anybody," John yelled out as he began to shed his first tear.

"You're lying to us, soldier. I already told you, she's told us everything," the man yelled.

"Keep your finger pointed at him, little girl, or he's a dead man," the agent screamed at Sofia.

She held her hand as still as she could. She didn't understand what the men were doing, but she complied with their demands, hoping that it would make them stop.

Attempting to stand up, the waist restraint pulled John back against the seat. Approaching from the darkness, another agent retrieved a knife from the sheath hanging upon his thigh. The deep voiced man grabbed Sofia by the hair, pulling her head back, forcing her to witness their demeaning acts.

Grabbing John by the collar, the man held the knife up high above his head. He was ready to thrust his blade into his captive's heart. Sofia's scream was inaudible through the mirrored window as she struggled to avoid seeing the murder of her companion. Her tormentor's smile reflecting above her was pure enjoyment in the moment.

With the knife plunging towards John's chest, Sofia closed her eyes, knowing that he could not survive the blow. As the tip of the blade came into contact with the outer layer of John's skin, the agent ceased in his action.

"If you want her to live, you'd better start giving us some real answers. You got me, soldier?" the agent growled at John.

"I don't know what to say. I don't know what you want from me." John cried.

"Do you want us to slit her throat right here in front of you?" the agent screamed into John's face.

As Sofia peered through her watery eyes, she could see that John was alive. The agent was holding the knife to an oozing puncture wound at the side of his neck.

"He's saying this was all your fault, that you seduced him into going along with your plan," an agent began to speak to her.

"He couldn't be saying that," Sofia wailed.

"Oh, yes he can... and he is. He's telling them who you really are: that you're a spy."

Sobbing uncontrollably, Sofia began to vomit upon the floor as two men approached from the blackness, unlocking the cuffs at her ankles and unbuckling the belts from around her waist and chest. Forced to stand upon her feet, she was so small and frail among such burly figures. One of the men placed his hand upon her back and looked at John, smiling in mocking derision.

"Where are you taking her?" John demanded.

"Far away from you. Her story's pretty solid. We're going to see how you like being the one taken advantage of. Some people are going to be pretty happy to see you tonight," the agent roared.

Sofia's attempts to turn to John one last time were hindered by her escorts.

"What are you going to do to him?" she cried.

"He's a criminal, he'll be getting what he deserves," was the answer.

Buckling under the weakness of her legs upon hearing those words, she was caught under the arms and dragged out of the cone of light and into the darkness.

"Wait. She's my friend," John said tearfully. "You can't do this to her."

"Those men know how to treat a girl right, unlike you. She's in good hands. You can stop your worrying," the agent said with a biting tone.

Grasping John by the back of the neck, an agent forced him to place his head between his knees while his partners assisted each other with the act of cuffing his hands behind his back. Removing the remaining restraints, John was unwillingly made to stand upon his feet as a gloved hand grasped the thick of his hair, raising him from his chair. With a heavy shove towards the blackness before him, he was led out of the room and into the cool, damp hallway.

As his legs began to give out under the mental anguish he was experiencing, John fell to his knees from where a forceful blow of a leather boot burrowed deep into his side. With the air blasting from his lungs, and the intense pain from the snapping of his ribs, he dropped backward onto his cuffed hands, gasping for breath and writhing in agony. Dragged into another large enclosure, he was dumped upon the floor while the men proceeded to cut and tear the clothing from his body, leaving him in the middle of the room bound and naked, curled up like a fetus ripped from its mother's womb.

Dressed in a light blue smock with a matching thigh-pocketed pant, a single male figure approached him with a small, leather container, which he set upon the floor. Unlatching the brackets upon its face, he lifted the top upon its hinges, pulling a tourniquet and needled syringe out from one of the drawers before tightly strapping the band around John's arm. Drawing several tubes of deep, dark blood from his vein, the man gently rolled the cylinders in between the palms of his hand before placing them into a slotted matrix inside the lower half of the case.

Grimacing in pain, John was pulled to his back, where two agents proceeded to restrain his legs. The man in blue pulled several items from his kit before pouring a cold, brown solution upon John's genitals. Pulling a pair of gloves over his hands, he tore open a long, flat rectangular package, from where he retrieved a lengthy rubber tube.

Grabbing John by the penis, the man fed the rubbery line into John's urethra, extracting a sample of urine that was captured in a small, plastic bag connected to the distal end of the tube. Mentally exhausted, John wanted to fight them off, but he could not find the physical strength to make the first move.

The man in blue placed the bag of urine into his case and closed the lid. Placing the cold, metal diaphragm of his stethoscope against John's back, he listened to the sounds of his breath. Standing up without a word, he walked out of the room followed by several other men.

Leaving John alone to cry and agonize by himself, the last remaining agent made his way towards the exit. The overhead lights blinked off. The dim, orange glow from the hall was the only source of illumination.

The savage cruelty by which the men spoke to Sofia had its objective based in the dehumanizing and humiliating of her entire being. Treated as if she were an animal, she was stripped of her clothes, probed for samples of blood and urine and placed into a brightly lit, glass chamber under the perversely watchful eyes of the agents. Attempting to cover her body with her arms, she curled up in the corner of the receptacle, weeping and ashamed.

A blast of cold water pierced the skin of her body. Like needles and thorns pouring forth from the faucets above her, she screamed out, her muscles constricting with a strangulating tension. Struggling under its freezing blanket of pain, gasping for a breath of air, Sofia crawled on her hands and knees, desperately feeling about for an area that was dry and warm. Her lips and fingers, purplish pale, her body shivering uncontrollably, she was on the verge of losing consciousness.

As the blackness of wasting away was nearing, a sudden shift in the temperature of the falling water became immediately noticeable. Sofia's mind began to clear, and she let out a deep sigh. The comforting warmth that she had been desperately seeking was finally showering down upon her.

At first it was a relief from the torment. Slipping down the drain in the center of the room, the cold water was fleeing away. Feeling the ease by which she could breathe again, Sofia rubbed her frigid arms and legs with the soothing liquid.

As the room began to fill with steam, the glass walls coated in moisture, hiding the evil eyes behind its drape. Standing upon her feet, Sofia sensed that there was something that was no longer pleasurable in the environmental change: the temperature of the water was increasing beyond a reasonable degree of easefulness.

The spray overhead was falling upon her with a light drizzle, and each drop was beginning to feel like the prick of a pin. As the pooling water commenced to bite at her feet, Sofia began banging her fists against the glass, begging to be let free. Clearing the moisture from the window, she found herself looking into the face of an arrogantly smiling agent. Backing away from the glass, she tipped her swollen feet out of the water by the toes, making every effort to rub away the searing welts that were forming about her back and head, and covering her arms.

A final spray of hot, scalding water dripped upon her neck followed immediately by the same cold rain of her first experience in the chamber. Falling to her knees for a second time, she continued screaming for a reprieve from the torment. Huddling back in the corner, horrified and brittle in heart, Sofia's teeth chattered from behind her pale skin. The terrible cycle of pain was about to go around once again.

The torturous event had been continuing for an immeasurable amount of time. Sofia's entire body was engulfed in a state of anguish as the last of the icy water finally emptied from the floor of the chamber. Curled up in the corner, her lips were as blue as her eyes, her skin as white as snow. The continued chattering of her teeth reverberated off the glassy walls. She lifted her head up as the entrance to her cell slid open, barely able to catch a short glimpse of the two agents that stepped in.

Grabbed by the arms, she was pulled to her feet and escorted out into the warm air of the compound.

"She's mine," one of the men growled.

"I've already claimed her for my own," another agent sneered, pushing his comrade aside.

A third agent entered into the room shouting, "Knock it off, both of you. Neither of you are getting her. She's *carrying*. Package her up and get her back to Basket Town ASAP. There's a few other women in the hold that need to go along as well."

Chapter Twenty-Eight

John awoke to the blinding brightness of the room's fluorescent lights. His wrists ached from the metal cuffs that were clenched tightly around the bones of his arms. Without any windows to determine the approximate time of day, he was not sure if he had slept for hours or minutes.

"Get off the floor," a deep voice demanded.

Startled to hear someone speak to him, as he thought that he was alone, John struggled to get up to his feet. Crawling to the nearest wall, he leaned into it, using it as an assisting device to help him stand upright.

Two men stood before him, their faces cold and far removed

from his suffering. Their haircuts were short and squared. Although one of them was expressed with a distinct scowl, the other lacked the snide cruelty of the agents that preceded him.

They were quite a unique couple. One was short and stocky, with a squared chin that gave the appearance of a man of fitness. The other was rather tall and lean, but he carried himself with a demeanor that was saturated with authority. Their uniforms were similar to the military fashion and very much unlike that of the Security attire. As they watched John gathering his balance, the shorter agent approached him, taking him by the arm.

"Can you walk, soldier?" he asked with a sense of calmness.

"Yes, sir," John replied.

"Good. Then let's move outside," he said.

The taller agent directed them towards the hall. John proceeded as directed, limping under the pain. He realized that he must have lacerated one of his feet during his move from the interrogation room, as he left smears of crimson paste behind with each step he made.

Passing by several Security agents that paid little attention to the three men, the lone captive was led through a labyrinth of tunnels and halls before finding himself presented at the bottom a long, winding stairwell. Neither of the men spoke a word. Hand gestures regarding directions were the only communication.

"Sir, where are we going?" John asked. But as silence was the only answer, he made no further inquiries.

The top of the stairwell led to a steel door with a scanner mounted beside it. The tall, thin agent peered into the eyepiece. The door unlocked. Held open by an agent on the other side, the three-man group proceeded through.

Escorted into what appeared to be a master control room, John was aghast at the system of surveillance used to monitor the people of this world. The room appeared to be hundreds of meters across. It was filled with more men and women than he could estimate. They seemed to do nothing but sit and stare at the thousands of black and white screens set in front of them, apparently linked to a camera network that covered the entire inhabited portions of the planet.

Directed around the entire perimeter of the monitoring center, leading to another stairwell, it appeared John was being purposefully led in this manner in order for him to take in the panoramic view through the single, continuous window that wrapped around the central Security hub. From what he could gather, they were situated atop of a grand mesa from which the compound overlooked three separate facilities.

Out the window at one side of the control room was a mining center, where an innumerable population of men labored under the heat of the Savior. Carts were manually pulled and pushed along their tracks, into and out of the deep tunnels that bore into the sides of the hills. Unending parties of men were elevator dropped deep into the mineshafts in one area, while on the opposite side of the facility others were simultaneously pulled out. Manually operated lifts were raising and lowering the gathered, raw materials along its intricate networks of ropes and pulleys. Taken from out of the planet's depths, the carts were emptied into their awaiting wooden crates before being hoisted upon the beds of the endlessly awaiting convoy of wheeled transporters.

Moving along to another side of the control room, John witnessed the expansive, airship center. Massive in breadth, it quite easily dwarfed the Labor facility by comparison of their respective sizes. Tens of thousands of launch pads littered the land with hundreds of rockets landing and lifting off every few seconds. Its warehouse array was vast and far-reaching. It spread out to such an immense distance that even from his high vantage point John could not see the other end of it as it disappeared over the horizon. Roving lines of variously sized vehicles were channeling soldiers and raw materials into the launch area with a seemingly perpetual continuity.

The third side of the control room overlooked a military training base where thousands of men and women were actively engaging in physical activities necessary to making a soldier fit for war. There were jogging formations in abundance, firing lines filled to capacity, obstacle courses over-run with trainees.

"Come this way," the voice of one of the officials said, directing him towards the final stairwell.

Leading them to the top of the staircase and through the door situated at its end, John was now standing inside a windowless room with a single table and three chairs: two on one side facing inward, and one on the other side, obviously meant for him. One of the military officials, calling for a Security officer below, made the request to have John released from his restraints.

As the officer entered the room, John avoided making any contact with the man's unseen eyes hidden behind his reflective visor. Unlocking the cuffs, the Security official allowed them to fall from John's wrists before removing himself from their presence.

"Have a seat, son," One of the men said. "I'm going to make this short and simple. We've been investigating the claims you made to the Security interrogators yesterday. That's when we came across this."

Receiving a sheet of paper from the hand of the military officer, John held it up to his eyes. As astonished as he was to see the photographs of himself and Sofia on an official, Blue Planet Security printout, he was more astounded by the fact that beneath their faces, written in a large, red font, were the words *Presumed*

Dead. Their faces were circled with ink so as to standout from among the several dozen other people whose images were set in rows and columns upon the page. A description below detailed the "*...kidnapping of the two children by one Mr. Eugene Sanders of the Class C Apartment complex*". According to the report, "*...a multi-vehicle collision on the Highway took the lives of twenty-eight men and women*", most of which seemed to have been unidentifiable, as "*the bodies were damaged beyond recognition*". The detailed report concluded with the "*elimination of the suspected target*"... Mr. Sanders was *gone*.

The paper brushed against John's thigh as he let his hand drop to his side. Mr. Sanders had died that day. "*Liberty awaits you, but stay away from the Red Xs*". Those were the last words he said to them.

"You two are very unique people, or, at least *you* are," the shorter, stockier official said, taking a seat in front of him. "Eighteen years old and living invisibly somewhere in the solar system. To your own people you apparently died, to the rest of the worlds you were unknown."

"Your home planet has accounted you for the dead," the taller agent chuckled, walking over and leaning against the wall. "But look, here you are: alive and well."

"You're probably wondering why we brought you here, aren't you?" the stockier agent continued. "I'm General Arlington and this is Second Lieutenant Corona. We've been sent here by a very influential individual who thinks that you may be someone of utmost importance."

"Don't play stupid with us, okay?" Lieutenant Corona interrupted. "We're a long way from home, and we'd like to get off this wasteland and back to the real world. So, when a question is asked of you, just answer it, do you understand?"

"Yes, sir," John responded.

"Now, just so you truly understand the importance of our inquiry, as far as military matters are concerned, there isn't very much that goes on above us that we aren't privy to. So if we're here, you'd better believe it's important. It's been reported Black-side that some strange events occurred in Basket Town shortly after you arrived. Do you know anything about it?" the General asked.

"No, sir," John replied.

"Well, we have a strong inkling that you do know something. Before entering this domain, when you left Planet Blue, did you ever visit the Star?"

"*Planet Blue*? I don't know what that is, sir," John said with all sincerity.

"You do know something, young man," the Lieutenant began to say before being cut off by his superior.

"How did you bring those people back to life?" the General interrupted.

"Bring those people back from *where*?" John asked with a tone of confusion.

"We told you," the Lieutenant yelled, "don't play stupid with us. We don't want to be here any longer than we have to, do you understand that?"

General Arlington held his hand up to the silencing of the Lieutenant. Continuing with his questioning, he asked, "Are you *the One* that these people have been waiting for?"

"Me? I don't think so, sir," John said. "I mean... I'm not really sure what you are talking about."

"The people here are very superstitious. They're certain that we're entering an era where a new type of, how shall we say it... *Leadership*, will come about. Are you a scout for *the One*?"

"No, sir... the One? I'm just a..."

"Is Sofia an agent for the One?"

"No, sir, she's just a..."

"About Eugene Sanders: did he ever mention anything about this world, Planet Raw?"

"No, sir, he..."

"Of all the places to visit, why did you choose this place?"

"When we boarded the ship, it brought us here," John said.

The General let out a sigh, looking over his shoulder at the lieutenant. He appeared frustrated, but patiently so. Turning back to John, he said, "We've processed the onboard data of the craft that you traveled on. It wasn't bound for this planet. Its destination was Golden World. Were you perhaps sent here to give these people a message?"

"No, sir, I just wanted some answers."

"Answers?" the General looked inquisitively at the Lieutenant as his inferior officer walked to the table, taking a seat beside him. "Answers to what?"

"I'm not really sure," John said ashamedly.

The two agents looked at each other, puzzled in their expressions.

"Can you raise the dead?" the Lieutenant asked.

"No, sir, I don't know what that is."

"An operator of the One is always supposed to tell the truth."

"Sir?" John responded with an expression of oddity.

"Are you an operator for this... this being?"

"No, sir."

"John, we have some terrible news for you," The General's voice was low and somber. "*Sofia's dead.*"

The words were numbing and surreal, the comprehension of which seemed unfathomable. John lifted the Security document back up to his eyes and stared at Sofia's picture for a moment. He could hear the Lieutenant chuckle under his breath.

"She's dead? What do you mean? No, she's not. She can't be."

"She was killed yesterday while being escorted to Basket Town."

"Killed? How?" John begged for an answer, his eyes filling with tears.

"The convoy she was riding with was struck by explosives hidden on the roadside," the General answered. "Everyone on board her transporter died."

Forming tiny puddles of warm liquid upon the table, the teardrops were rolling down John's cheeks, falling off of the tip of his chin. With the palm of one of his hands he pressed hard against his eyes, covering his shame, while the paper crumpled between his fingers in the other.

"Do you think that you could bring her back if we were to take you to her body?" the General asked.

John's thoughts were in disarray, filled with the images of Sofia in the interrogation room pointing at him. How could he answer such a foolish question? Why were they asking him such nonsense, he thought. He remained silent, his throat muscles clamped down upon his airway, suffocating and wrenching. He was smothering under the intense desire to be by Sofia's side, but all he could do was cry.

"John," the Lieutenant said, "we'll take you to her right now if you can bring her back from the dead."

John did not respond. Recognizing the intense distress that they had brought to him, the two men ceased with the interrogation. John wept alone, paying little attention to the agents as they stood up and walked to the far corner of the room, quietly conversing with each other.

"I'm so sorry, Sofia. I'm so sorry." He whispered under his breath.

The door to the room swung open under the heavy hand of the Base Commander. Accompanied by several armed agents, he entered in with a broad chest and a heavy chin held high. After saluting his superiors he proceeded to speak, "Have you come to any conclusions regarding the young man? Is he *the One*?"

"We're not absolutely certain on the closure of the case, but we're pretty sure that he's not the man we're looking for," the General answered.

"And, we're at least certain that he's not a threat to Black in anyway," the Lieutenant added.

"Very good, then," the Commander said. "So, are we going to leave him here? And if so, what is the wish of Headquarters as to where he shall go? Should I put him in the mines?"

"Mining might not be a good idea," the General said shaking his head. "Considering the rumors going around, he might have a negative influence on certain members of the Underground."

"Then what do you suggest that I do with him?

"He understands that the girl's dead."

"I, see."

"So, perhaps *Kill Core Training*. It'll harden his mind, and wipe away any innocence that he has left. Whether he happens to be or not, although it is very unlikely, an agent of the One, you could always assign him to a Sweeper squad when he finishes the course. It's certain to numb his mind, destroy his soul," the General smiled.

"Yes, that's very good," said the Commander, with a laugh.

Like thorns in his side, the three officers words were piercing and ill compassioned. They had no care for the life of his lost love. John did not understand what exactly it was they were talking about, but he understood, in at least a rudimentary sense the term *Kill Core Training*. Whatever the indoctrination was he was about to receive, by the title alone he wanted nothing to do with it.

CHAPTER TWENTY-NINE

The beams of the Savior dripped through the holes in the cardboard ceiling, illuminating the room with dozens of His long, thin shafts of light. The air was stale and dry, soaked with the smell of death. Wiping the sweat from her brow, Sofia sat at the edge of a makeshift cot drinking water from a rusty, food storage can.

It had only been a little more than twenty-four hours since she arrived in Basket Town, but her presence had not gone by without notice this time around. On the day that she was released from the custody of the Security agents and thrown onto the filthy dirt of the city streets, the eyes of the women were there, watching her every move. As the Security transporter had driven off, leaving her alone in the presence of so many strangers, Sofia had found herself suddenly surrounded by the masses reaching out to her and rubbing their hands upon her head, her back, her arms... anywhere they could touch. They had been pleading for her *healing power*.

Weaving a band of dried strip of stalk through her basket, the woman seated on the floor in front of her worked quietly repairing a hole in its side. Her hands were quick and delicate, moving with the gracefulness of the years of experience with her craft.

Swallowing down the last of the warm, salty water, Sofia placed the can upon her lap.

"Thank-you for the drink," she said.

Setting her project on the floor, the woman smiled as she took the can from Sofia's hands. Standing up, she walked it over to a cloth-covered window on the other side of the room. Pushing aside the covering, the light entered in, revealing the woman's protruding abdomen, which seemed so out of sorts in comparison to the bony, thinness of her arms and legs, the sunken skin of her cheeks and eyes. Dropping the improvised cup outside, it fell into a pile of refuse in the trash littered alley below.

Returning back to Sofia, the woman took a seat beside her on the cot, appearing uncomfortable and nervous by Sofia's close presence. As the stranger made an awkward attempt to look at her, Sofia passed her a friendly smile, but she was too shy to make eye contact, and she quickly turned her head away.

"Your skin is so smooth and young. Are you from the Savior?" Sofia's odd host asked of her with a hint of embarrassment.

Sofia rubbed her hand upon her own rosy cheek, finding it quite queer that the woman seemed so enamored by the tone of her flesh, not to mention that she had made a reference to a place known as Savior.

"Um, no," she answered. "I'm actually from Labor."

The woman took Sofia by the hand. Opening her palm, she revealed its smooth, pink surface. The woman's deep, black skin contrasted heavily against Sofia's fair tone.

"You don't look like you've labored much," she commented, comparing her own discolored, calluses to Sofia's youthful tenderness.

"I'm sorry," Sofia smiled. "I didn't mean that I work hard. Labor is where my home is. That's its name."

"Oh, I see," the woman said, turning her face away as if she was feeling ridiculed by her own comment.

"I do want to thank you for bringing me to your home, though. It's very," Sofia paused, "*unique.*"

"It is very well made, isn't it?" The woman smiled as she looked around the ragged apartment. "It used to belong to a woman by the name of Sage many years ago that bore thirteen children here."

"Wow. Really? That's quite a lot of children." Sofia said. "Where is she now?"

"She became barren," the woman explained. "Eventually the Security found out and sent her to die on Red."

"Is Red where the old people go? In Labor we called it Restful Haven."

Seemingly taken aback by Sofia's ignorance, the woman looked at her in a curious manner.

"Red is where the war is. Everyone, unless they die here first from an accident or something worse, ends up dying in the war."

"So there's a war being fought here, too?" Sofia asked with amazement.

"Here? No. On Red," the woman corrected her.

Confused as to what exactly she was talking about, Sofia chose to ignore it. She was about to open her mouth to change the subject when the woman asked her, "How far along are you?"

It was another bewildering question, to which Sofia respond-ed, "From home? Well, I never thought about it, but I guess a million…"

"Oh, no," she interrupted with a nervous giggle. "I meant for your baby."

"My *baby*? I don't have a baby," Sofia said, reacting to the wom-en's seemingly absurd line of questioning.

Rather perplexed in her expression, the woman placed her hand upon Sofia's abdomen.

"They wouldn't have brought you back here if you weren't with child. This is where we bear the children and work the land for the wealthy. You *must* be carrying."

Carrying. What a strange thing to say, Sofia thought. It was the same term used by the agents on the day she was sent to Bas-ket Town.

Walking across the room, the woman left her side, picking up another rusted can from the corner and taking a sip from it. It seemed as if she did not want to talk anymore. She sat down upon the floor giving Sofia her back. But after a moment she said, "Thank you for what you've done for me."

Sofia did not understand why the woman was giving thanks to her. Standing from the cot and walking across the creaking floor, Sofia stepped beside her and placed her hand upon the woman's shoulder.

"I'm the one that should be thanking you," Sofia said. "When all those women were surrounding me yesterday, I didn't know what I was going…"

"They weren't trying to hurt you," the woman interrupted. "They only wanted you to heal them… and to raise their loved ones from the dead."

A fearful churning of her stomach accompanied the terrible thoughts of Sofia's mind that the woman sitting in front of her was insane. How to answer such a statement, she did not know. Healing the dead, she thought to herself, what in Labor does that mean?

After considering the trauma she would probably sustain if she were to jump out of the window to make an escape, she left off with the plan and asked, "Heal their dead? I'm not sure I understand. What do you mean heal their dead?"

"It's all part of the change that's coming. The day when *He* returns for us," the woman said.

As the woman placed her hand upon her own abdomen, Sofia took a few steps back. It was quite obvious to her now, that the woman had left her side to be alone, to hide her tears.

"I was among the dead when you arrived here by the airship," she confessed. "The presence of you and your mate brought me back. Many people believe that you two are part of the New Beginning."

Straightening up the shirt collar of his new, black uniform, John was barefoot upon the cold, concrete floor of the military installation's holding cell. Nervously limping back and forth, he knew that whatever training he was being forced into was certain to begin shortly, as the two high-ranking officials had ordered it to happen before they departed back to their home planet.

Upon his reception of the order from his superiors, the Base Commander had seemed quite pleased with their decision to place John in the Kill Core facility of the training compound. He wasted little time moving him through the process in order to get him started immediately.

Since his return to the tunnel system, retracing his steps back through the control room, John had not seen the light of the

Savior for several hours. He had been escorted into the military's training grounds where he received a new set of fatigues. Ever since that time, he had been held in the cell in which he currently found himself waiting.

The silence made the moment all the more anguishing to his soul, as he could do nothing but think. He thought about Sofia. He thought about their time in the forests outside Labor. He thought about the fact that she no longer existed. The image of her frail and petite person, fearfully looking into his eyes, pointing directly at him, as if she were accusing him of some misdeed, was seared upon his brain. It was ten fold worse than the intense burning in his legs from his continual movement, and the sharp stabbings at his side from his fractured ribs. Almost cathartic in nature, as the pain seemed justly deserved as a punishment for all the suffering he had caused, it kept him going. He needed to suffer, too.

The longer he was held, the more he thought. The more he thought, the stronger his anger grew towards the men that were the cause of her death. He was turning his fears into hatred. It helped to keep him warm.

The door to the cell suddenly opened, causing John to put an end to his pacing. Approached by a heavily armored, military agent, John stood in his place. Without saying a word, the man shoved him to the ground and walked out, leaving him alone once again.

Standing back upon his feet, John stared at the door, expecting that the agent would return again. But after several minutes of looking upon the flat aspect of the exit, he gave up waiting and returned back to his tormented sauntering.

It was not long before the door once again opened to the same robotic agent. After performing the identical action upon John, he left the room in the same manner. The game continued for the next several hours, with the violence by which the man entered escalating with each encounter.

The final straw came when the agent entered in with a club in his hand. Raising it above his head, about to bring down a deadly blow, John rushed upon him, grabbing him by the legs, toppling him to the floor. Racking the wooden stick upon John's back, the agent fought to regain his footing. Swinging a fist into his throat, John forced the agent to drop his club. Clenching his neck and gasping for air, the man crawled upon the floor retreating from the fight. With a heavy grasp of the chin of his helmet, John tore the man's head backwards, ripping the head protector off, the chinstrap shearing away the man's skin.

As the agent rolled over crawling upon his elbows and knees, John scurried towards the wooden baton that had fallen upon the floor less than a meter away. Wrapping it within his fist, he turned back upon his enemy with a hard-set determination to kill him.

His swing was intentional, and in the fullness of his strength he attacked. The shaft of the baton was about to make contact with the back of the agent's head when John's arm was stopped mid-flight as the dart of a taser gun bore into his back. A current of electricity pulsated throughout his body, freezing his muscles and dropping him to the ground.

The military personnel that entered the room stepped over their motionless victim, assisting their fellow agent to his feet and walking him out of the room. As the last soldier proceeded to make his exit, he pulled the cables from his taser letting them fall to the floor.

Tactile sensation was beginning to return back to John's legs and arms. As he was sealed once again inside his cell, alone and sore, he gazed upon the reflective goggles of the last agent to leave the room, making eye contact as it were. The opportunity for revenge would come again... it was only a matter of time.

Sofia could still hardly believe the words that had entered her ears just a few days prior. To think that she was carrying a child inside of her was a miracle that even her own wild imagination could never have conceived. She had not started experiencing any noticeable changes with her body as of yet, and the more she thought on the idea of being pregnant, the more she concentrated on feeling the child inside of her, although nothing seemed to come of it.

She was now gowned in the cultural, colorful dress of the women of Basket Town, and fitted with a facial scarf to help cover her fair skin while they worked the fields under the Savior's rays. She obeyed the request of her companion, Maryanne, the black-skinned woman, staying close by her side as they gathered fruit together, knowing that Maryanne was not only looking out for her best interest, but that she was a native to the town. Her experience made her a trusted resource.

It was difficult being out in the streets. Thronged at every corner by the women of the city, Sofia was much more comfortable in the fields, where there were fewer citizens, both living and dead. Although the work was laborious, and she was still the focus of attention wherever she went, Sofia found it much easier to acclimate to the eyes that were constantly upon her, rather than the hands that touched her.

The Security vehicles rolled along the dirt roads on the outskirts of the flatlands, kicking up their billowing tails of thick, brown dust as they made their circuits around the perimeter of the city and through the farmlands. For the most part, the agents seemed to know which women were untouchable and which ones were not, although Maryanne said the rule only applied to certain times of the year. According to her command,

Sofia gave special attention to be sure to never make eye contact with any of them.

On a few occasions they were assigned to work the fields at the edge of the city, towards the rising Savior. The base that she and John had made their initial landing was still sitting lonely on the distant hilltop. Over its high wall, the tip of their air transporter was barely visible. But after a few days it was gone.

During the cool of the night, hidden within the thin, shanty walls of Maryanne's abode, Sofia made every attempt to busy her mind, to keep it from wandering too deeply. She began learning the art of weaving, working with her hands in the dim flickering of the lamplight. The nighttime was the only time when no one else but Maryanne was present. Sofia missed John with a passion. Reminiscing of him and their adventures helped ease the pain of his absence. As the cool night's breeze would often blow aside the tattered, cloth covering of the window, she would occasionally catch glimpses of the wishing stars... *oh, how she hated them.*

Due to the fact that her companion was not afforded the people skills that Sofia had obtained while living in Labor, the woman remained quiet and reserved during the beginning stages of their relationship. Shying away from discussing very many details about her own life, her likes and dislikes or anything else for that matter, Maryanne was a good listener, a characteristic of a friend that Sofia subconsciously needed to help her through the daily stresses of being separated from her love. But after a few days of accompaniment with Sofia, Maryanne seemed to feel a little more comfortable in her presence, speaking more openly, yet in a rather secretive manner.

One cool night, while sleeping as soundly as she possibly could under the circumstances, Sofia awoke to the soft, voiced whispers of her new companion.

"Sofia, I need to tell you something," she said.

Sofia knew immediately by Maryanne's tone of urgency that she had some news of great importance to tell her. Sitting up at the edge of the cot, she rubbed the blurriness from her eyes.

"What's the matter, Maryanne?" she whispered.

Maryanne was hesitant at first, nervous and stuttering. Speaking to Sofia about the secretive details of John's whereabouts, it was not long before she settled down, expressing her thoughts with more clarity. She had a contact somewhere within the Security that informed her that John was in lockdown in the military training center. Although she was not privy to any of the finer specifics of his purpose in being there, Maryanne was certain that he was being trained into something that would undoubtedly be incredibly taxing upon his spiritual well-being. In fact, according to her source, John was on schedule to be transferred to the inner facility of the training center within the week. That is the place where, she said, *"men become monsters"*.

Sofia's emotions were a mix of joy and sorrow. She was thankful to know that her love was still alive, but her heart was still downtrodden by the painful words regarding his horrible situation. She could not bear the fact that she possessed the knowledge that somewhere, beyond the flatlands and over the horizon, John was suffering under the hands of the Security. Placing the deadly potentials and dangers awaiting him into the inner recesses of her mind, Sofia attempted to forget all of John's difficulties, instead concentrating on the fact that they could one day be reunited. She knew John more intimately than any other person. He was strong in spirit, rugged in mind. And he would fight every effort of his captors to change him for the worse.

Sofia struggled to fall asleep after the news that Maryanne had brought her. Her thoughts were a tangled mess of hardship and happiness. She finally drifted off into a light rest a short time before the Savior was to make his presence known. Under Maryanne's wishes, she was left alone for the rest of the morning, allowing her to obtain the rest that her body so desperately needed.

CHAPTER THIRTY

It had been a heavy day of gathering and transferring of produce from the great fields of the flatlands. After returning to Maryanne's home, Sofia, even after a half-day's labor, was far too exhausted to work anymore with her hands. After sponge bathing her arms and legs behind the veil in the corner of the room, she climbed onto her cot and immediately fell into a deep sleep.

The soft whispers entering through the window on the opposing wall from where Sofia lay were like sheets of water on a stormy day, unsettling and too random to allow for a mind's rest. As her eyes opened, she found herself staring at the ceiling, unsure at first of what it was that had caused her to suddenly awaken from such a dreamy state. Sitting up in bed, Sofia was about to call out to Maryanne when she realized that her companion's bed was empty. She was nowhere to be seen in the room.

The whispers from the window began to flow once again. As the initial fear of the unknown began to wane, Sofia's curiosity was piqued. Throwing aside the thin, course sheet from off of her legs, she began to quietly make her way across the room.

At the midway point to the rag-covered opening in the wall, the creaking of the wood flooring beneath her feet became an immediate concern. Its sound would certainly give away the fact that she was awake. Choosing the safer route, her adventurous side stifled long ago by her terrible experiences, Sofia returned back to her cot, sitting down and waiting in the darkness for the strangers to leave.

The time was moving by at a sluggish pace. It seemed as if the long exchange of words would continue throughout the rest of the night. Just as Sofia was about to give-up the wait, the fading sounds of the strangers' footsteps indicated that they were departing from each other. Hearing someone enter into the room downstairs, she quickly slipped back into the cot, drawing up the covers.

A vehicle from the streets outside, indicated in all likelihood by the familiar sound of its rumbling engine, a Security transporter, drove off into the distance just before Maryanne entered through the door. Quietly making her way across the room, she climbed into her bed without saying a word.

Considering that Maryanne hardly ever spoke with anyone in the community, as far as Sofia had seen, she assumed that the person driving off must have been the "contact" that Maryanne was getting her information from. As her companion seemed to fall fast asleep, Sofia did not attempt to press her on the subject of her encounter. It was, after all, none of her business.

It had been over a week since John had been able to procure any *real* sleep. Having been transferred to another cell somewhere on the training grounds several nights ago, there were rare occasions where he was able to nod off momentarily before being interrupted by the harsh words of the military personnel. Although his hearing seemed to be in tune to the sensual world, his vision seemed out of synch. Unusually appearing apparitions were becoming the norm. The walls were chronically in a slow state of movement, appearing to breathe, inhaling and exhaling around him. Every effort to close his eyes to regain his inner balance was met with a hurtful end from one of the soldiers waiting outside. No longer willing or able to fight, John gave into the demands of each man that entered the room, even apologizing to them whenever they pushed him to the ground or threatened him with harm.

He had not seen a Security agent for quite some time. It appeared as if the military had taken full control of his person. He attempted in vain to scrawl into the forearm of his skin the days that had passed since he had last seen Sofia, but without any access to the Savior, he lacked the ability to discern whether it was day or night. Differentiating between minutes and hours had become nearly impossible.

The door to his cell opened and two soldiers stepped in.

"Come with us," one of them demanded.

Lifting himself up, John held his hands out, giving the men the opportunity to place the cuffs on his wrists without any resistance.

"That won't be necessary," one of the soldiers replied.

As they proceeded through the door, John followed close behind. Entering into the hall, he was now standing in a narrow tunnel with barely enough room between the walls for the two soldiers to walk side-by-side. Leading him away from his prison cell, the two men seemed unconcerned about escorting an unshackled prisoner. Other than the batons that they held in their hands, they appeared to be unarmed.

The light at the end of the tunnel filtering between the edges of the silhouettes of the two men was bright and powerful. John was unable to distinguish the nature of it, whether Savior or artificial. But, he thought, it made little difference what the source of it was, as his destiny was being effectuated without any consideration of his own desires.

As they neared the exit point, John recognized the Savior as the source of the intensity. The brightness was growing exponentially with each step, along with the sudden rising temperature.

Greeted with the blindingly reflective sand of the desert valleys as they departed from the tunnel, the three men descended the winding, concrete stairway that led to the bustling training grounds below.

Gunfire was exploding rampantly throughout the region in never ending volleys, intermittently overshadowed by the booming sounds of explosive ordinance. The training center was much larger than it had first appeared to John from the windows of the control room. Fenced around its perimeter with a barbed wire structure, its numerous stations interconnected through a maze-like network of trenches that were filled with soldiers performing various drills.

As they walked off the last step and entered into the crowds of uniformed men and women that marched along in strict fashion, John noticed that he was the only person in a black uniform, the only soldier unattached to a larger unit. His escorts seldom checked his presence. He figured that they knew he had nowhere to run.

Through the ceilingless corridors they walked, continuing past several firing ranges and hand-to-hand combat sessions. Platoons of soldiers passed them by, singing cadence and moving through the masses as a single, organic unit. Still the only soldier dressed in his peculiar fatigues, John was beginning to wonder all the more as to what the purpose of his particular training would be.

Rounding a sharp corner, they walked under an overhead sign sporting a symbol of a broomstick with its bound sweeping-fibers dripping with blood. The words etched across the bottom read: *Under the Rug.*

The trench terminated at a heavily guarded gate at which the three men came to a halt. One of his escorts walked over to the scanner on the wall. Peering into it, the screeching buzz of the locks released.

Flakes of rust borne metal fell from its bars as the gate began to swing open. Two soldiers, dressed in the similar black uniform as John, only striped like a tiger with streaks of red, stepped through the threshold.

"We'll take him from here, fellas." one of them said.

As his former escorts turned to leave, John stood in silence before his two newly assigned captors. Standing side by side, John caught a glimpse of their names embroidered above the left breast pockets of their shirts. The one standing to his left was Michaels. The one to his right was Crawford.

Crawford was a middle-aged soldier with a short military cut and narrow shoulders. His eyes were heavily bagged and sinister-looking under the natural downturn of his thick brows. His nose was abnormally hooked, and seemed a perfect fit for his hunched back. He lacked the stiffness more commonly characteristic of a trained individual. His partner, Michaels, on the other hand, was nearly the same build. Similar in demeanor, as if the two men were borne from the same mold, but Michaels was probably half the age of his superior.

"You're just in time for the fun," Michaels said with a laugh.

Taking John by the arm, he jerked him forward, leading him through the gateway.

"We've got a lot of toys for you to play with today," Crawford replied.

As they walked through the threshold and into the first courtyard, the gate began to close behind them. Crawford spun John around by the shoulders making him watch as the only door to the outside world closed him in.

After initiating its automated locks, he whispered into John's ear, "You won't be seeing the outside of that gate for a long, long time."

Forced to turn around once again, John was pointed directly at a stairwell that descended underground at the other end of the quadrangle. It looked to be their objective for the moment. With a shove at his back, the soldiers hurried him ahead, pressing him along the concrete path that terminated at its entrance. Seemingly under the pressure of a time constraint of which John knew nothing about, they urged him with threats of harm to keep up with them, pulling him along by the sleeves of his shirt, kicking at his feet and tripping him to the ground, dragging him by the scruff of his collar.

Into the stairwell they entered, descending into the bunker below, where the men began to pick up the pace. Flipping on the electronic lanterns that they had strapped to their belts, the walls around them became a living mural of shadows that created a disorienting effect upon the senses.

Down a tunnel and into a dark room they went, with John struggling to maintain his balance. The laughter and howling of the two men in their jubilatory glee created a mood of pure dread. Lit up only at the end in which they had suddenly come to a standstill, the room was cold and dry. His tormentors walked around him, their lights shining in his face caused a deep burning to his eyes. As they gave him a reprieve from the brightness, John could see that there was a single, metal bench bolted to the floor in front of him. Empty and sterile, it was the only piece of furniture in the room as far as he could tell.

As Crawford disappeared into the darkness, John could hear him performing an action that sounded like the flipping of switches. The sudden flickering of several lights overhead gave a brief, but indiscernible view of the room.

The lights stabilized, growing brighter by the moment, until his surroundings were glowing white. John's newly found visibility allowed him to see that he was standing at the head of an indoor shooting range. The smell of fresh paint that emanated from its shimmering, reflective walls gave the appearance of a recent construction.

The far end of the room was, according to the distance markers set upon the floor, three hundred meters away. John could make out a single, steel door with a central locking mechanism situated on its perpendicular wall. Between him and the three hundred meter sign, standing erect in fifty-meter intervals, were several rectangular shooting targets with human silhouettes imprinted upon their faces.

Returning back with a rifle in hand, Crawford shouldered the weapon, taking careful aim at John's head as he approached him. Lifting his hands in the air, John coward back, causing the two men to burst into laughter.

"This is *your* rifle, boy," Crawford said. "Don't be afraid of it."

A sudden blow to the gut from Michaels caused John to double over, falling to his knees. Removing a leather strap out of the cargo pocket of his pant leg, along with a metallic roll, Crawford leaned over his victim.

"Don't move," he said with a laugh. "This isn't going to hurt me at all."

Wrapping the strap around John's neck and fixing its latch, securing it with a miniature padlock, Crawford proceeded to pull out a knife, ripping through the back of John's shirt and exposing his spine. Unraveling the metallic strip and tearing away the paper lining that was held to one of its sides, he then placed it on John's back, pressing and molding it into the contours of each vertebra. The two wires dangling from the neck collar were connected to the strip and tucked away at the collar's base.

After completing the task, the men stepped away, allowing John the time he needed to catch his breath and stand back upon his feet.

"Listen here, little dog," Michaels said, as he bent over and whispered in John's ear. "You aren't going to do anything unless we tell you to. Got it?"

Still reeling under the shock of the blow, John was about to answer him when a sudden pulse of electricity ripped through his body, dropping him back to the floor.

"This is nothing compared to the pain that we will put you through if you do not listen to us," Crawford screamed into his ear.

"Thirty-six weeks, John," Michaels laughed. "We've got you for thirty-six weeks. Every day is going to be a living hell for you."

The electrical activity had ceased. Being hoisted up to his feet gave him a flashback to the beatings that the Monster used to dish out. The cruelty of the men was too similar: they behaved in the same manner as the Monster. They cursed in the same manner. They yelled and screamed in the same manner. They even held to the same wicked expressions as the Monster.

"Take the weapon and shoot the targets," Crawford said as he set the rifle down upon the table. "We know that you already know how to do that."

"Do not charge that bolt until we're clear, do you understand?" Michaels screamed.

"Yes, sir," John moaned in reply.

The two men started towards the exit when Michaels turned back and said, "Remember, John, we'll always be watching you. You can't get away from us."

He could hear the door slam shut behind him, followed by the initiation of its lock. It was not long before the static from an overhead speaker began to crackle throughout the room, followed by Michaels' voice, loud and clear.

"Get up, now. Charge your weapon... and have fun shooting," His laughter barely drowned out the hysterical burst from Crawford. "And, John, make sure you *kill* every target out there, or you'll feel the pain."

Dragging himself to the table, John lifted the rifle from its sterile surface. It was the same type of weapon he had used for shooting practice back on Labor. Pulling back the charging handle, he chambered the first round of the magazine. Taking aim at the hundred-yard silhouette, its blackness contrasted heavily against the bright sterility of the room, John took in a deep breath. Squeezing the trigger, he fired off a single shot. As the bullet bore a hole through the target's "chest", John let the rifle's sights drop, startled at the red, misty cloud that exploded out the back of the cardboard image.

"Pretend that these are the men that killed Sofia, John. What would you like to do to them?" Crawford's voice echoed. "Don't stop shooting. Kill the targets, John."

Shouldering the weapon once again, he took aim at the fifty-yard silhouette and fired off another round. As the bullet impacted the targets "head", an audibly hollow crack resounded throughout the room with the accompaniment of tissue and bone and a similar blood spray blowing out the back. He looked at the receiver of the rifle, dropping the magazine to inspect the cartridges inside. Seeing nothing askew, he replaced it, bringing the weapon back to his shoulder.

"You should have seen Sofia drowning in her own blood that day, John. It was so, so terrible. I wish you could have been there."

John fired another shot towards one of the two hundred-yard targets followed by a similar result.

"She cried so hard, 'John, John. Help me.'"

John fired off several more rounds with the resultant blood and tissue littering the floor of the range.

"She blamed you for her ills, John. You know it was your fault. Remember when she pointed you out as the reason for her suffering?"

He fired more rapidly, tearing into the "flesh" of the targets, gutting them thoroughly, until the rifle's bolt locked open and the magazine was empty.

"Now, have a walk to the wall on the other side," Crawford demanded.

John took a moment to lower the weapon's sights from his eyes.

"Go ahead, have a look at your *kills*," Michaels arrantly goaded him.

The walls and ceiling around the targets were splattered with crimson droplets and clotted tissue. The floor was a thick stew of bloody meat and bone. Dangling the rifle across the front of his thighs, John began the hazy, dream-like trek towards the carnage.

Growing steadily closer, he could see that the gore was spread across the entire range. The fifty-yard silhouette was just within reach. The paper target itself was beginning to saturate around its "head", dripping down its "body".

As he pulled up alongside the ranged milestone, he felt that near-blackness of the mind approaching as he took in the sight of the dead men and women strapped to the frames behind the targets. Bound hand-and-foot and taped across their mouths, their bullet-destroyed bodies leaked their life sustaining fluids upon the floor.

"Keep walking to the back wall, murderer, then look back and revel at your great accomplishment," the cruel voice of Michaels belched out.

The rifle's forearm slid from his hand, held up by the pistol grip of the other as John fell to his knees. In his disobedience, he brought the electrical bolt of insubordination branching through his brain and the nerves of his spinal cord, dropping him cold and motionless upon the floor.

"Let's try that again. Get up and walk," Michaels' voice boomed through the speaker.

Pulling himself up by the metal bars of the target beside him, John stood upon his feet, his legs jittery and weak. Dragging the barrel of his rifle through the coagulating pools as he obeyed their command, he instinctively vomited on the front of his shirt. A tingle of electricity ran up his spine. They were toying with him. Ignoring the laughter dripping through the speakers, he kept moving. He had to, or else the pain would come again.

His objective was the opposing wall, and that was where he set his eyes. In his periphery were the dead. He couldn't escape them. He walked the path of death between his victims. Hollow and lifeless, John was no different than the empty corpses strung up around him.

Upon reaching the wall, he stretched forth his hand, touching its speckled, cold surface. The effects of his blood-soaked shooting spree were behind him. Placing his sweat-beaded head upon it, the fumes of its fresh coat of paint helped to subdue the iron smell at his back.

"Turn around, John," Michaels demanded.

Wiping his forehead across his outstretched arm, he refused to look back. The violence that he had caused was innocently initiated, he thought. He would never have committed such an atrocity had he not been tricked into it. But all the philosophical musings in the world could not alleviate the fact of the matter: they died by his hands.

"Turn around, now!"

"I can't," he whispered.

The sudden jolt of a thousand needles burrowed into his brain as he once again fell, convulsing uncontrollably, to the floor.

"No, you can... and you will," Michaels screamed through the speakers.

As the electricity abated, John scooped up his rifle by the sling and struggled to his feet. Turning to face his audience, the loud speakers began to fill the room with the music of the brass horns and stringed instruments, similar to that of which he and Sofia used to listen to back in their home on Labor. The torn and broken bodies of the dead stared back at him as if he were on trial.

"Look upon this man, women of Basket Town and men of the mines," Crawford laughed through the loudspeaker. "This is your god. Some of you were witnesses to his powers of life, now behold, death is in his hands."

CHAPTER THIRTY-ONE

The tenderness of Sofia's chest made the sponge bath less inviting. She was sweaty and uncomfortably coated with the usual thick layers of dust that had seeped through her clothes and onto her skin throughout the course of the day. After allowing the water to dribble down her body, picking up bits of debris on its way into the tin pan in which she stood, it was not long before she felt at least a little more refreshed.

Her stomach was empty, but she was not in the mood for the consumption of anything. She awoke this morning with a burning nausea that had only grown more intense with each passing hour, but began to settle out by midday. A few crackers and a little water, that was the extent of Sofia's intake since arriving home. After clothing herself in a freshly, Savior-dried skirt and top, she fell upon her cot, rubbing the aching muscles of her legs.

The fieldwork seemed more fatiguing than it had been in the recent past. Sleep was continually on her mind during the entirety of the day. Instead of breaking for lunches, Sofia was spending her mealtimes in the shade of the fruit trees, napping away. She would fall asleep the moment her head touched the grassy ground. Oftentimes, the last thing she would remember seeing before being woken up by Maryanne, were the multitudes of thin streaks crossing the sky above.

It had been three weeks since her last contact with John. Her female companion had not received any more news about his health, mentally or physically. After questioning Maryanne as to how she had obtained the information about him in the first place, Sofia was met with a curiously blank stare. For some reason she knew that Maryanne would eventually tell her about her *source*, and that more news of John would be incoming. But it was the anticipation regarding her love that was the most difficult aspect of living at all.

"Here, take this," Michaels shouted, handing John a new rifle.

It was unlike the one that he had been using. Shorter in length, it was unusually light, even for a weapon of its size.

"You'd better shoot fast," Crawford sneered. "Who knows, these may have been the ones that killed Sofia."

With their usual laughter, the men hastened out of the room with Michaels closing the heavy, steel door behind them. The radial latch was turned on its center, engaging the locking hubs. John was left all alone in the kill house.

After a minute of waiting, the soldier's voice blared through the overhead speaker, "You've got ninety seconds to eliminate all of them. If there's more than one left, the gas goes on, and every one of you will be coughing your lungs out."

The overhead lights at the mid-way point in the room flashed on, revealing once again the piles of both fresh and decayed bodies that John had been forced to use as targets over the past several weeks. The once clean walls and floors were now pockmarked with bullet holes and splattered with layers of dried blood and fleshy fragments. Each hour he had to remove the men and women from the target-frames and dump them wherever he saw fit. Then he had to endure the pain of watching more innocent victims, crying and vomiting their way onto the range, strapped into place by their escorting captors, left alone like worthless meat for him to devour. At night he slept among the dead. They were his constant companions. Death never left his side.

The paper target coverings for his victims were no longer used. That was part of the conditioning of the soul that was necessary in the beginning. He now had to look them in their eyes while he pulled the trigger. Their mouths were no longer taped shut, drowning out their screams. That was required to help ease him into the savage beast that he was becoming. Death came fast and furious once the shooting began. Acquiring and eliminating his targets was now a rote maneuver: ten targets, ten shots, seven seconds, twenty targets, twenty shots, fifteen seconds. There was no longer any thought required by him, he could practically perform the task of ending a man's life in his sleep.

The screaming men and women that hung before him were no different than the last set, or the set that preceded them. After hundreds upon hundreds of kills, they were becoming merely sacks of fluids with sounds emanating from them. John had to force his mind to accept that they were non-human, otherwise there was no way he could endure what he was doing.

The smell of rotting carcasses heavily engulfed the stale air of the range, but John had grown accustomed to it. It no longer bothered him. Suicide was ruled out as an option from the very start, as the electricity would flow the moment he attempted to place the barrel of his firearm anywhere near his head.

The new day had brought with it an unusual test from Crawford and Michaels: ninety seconds, four targets to eliminate, a feat that seemed laughably simple. Ninety seconds. That's a long time, John thought, lifting the rifle to his shoulder. As he began to take aim, the volume of angst among his prey began to rise. After placing the front sight of his weapon upon the first target, he was ready to commence with the test. As he began to place tension upon the trigger, he could hear what sounded like the door at the back of the range bursting open followed by shouts of various inflections. Several soldiers were rushing inside, taking cover behind the bodies of the dead.

With the crack of a pistol, a bullet whizzed past John's head, flattening out like a lead pancake against the thick steel door behind him before falling to the concrete floor. John's instincts took over and he began running towards the nearest pile of corpses. Leaning into the bodies, he could feel the vibrations against his shoulder as several bullets burrowed deep into the thick of his fleshy cover. Peering around the corners of the decaying and crumbling heads, he could make out the movement of four soldiers, two of which were moving towards his flank. Their weapons were drawn and their eyes appeared unnaturally fearful. Another shot tore into the skull of his cover, sending brain matter and bony fragments splashing into his face.

Wiping the blood from his eyes, John dropped his weapon's magazine into his hand. Michaels had left him only three rounds. He thought the firearm felt too light. That rotten, little... John thought, as he locked it back into the receiver's well. Pulling the charging handle, he chambered one of the few cartridges available to him.

"Thirty seconds passed, John. You'd better move fast," Crawford mocked.

The shouting of his enemies was intense, drowning out the screams of the living targets that hung across the range. The actions and the unusual terms that these so-called soldiers were using in their amateurish communications were a dead giveaway that they were miners and Basket Town women fighting for their lives, not formally trained individuals as their uniforms were made to imply. It helped him that they were unintentionally revealing their locations. Every scream, every shot, was an invisible path that John would use to lead him to the kill.

Raising the rifle up to his cheek John listened to the footsteps of the lead man as he cautiously approached his position. Some of the hanging targets were urging the miner to move faster, cautioning him as to John's whereabouts. The enemy was in close range now, perhaps within three meters or less, he thought.

"Thirty seconds to gas," the voice blared through the loudspeaker.

John silently peered over his rifle's sights. Strafing out of his cover and firing in a single swift motion, the shot tore into the man's head, dropping his body to the ground. Lifeless and bathing in his pooling gore, his death sent the hanging targets into a wave of terrified howling.

Attempting to run for cover, the other "soldiers" fled in a disorderly display of wild commotion, blindly firing their handguns towards John's general direction. Wildly spraying throughout the room, their bullets unintentionally pierced the walls, the dead piles and the living targets.

Taking careful aim, a second man fell in tune with the echoing report of John's rifle. Then the third, a woman, flipped head over heals after the bullet's impact, another addition to the rotting mess that surrounded her body.

Running towards his first fallen victim, John threw his rifle down and slid through the blood. Scooping up the man's pistol, he controllably blew off cover-fire while attempting to reach another pile of death for safety.

As he checked the magazine's cartridge quantity, he heard a single shot fired from the enemy's direction, but there was no discernable impact of the bullet anywhere near him.

As more than thirty seconds passed, John waited in accepted anticipation for the incoming gas of doom to fill his lungs. He was ready to suffer... but his time did not come.

"I guess you scared her to death, John," Crawford's voice belched out in disgust. "That's too bad. Now finish off the rest of the targets so we can get onto the next phase in your training."

Pulling himself up by the arm of one of the corpses piled in front of him, John could see the last remaining "soldier" lying between the stacks of destroyed lives. The self-inflicted wound at the side of the woman's head was evidence that she never intended to do him any harm. He tried to remain emotionless, but he found it difficult to hide his feelings when his soul, his essence of being *John*, was so close to being lost.

The moisture was building up at the inner corners of his eyes as he gathered up the pistols of the Planet's fallen citizens. Ignoring the pleading cries of his "targets", he wiped away the tears for the last time and walked over to the bench, dropping the weapons down upon it.

"Hurry up. We don't have all day," Michaels urged him with sadistic anticipation.

Dropping the magazine of one of the pistols, he checked its cartridge count and placed it back into the receiver. As he lifted the weapon, placing his sights on the first of several targets, the screaming and wailing heightened. With a moment of inaction on his part, John knew the electrical shock would soon be upon him. He would eventually give in to their torturous methods and take the lives of these innocents. It was one of the one few things in his life that he could be sure of. But as he stood there, a conductor of the symphony of pain, the orchestra of screams should have been deafening, but he couldn't hear a sound.

The reddened tenderness caused by the acne that had grown upon Sofia's fair skin was rather disturbing at first sight. Maryanne had told her that it was a normal part of the pregnancy and that it would probably clear up some time in the near future, before the baby was born. Not the type of person possessing a characteristic vanity, Sofia still wanted to be attractive to John, even on the aesthetic level. Her breasts were sore and swollen, as well. And, although there was very little she could do to contain it, she felt the pangs of hunger almost every second of the day.

Checking the tick-marks that she had scraped onto one of the hidden bars underneath the mattress of her cot, Sofia counted out seventy-seven days without her love. Other than the original news that Maryanne had given to her several weeks earlier, there was nothing more that her *contact* could tell her about John's condition or whereabouts.

Depression was difficult to fight against, and crying herself to sleep was more and more becoming the only way she could obtain the rest that her body required of her. The fieldwork was also becoming stale and repetitive. And the frequent urination that she was beginning to experience was making it difficult to keep her mind busy at the tasks that she was assigned to.

Maryanne seemed to notice that Sofia was going further under the weather with each passing day. Sofia had heard her whispering on several occasions during the night meetings with her *contact*, stating to him that it was imperative that he find something out about John's present condition in order to soothe Sofia's heart and mind. And while the agent was agreeable as to Maryanne's request, his frequent nighttime visits were of little value in that regard.

Fearful of losing her to the darkness of overwhelming grief, one night Maryanne confided in Sofia about her involvement with several members of the Security, especially her contact and dedicated mate, Stephen, and the secretive organization that was networking throughout the various levels of the planet's governing agencies. She explained to her that, within the currently governing command pyramids, there were hundreds of men and women working to overthrow the powers-that-be from the top down.

"Several well-placed individuals," Maryanne told her, "are attempting to obtain the identities and the locations of the leaders of a place called Golden World, to bring them to justice."

Maryanne went on to explain about the workings of Basket Town. And, although it was poverty stricken and violent, "There are places far worse than here," she said. "Where there is no light of hope."

To live in Basket Town, Maryanne explained, a woman only needed to be fertile. Once she passed her time, she was sent to die at a place called Red. Some believe this to be another planet, some a distant part of their own world, others, a euphemism for extermination.

The Security agents were the ones that executed all the orders against the citizenry. Although they could have any woman in the town at any time they chose, their leaders enjoyed marking out certain days at random throughout the year for letting all the agents loose upon the city. The women called them Savage Days. The agents called it *R&R*. During these terrifying times, convoys of transporters would roll into the city, releasing thousands of agents from their iron bellies. Any woman that did not appear to be carrying was supposed to be free game. But as the years went by, most of the agents would ravage any woman they came across, whether she was carrying or not. But Stephen was among those men that refused to add to the miserable existences of the citizenry of the town.

During one of the Days of Savagery, she told Sofia, he found her while she was hidden among the refuse of an alleyway. Speaking kindly to her, he soon convinced her that he would do her no harm, and he soon became, not only her personal contact, but also her confidant, avowed husband and doorway into the secretive underworld.

As the years went by, they bore several male offspring, but there was no possible way for them to keep the children from eventually being taken during the raids.

"But these days will change," she said. "Everything will become what it had once been, only better."

After her short synopsis regarding the current situation, Maryanne's tale took them back to the alleged roots of all their problems. Intrigued with her story, Sofia listened, wide-eyed, but skeptical.

Seemingly fantasy in nature and bordering on the mythological, Maryanne began by recounting the tales of the other worlds that she had become learned in through her childhood upbringing and the small details that she gathered during her encounters with Stephen: a Red Planet where war continually unfolded, and another world, called Golden, where, it was assumed, the richest of men and women were gathered. She even seemed to be mentioning Labor by the description she was giving, but she called it Blue.

Upon hearing the names *Red* and *Golden*, Sofia interrupted her, explaining that she and John had come across thousands of crates bound for these two places. She explained how they thought that they were merely cities that existed somewhere on Labor's planet. Giving a brief account of her and John's journey on the flying craft and their *home* hidden in the woods, she described the weapons of war that they had found inside the crates marked *Red*, and the sweet treats that she and John shared together from Golden's boxes, one of the many luxuries of the short-lived experiences that the two of them had together.

The stories that Maryanne had been handed down were seemingly reassured in their truths by the affirmation of Sofia's own words. She had been shown the blacked out names that had once been stenciled on the walls of their room and on the wood panels of the buildings outside. Maryanne also had Sofia's description of the crates stored in the air transporter and of those hauled on the backs of the vehicles of Sofia's native planet.

Seemingly relieved to know that her mother had not given her the watered-down analogical version, or the simplistic, localized account, Maryanne appeared to feel more confident in her presentation.

She continued with her narrative well into the night. According to the commonly held belief of the women of Basket Town, though, not all of them, she stressed, there was the same line of thinking regarding these other worlds: Red Planet's wars were planned and executed under the strict terms of the ruling class so as to be perpetual in nature.

"It's believed that it's a method," she said, "for keeping the population in fear, and its growth under control. It's also a means for entertaining the blood lust of the wealthy."

"It was said to exist with a soil of a deep burgundy hue, its waters run red, like the blood of the billions of men and women slain upon it over ages unknown."

While layers of similar stories with varying details obscured its ancient history, Maryanne unfolded the story to Sofia according to the traditions that her own mother had taught her.

"Red Planet," she explained, "was once a thriving world filled with peaceful cities and villages that functioned in a spiritual and economic security under the Ruler of Goodness. It was eventually overthrown by a foreign military that was motivated by power and greed."

Taking Sofia by the hand, Maryanne walked her over to the window, pulling back its cloth covering and revealing the millions of stars twinkling in the night sky, and the thousands of *wishing stars* that polluted its beauty.

"They invaded from an unknown planet hidden deep within the blackness of space."

She went on to describe "the corralling of the conquered peoples into the military's great transporters, sending them to the planet Raw, where they were further separated according to their sexes. The women were settled into what would come to be known, after hundreds, if not thousands, of years, as Basket Town, while the men were forced deep into the underground to mine for necessary elements."

"Raw was the name designated to the planet upon which we now live. It was so called due to the vast amounts of usable resources that exist in its valleys and hills. It also houses an immense water system that only flows near the soil's surface under the flatlands, giving that area its fertility."

"It was under this prodigious project," Maryanne continued to explain, "that the industry of Planet Blue came into existence. The brightest, most intelligent of the peoples were sent to its walled domain to engineer the weapons for war, and oversee the construction of the tools and systems that would keep the economies functioning in their proper orders."

"It was the workings of the laboring classes of Red, Blue and Raw that would keep the peoples of Golden World bathing in their unending luxury, oblivious to the sufferings of their subjects, wild and extravagant in their living, morally bankrupt in their souls."

"In order to keep their materialism alive, they knew that they needed to keep their slaves' population growing," she continued to explain.

"The self-anointed overseers allowed for festivals several times a year, permitting the conquered men and women to unite for one week per event. As the growth of the peoples began to exceed their expectations, however, the multi-annual times of meeting were put to an end, and the ruling military was given the task of making sure that the population would remain true to their original plans."

"As for the benevolent Ruler and his son, it was said that they fled into the burning heat of the Great Star, along with their armies. There, the Soldiers of Goodness await their orders to seize back their Ruler's position among the heavenly bodies. The existing governing agency would continue its dominion until the time of their return: the day when the Ruler would become Savior, and would restore peace once again."

Sofia hung on every word that Maryanne spoke. As they communed together late into the night and early into the next morning, Sofia found her stories to be almost too incredible to be true, yet they were exhilarating to her soul. A history of which she had never known, an explanation for her whole existence was being delineated to her. Her only wish was that John could be by her side, listening. These, she believed, were the answers that he had been seeking.

By the seventeenth week, John had taken the lives of more people than all the personal contacts he had ever made during his entire life in Labor. His heart was like a rock in the snow, cold and hard. His mind was a microcosm of hatred.

Released from his shooting-range, *room-of-death*, permitted into the training facility outside, it was near impossible to remove the images of the bloodied bodies that had accumulated and bunked with him over the past four months. Everything in the world had some bizarre sort of related morphology about it that was reminiscent of the eyes, the splatter and the puddles of his *room*.

Escorted by Crawford and Michaels to the Red Simulator, he had finally graduated to the third tier of his training. Taking hold of his new uniform, John removed his crusty, wretched, blood stained attire, letting them crumble to the floor, gathering at his ankles and feet. He was only a few short weeks away from attaining the official status of an agent of a Sweep Team. For all it was worth, other than killing, John still had no idea what their ultimate purpose was.

Naked for only a moment, he was commanded to remain still with his arms held straight out in front of him, his palms in the supine position. Michaels approached him with a machine held in his hand that resembled a pistol. Pointing its "barrel" at an angle to John's open hand, it made contact with him. With a pneumatic puff of air, it injected a metallic device under his skin, not much larger than a grain of rice.

With a motion to commence, John pulled on his newly awarded shirt and pant. As the last button was eased through its hole below the collar, he was now adorned with the tiger-stripes of deadly black with slashes of red. His *mission* was changing, his trainers informed him. Although he would still sleep in the *room-of-death*, his training was moving into the practical realm: he would now learn to survive and kill under difficult circumstances and in harsh conditions. Poisoned and polluted environments would become the norm. He would learn to bring death to those hiding in complete darkness where goggled, night-seeing devices were necessary. The art of tracking and hunting for those that were deserters of the battlefields would be his primary objective. He was becoming a member of an elite unit, a living Monster.

The Simulator was just ahead. The sign above the palm scanner indicated that it was the place where he needed to present his ticket in order to pass through. With a quick wave of his hand into its red, glowing camera, John was now more than ready to enter its arena.

Like tiny bubbles popping in her belly, Sofia could feel the first movements of the child she was carrying inside of her. Placing her hand upon her abdomen, she thought it strange that she was unable to sense the activity that was taking place just underneath the skin.

"Maryanne," she giggled, "it tickles when he moves."

Maryanne dropped the last of the fruit into her basket. After adjusting the cloth carrier that wrapped over one of her shoulders and under her other arm, she pulled her breast from the mouth of her infant son and briskly walked over to Sofia, who had settled for a break in the shade of one of the orchard's trees.

"When that child begins to kick with a passion, you'll remember these days with more fondness than you can imagine," she said, kneeling down and rubbing Sofia's shoulder.

"I'll feel him more and more from this time on, won't I?"

"The more he grows within you, the sharper his kicking gets, and the stronger will your love be for him."

With a sweet smile, Maryanne strolled back to her basket, waiting until a nearby, roving Security vehicle was out of sight before reaching down and extracting a thin-skinned piece of fruit for Sofia.

"Here," she called out. "Catch."

The yellow-green ball sailed through the air, landing in Sofia's cupped hands. Rubbing it clean on her shirtsleeve, she closed her eyes, biting into it and savoring its sweetness. Her hearing seemed more in tune to the world. The child cooing in Maryanne's arms was so loud and vibrant. Then she thought about John. It had been so long since she had heard anything new.

"Wherever he is right now," she pleaded to the Savior above, "please, keep him safe."

Passing through the familiar passageway on the far side of the secretive training grounds for the second week, John stepped through the threshold with the usual motions. Performing the wave of his bloodstained hand over the scanner before proceeding further, he waited beside the computer's terminal. The green light on the wall gave the visual affirmation that he was cleared to enter. With the opening of its security doors, he and his regular chaperones proceeded into the Simulator's holding cell.

The Simulator was a wide-open expanse of land, approximately three to four thousand meters square, bordered by electrical fencing and layers of razor wire. The terrain was rough and rolling, and coated with strange red sand that was obviously not indigenous to the planet.

Those that died in the Simulator were left in the places where they fell, littering the landscape in various stages of decay, adding more sense of *realism* to the world, giving a closer approximation to the land in which John would actually be working. The scorched transporters and weapons of war of the dead were also left in place. Again, adding to the simulated effect. It was here that the "targets" were a true threat, as they were free to run and hide, having at their disposals the weapons of their individual choices, as well as the weapons of their fallen comrades.

After thirty minutes of being released into the wild, the chase was on. John was finally free, let loose into the open expanse, unbound and uninhibited by his electrical collar or the voices of his tormentors screaming through the speakers. Having lost his moral point of reference long ago, death was seen as a means and not an end, and he purposed to himself that killing everyone was justified. That was, after all, the only assurance he had to fulfilling his self-promised revenge for the death of his life's mate. Kill the so-called innocent as well as the so-called guilty. Who could tell the difference between the two, anyway? Sweep everyone up in a single wave of death. Her murderers would get their due justice. Nothing else mattered... just kill them all.

Taking the lives of the men and women on the battlefield was much simpler than fighting it out with the moving "targets" in the claustrophobic confines of the indoor range. In the Simulator they could be eliminated at much greater distances, and better yet, they could be toyed with for hours: made to suffer, as Crawford had said Sofia suffered.

On this particular day, the Savior was beating down hard and hot. Drizzled with sweat, his cloth, facial covering flapping in the wind, John wiped his forehead with the sleeve of his shirt and crawled across a wind swept knoll. Gathering up the ammo from the rifle of his latest victim, his eyes followed the tracks of the dead woman's companions that disappeared over the hill and into the dried waterway that he knew existed on the other side. By the deep indentation at the toe end of the footprints, he could tell they were running. He knew for certain that they were not waiting around to ambush him.

With the butt end of the rifle to the ground, he grasped its barrel and assisted himself to his feet. Glancing over his shoulder, back towards the corpse lying face first in the blood-soaked sand beneath it, he scanned his eyes across the horizon.

"Sacks of fluids wrapped around sticks of calcium," he mumbled. "Baking under the skyward star."

Picking up the path of his prey, back dropped by a pale blue sky slashed with hair thin contrails, John disappeared over the sand blown hill with his rifle resting on his shoulder.

As the Savior reached its peak, three consecutive reports echoed throughout the Simulator... it was just another afternoon for the Sweeper on the open range.

CHAPTER THIRTY-TWO

Rubbing her protruding belly in her reflection in the pooling water, Sofia was amazed at how much she, as well as the baby, had grown in just over six months. The pressure on her pelvis was quite humbling while she was standing. Looking around at all the women in the field that were either much larger than she, or else were in the process of nursing, the feelings of envy of which Sofia was experiencing over their strength and heartiness was most deserving.

By mid-afternoon the suffocating heat was mixed with terribly high moisture content that strained Sofia's breathing, adding to the stress of her already compromised diaphragm. Exhausted and hungry, her feet and ankles pitting under the swelling, she hoped that the birth of her child would be over soon. But she knew, according to Maryanne's experiences, that she was only two-thirds of the way there.

The nighttime came all too slowly. Having bathed and changed into a thin, cool sleeping gown, Sofia found it difficult to obtain a position of comfort upon her bed. Although it was quite apparent that her cot was hardly designed to give respite for a woman in her condition, she concentrated on guiding her thoughts elsewhere, hoping to fall asleep before too long.

After a lengthy span of time, Sofia's eyes were still wide open. She gave into the fact that she would not be resting well for quite some time. Tossing and turning throughout the rest of the night, she knew very well that the morning would find her worn and fragile.

As the afternoon of the next day presented, the Savior's heat was falling with the ferocity unseen on any of the preceding afternoons. Moving through a busy intersection, her basket held upon her head, Sofia was able to keep up with Maryanne for the most part, only losing sight of her momentarily in the bustling droves and grasping hands.

As they reached the drop-off point for their produce, a convoy of Security transporters began to pull into the town, causing an unsettling wave of emotion to rumble through the streets. Maryanne let her basket roll off of her head and onto the ground.

"Drop your basket and follow me," she said, taking Sofia by the arm. "Don't look back at them, just walk calmly."

Obeying her friend, Sofia followed Maryanne's lead. At first the masses, taken by surprise, began moving away in the same calm manner. But after a moment, the grind of the metal doors swinging open, and the extricating of the agents rushing from their vehicles, caused a sudden panic to erupt.

As hundreds of women behind them, screaming and flailing, were taken to the ground by the ravages of the Security madness, Maryanne struggled to keep her grasp on Sofia's arm. She began to move well beyond Sofia's current abilities, steadily leaving her behind.

"Sofia, don't fall back. We need to get out of here," she yelled.

Out of breath and losing sight of her friend, Sofia stayed on the path that Maryanne had set.

"Maryanne, wait for me," she screamed as her companion veered off the street, entering into one of the garbage filled alleyways.

"Not now, Sofia. We just need to keep moving," Sofia heard Maryanne say as she rounded the corner and fell out of view.

Entering into the narrow-walled pathway, Sofia found Maryanne leaning over her knees, panting and out of breath. Her child, Matthew, crying and scared, was the driving force that made her leave Sofia so far behind.

"Sorry," she was able to say, before inhaling deeply. "Let's keep moving."

Seemingly familiar with the route she was taking, Maryanne did not hesitate to turn down any particular corner when faced with several branching paths. The distressing cries from beyond the walls of the buildings grew ever more grievous. The deeper they moved into the city, the more vigorously Maryanne seemed to push Sofia towards their goal. With the tearing of tires skidding through the dirt, Sofia could hear the Security transporters racing through the roadways, roaring around the corners, barreling into the crowds, followed by the shrieks of unforgiving terror.

After working their way through several twists and narrow turns, they were about to exit the alleyway and enter into the calamitous crowded streets. Maryanne peaked around the corners of the building. Like wild animals whose bodies were under the automated control of their fears, the masses of women were desperately attempting to force themselves into any of the nearby structures that they could find. Stepping upon each other, pushing and shoving, fighting to avoid being captured by the gangs of black-uniformed men preying upon them, she could see that the fleeing crowds were, in their haste to escape, trampling upon several unresponsive bodies.

Spying out a narrow clearing through the throng, Maryanne took Sofia by the hand, urging her to run with her to another alleyway on the other side. Moving perpendicular to the fast flowing river of bodies, they were thrown around in the chaos, momentarily separated.

"Sofia," Maryanne screamed, as she pushed against the heaviness of the panicked citizenry. "Where are you?"

Falling to the dirt road, Sofia wrapped her arms around her abdomen, protecting her child. Tripping over her, several women crashed to the street beside her, bringing several others down with them. The dust in the air was thick and burdensome, causing the Savior's light to appear as a hazy, glowing fog of yellowish-orange brightness. As Sofia pulled herself to her knees, she felt a hand grasping her by the shoulder of her shirt. Looking up and expecting the worst, she could see the blackened silhouette of Maryanne tugging at her.

"Sofia," Maryanne cried with breathless relief. "I thought you were gone."

Helping her to her feet, Maryanne threw Sofia's arm around her shoulder and assisted her out of harms way. Nearly stumbling upon each other, they entered back into the maze of rotting food, soiled papers and old cans. Leading them to a dead end, Maryanne dropped to her knees and began digging through the garbage in a desperate search for something hidden beneath it.

"What are you looking for?" Sofia asked in a tearful panic, while being overwhelmed by the insanity rising up in the village.

Paying no attention to her question, Maryanne kept digging through the debris, feeling around for the distinct hard surface that would bring them to safety.

"It's somewhere around here. Where is it?" she mumbled to herself, blindly groping under the layers of waste.

Like a tin can bouncing off a thick metal plate, Sofia heard Maryanne as she made a disturbance upon something.

"I found it," she said with cautionary jubilation. "But, we need to crawl into this mess, that way the door will stay covered after we go in."

Leading Sofia by the hand, Maryanne helped her to her knees and began manipulating the garbage around them, forming a small tunnel with a pathway leading into the darkness of the piled up refuse. Scooting upon her side at Maryanne's request, Sofia squirmed her way feet first into the opening, inching herself towards a metal disc at the far end of the channel. Maryanne edged past her, reaching out and turning the handle that was set into the groove upon the disc's surface. It was a somewhat familiar sight to Sofia, as it was not unlike the manhole covers that she used to see on the streets of Labor. Sliding the plate to the side, Maryanne exposed the blackness of a hidden room beneath them.

"There's a ladder in there somewhere," she said, reaching out her hand for assistance. "Let me help you down first so that I can close the door behind us."

Feeling the first rung under her foot, Sofia slowly entered the darkness of the pit. Descending blindly under Maryanne's trustful watch, it was quite the distance before she finally felt the solid, dirt floor beneath her.

"I'm at the bottom, Mary," Sofia's voice reverberated in the hollowed enclosure. "Are there any lights down here?"

Sliding the overhead plate shut over them with an audible closure of the lock, Sofia could hear Maryanne's shoes clanking on the metal steps of the ladder.

"Don't move around. I know right where everything is. As soon as I get down there I'll turn them on," she said.

Hearing her feet crunching upon the pebbles that littered the ground, Sofia listened as Maryanne made her way across the room. With the flick of a switch, the dim lights set upon the walls began to glow.

As the room came into view, Sofia found herself standing in the middle of a relatively small, rectangular bunker. Its walls were made of old, crumbling concrete saturated with dried, rusty watermarks that had once dripped from the ceiling long ago. It reminded her of the interrogation room from where she had last seen John.

Shelving units, bolted in place on two of the walls, supported five clay jars that were set neatly upon them. Each one appeared to have a placard with a word etched into it of which the flickering lights ultimately obscured.

"Remember the *Savage Days* I told you about?" rhetorically asked Maryanne.

"It's much worse than I ever imagined," Sofia responded looking towards the exit above her. "Much worse."

Walking over to one of the sets of jars at the far side of the room, Maryanne picked up one of the containers and said, "Boys, I'd like you to meet my friend, Sofia."

As Maryanne held it out to her, the light reflected off of its dull surface. Sofia could see the crudely engraved name of *Samuel* scraped into the metallic plate glued to its base.

Placing it back upon its shelf, Maryanne walked beside each jar, continuing with her introductions, "And this is Frederick. And this is Thomas. Say, 'Hello', Thomas. And here's Joel. And last, but not least, Adam. These are my children, and this is my hiding place during the Savage Days. Stephen helped me find it."

Sofia could see the watering of Maryanne's eyes, and immediately understood that this was a private, and holy place for her.

"Thank you for allowing me to be here," she said.

"You're like a sister to me," Maryanne responded. "You're always welcome here."

Walking up to Sofia and wrapping her arms around her, she laid her head upon Sofia's shoulder and began to cry. She sobbed and wept for an extended period of time.

"Stephen had a contact that died long ago on Red. He recovered the identifiers from our sons each time they fell in battle. He said they wouldn't fight. They just stood in their places and let themselves die. They just stood there while men gunned them down."

Sofia had not seen Maryanne in a state of anguish before. She always assumed that the women of Basket Town were hardened against showing their feelings for their young. But as the hours passed, Maryanne spent their time reminiscing about the early days of her children's lives. She expressed the hope that she had for their safety, and that their lives would be such that their belief in the Savior would, in the end, bring them to her once again.

She explained that the negative effects upon her faith in seeing the return of any such goodness to the world was compounded with each of the deaths of her sons. It was only through Stephen's encouraging words, as the data regarding Golden's rulers picked up over the years, that she was able to finally pull herself out of the depressed rut that she had fallen into. But there was never any hope of ever having the emptiness in her heart filled after the loss of her children. It was only through the encounter with Sofia, Maryanne went on to explain, that her outlook on the future became brighter and the light returned, as her and John's appearance in Basket Town had brought her back from the dead.

With only two weeks left to complete his training, John was anticipating that his final day in the Simulator would be an actual representation of the world of Red that he would be experiencing once he received his orders for deployment. Michaels and Crawford had been playing along with him as team members on its bloody sands for the past several days, allowing him to give the orders and set the tempo for the kills. The increase in the volume of the "deserters" had grown significantly, and John and his group were tasked with eliminating crews of "soldiers" consisting of men and women that outnumbered them at least eight to one.

The Simulator had been consistently evolving more and more into a miniature battlefield throughout the progression of the exercises. The exploding bodies and constant barrages of incoming fire made the adrenalin fill the veins, the senses more keen. It was John's own little war, narrow and confined, such as that with which he fought daily in his mind.

The final test of elimination had been set into motion not less than two hours ago. John was prone in the sand, inching his way up an embankment, trying to get a better feel for the enemy's position. Crawford and Michaels were hunkered down at the bottom of a nearby knoll awaiting their orders.

Using, the torn and broken lower extremities of one of the dead for cover, John peered through the holes in the flesh, spying out the rocky outcropping that was a common area for the prey to take refuge.

After several minutes of patiently waiting, he caught sight of a single movement from the shade of a boulder: the flapping facial scarf of one of the deserters whipping momentarily into the air. Crawling back down the embankment, he duck-walked his way to his "team".

"We need to make a three way split," he said.

"Whatever you say, boss," Crawford replied.

"Just don't get us killed," Michaels retorted. "Make sure you know what you're getting us into."

John detailed the three paths that each one of them would take in order to surround the deserters' fortification. The team would form a triangle around the holdout that would allow the crossfire to catch everyone in its net. The plan was approved by both of his instructors as a legitimate answer to the problem. If they pulled it off it would be John's final test in the Simulator. With their orders doled out, the three men split their ways and began their slow, steady courses towards their assigned positions.

After being separated for a minute, Michaels called back to John, "Hey, Sweeper!"

Taken by surprise by the sudden change in tone, John glanced back over his shoulder. Michaels and Crawford both gave a thumbs-up, smiling out of the corners of their mouths. They were proud of him, as if he had been the son of their creation. John returned the hand gesture, but saved the smile for another time.

The rocky formation stood approximately four hundred meters towards the rising of the Great Star. Camouflaged with the blood of a fallen "soldier", John moved along the crimson sand, slithering through the carcasses and burnt out vehicles. Through his binoculars he could see Michaels head, like a tiny pin top, bobbing and weaving along the opposing ridge as he made his way towards his appointed place.

The accumulating anxiety of the deserters was growing ever more strenuous on their shoulders, as they seemed to be peering out from the rocks with a greater frequency. It was as if they knew their end was at hand.

After nearly an hour the two men called in through John's earpiece that they were in position. The visibility was phenomenal regarding their victims. As the recon data began streaming in from his team members regarding the targets within their respective sights, John understood that Crawford and Michaels were situated in such a manner as to allow them to see several soldiers of which the other could not. Once the shots began to fly, there was no hope for any of those in hiding to escape.

"Whenever you're ready, just give the word, Killer," Crawford's voice crackled in John's ear.

John snarled with irritation. He hated the man. Pulling his scoped rifle up to his cheek, he could make out a young male with his hand pressed down on the shoulders of one of his women comrades. His protective posture with regards to her safety was intriguing. Finding it difficult to keep them within his sights as they bobbed up and down searching for their pursuers, he took in a deep breath, leaving them alone and placing the crosshairs on the armed man kneeling at their side.

"On my shot," he said, exhaling into the mic. "Three..."
His fingertip rubbed the hot steel of the trigger.

"Two..."

Observing the heat waves rising along his line of sight, shimmering horizontal then vertical, then back to the horizon, John steadied his aim, compensating for the wind and for the bullet's drop. Aiming high and to the right of the target he and his weapon were one, an organic whole.

"One..."

Squeezing the trigger, the hammer dropped, initiating the chemical reaction within the compound contained in the primer. With a flash of powder the bullet propelled from the muzzle, roaring across the blood-wasted battlegrounds. It entered into the rocky formation, sailing above the heads of the deserters, rocketing towards its primary destination. Tearing apart the air in its path, it bid farewell to the enemy's fortification as it retreated from the towering boulders, leaving them behind and sailing across the open valley. Finally making contact with its intended victim, it burrowed deep into the head of Crawford, exiting out the posterior aspect of his skull with a cloudy, red mist.

John watched his body crumpling over, disappearing somewhere on the other side of the ridge where he had been perched seconds earlier. His *instructor* was now nowhere to be seen.

Unaware of his fallen comrade, Michaels continued to fire into the enemy, dropping dead each man with every single bullet that left his barrel. In a display of panic, the men and women fled from their rocky coverings like the scattering of ants when their hill is exposed to pooling water.

Peering through his scope, John watched the terrified couple as they worked their way to the base of the outcropping. Two shots echoed from the direction of Michael's position. Two bodies fell. The woman appeared to be alive, crawling upon her bleeding belly, reaching out for her dead companion. Another echoing blast and she became motionless. Taking aim at the other fleeing members of the group, John began to take them down one-by-one, until they were no more.

"I think we got 'em all, John," Michaels whooped. "What a blast. It never gets old, does it?"

"No, it doesn't," John replied.

"Hey, Crawford, how many did you get?" Michaels laughed, but there was no response. "Crawford, are you there?"

"Crawford, it's John. Everything alright?" John said into the mic, feigning to be concerned.

"I'm trying to scope him out, John. I can't find him anywhere," Michaels said with concern.

Pulling Michaels up in the crosshairs, John could see that he was desperately scanning about for his friend.

"I'll meet you at the rocks," he said. "We need to stick together to find him. Maybe one of the targets got away."

After a long pause, Michaels voice came through, "Roger that."

Sliding the rifle to his back, John pulled himself up and headed towards his rocky destiny. Withdrawing his sidearm with a partial pullback of the weapon's slide, he made certain it was charged and ready to go.

With the firearm held by his thigh, he walked through the wasteland with his eye on the speckled dot named Michaels that was cautiously making its way towards the same destination from the distant, sandy formations. Sweaty and calloused, the palm of John's hands found no relief from the heat. His knuckles whitened under the heavy clenching of his fist around the pistol. He had waited six months for this day... six long months.

Entering into the cleft of the outcropping, Michaels stepped out from between two large boulders.

"I can't believe they got him. Twenty years in this business. I didn't think..."

The report of John's handgun put a stop to his mouth. The man fell to the ground gasping under the pain and pressing against the bone-fragmented hole that had formed through his kneecap. The smoke from John's barrel seeped from the muzzle as he moved closer, becoming more intimate with his latest victim.

Sliding the rifle from his back, Michaels made a desperate attempt for the trigger, but he was not quick enough. Met with another heavy explosion of John's pistol, the bullet tore through Michaels' elbow, leaving his forearm dangling like a bough snapped from the trunk of a tree. He screamed under the intense burning, grabbing at the remnants of his arm.

"You two told me in so much detail about Sofia's death, remember?" John asked with cold rhetoric.

"We didn't have anything to do with that, John. Really, we didn't," Michaels cried.

"But with the kind of detail that you did have, you must have been eye witnesses to the sufferings of her last day, right?"

"Look, John, it's what we were told. You've got to believe me. I don't know anything else about her. Just let me live, and I'll say the deserters did this to us, okay? I promise. Just let..."

Another report echoed throughout the walls of the outcropping as Michaels screamed out in pain. Holstering his weapon, John pulled his knife from the sheath at the small of his back. Its sharp, blackened blade swayed back and forth to the rhythm of his gait as he slowly closed in.

Michaels fought to scoot away, but his broken, bloody stumps were of no use, he was unable to move. John stepped into his personal space with a sudden burst of rage. Grabbing his enemy by the hair, he thrust the edged weapon deep into the side of Michaels' skull, using it as a handle to manipulate his instructor's head around. Twisting it back he forced the man to look him in the eyes.

"I know you're in pain, comrade. But from what you people have done to me, this is nothing in comparison. My whole existence *is pain*."

Handing Michaels the smile that he owed him, John ripped the knife out, slashing it across the throat and thrusting him to the sand to finish his last moments of life gurgling and choking in his own blood. After wiping the blade off, smearing the liquid life upon the dying man's shirt, John slid the knife back into its sheath.

Leaving the dead behind, John climbed into the rocky fortification, lifting up a rifle from the hand of one of the deceased soldiers. Turning it back upon himself, he fired a single shot into the flesh of his thigh, and then another into his gut.

The red stream of life dripping from his body felt thick and warm. Blanketed under the heat of the Great Star above, John felt the claustrophobic suffocation that sometimes came to him during the lonely nights in his Room of Death. Holding pressure to the wounds, he clicked his microphone on, transmitting to the Sweeper Training Headquarters, informing them of the casualties and the hard fought exchange that took place between his team and the enemy.

"I'm wounded, sir," John panted into the microphone. "I think they got Michaels and Crawford. I need help."

It was only a matter of time before a medical team would be escorted to his position. He had to keep his story straight. His only hope, now, was that he had passed the final test.

The squeezing sensation around the abdomen that Sofia was feeling was, according to Maryanne, a normal part of the process of carrying a child in the womb. It was a natural reminder from her body for the past two and a half months, letting her know that the birth was coming sooner rather than later.

"It's telling you that it's time to get mentally prepared," Maryanne would say.

As the intensity of the contractions had, over the past few days, been increasing in duration, Sofia was beginning to feel the anxiety about the delivery.

"Don't worry. I promise I'll be there to help you through it," Maryanne said, repeating her words in the same manner as she had done on many past occasions.

Sofia shuffled her feet upon the floor as they hung over the side of her cot. She was not particularly fond of pain. Having been a witness to Maryanne's recent birth, she was not all that certain that she could endure the suffering in the way that Maryanne did, and with such grace, to boot.

Sitting on a wooden box in the corner of the room breastfeeding her child, Maryanne rocked back and forth with quiet contentment. Yet, with the bags under her eyes, she seemed so exhausted.

As another contraction pulled at the underside of Sofia's abdomen, she took in a deep breath and closed her eyes. Concentrating her mind's eye on the forests of Labor, she walked herself through the tall grass and blooming flowers, holding hands with her dear friend, John. She could almost hear his voice, as real as the audible thumping of her heart pounding in her ears. The heavy aromatic fragrance of life that only existed in that wilderness was so vivid that she began to feel the soreness around her sinuses as she held back the desire to cry.

As the pain subsided, she opened her eyes to the reality of the present world.

"Is it as bad as it looks... the pain, I mean?" Sofia asked.

Maryanne removed the sleeping child's mouth from her chest and covered herself while continuing the soothing rocking motion of the baby that she held in her arms.

"I honestly don't know how to describe what it's like," she said. "During the birth, I guess you could say that your whole being is pain, there's no way to escape it... you just hurt. But, after your little one enters the world, it's gone, as if it never existed. You'll look at that child, with its cord still connected to you, and its purple skin," she laughed. "You'll be so happy you won't even consider the suffering that you'd just gone through."

To Sofia, Maryanne's words seemed so few, yet they were always so thoughtful. Her soft-spoken spirit was a blessed comfort. She was thankful that Providence had brought them together. But the anxiety she was experiencing from the impending birth, and the lost hope of ever hearing from John again, was still an overwhelming burden on her shoulders.

"I'm so glad you'll be with me on that day, Mary, because I'm so scared," Sofia confided.

Seeing the tears welling up in Sofia's eyes, Maryanne pulled herself up from her chair. Walking over to her, she took a seat beside her on the cot. Leaning against her, Sofia placed her head upon Maryanne's shoulder. The high-pitched sighs that fell from the blanket-bundled child sleeping upon Maryanne's lap were a soothing relief. She wanted to accept the fact that there would not be any more news forthcoming from Maryanne's contact, Stephen, regarding John's whereabouts and his well being, but she could not give up the hope that they would some day be together.

The two women continued to sit beside one another until late into the night without a word being spoken. Sometimes silence can communicate better than words.

CHAPTER THIRTY-THREE

The transporter rumbled under the roaring of the engines as its thrusters fought against the incoming planet's gravitational pull. With his rifle slung over his shoulder, John stood among the thousands of Sweep Team members packed into the various levels of the aircraft, awaiting their touchdown on planet Red. Dressed in their black and red fatigues, they were weighed down under their heavily armored chest plates and helmets.

Thirty-eight weeks of hell. Thirty-eight weeks of death. John could feel the anxiety in his gut, wondering what he was going to find once the doors swung open and they hit the dirt. If all the carnage of the past nine months was leading up to this, John knew that there were no deserters escaping from the violent storm that he was about to bring in.

Looking about at the mirrored images of his own masked visage reflecting off the face protectors adorned on all the members of his exclusive society, John could sense by the shuffling of feet and the rubbing of fingers that they were feeling the same anticipatory rage inside. None of them would have chosen this kind of life for themselves. It had to be forced upon them, just as it was upon him... and someone had to pay for it.

Pulling at the bright, red fruit growing off the vine in the shadows of her lantern during the cool, early morning, Sofia doubled over under the stretching pain squeezing her around the abdomen. Seeing her in such an immediate distress, Maryanne dropped her basket, running through the orchard to be by her side.

"What's the matter, dear? Are you okay?" she asked, rubbing her back.

"The pain keeps getting worse, Mary. It's hard to breathe when it comes," Sofia said as the pain began to subside.

Waving for help from the other women in their produce gathering party, Maryanne began to make arrangements for her and Sofia's departure. Leaving their baskets in the care of their fellow workers, she placed Sofia's arm over her own shoulders, picked up the rusty lamp by its swiveling handle and began leading her in the first of many steps in their long walk home.

The deafening noise of the engines was reaching its peak, and contact with the surface was imminent. The Simulator's killing fields were about to be put to the test.

With his knees buckling under the strain of landing, John bumped up against several of the Sweep members among which he was surrounded. There were no words spoken. They were like robots, cold and without emotion.

The hydraulic locks of the ship's hull began to release. The mouth of the door's hubs lifted from their sockets. The anxiousness to get on with the work was apparent in the posturing of every man present.

The ceiling door opened above, and the Sweep agents from the upper decks began descending the ladder, preparing to embark on their murderous missions. The clanking of their boots against the metal rungs brought back memories of Sofia, when the two of them had ascended that identical ladder several months prior. He had followed her through the top door and, upon closing its hatch, he held her... John immediately quashed the thought. It was too painful. Pain needed to be turned to hate. Hate was easier to deal with.

The red sand blowing in from the opening under the rising, bay door gathered at their feet. Grinding it under the toe of his boot, John felt the familiarity of being in the Simulator, as it had apparently been filled with the Red planet's exported gravel, adding to its pre-planned realism.

The bars of light sifting through the silhouetted figures standing in front of him, waiting to exit the ship, were much too bright and unnaturally white to be falling from the Great Star in the sky. As the agents began to make their way out the door, the joints of John's fingers cracked under the sweating grip by which he held his rifle.

Moving at a crawling pace towards the exit, he could now see that the brightness was coming from the operating base's mounted lamps, just as he had suspected. Descending the ramp to gather with the troops of Sweepers outside, he took a moment to look to the sky above: it was filled with stars.

The base appeared to be situated on a steep hilltop or relatively short mountain. But, due to the surrounding walls, John was unable to see what was happening outside of the installation. Thumping explosions vibrated in the hollow of his chest, and the war cries and machine gun fire of hundreds of thousands, if not millions, of men and women could be heard rising from the valley below.

Forced into a single file line, the agents were separated into various sized parties before being escorted outside of the compound. John was assigned to a four-man squad led by one Sergeant Madison. The other two men, Goldman and Roberts, were as equally unknown to John as was his squad leader. As all the men were dressed in full gear, there were no discerning features to distinguish one man from another, with the exception of the nametags embroidered on their chests.

Yelling to the Sergeant through the microphone that he wore across his neck, a lower ranked officer was barking out orders, muffled and incomprehensible due to the thundering blasts from the valley. According to the officer's hand gestures and the movements of his lips, they were being assigned to an off-road transporter that was located in the Security Zone approximately one hundred meters downhill.

Motioning with his rifle for their attention and cooperation, the Sergeant directed his men to receive his attention. John and the other two men fell in line in front of him.

"We're assigned to watch for deserters from above the Valley of Blood. Anything more than a three or four-man group we call in for further orders, otherwise, it's hunting time," he said through their earpieces.

Sofia fell to her knees just outside of the entrance to the apartment. Groaning under the pain, Maryanne huddled over her, doing her best to comfort her during her periods of suffering.

As she regained her composure with the easing of the stress, she took a deep breath and stepped inside. The musty odor of death was more pronounced than ever, and having become accustomed to it over the past several months, Sofia was surprised to find her sense of smell so heightened, and her propensity towards nausea so easily triggered. The stairs leading to their room above seemed so steep and uninviting, but the cot waiting for her on the other side of the door, despite all its shortcomings, would be a wonderful comfort.

After a dreadfully difficult time of conquering the stairwell, they finally reached their room. Falling onto its semi-soft springs, Sofia lifted her legs onto the bed. She attempted to relax, but she felt the tugging pains beginning all over again.

The mountaintop upon which their base was situated was steeper and higher than the ones below, and gave a full view of the entire battleground. As they made their way to the base's edge, John and his assigned team were finally able to see the war being fought firsthand. The Valley of Blood appeared to be divided into two distinct areas. It was, according to the deaths John was witnessing, living up to its name.

Two military bases were situated on the ridges of two opposing ranges of steep, rocky hills, each with their own respective, over-active, air transporter systems. They faced one another from across an open wasteland by approximately four thousand meters. Watching from his vantage point was like witnessing a sick game that was being played out by the warped and twisted mind of Insanity itself. Hundreds of thousands of men and women were standing in rows and columns of formations, blanketing the faces of the hills directly across from each other. With the echoing blow of an unseen battle horn filling the valley with its wailing, the multitude of formations descended upon the waves of their own battle cries, firing their weapons wildly, charging blindly to their deaths.

Sitting on the hood of their assigned transporter, John sat beside the Sergeant, looking through a pair of handheld binoculars. There was no order to the battle. Each soldier appeared to be emptying his or her rifle before using it as a club or an instrument for stabbing. The soldiers in the distal formations, still waiting their turns to descend into battle, were throwing explosive devices into the valley, sending body parts and whole corpses, as well as their own fellow mates, hurdling through the air. Piled up thick, and forming a coagulating pool of blood at the valley's basin, floated millions of fallen soldiers, bloated and pale and torn to pieces.

As the hours passed by with only large groups of deserters to call in, one of the squad members drew out his rifle in boredom and began firing into the carnage of the valley. They all knew very well that the distance was too far for him to make contact, but his actions were understandable under the monotonous circumstances, and the Sergeant refrained from keeping the Sweeper back from venting his frustration.

Attempting to track his squad mate's bullets, John spied out a small group of soldiers commandeering a transporter and driving off into the blood red hills towards the rising of the Great Star.

"I've just caught sight of three individuals making a run," he said to the Sergeant.

Handing over the binoculars to his superior, John swung his rifle from off of his back, anticipating further orders. With their team leader scanning the area below, Goldman, anxious to get into the fight, said, "What do you see? Are we red light, Sarge?"

"I see 'em," the Sergeant mumbled. "It's killing time."

Howling and laughing as they hopped down from the roof of their off-road vehicle, Goldman and Roberts hustled to get into the hunt, throwing themselves through the doorways of the transporter. The Sergeant handed back the binoculars to John as the two of them slid off the hood. Taking their seats inside, they buckled in, preparing for the rough ride ahead.

As the engine kicked on, Roberts threw the transporter into gear, and began driving them down the steep, dirt road that descended the mountain. Guiding them towards the deserters' last known position, John poked his head out of the window searching for the tire tracks that would lead them to the kill. As they appeared to be heading in the direction of the solar rise, the Sergeant commented that they were probably trying to make their way to the Old World ruins, but that the fuel cells of the war machines were never filled to capacity due to such a high potential for soldiers to attempt escape.

"They won't get far," He assured them. "Nobody ever does."

Wringing the towels and sheets out as she pulled them from the boiling water with her gloved hands, Maryanne was making all the preparations necessary for the birth of Sofia's child. Covering the floor with the stained, thin cloth, she attempted to make the room as clean as she possibly could within such a filthy environment.

With both of their cots situated alongside each other forming one large bed, Sofia had a much larger area to spread out on. As she lay on her back, the long shadows cast upon the ceiling by Maryanne as she moved past the lantern and through the room, busy at her work, appeared like alien clouds gathering in the night sky. The pain was growing stronger and more frequent. With the cloth removed from their only window to the world outside, Sofia could see the dispersing haze of light gathering in the sky as the Savior was about to make his entrance.

As they rounded the base of the mountain, the tracks to the escapees' vehicle were quite lengthy, and it appeared as though they may have had more fuel in the vehicle than the Sergeant had anticipated. As his team leader lifted the visor from his face, John had his first glimpse of the man. He was middle-aged, probably in his late thirties, with facial hair that seemed far grayer than he would have expected. By the creases of his forehead and the scowl of his brow, he was as equally hardened as Crawford and Michaels, perhaps even the Monster himself. Lifting the binoculars to his eyes, the Sergeant peered at the horizon in the direction of the bluish-purple sky, beyond the red sand hills, where pillars of black smoke arose from the ruins. Placing the viewing apparatus on his lap, he closed his face shield and ordered Roberts to continue driving.

The clarity of the redness of the sand was becoming more pronounced with each passing minute as the brightness over the hills indicated the nearness of daylight. The ruins, according to Goldman, who had been incessantly blabbing into his microphone, were situated on the other side of the ridge.

"I've only seen a few stragglers actually make it out this far," he commented. "They're usually too dehydrated and beat to continue fighting, though."

The trail of rubescent dust following their transporter was too easily marked out from a distant vantage point. Knowing that there was a possibility that the deserters would be waiting in ambush, the Sergeant ordered Roberts to stop the vehicle: they would be hoofing the remaining distance to the targets.

With all the preparations complete, it was now only a matter of time before the child would be entering the world. Maryanne had pulled her wooden-box seat under the sheets, situating it at the bedside near Sofia's head. Sweating profusely under the dense, moist heat of the room, Maryanne used a soft, damp cloth to cool Sofia down.

"We're getting so close now," she smiled.

Dipping the cloth into the can of cool water at her feet, Maryanne flinched under the sharp pinching of Sofia's hand as she took hold of her wrist. Her contractions were now only a few minutes apart.

Low crawling to the peak of the hill, the four men kept a safe distance from one another, preparing to return fire should it become necessary. They had reached the edge of the ruins, and John could see what had once been, in the distant past, a thriving metropolis similar to Labor, only much greater in extent and height. Although it may have been awe-inspiring at one time, it was now an empty shell of a city under the unforgiving hand of war. Still used for urban battles to entertain the powers-that-be, the fires and billowing smoke of destruction seemed to be in a perpetual state of burning.

Retracting the face protectors back, as ordered by the Sergeant, each man pulled his gas mask from the pouch hanging upon his hip before sliding it into place. Inhaling and exhaling, the seals of their masks were complete. At his further command, the team members retrieved a single canister from their vests, throwing them into the nearby buildings.

At the sound of the popping explosions that indicated the release of the poison into the air, the agents were brought to their feet and ordered to commence the hunt. Stalking in a "V" formation, they existed as a single unit, a single entity: a killing machine. Somewhere hidden in the skeletal remains of the ancient city, the four men were running for their lives. Their bleeding hearts were the trophies of Sweeper society.

Picking up the embedded tracks left by the feet of the deserters in the ash and sand, the team members cautiously peered around every corner and over every wall. Wherever the boot prints led them, the team would follow.

The distant thundering of explosions and snapping machine guns, the local crackling fires of burning vehicles and gelled fuel, these were the only sounds audible in the city. The blood gurgling coughs of the choking escapees that they had expected to hear never materialized. The Sergeant ordered more canisters of the fatal gas to be administered in the streets and alleys ahead of them. He wanted the poison to fill the air, to fill the buildings, to flow on the rooftops, anywhere that was a potential hiding place.

Wandering deeper into the city under the cloak of the thin, hazy smoke, the rising complexes surrounding them appeared to have been built steadily taller. A portion of the inner hub of the city became visible between the walls of the rising structures that lined the streets as they made their way through another cross-section. The rotted frames of the skyscrapers, packed together at the central aspect of the long-deceased metropolis, were still several kilometers inward. It seemed to John as if their prey could be anywhere, and yet nowhere. He was feeling the frustration and anger of defeat, knowing that the deserters had got the best of them.

The heavens above were beginning to change to a lighter shade of blue, leaving the purple haze of the early morning behind and blotting out the last remaining stars. The Great Star of the sky was soon to be presenting itself, and with it the discomfort of the heat that would build up under the agents' armored gear.

With the crack of a rifle, and the ricocheting buzz that accompanied the bullet as it bit into the concrete wall next to Goldman's head, the Sergeant yelled into his microphone, "Everyone down!"

Grabbing Goldman by the shoulder, the Sergeant pulled him into a building on the opposite side of the street.

Taking cover beside Roberts, set between the walls of a narrow alleyway, John attempted to peek his head around the corner, hoping to catch a glimpse of the shooter. The concrete exploded into a chalky puff of dust and debris as another piece of lead slammed into the wall only a few centimeters from his mask-covered face.

"We need to split up," John whispered through his microphone. "Let me take Roberts. We'll move along this side of the street. We might be able to take their flank."

Hidden deep within the debris of the old apartment complex, Goldman and the Sergeant sat in silence. Contemplating John's suggestion, the Team Leader tried to consider the possibilities of the action.

Leaning against the wall, John and Roberts slid down to the rubble-covered floor of the alley. While awaiting their orders, another crack of a rifle rang out, and the bullet embedded into the corner a meter from their position. The crackling of their earpieces indicated that the Sergeant was about to give his command.

"We're pinned down in here," he said. "See what you can do."

With a thumbs-up, Roberts patted John on the back.

"Let's do it," he said.

Duck-walking to the end of the building, they made their way through the alley. Climbing through a hole that had been blasted into the side of the structure at one point in its long exhausted past, the two of them entered in.

Working their way towards the shooter's direction, the two-man team scuttled through several rooms before reaching their exit. Out through the window frame they climbed, back into another alleyway. Another shot fired, apparently directed towards Goldman and the Sergeant. It would take time, John thought, but with such amateurish gunplay at work, he and Roberts would soon make an end to their annoying targets.

Screaming under the intensity of the pain, Sofia's head was beginning to spin.

"You need to slow your breathing down," Maryanne urged. "You're going pass out."

"Okay," she panted. "I'm sorry. It just hurts so much."

As the squeezing of the contraction faded, Sofia rolled onto her side, attempting to stand upon her feet.

"I need to get up, my back's hurting."

Maryanne wrapped her arms around Sofia's waist, placing most of the pressure at the small of her back. As the contractions began again, Sofia began her tachypneic breathing while Maryanne increased the force against her lumbar region.

The Savior was just peeking over the edge of the hills, bringing its warming rays of light upon the city's cardboard rooftops. The women of the town had long ago busied themselves with their daily routines. The crowds of the streets were now openly visible. From the direction of the flatlands, the cottony rise of dust from the speeding transporters heading into Basket Town were an unusual sight at such an early hour of the day.

Several women, upon seeing the Security vehicles heading towards the city, began forsaking their fieldwork, shouting out the alarm towards the other groups of women. Lifting their heads from their work, the women downrange turned towards the city, hollering out, alerting the next group in line. As the distress calls reached the edge of the city, the cries grew louder as nearly every woman, upon hearing the warning calls, lifted their voices in a chorus of admonition.

Floating upon the breeze through the window, the melodic monition fell upon Maryanne's ears.

"They're coming," she said under her breath.

Moaning in agony, Sofia returned to the cot. With her arms shivering under the stress, Maryanne knew that the child was going to be born any minute and that the Security forces would not be far behind, perhaps even present for the birth itself.

The echoing shot taken at the Sergeant and Goldman had initiated from a rifle directly above the heads of John and Roberts. Three distinct voices, apparently muffled under their gas masks, were calling out targeting positions for the sniper. Moving further into the old, fragile apartment building, John and his partner were silent and focused. The voices could be heard falling down the plaster and concrete littered stairwell leading up to them.

Turning off their microphones, the two-man assassin team toe-stepped their way up the stairwell, taking extra precaution not to disturb any of the debris that lay at their feet. The light of the Savior was beginning to seep into the room as they reached the top of the staircase. Hidden behind a cloth-covered banister that blocked their view from the team of deserters, the two men placed their eyes against the holes punched into the cloth's side and peered through the tattered railing.

The feeling of pushing was so overwhelming that Sofia could not stand to wait any longer. Screaming in pain, blood and liquid poured forth from her birthing area.

"He's almost here, Sofia. Keep pushing," Maryanne encouraged her, holding out her towel wrapped arms between Sofia's legs.

The warning cries of the streets outside were at a deafening volume as the transporters pulled up to the curb of their abode. Maryanne looked back over her shoulders, anticipating their presence. She knew they would be kicking in the door any minute.

The beams of light entering through the wounds of the building were falling upon the three-man sniper team. With the deserter's backs facing them, John and Roberts could see, to their surprise, set between two soldiers dressed in their military battle dress, the sniper lying prone on the floor, fully clothed in Sweeper attire.

As Roberts turned to look at John, his boot knocked a piece of concrete over the edge of the stairs, alerting their foes. John lifted the barrel of his rifle over the railing. Pulling the trigger, he opened fire, blindly emptying his magazine into the direction of the enemy. Roberts, throwing a flash-bang grenade over the railing ducked his head down, yelling, "Grenade!"

As the blinding explosion rocked the walls, raining down chunks of plaster and concrete into the room, John let his rifle fall back, swinging across his shoulder upon its sling, while he retrieved the handgun holstered upon his hip. With Roberts in tow, the two men moved into the room, saturated with the hot bars of light filtering through the heavy clouds of dust kicked up by the skirmish. With several shots to the head and torso, the Sweeper agent fell to his death. The eyes and ears of the two remaining soldiers were in a state of neural confusion. John and Roberts blocked the Savior's light from their faces as they stepped in front of them. The men appeared to be willingly kneeling down, giving themselves into their captor's hands.

As the child's head began to crown, Maryanne heard the thumping of fists on the door behind her, followed by the demand to immediately open it. Through the thin strips of light falling from the ceiling, the dust pulsated off the walls with each knock of the agent outside. Sofia, too overwhelmed by the pain to hear the commotion, continued to push, feeling the movement of the child as he prepared to make his entrance into the world.

With her baby's head completely free and exposed, the Savior's rise brought the needed heat and soft brightness to bear upon him. His shoulders were beginning to pass through her vaginal canal when the door burst open to the sounds of men yelling and boots pounding.

"Get on the floor, now," The agents yelled with their guns drawn.

Ignoring their demands, Maryanne continued encouraging Sofia with the birth.

The two deserters did not plead for their lives. They did not even blink as they cast their eyes up to the Great Star above. At the moment that John and Roberts pulled their triggers, John was almost certain that he saw the men smile. As the bullets tore into their heads, their bodies folded in upon themselves to the floor like cloth, bleeding out their life's worth. They had become like the city, empty shells, nothing more.

With her final push, Sofia heard the cry of her child for the first time. Seeing Maryanne at the end of the cot, her baby wrapped in the towel, she held her arms up to take hold of him.

Like bright vines of a forest of light, the Savior's beams filled the room through the holes in the ceiling.

"Put the child down and get on the floor," came the demand once again from behind Maryanne.

Maryanne could not obey his orders, and defying them, she began to present the newborn to his mother. As the bundled package was about to be delivered into Sofia's hands, two electrified prongs veering towards Maryanne's back followed by a puff of smoke from the barrel of the agent's taser.

The barbed needles sailed through the air, whizzing through the shadows of the ceiling, inline with their target. Sofia could feel the warmth of the child through the thin cloth of the towel as he fell into her arms.

As the wired darts entered into the falling particles of light, they stopped mid-flight, tumbling to the floor. Maryanne turned around to look at the man that had just fired the weapon.

"This is not your child," she said, falling to her knees and looking to the Savior above. "Please, don't let them take him."

Throwing down the taser, the commanding agent ordered his awaiting Security personnel to arrest the two women and to separate them from the child, taking extra care to be sure that they were not transported back to their headquarters together.

Sofia screamed out as the men began to approach them, "You're not taking my baby!"

Closing in on Maryanne, the first agent entered into the light. Like a bubble bursting in the air, he exploded with a glorious mist of crimson spray of flesh and bone, painting the ceiling and walls, blowing holes through the cardboard, allowing more light to enter in.

Staring in disbelief, Sofia's face was splattered with the ruby dots of the Savior's wrath, while the crying bundle in her arms was a speckled display of the things to come.

Pushing his way out the door in order to flee from the macabre incident, a light ray fell on the commanding agent, and in an instant, he was gone, coating the doorway and stairwell outside with the remnants of his lost being. As the Savior's particles filtered in through their newly found portals, the annihilation followed down the stairwell like a chain of timed death: one explosion followed another until the living were no more, and the dripping enclosure was all that remained of them.

Waiting beside their transporters, witnesses to the destruction from within, the remaining agents attempted to rush through the crowds, pushing the women to the ground in their desperate attempts to escape. But they were met with the same fate as their comrades. As the burning sphere of the sky arose above the rooftops, their bodily structures polluted the women around them.

Driving back to their mountainous compound, John thought deeply about his first run-in with a group of real deserters. Unlike the Simulator, these seemed to be true soldiers. They were trained in weapons usage and military linguistics, and they were not afraid to kill. But more importantly, there was a hole in the Sweeper community. One of their members was working against it. What was he hoping to accomplish, John wondered. What purpose was there in running?

The drive back to the base was without incident. They had not come across any more deserters, as was expected. Climbing up the steep incline, leading them to their lookout station, John watched the continuing battle of the valley out the back window of the vehicle. There were more men and women dying and fighting in that arena than all the people of Labor combined. Where could they all be coming from?

Careful to avoid slipping on the stairs, Sofia held a towel between her hand and the blood soaked rail. With a sheet wrapped over her and the child, catching the dripping flesh that fell in sticky chunks from the ceiling, she would have to wait until they were outside before throwing it off of them. With Maryanne and her child accompanying them, they exited the building, pausing for a moment at the edge of the convoy of empty transporters parked along the sidewalk.

The streets were awash in watery red fluids and pinkish-white flesh. The usual, stifling mass of women that commonly walked through them was nowhere to be found: the city was barren. Everyone was in hiding.

A transporter at the furthest visible end of the city rounded a corner. Its driver, seeing them standing in the street, began speeding in their direction, bearing down on the vehicle's horn.

"What are we going to do, Mary?" Sofia cried, feeling her warm blood dripping down her legs, forming puddles around her feet.

Taking Sofia by the arm, she pulled her around the abandoned vehicles lining the street.

"Let's go this way. Maybe we can lose them in the alleys."

Entering between the buildings, Sofia doubled over again, feeling the contractions of birth once more.

"Maryanne," she screamed.

Pulling her gown aside, Maryanne could see that in her haste, she had not cut the child's cord, and Sofia was beginning to pass the second birth. Hearing the oncoming vehicle, Maryanne was panicked as to what to do. Sofia needed to be in a cleaner environment, and they needed something to cut the child loose that would not cause him to get an infection. She walked Sofia as delicately as she could around the corner, deeper into the filth of the alley, hoping that the Security agents had not seen them as they sneaked away.

With a rumbling stop, the transporter's squeaking brakes brought it to a sudden end just outside their hiding place. There were no splashing explosions this time, no screaming, no opening of its metallic door accompanied by the stomping of boots. As she waited, rubbing Sofia's back while rocking her own child to keep the silence, she heard a voice coming from inside their apartment building.

"Maryanne! Maryanne, where are you?"

It was Stephen yelling from their upstairs window! His voice brought an immediate sigh of relief. Whispering into Sofia's ear, Maryanne said, "Wait here, I'm going to get help."

Running out into the street, Sofia could hear her calling to her mate, "Stephen! I'm here, Stephen."

She could hear them uniting just around the corner. Maryanne was in a terribly contradictory emotive state of happiness and fear. She was crying and babbling hysterically, while Stephen attempted to console her.

With her legs growing weaker, and the tightening contractions returning, Sofia searched for a clearing among the garbage that was piled up to her knees. Unable to find a suitably clean area, she held her child securely, sitting down in the place where she stood. Holding him up, she finally had a chance to look into his eyes. They were so blue and his cheeks so pink. His cry was sweet and tenderly soft. Under the blinding light of the Savior, she held the child close to her while the squeezing of her abdomen intensified. He was the offspring of her and John. Holding the child was like holding him. The world seemed to be falling apart around her, but nothing else mattered. What an adventure this has been, she thought.

Chapter Thirty-Four

As the years went by, John was beginning to sense that the battles with the deserters were slowly, but steadily, intensifying. Their ranks appeared to be better trained, more adept at survival, more organized and self-determined. Most of the Sweep members attributed it to an evolving state of awareness that was growing inside the bio-engineered men and women being sent into the Valley. The chief rumor floating around detailed a training facility, a secretive complex known as Planet Wasp Nest. Although that was the prevailing view on the matter in discreet conversation, it was not held in high regards within the circles of public discourse.

Wasp Nest was not, according to the questionable information disseminated among the rank and file and those agents less privileged in regards to security clearance and classified information, a planet as such. It was believed rather, to be a hub of moon-sized asteroids where there supposedly existed the mass production of genetically altered peoples created with the sole purpose of dying in the Valley of Blood.

The passing of time had brought John into contact with several well-placed individuals with a more intimate knowledge of the deeper aspects of the governing agencies. Through one of his sources he learned of the intricate details and behind-the-scenes functions of the military's more secretive entities.

The Security on Raw, as John came to find out, was its own entity, left out of the loop as to what the military was engaging in. Although the top brass used them to bring certain men and women in for questioning, what was done with the prisoners afterwards was strictly a military operation.

When John first came to the understanding of the heinousness that was the underbelly of his training, he all the more resented his former "instructors". Although he wished that he had applied more pain to Crawford before shooting him from such a non-intimate distance, Michaels, he believed, received his due reward... for the most part, anyway.

The following years in his initial function as a Sweep operator began with a state of mind full of contradictory emotion. But with the passing of time, John eventually, with the exception of a few transient moments, blocked out all the heartbreaking thoughts of Sofia and the wonderful days they had spent together.

He began by turning his sadness into hatred, his love into hatred. Everything he ever cared about was ripped away from him and annihilated. He alone was left to wallow in his guilt. With all of his emotions exchanged for the heart-searing anger that pulsated within him, John found acceptance and comfort in the open arms of the Sweeper Society and their murderous ways.

Burning under the stress from the thick, black smoke that blew across the city ruins, John's eyes were moist with tears as his helmet's face protector did little to filter out the polluted air. As part of a larger Sweeper force than he was used to, he and his crew kept their heads low, crouching beside the crumbling walls and waiting for their next order.

During the late morning, pre-op briefing, Sweep Command had informed all active units that a monumental breach had occurred in the Valley of Blood. In the ensuing battle, cloaked under the darkness of the early dawn, a rebel faction had staged an uprising.

Entire formations of deserters had simultaneously fled the Valley for the first time in the history of the war, commandeering hundreds of vehicles and fleeing to different parts of the planet with an innumerable cache of weapons and ammunition. The organization with which they were operating seemed far too complex, to John's mind, to be carried out by mere grunts thrown into a foreign war. It had to have been facilitated by someone with insider knowledge of how the Valley operated and what its surroundings held in regards to resources and vantage points.

Much to John's chagrin, the briefing had brought more terrible news other than the uprising itself: the order to forego the use of poison gas, a primary tool in the Sweeper arsenal. The reason for its discontinuation was, to John, a blur at best, but it ran along the lines of *"safeguarding against friendly casualties"*. In order to light-en their loads, several operators, seeing their filtering masks as an added burden to their already heavy load, chose to leave them behind, contrary to John's stance in the matter.

Splitting up and heading out into numerous parties, the Sweeper's numbers were thin and diluted down as they pursued the deserters far from the Valley and into the ruinous, ancient environments. Outnumbered and out-gunned, their training had not prepared them for the full-scale warfare they were getting themselves into.

Sweep-Team Alpha had begun their retreat from the buildings just ahead of John's position. From his cover behind the concrete structure he could hear the rhythmic bouncing of the gear against their bodies. Moving to the open, rubble-strewn streets in a parade of clinking metal, John used their sounds, coupled with the tempo of the crunching rocks and debris under their boots, to judge their distance and gauge their motives.

Within a few seconds time, the Command Center's radioman came over the earpiece confirming his suspicion: John and his men needed to lay down covering fire for the fleeting team. Lifting their rifles over the wall on his command, he ordered his men to place suppression fire towards the enemy's lines.

There was an initial pause, a moment of confused silence as his team was unable to locate any targets that were in need of their suppressive service. But a crack from a deserter's rifle changed everything. And within a fraction of a second the world around them exploded into a hail of small arms fire.

Before they could even squeeze off a handful of rounds, all the men under John's command fell to the ground as a chain of explosions sent the bodies of Alpha Team's members tearing into meaty particles. The entire crew was wiped out in a single volley.

Lifting his reflective visor, the smell of destruction, like burning rubber, hung heavily in his nostrils. The stuffiness of the helmet's shield was too suffocating to keep it hanging over his face. Pulling out a map from his hip pocket, John traced the assumed position of the enemy's X-Y coordinates.

"Requesting to gas ahead of position: maploc three-one-echo! How do you copy, Command?" he spoke into his microphone.

The only answer was static.

"Request repeat: gas ahead of position maploc: three-one-echo!" Do you copy, Command?"

After a few seconds of radio silence, John looked up the line at the battle-hardened faces that existed through the open facial coverings of his team members. Shaking their heads and cursing the Command, they silenced themselves as a voice aired through their ears, "We copy loud and clear."

There was another static-filled moment of silence, followed by, "That's a negative. Do not smoke them out. Repeat. Do not smoke them out. How do you copy? Over."

Clearing his throat, he spit on the ground.

"Roger that," he grumbled.

A unit from the rear line crouch-walked their way to John's team. They were a Sweeper party of three. A unit similar to the one John was commonly assigned to. The team's leader, Sergeant Carlson, yelled as he closed in on them, "I think they want them captured alive. What do you think, John?"

"Alive?" He responded, panning his eyes across his men. "Nobody's getting out of here alive."

The great star-of-the-sky's brightness reflected off the crystalline water of the contrails that were pinned high in the atmosphere. By the purpling haze of light filling up at the horizon, every man knew that the daylight of Red was only a few more hours short of giving way to the darkness. Without any night vision devices on hand, John understood the severity of their predicament, the advantage they would be giving to the enemy if they did not move quickly to secure a base of operation closer to the area in which they were holding out.

With the order to commence, his and Carlson's teams expedited their transition into the ruins. Divided into several two-man groups, John ordered his teams to move cautiously under the watchful cover of every other member. Heavily organized and methodically advancing, they headed towards the towers of the city's central hub, visibly peeking over the ruinous heaps and crumbling, skeletal frames of their surroundings.

John considered the distance on his map. If they did not run into anything to hinder them, they would arrive at the first of the great towers by last light at best, or in the early darkness at worst.

As the light of the sky was beginning to dim, the Sweepers reached the border of the inner city. Constantly slowed down throughout the day by intermittent shots fired from the distant buildings, John was relieved that they had made the journey in such a short span of time, and without any casualties to boot. Each member of his team was feeling the exhaustion of the trek. Dehydrated and parched with thirst, under duress from their weariness, they had to take extra precautions with silence and motion due to the close proximity of the enemy, as they searched for a secure place to pass the night away.

The darkness had unfolded itself over them like a hostile sheet of fabricated nightmares. John sat with his rifle on his lap leaning behind the cover of a wall, just below a blown out window frame.

Listening to the radio chatter through his earpiece, he began cursing the Command for letting his men get into such a plight. Gassing the deserters would have brought the whole fiasco to a closure long ago, he thought.

Central Command had discounted the enemy's size and strength during the morning's battle analysis, resulting in every Sweep teams' overconfidence and lack of preparedness with regards to their posturing and necessary equipment. As far as John was concerned, the blood of Sweep members was on their hands.

Over the airwaves, the screams and mutilating deaths of his comrades fighting the deserters in other, distant parts of the planet poured through in volleys of mentally torturous waves. They were a constant reminder for all the men of his command to keep themselves vigilant, even with the grueling heat and nagging desire to rest tugging at their minds and tearing down their bodies.

After listening to the minute-by-minute updates on the open channel for several hours, dozens of raging gun battles and countless skirmishes had yielded nothing of significance: no Sweeper teams were able to report the capture of a single Valley fighter, but the casualties were mounting up among those of John's own community.

Having no idea as to the size of the enemy force they were soon to be facing, he was beginning to feel the nudge of anxiety in his gut. Was it a whole formation waiting for them out there? Or, was it merely a single unit with a strong, well-informed leader? There was no way he could tell, and Command was not helping them in any way. *Turn the fear into hate*, the motto rang in his ears. He followed it hard. He hated the deserters with a passion. Killing them would be a joy, if only he could find them. He was doing it for Sofia, after all, if he remembered correctly. That was the reason, he thought to himself, wasn't it? She had been his love, his life, his... like coals of fire, so the baser emotions fueled his anger. He pushed the thought from his mind, another morsel of that past life that had somehow managed to remain hidden in the cracks and crevices of his brain. He despised it. It made him soft and weak. Weakness needed to be dealt with. It was an energy that needed to be refocused into a new form: hatred towards the enemy. It was the guiding factor that had kept him alive for so long... if his existence could be called *living* at all.

The tips of the buildings of the inner city were feeling the heat of the Great Star as it arose over the horizon, touching the skyscrapers reaching up to the skies. Due to the heights of the structures, they seemingly existed among the unusually high quantity of contrails that crossed through the blue-green expanse. In order to get an upper hand on the situation, the team leaders, John and Carlson, had agreed to a pre-dawn excursion, with the idea that they would secure a safe zone long before the enemy had knowledge of their intentions. Seeing the revealing glow of light descending upon them, the Sweepers picked up the pace, moving into the shadows of the buildings, staying within close proximity to immediate cover in case of incoming arms fire.

Amazed at the ingenuity of the mind of man, John had never seen such towering monstrosities before. In his nearly twelve years on the planet, this was the first time he had ever stepped foot so deeply into the ruins. Packed together with such close proximity, the designed layout of the city vaguely reminded him of that other world of his, the distant past that he had once belonged to: Labor, *where the light of the Star was not permitted in.* He dropped his eyes from their skyward gaze: nostalgia was evil. He had to kill it before it killed him.

Entering into the lobby of what had once been a business construct, John could see the faintly visible brass letters that were set into the concrete on one of its walls. The structure was once known by the name *Adelaide and Sons, Incorporated.*

Ordering his team to clear the area and move to higher ground, they swept through each of the first floor's adjacent rooms before ascending the stairwells leading to the upper levels. Taking up tactical positions at the mid-point of the building, they were approximately forty stories above the ground before they settled in.

Carlson's team had moved into the building across the street, setting up its own base of operations. Their plan was to head to the roof of the skyscraper, hoping to gain a better view of the enemy. After nearly forty-five minutes, the leader of the three-man team reported his findings to John.

"There's no advantage from this high point. The buildings are too close together to see anything other than the next one in line. Over," Carlson said.

"Alright. Rendezvous with me at the Adelaide lobby. We'll set this place up as our command post and go from there. Over," John responded into his microphone.

As Carlson affirmed his message, John peeked out the window. The morning had brought an eerie calmness with it, as there were no snipers frustrating his team with random potshots, no explosive eruptions of resistance, not even a hint of breeze existed to rustle the dust into the air. The deserters were up to something, John thought. Their inaction, coupled with the mood set by the stillness in the wind, was a witness to their scheming.

Continuing the anticipated wait, the seconds hand on John's watch unrelentingly ticked by. It had been nearly forty-five minutes since he had sent a small unit to meet Carlson and his men downstairs, and nearly an hour had passed from the time that he had heard the last words from Carlson himself.

Taking another peak out the window, he spied out from the edge of his field of view the movement of an unnatural entity in the streets below. His binocular brought the culprit vividly into view. It appeared that a deserter scout was advancing towards their position, moving haphazardly from cover to cover.

Apparently unaware that he was being watched, the soldier's actions were novice at best, and poorly executed. He was the only moving object in a world that existed with the stillness of a painting.

John immediately assumed his presence to be a trap. Radioing to the men down below, he informed them of the incoming enemy, but refused their request for engagement: the peculiarity of their predicament required a careful balance in his consideration of the use of force against those potential advantages that forbearance could sometimes procure.

Like a spider in a dark room that had just been exposed to light, the scout scrambled through the rubble in a disorderly fashion. He appeared to be a man in mental turmoil. Eventually making his way between the Adelaide building and the structure that Carlson was last heard from, he held his position, leaning against the twisted, metal frame of a burnt out transporter.

Observing the event through the sights of their rifles, John's men remained in their hidden locations throughout the lobby. As the unarmed man ran to cover amongst the debris of a fallen wall across the street, a pile that lay just outside the building's blown-out doorway, several of the men began to apply the tension to their triggers, anticipating the kill.

Removing his backpack, the deserter undid the straps of its cover and reached inside, unknowingly so near to death should he make the wrong move. In the same manner that the scout's hand entered the sack, so it returned: empty. He pulled the straps back over his shoulders. After cautiously looking around, he disappeared inside Carlson's stronghold.

"Carlson, you've got a single individual making his way to your location," John spoke with urgency into his microphone.

There was no response, not even a hint of static.

"Carlson. I repeat. You've got a single individual making his way to your location. Do you copy?"

Again, there was no reply. Switching his radio to the open channel John received nothing but silence. Realizing that the communication was either jammed or that Sweeper Command had been overrun, he called out to the two men in the adjacent room, informing them of their current situation. John took a minor comfort in hearing the message shouting down the line and into the other rooms: his team was still intact, but initiating orders would no longer be done through the silent whispers of their individual communication devices.

As the heat of the morning was beginning to rise in conjunction with the Great Star of the sky, John wiped the sweat from his brow, handing his rifle to the agent kneeling at his side. Removing the binoculars from his vest pocket, he intended to scan through the windows of the opposing building, hoping to get a glimpse of Carlson's team or, perhaps, of the scout that was now in their midst.

The eyecups had just made contact with the sockets of his skull when the roaring billow of flames and scattering fragments of concrete exploded out the sides of the skyscraper, tearing away the walls and structural integrity from the lobby below. The destruction arose approximately twenty stories upward.

As the entire team stationed on his floor abandoned their posts, rushing to the aid of John and the other men exposed to the detonation, the din of twisting metal and crumbling concrete accompanying the swaying building across the street filled the air with its ominous tune.

Tipping towards its side, a thunderous wave of ashen, gray cloud blew through the windows as the tower crumbled into another building across the way, disintegrating the two structures into a single mantle of wreckage. Before pulling his face shield down, John shouted the order for his men to retreat to the lobby floor.

With their visibility obscured, the agents groped around, calling out names and positions until they had transitioned into a single file line, one hand on the shoulder of the man in front of him, the other hand on the grips of their rifles. There was no way to expedite the move. Everything would have to be done with a slow, methodical order until they were in the clear. Yelling out to the agents John had earlier sent down to meet Carlson's team, the lead man was cautious not to become the first casualty by way of friendly fire.

Entering the lobby was a disorienting action, as the grayed-out world was so different in appearance from their first encounter with it. The street outside was fogged from existence. The city in general seemed to have been turned into a black and white photograph with its sharply contrasted bi-colored stains splashed upon its image.

Shouting for his team to hold position, John could hear his order moving up the line in the echoing of various inflections and pitches of the agent's voices, bringing the team's advancement to a standstill. Using their shoulders to keep his path, John worked his way to the front of their train. Once in position, he shouted over his shoulder giving the command to resume their egress from the Adelaide. Leading his men into the smoky world outside, his plan was to backtrack their way to safety, to wait for the dust to settle before re-advancing upon the enemy.

Surrounded by the thickness of the outdoor atmosphere, the visibility was less than an arm's length from the tip of his nose. Through his visor, John could see the hazy particles and debris gently hovering around his field of view, floating around his head like fish in a pond. Looking back he could just make out his own reflection in the facemask of the agent following close behind him.

After a moment of time had elapsed, he realized how disoriented he was without his sense of sight. It was difficult to gauge with any degree of accuracy the distance they had traveled or the amount of time that had passed since their extrication from the building. At the slow, steady pace at which they were moving, John figured that they must have crossed somewhere just over ten meters, but he was certain it was well under twenty.

In the eerie quiet of the ashen cloud, as if a beetle whizzed by his ear, John could hear the buzzing of an unseen object passing between him and the agent to his rear. A peculiar snap reverberated from behind him. He felt the agent's hand slip down his back, followed by a heavy thud at his feet.

Stopping to look back, the smog was too thick to clearly visualize anything with any distinction, but he could make out the silhouette of the agent lying on the ground. Before his mind could inform his muscles to react, causing him to kneel down and assist his fallen comrade, another snap resounded from the thickness before him, accompanied by a spray of bloody droplets across his visor, and the gurgled drowning of one of his unseen men.

"Take cover," John yelled, dropping prone to his elbows and knees, crawling blindly through the street.

The quietness within the dusty shroud suddenly exploded into flashes of dispersed lights and bursts of automatic weapons. Screams of agony and cursing arose with the wildly returning fire of the Sweeper agents throwing the lead from their weapons in the general directions of the incoming attack.

"Fall back," John yelled, but his voice was overcome by the intensity of the din, and the loss of electronic communication had left each man to his own fate. Firing in a rash and uncontrolled manner behind him, John retreated from the fight, running back down the street that had led them to the Adelaide building the day before.

Lost in the haze and temporarily devoid of rationalization, he stumbled through the rubble, confused and tormented for abandoning his post in the manner that he did. Tripping to the ground and rolling down an embankment of debris, he abruptly found himself lying beside the torn up carcass of the deserter scout. His face had been torn from his skull and he was missing both the limbs on his left side. The explosive that he had planted had done its job too well.

Sitting up, John could hear the humming of the bullets overhead. The battle was playing out a short distance away. Sweeper Command was either staying silent and out of the fight, or else John was alone, and currently without a functional chain of command that he was being held accountable to.

Searching the man's body, he felt a gasmask pouch pinned underneath the dead weight. Rolling the corpse onto its back he removed the scout's filtering device from its satchel and opened his own facial visor. The particulate matter of the air entering his lungs caused him to cough and choke. He placed the mask upon his face and sealed it against his skin. Removing the gas canisters that the soldier had attached to his vest, John clipped them to the loops on his own chest armor, keeping the last two in each hand. It was time to play by the Sweeper's rules.

The automatic fire from the deserters still raged fiercely against the few remaining agents holed up inside the Adelaide building. The cloud of dust was beginning to settle, and the visibility was such, that the men and women closing in upon them appeared as shadows scurrying about in the silhouetted hills of rubble strewn across the streets outside.

With the clanking of several cans rolling into the middle of the street, followed by the eruptive popping of their triggering mechanisms, the deadly gas began to evacuate into the surrounding atmosphere.

"Gas," came the screams of the deserters.

The exclamation was repeated throughout the immediate vicinity by a quantity of soldiers greater than John had anticipated. They were not a mere squad, nor a platoon size unit. He, along with the last few men under his command, was facing a formation, perhaps two. Tossing out a few more canisters, he advanced his way to an opposing street that ran parallel to the Adelaide, taking up a position in a building to the rear of the enemy.

With the gas forcing them back, John was able to observe them from his hidden vantage point. They were fleeing to their awaiting transporters, speeding off in the opposite direction from his position. Removing his map from his pocket, John could see that they were escaping towards the distant Red deserts, which began approximately twenty kilometers to the far side of the ruins.

As the last two squads of deserters struggled over the wreckage of the fallen building, the first four-man team to scale the destruction sprinted to one of their awaiting machines. With a dust trail following close behind it, the retreating vehicle disappeared into the ruins, leaving the few remaining survivors without support. John could tell by the manner in which the former squad had hastened in their escape, showing little regard for those unable to keep up, that they would not be returning to help, even if the last of the soldiers required it.

Raising his rifle to his shoulder, he hesitated to pull the trigger until all the rebels had exposed themselves in the open. The two members standing at the top of the ruinous heap were approximately three hundred fifty meters out. They appeared to be waiting for the rest of their team before making the final dash. Assisting one of their wounded comrades over the rubble, they were finally exposed... and alone.

With a limping gait, an injured soldier draped his arms over the shoulders of both a female deserter on one side and a male on the other. Behind them, another female carrying several weapons over her shoulders covered their rear. John steadied his aim, keeping his iron sights covering the body of his already suffering target. He was wholly prepared to place a bullet into the man's mask-covered face.

As they reached the base of the mound, John squeezed the trigger, sending a single projectile spinning from the muzzle of his rifle. The explosive impact of ruby mist dropped the wounded deserter dead in his tracks, bringing his two helpers to the ground with him. Firing off another shot, he watched the female at the rear fall to her knees, writhing in pain as she grasped at her leg.

As John was about to release the death blow into her body, a shot from the last remaining male soldier whizzed past his head, ricocheting off the wall behind him. Rushing to take cover inside the building, he headed down the stairwell leading to the street below.

Cautiously clearing the exit, he ran behind the charred and rusty remains of an old vehicle just outside. As he peered around its edge, he caught a glimpse of one of the deserters ducking down on the other side of the high-walled remains of an ancient courtyard another three hundred meters along his line of sight.

Advancing to a low-lying wall twenty meters ahead, John was able to gain the advantage of concealment and mystery, allowing him to close in on his unsuspecting prey. Firing into the air in order to keep them constantly guessing as to the number of men they were fighting, John was testing their psychological strength, initiating the tormenting trials upon his enemies that he had learned through his years of practical application on the battlefield. He knew that the growing anxiety would skew their judgment, causing them to make mistakes. Eventually, their fear would allow him to narrow the gap between them to such an extent that they would be dead before they even knew he was in their presence.

After nearly forty minutes of cautiously progressing towards their holdout, John was finally within a stone's throw of the courtyard. Pulling the last two canisters of poison from his vest, he removed the pins. Pulling his arm back, he hurled them in one at a time.

As the explosive follow-up indicated that the gas was being released, John waited for the visible, rising cloud of death before moving to finish them off.

Kneeling down and pressing his shoulder against the broken wall of concrete he was using for cover, the shadows of the buildings overhead slowly began drawing back towards the Great Star. Reaching its arms over the city, the Giver of Light dropped its particles upon the gray and deadly streets.

A soft breeze began to develop, rustling the papers and ashen soot that littered John's surroundings. It was the first time since he had entered the ruins that the stillness of the air had been naturally broken. Feeling the warmth of the Savior running along his shoulders as its illuminating essence continued up towards the skin of his arms, John pulled his sleeves into his hand, covering himself from its rays.

The rising plume from the courtyard signaled to him that the target environment was saturated with his murderous chemical. Gripping his weapon tightly, he prepared to make his move.

Raising the rifle to his shoulder, John stood from his cover, advancing the last ten meters towards the threshold of the courtyard, surveying its entrance and noting the details of its outer walls. There was no disturbance from within: no coughing, no movement. From his crouched, battle-ready stance, he fast-walked up the sidewalk leading to the open entryway, keeping a steady aim, ready to engage, or rather, destroy, the first deserter he came into contact with.

Each step forward was like a rhythmical drum, the beat of which was orchestrating the crescendo of the soft breeze as it began to dance to his tempo. Picking up speed, it swirled the gaseous cloud through the air.

Recognizing the potential for diluting its potency and effectiveness upon his adversaries, John realized that he only had seconds before losing his advantageous ground. Leaping over the corpse of his first victim, he subconsciously gave his own body over to the spell of rote motions.

Entering through the walkway, the breeze suddenly became a strong gust of air that lifted the thick fog of poison into the heights above, swirling it into the windows and gaping wounds of the war torn structures of the city street. With a cleared visibility,

John was able to catch a glimpse of movement out of the corner of the circular eyepiece of his chemical respirator. Rotating his rifle's sights towards the stirring creature, he found himself staring down the barrel at a bleeding woman lying on the ground, her muffled scream barely audible through the fogged lenses of her gasmask.

The light of the Savior fell upon her as he squeezed the trigger. He heard the crack of his rifle. Through the aperture of his rear sight, he fell into a hypnotic awareness of the bullet as it traveled mid-flight, a sluggish motion of surreal imagery of a projectile shattering into a cloud of particles. Splattering into the concrete behind her, the woman's unblemished silhouette was the resultant effect: an ornamental mural etched upon the wall. Without hesitation, he squeezed the trigger again. As he heard the audible crack of the shot, the stock end of a deserter's rifle caught him across the back of his helmet, breaking the strap of his mask, sending his next bullet to bury itself deep into the ground beside the woman's leg.

Crashing to his knees upon the fragmented slab beneath his feet, John's respirator followed close behind, slamming down beside his knee. The reflective face protector of his helmet subsequently fell into its closed position, covering his face.

Partially dazed, but still running on years of repetitive conditioning, John pulled the knife from the small of his back, stabbing and slashing wildly behind him, thrusting the dagger into the belly of the deserter that had struck him. Ripping the knife out, he slashed it again across the cheek of the man's gas mask causing his enemy to fall backwards, dropping his weapon and screaming out in pain.

Lifting the knife above his head, John prepared to plunge it into the man's heart. The pain in his skull and the throbbing of his neck were justification enough for him to eliminate the rebel from the living.

As the blade made its downward fall, an explosive impact against John's face-shield sent heavy shards of its fibrous material ripping into the skin of his face and the side of his head, tearing away the lobe of his right ear, staggering him with its deafening ring.

Momentarily disoriented by the blow, John stumbled about, shielding his eyes. He could feel the warmth of his own blood oozing from his facial wounds and smearing across the palms of his hands. Through the spaces between his fingers he could see the only deserter that he had not wounded, pistol at the ready. Her hands were trembling and struggling to keep her aim. Her dampened, distressed cry was scarcely audible through the thick rubber of her respirator. His own hearing and sight had been amazingly spared from harm.

Feigning to be struck blind by her bullet, John continued to stumble around moaning and screaming, inconspicuously inching himself closer to her. The woman appeared to be falling for his act. As her weapon began to lower, her attention moved to her wounded mate that lay at her feet.

With her arm within reach, John grabbed the soldier by the wrist, tearing the firearm from her hand and jerking her towards him before throwing her down. She hit the ground hard, landing beside her wounded female companion.

Taking aim at the writhing man groaning at the end of his barrel, John's passing glance caught the eyes of the woman that had shot him. She was staring deep into his soul, as if to plead with him for mercy. She was exactly where he wanted her: witnessing the end of her comrades. He could see the terror in her expression, horrified from behind the plastic windows of her mask. The satisfaction he was experiencing warranted the dramatic delay in all of their executions.

Behind her, the other woman continued to bleed out from her leg, laboring to unstrap her respirator. Panting, pale and sweaty, she deserved her pain, he thought.

As the latches of her mask unhinged under the trembling of her frail, weak fingers, it fell from her face. John stepped back, dropping his aim. In all the years of peering into the eyes of death, he had somehow found himself gazing once again into the familiar sky-blue eyes of a life once lost.

"Don't shoot, John," she spoke through the quivering lips beneath her tears. "It's me, Sofia."

Overcome with amazement and a sudden sense of dread, John looked about in the courtyard, visually taking in the familiarity of the battlefield destruction: it was something real, something that could ground him in reality. All he needed was an item of material value to let him know that he was merely hallucinating.

The womanly apparition appeared all too veritable, too genuine. He could not look into its eyes again without killing it. Raising his pistol towards its head, he fired a single shot. The bullet exited the darkness of the barrel, entering into the world of light. And, just as some unseen force thwarted John's previous attempts, so too did this projectile's end come in the same manner, shattering into a million pieces before his eyes.

As if there was a beckoning from above, John turned his face to the Savior, and began to curse. He was hallucinating... there was no other way to explain what he had just seen.

Over the shoulder of Maryanne, John was standing in the rays of light that fell through the splintered beams that crossed over the yard. Sofia wanted nothing more than to run to his arms and hold him. Ignoring the pains from the wounds in her leg, she fought against her body's desire to stay and rest, giving in to the yearning of her heart.

"John," she called to him. "Please, come to me."

Slipping his helmet off his head, John let it drop to the ground. It landed at his feet, settling beside a crack in the concrete through which a tuft of red grass had grown. Rolling away from him, it settled beside the crimson pool that formed under the dripping blood from the deserter that was struggling to his knees behind him. The hatred was burning him up. He had no desire to give into his wishful thinking. Closing his eyes would make it all go away, he thought.

Undoing the straps that were tangled in her hair, Maryanne crawled beside Sofia. Removing her gasmask, she motioned to her mate, Stephen to remain still.

"That's John, Mary," Sofia said. "He's here to save me."

Removing the backpack from her shoulders, Maryanne unsnapped the pouch on its side, pulling out a small folding knife.

"You're hurt, dear," she said nervously, trying not to call the Sweeper's attention to them. "You're going to be alright, Sofia. We just need to stop the bleeding."

Tearing through Sofia's pant leg, Maryanne exposed the extensiveness of her wounds. Placing a thick, gauze padding upon the gaping holes, she moved Sofia's hands upon the thick pile of absorbent, encouraging her to keep the pressure needed to help alleviate the flow.

"I need to go help Stephen, okay? I'll be right back," Maryanne said, removing her hands from tending to the sites where John's bullet had entered and passed through.

"Maryanne, go get John for me, please," Sofia wept. "I need him by my side."

"I'm sure you do, dear, but not right now. You just keep the pressure on your leg, okay?" she whispered, as she unzipped the top of her sack, anxiously looking over her shoulder at the murderer standing behind her. Maryanne knew all too well what these men were capable of. Whether or not this man was actually Sofia's lost mate made no difference to her. She wanted nothing to do with him.

With her trembling hands, Maryanne apprehensively gathered up the medical supplies necessary to attend to Stephen's wounds. Avoiding any hint of eye contact with the agent, she stood up. Staring at the ground, she began walking towards her comrade.

As she was about to pass by the courtyard's entryway, three men entered through with their guns drawn. Their visors reflected the terror of her expression. Dropping her provisions, Maryanne stood motionless in the firing line of the surviving agents of John's Sweeper team.

"Sit down," one of the men whispered the command, motioning for her to move away from him.

Maryanne immediately obeyed, stepping back and lowering herself back down beside Sofia.

The second agent, seeing John standing with his face to the sky, bleeding from his torn skin and lacerated forehead, kept his sights on Stephen as he moved towards his team leader.

"Is everything alright, John?" he asked.

"I'm not sure," John stuttered, lowering his head towards his three captives.

Touching the torn skin of his ear, John felt the coagulated thickness of his liquid life dripping from his wounds. Wiping his hand across his shirt, the blood smeared, settling upon the creases of its fabric.

"I'm wounded," he said, as his eyes met Sofia's once again.

"Are we going to eliminate them, or are we going to drag them along with us?" the agent asked, unconcerned about his Sergeant's trauma.

Writhing and suffering, Steven's contorted image reflected off of the blued metal of John's pistol as he raised it up from beside his thigh. John could feel the rising burn of anger and hate filling his mind, running through his veins, drawing out from the pores of his skin.

A fool had once called him a god, yet he had not done the deeds of a god. He had not created anything. He had only taken away. What kind of god does that make him? He had been deceived. A god could never be deceived. Sofia was alive. They knew it all along. The flames filled his eyes. They all knew it.

The cause of all her sufferings of the past: that is what I am, John thought. Sofia's bleeding out of a wound caused by my hands. What have I done to cause others to want me to suffer so much? "What had *she* done?" he whispered

Like a thunder's roaring riding upon the tails of lightening, the searing scorn of a decade of destruction poured through him. Three shots fired, three men fell... just like they taught him.

Before the last agent's hollowed corpse could hit the ground, John's pistol landed at his feet.

Staggering over to Sofia, he reached down, tearing the medic's kit from the body of one of his dead comrades as he passed him by. Kneeling down beside her wounded, leg John unzipped the satchel. Removing the rapid-clot material from its paper shell, he placed it into the openings of her wounds. After wrapping a dressing around her injured extremity, he looked into her eyes, worn and tired. There were no words exchanged. Sofia just smiled, watery-eyed and pale. The soothing blanket of her embrace was the first step in a long run leading to the healing of his soul.

CHAPTER THIRTY-FIVE

Maryanne was not quite as forgiving and accepting of John's presence as Stephen and Sofia. As he took the helm of their vehicle, racing it through the city streets of the ruins, speeding and weaving wildly through the debris, John's rough handling of the transporter reminded her of the carelessness of the Security personnel that she used to see blazing their deadly paths through the streets of Basket Town. Having been several years since dealing with those awful experiences, the jarring drive was bringing back all the painful memories of her past.

Struggling to keep the threaded needle steady under the rugged conditions, Maryanne pulled the sharp tip through Stephen's skin as she unevenly sutured close the stab wounds inflicted by John. Although her mate's years of experience under Raw's Security had, up to this time, seemingly purged his mind of reacting to painful stimuli, Maryanne was left feeling a sense of cold nausea with each piercing of the jag. For the first time in their lives together, he was writhing with discomfort.

Lying across one of the side seats with his mate kneeling beside him on the floor, Stephen was cognizant, despite his misery, of the presence of John and Sofia. He was making a conscience effort to maintain control of his outward suffering to the best of his ability.

As John cornered the vehicle around the edge of a fallen building, Maryanne slid across the puddles of Stephen's blood, leaving a smeared track in her wake as she slammed into the opposing side of the transporter. Glaring over her shoulder, she pulled herself back to Stephen's side. The intensity of John's demeanor, not to mention his Agency history, was giving her cause for the increasing suspicion she was beginning to hold regarding his motives in helping them. Seeing Sofia sitting beside him was effecting a burning in her gut. He was obviously experienced behind the wheel, swerving between the waste, running it at top speed while constantly looking back to be sure that they were not being followed... but he was still a Sweeper. The hatred in his eyes bore witness to it.

Exiting the ruins and entering the red sands of the desert, John spied out several air transporters rising high into the atmosphere. The burning blue-white lights of their glow were like shimmering stars visible in the afternoon sky. Following close behind, the billowing smoke of another group of transporters preparing for lift-off was filling the valley just over the peaks, leading John to their point of arrival.

"Where are all those tranporters headed?" John yelled over the rumbling of their engine as he leaned over the steering wheel, gazing up at the thick white contrails.

"Each one's heading towards one of the asteroids that exists on the other side of Raw," Stephen returned answer, cringing under Maryanne's handiwork. "Central's been working on this plan for years. We're finally getting our chance to change things to our advantage."

"But, why the asteroids? Why are they going there?" John asked.

With an expression of disapproval on her face, Maryanne shook her head at Stephen's revealing statements, discreetly mouthing the word *No* in his direction. Shrugging off her concerns, he gave into John's inquisitiveness, grasping in his mind the importance of having a hardened Sweeper on their side.

"Central believes that Golden Planet may exist on one of them. Before the failed uprising on Raw, intelligence was gathered about several military operations taking place in the belt. They think Golden's hidden in there somewhere, tucked away in the crevices of one of those giant rocks."

As the glowing tails of the rising pillars disappeared into the bluish-green of the heavens, John could not help but think back to the day when he and Sofia had entered into the transporter on Labor, completely unaware of the future events that their actions would bring upon them. But the thoughts did not bring back feelings of peacefulness and innocence. Instead, just as he was conditioned to, the images of his mind brought frustration and murderous anger.

"Is there a base over those hills?" he asked, trying to ignore the mental pictures of his past.

"No. Central programmed several stolen airships from Raw, engineering them to land there. Each one is a one-way ticket once it takes off."

"So there's no way to bring them back?"

"It's not that," Stephen paused. "We're anticipating that Golden's forces will prevent most of us from coming home."

"So, you're going there to die?" John asked with amazement at the foolishness of the plan.

"We're going there to reconnoiter. We need specific data concerning Golden's leaders and their primary governing order. It's the only way to defeat them. Every one of us volunteered for these missions, John. We're well aware of the dangers."

Finding it hard to believe that Sofia could get caught up in such a venture, as she was so passive and mindful of the living, he asked her, "Were you going with them?"

It was John's first words to her. Speaking with him for the first time since their last meaningful discourse on that dreadful street in Basket Town, she found it was difficult to express her thoughts verbally. After so many years apart it felt like a dream. It seemed as if at any moment Maryanne's voice would pull her from the world of sleep, back into the violently convulsing reality from which she had known for too long.

"No, John. They were helping me escape. They've arranged a special transporter for me... for us, now. Can you believe it? It's going to take us back home."

Home. John could hardly remember what the word meant on a conceptual level, let alone on an existential one.

"Back to Labor?" he asked.

"Yes. That's where I was headed. I was going to go to our old home in the woods, knowing that, when you were able to, you would go there to find me."

Long lost feelings of sadness and love, emotions of which John had not known for years, attempted to touch him anew. But the cold, unforgiving transformation that had held him captive for so long would not allow it. Ignoring her involvement of him in her plans to return to Labor, he instead delineated the conversation into the obscure.

"I have so many questions, Sofia. I don't even know where to begin," he said.

"I have just as many questions for you, too," she said. "But, for now, I just want you to pay attention to me, okay? Just keep driving, but listen."

Nodding in the affirmative, John was about to add a condition to his agreement, but Sofia cut him off mid-sentence.

"Please, promise me you won't say a word until I'm finished."

Agreeing to her plea with another nod of his head, John felt the gnawing pain of seeing her so aged, not having been by her side during the passing of so long a time. Her youthful beauty was still there... but then again, it was not. He wanted to reach his arm out to her, to hold... the burning anger of converted weakness was filling his mind. Like a well-programmed machine, he returned to his driving.

Knotting off the last bit of thread and cutting it short with her teeth, Maryanne listened to the driver's side conversation from over her shoulder. She wiped the blood from Stephen's body with a damp cloth. Feeling the attention to his wounds waning, Stephen lifted his head as John was nodding to Sofia. Tears were rolling down her cheeks, but he was doing nothing to alleviate them.

"I never gave up the hope that you were alive." Sofia whispered to him. "The days were so hot, and the nights were so cold and lonely, but you were always by my side. We may have been apart for many years, but the Savior allowed me to have you near... near in the person of our son."

Opening his mouth, John was about to ask her if he understood her statement correctly. But Sofia quickly touched a trembling finger to his lips, shaking her head in disapproval. As promised, he returned his eyes to the rolling hills of flowing red sand, keeping the vehicle in its straight path, and remained silent.

Sitting back in her seat, Sofia continued, "It's true. We had a son, John. His eyes were blue, like mine, but his lips and chin were yours. While I carried him within me, you were there. Every time I would look at him after he was born, I was, in some way, looking at you. I even named him after you."

Maryanne realized that Stephen was watching her. He had caught her eavesdropping, and her watery eyes were revealing the anguish of her heart as she listened to her friend explaining the all-to-familiar tragedy of losing a child. Pulling Maryanne close to him, she laid her head down upon his chest. Together they listened to Sofia as she spoke so intimately from her heart.

"He was so beautiful, dear."

A faint smile formed at the corner of her mouth.

"I wish you could have seen him. He had such a radiant smile. He almost never cried."

A blade of the Savior's light slipped through the window, splashing across the dashboard and spilling onto the steering wheel, crossing John's fingers. Sofia watched it changing the shapes of the shadows that surrounded it, casting a sharply defined edge across its path.

"So many people believed that he was actually the One that would change the world. It's so odd to think that anybody would... Strange events took place around him, even while he was in my womb, in the days when we had no idea that he was there."

Sofia paused, contemplating upon the moments with her child. But after a moment she realized that she had not finished her story, and so she continued.

"He's gone now," she said. "But, he never died."

Listening with a subtle hint of disbelief touching him at the back of his mind, John was feeling a growing sense of morbid sadness at their loss. He thought he felt that love that he once had, but again, the wall of fire, the mental restructuring that his mind had been forced through, took control, allowing it to last for only a brief moment before burning up into oblivion.

Sofia sat in silence. Her mind was caught in the moment of the time long past of which she was speaking of.

"What happened to him, Sofia?" John asked, for some reason of which he himself did not understand.

Maybe it was to make more sense out of the violence, or the search for something deeper regarding the strange events that surrounded the child. Either way, it was another life ruined by the strands of time of which he had threaded.

"He just disappeared one day," she replied.

Looking out through her reflection on the passenger side window, Sofia stared at the passing hills and open desert.

"It was such a wild morning. Maryanne and I went into hiding after his birth. Something terribly bizarre happened in the room that day. It was just so odd and frightening."

She was speaking too vaguely for John to fully appreciate the situation of which she was recalling, to comprehend the depth of her story. But even if she had the ability to detail the events more clearly, John's heart was far too concealed under its cloak of blackness to be reached on any emotive level.

"There was so much blood," she continued. "The men that... I'm not really certain what happened that morning. But, it had been several years after his birth when the people began to riot. The battles with Raw's Security forces were taking place on a daily basis. They were making their raids in the housing district when we were found in the hidden place that Stephen had built for Maryanne."

Speaking in stuttering, seemingly disorganized statements, Sofia found it virtually impossible to explain with words the events that had transpired on that fateful day. She tried her best, but only Maryanne and Stephen, as witnesses to the events, could appreciate what she was describing.

"They came into the room for him. He was nearly a young man at the time. There was so much shouting and screaming everywhere. I tried to grab his hand. I tried to pull him away, but... it was so... odd. The brightest light I've ever seen filled the room, but we were safe to look into it. It blinded the Security agents, John, but it didn't harm Mary or me. It was... odd, so odd. When the light disappeared, all the agents fell down dead... and he was gone. Just like that... gone."

Her lips were trembling like the finger that she had placed upon his mouth just moments earlier.

"He was so golden, John. So beautiful."

Trying to reconcile in his mind the hatred that had built up inside of him with that desire to make everything right regarding his past mistakes, John could not help but feel the aches of hopelessness. There was nothing he could do to change what had already been done. He had a son that he would never meet... but the wall of indignation built up in his heart would not allow him beyond that objective fact.

As the light of the Savior bent through the window, it reflected off the glass in such a way that it caught John at the edge of his eye. Piercing through his pupil, it touched the nerves at the back of the orb. He was golden, John thought. *Golden.*

Jamming his foot into the brake, the transporter slid sideways, skidding through the sand. Throwing her hands on the metal bar mounted to the dash in front of her, Sofia braced herself against the sudden change in the vehicle's motion. She could feel the dull thud of Maryanne's body ramming into the rear of her seat. Grinding to an abrupt stop far from their destination, the vehicle became engulfed within its trailing red tail of dust.

"What's going on?" Stephen shouted from the bench.

Looking over the seat, John's expression was difficult to interpret as he unbuckled himself and began to rise. Maryanne crawled away from him, huddling close to Stephen, believing that the Sweeper was about to show his true deadly nature.

"Golden," John said, climbing into the back of the transporter. "I know where you can find it. Those ships are heading to the wrong place. Is there any way to notify Central?"

"Well, yes," Stephen stuttered, sensing the dread that was consuming his companion. "I have a com-system in my rucksack. What's going on, John?"

"Those men and women are being sent to their deaths. They're not going to find anything of worth on those asteroids. There's nothing but soldier farms there."

"Soldier farms?" Stephen questioned. "What are you...?"

"Yes, soldier farms. It's called the Wasp Nest. They breed people out there strictly for the sake of dying in the battles here on Red."

"No, John. That's what they were doing on Raw. They..."

"Stephen, listen to me. Think about it. The war's perpetual. It never ends. Do you really think that they can produce that many soldiers in Basket Town?"

Contemplating John's words, Stephen sat for a moment in silence.

"But you say that you know where Golden is?" he asked.

"I do... but not exactly. There's a handheld computer that Sofia and I brought with us to Raw many years ago. Wherever they took our belongings on that day, you'll probably find that computer. It had the destination to Raw in it. That's how we got there."

"But what about Golden?" Stephen questioned further.

"The cargo bay was full of crates labeled for that planet as well as this one. That ship was supposed to go there, and then, after dropping off Golden's cargo, it was destined for here..."

"But it never had a chance to make it that far," Stephen continued. "I need to get the radio."

"Wait," Maryanne interrupted. "Are you sure about this, Stephen?"

Her look of distrust was apparent. John was a man of blood. But Stephen knew that if he were not a willing defector, their whole squad would have been dead long ago. Placing Maryanne's suspicions aside once again, to her dismay Stephen said to her, "I trust him."

Bowing her head in disapproval, Maryanne slipped her hand off the top of his palm and looked away. Sitting up and hobbling to the rear of the vehicle, Stephen unhooked his backpack from the rack, throwing it to the floor. Unzipping its main compartment, he removed the communications device and set it down. Picking up the transceiver, he turned some dials on its face and began an attempt to make contact with his superiors.

"Central, this is Commander Stephen James of Gamma Formation, Red side, under operation Crimson Flow. How copy?"

There was a moment of radio silence during which Stephen glanced at John. He was sitting at the edge of the driver's seat beside Sofia, waiting impatiently for a response.

After a few seconds, a repeat of his words into the mic resulted in the same outcome, and he began to wonder if they were still operational. With a sigh of frustration, Stephen was about to make one last attempt when a static-riddled voice came through the speaker.

"Commander James, this is Central. Over."

With a deep sigh of relief, the commander put the microphone to his mouth.

"Central, we have a defecting Sweep agent on board ground transportation heading to air rendezvous. How copy?" After a moment of silence the voice returned, "This is Central. Say again. Over."

"Central, repeating: we have a defecting Sweep agent on board ground transportation heading to air rendezvous. How copy?"

There was another momentary pause.

"Copy that, Commander. Can you confirm the identity of the prisoner?"

"Affirmative. Confirmation of agent is in process. Standby. Please note: Sweeper is not a prisoner. It is a defecting product, and is in the process of supporting ground recon. Over."

"Copy that, Commander. Awaiting agent data. Over."

Unfolding the knife that he removed from his shirt pocket, Stephen held his hand out to John and said, "Come over here."

John left Sofia's side, approaching Stephen with cautious suspicion. Maryanne watched him as he knelt down beside the radio.

"Give me your hand," Stephen said, taking hold of John's wrist and placing his palm upward, facing it into the tip of his blade.

Looking him in the eyes, Stephen said, "Don't move. I just need to retrieve something from you."

With a nod of his head, John felt the blade dig deep into his palm. He could feel the warmth of his blood dripping from his hand onto the floor.

"Hold still. I can feel it, it's just a little deeper."

The knife's metal tip vibrated off of a metallic object hidden beneath the hardened layers of his skin. John understood that he was attempting to recover the security chip placed there during his Sweeper training. As Stephen pried the rice shaped article out, John felt a strange release fall from him, as if a layer of low-level energy had been peeled away from his body.

Wiping it clean, Stephen placed the Identifier into a slot at the side of the com-system and plugged in several codes into the keyboard mounted on the machine's lower half. Picking up the transceiver, Stephen said, "Central this is Commander James. How copy?"

"Commander, this is Central. Go ahead."

"Central, data on Sweeper incoming. Over."

"Copy that."

Although Maryanne was steaming over his trustfulness of the Sweeper, Stephen understood her position. If John was speaking the truth, they might be able to end the war without much bloodshed. But, if he was deceiving them, as she believed he was, which was very much a possibility considering his apparent indifference to Sofia's story of the loss of their child, then his trust in John could have a tremendously negative repercussion in their attempts to gain universal control. Times were desperate. He had to make an executive battlefield decision and act accordingly.

Wrapping a dressing around his hand, John returned to his seat up front. Maryanne gave a gestured look at Stephen as if to ask him, "Well, what are we going to do, now?"

After considering his options he drew the mic to his mouth.

"Central I need access to General Montgomery ASAP regarding actual operation target location according to Sweep informant. This is a high priority affair. Over"

CHAPTER THIRTY-SIX

The armored transporter rounded the base of the sandy hill just outside the launch area. Three towering machines stood at the ready, surrounded by the scattering of abandoned vehicles left behind by the recon teams in their haste to take to the skies. The numerous scorched, black circles of melted sand, the effects of the blasts of the recently departed airships, were an immense contrast to the red rolling hills and desert that surrounded them. As John made the final approach, a distant, lone individual standing at the foot of the ramp leading up to one of the air transporters waved him down.

Kneeling between the two front seats, Stephen directed John to their awaiting guide.

"That's our man," he said. "We need to get our gear ready. Sofia help Maryanne get the packs by the door."

Expecting a word of resistance from John, as she assumed that they were leaving for Labor and had no further need of their military accoutrements, Sofia stood up, but waited a moment before vacating her seat. But nothing appeared to be forthcoming from him, as he did not seem to take notice of her. The scab-covered wounds on John's ear and face, filthy, open to the air and in terrible need of attention, were quite unnoticeable up to now. As they were most befitting of his distancing demeanor, Sofia turned away from him, dropping her chin in disappointment. Stephen stepped aside in order to make room for her to pass by before taking the seat up front. Sofia continued to walk off without saying a word. John's injuries would have to wait.

"So, what's the plan, Commander?" John asked as Stephen took a seat beside him.

"I'm not exactly sure. Command wrote on the com-system that communication wasn't secure enough. Our orders are with that man down there," he said, motioning with his eyes to the awaiting soldier.

As Sofia reached the back of the vehicle, she pulled her pack from the hook on the wall. Crawling upon her knees to keep her balance during the turbulent drive, she was about to drag it to the doorway when Maryanne took hold of her by the arm.

"Do you still trust him, Sofia?" she whispered.

Finding it difficult to make eye contact with her due to the forceful nature of her tone, Sofia nodded her head, saying, "I know he's a little different from the last time I saw him. And I know that you don't trust him, but..."

"But, nothing," Maryanne interrupted. "He didn't even flinch when you mentioned your son to him. I think he's working against us."

Lifting her eyes to Maryanne's was not an easy task, especially while such harsh words against John were falling from her mouth. As one who had a disdain for confrontation, Sofia found it difficult on most occasions to speak her mind, but she was not about to let Maryanne lash out in such a manner.

"No, Mary," she said. "You're wrong. I don't fully understand what he's been through, and neither do you. But I love him. And, I know deep down inside, John is still the same man he used to be. It may take some time, but he'll come back."

She began to turn away, taking up her backpack and leaving the antagonistic woman to her skeptical views, but Maryanne took hold of her shoulder, forcefully restraining Sofia against her will.

"Step outside of your fantasy world, Sofia," she said with a spiteful whisper, making sure that the men up front were not aware of their conversation. "Take a good look around. You two were living a dream. The world that you built up in the forests of Blue, it wasn't real... this is real."

Yanking herself free, Sofia brushed off Maryanne's hand, saying, "It was real, Mary. As sure as the Savior is real, and as sure as He helped us when we didn't understand the reality of His being. That home in the forest was real."

"It wasn't. You just got lucky finding your way there," Maryanne snapped.

"Lucky? Mary, how can you say that? We were sent there by..."

"It was just luck," Maryanne said, shaking her head.

For a moment Sofia was speechless. But the reality of the fact that Maryanne had said the words was settling in. Taking up the shoulder straps of her pack, she said to her, "This war has hardened you. You're no different than he is. I love you, Mary. You're like a sister to me. But I won't stand for you to talk to me like that."

Turning back for the last time, with a tearful eye Sofia dragged her baggage away. Maryanne continued to stare at her, expecting her to look back, but she did not. The distinct voices of John and Stephen conversing together were like scalding water poured upon her heart. The war had changed everyone.

As tall as the air vehicles appeared through the front windshield, they seemed to John to have lost their intimidating appeal after his experiences with the skyscrapers in the ruins. Pulling alongside the awaiting deserter, he cut the engine and exited his seat, following Stephen to the rear of their transporter.

The Savior was beating down hot and heavy as the steel door to their armored machine lifted open. Stepping out onto the desert sands, the hum of the idling rockets filling the air, the four passengers made their final exit from the vehicle's stifling confinement.

The last of the deserters approached them, introducing himself as one Captain Banks, a former high-ranking agent from the Security force on Raw. He was a much more mature appearing gentleman than John would have expected to see committed to such a physically laborious duty as a recon mission. His facial features and age-whitened hair were an obvious distraction from the well-maintained musculature of his body.

Stephen, familiar with the Captain from their past Security details, was apprehensive at first. He questioned Banks as to why, of all the other officers, he was the one chosen to stay behind. The Captain explained that he had volunteered after receiving a security message from Central. He went on to explain that, after he had read the dispatch, he realized that a well experienced leader would be needed to complete the task at hand, and without hesitation he insisted that Stephen step down from his duty as Mission Commander, allowing him to take over. Initially, Stephen seemed at odds with the idea. But after reading the message himself and hearing further details of the rationale of Central's thinking, he willingly conceded his post. With Mission Command being turned over to Banks, John watched as the two officers shook hands before making his request.

"Would you let me look at the letter?" he asked, but the Captain refused.

"It contains highly sensitive material," Banks said "I can only divulge its contents to those with a high-level security clearance. But I can tell you that Central did locate your little device. And it has made a huge impact on our plans."

Motioning to Stephen and Maryanne to follow him, the two operators excused themselves from John and Sofia, accompanying their newly assigned Commander up the ramp of one of the airships for a private chat. John folded his arms and watched them as they disappeared into the transporter's storage bay. There was something about the Captain that did not sit well with him.

Taking John by the hand, Sofia pulled him to the open door of the transporter, sitting down on the step of the threshold.

"I've missed you so much, John. I can't believe we'll finally be able to go back to our home," she said. "I knew this day would come. I prayed for it so often."

Disconnected from the conversation, John waited impatiently for the return of his newly found superiors.

"Do you look forward to reading again?" Sofia asked.

Hearing her speaking, but unable to keep his attention, he heard the words from her mouth, but did not discern the particulars of her question. He felt like two creatures in a single body: one yearning to be with his wife, the other desiring to push her away.

The latter was the victor in the psychological battle.

"Uh, yeah. I mean, no. Not really," he stuttered.

"Well, I do," she continued. "I can't wait to get back to our bed, Do you remember...?"

"No, I don't, Sofia. I don't really remember anything," John snapped. "I know that you can't understand it. I'm like a dead man inside. I've done things that you would not believe... that I wouldn't want you to believe."

"I do understand. I really do."

"No. You don't," he yelled, slamming his fist into the side of the ground vehicle's cabin. "You couldn't possibly understand. I have something inside of me, tearing at me everyday. It never goes away. Ever."

Sofia stood up, placing her hand upon his shoulder. She moved closer to him, she longed to be at his side. But he stepped away. It was as if her touch was mere dust as he brushed her aside.

"Don't do that, please. I can tell you I love you. I know I do. But, I just don't know what it is to live anymore," he said.

Backing away, Sofia turned from his face as she tried to hide her emotions. John let his head hit into the cab of the transporter. He was unsuccessfully attempting to relax the anger away.

A witness once more to her sorrow, Maryanne walked out of the airship with Stephen and the Captain just as Sofia turned aside from John. Although she missed the details of their ordeal, in her heart she was glad to finally see Sophia get a glimpse of the Sweeper's soul. It was apparently just as she had suspected: cold and hardened.

"You two need to get on that ship," Stephen said, pointing to the rumbling column of steel waiting to make its departure from the planet. "It's programmed to take you far below your crash-site home. And with plenty of provisions to get you there comfortably and safely."

John was leaning against the wheeled vehicle, and Sofia wondered whether or not he was ready to make the trip with her. Lifting his head from the hot, metal plating of the transporter he stared at the Commander in silence.

"Are you ready to leave?" Stephen asked him.

"You're going to Golden, aren't you?" John asked to the silence of Stephen and the Captain. "There's someone there: the cause of all the troubles of the worlds. This is a death-card mission, isn't it?"

As if they were children caught in a lie, the two officers looked at one another, then back at John.

"It's *sensitive* data, John," Captain Banks said. "I can't say whether you're right or not."

"I know that's what you're going to do," John responded. "And I can tell just by looking at the two of you that neither of you were made for the job. It's not in your eyes."

"What are you talking about, John?" the Captain asked.

"You know what I'm talking about, Banks," John said, pointing at him with the fierceness that Sweepers were notorious for.

Sofia could not comprehend what they were arguing about, what it was that John was accusing them of being too incompetent of performing, but she felt the full breadth of rage that had consumed him. She began to understand Maryanne's fears a little better, as she began to fear him, too.

"There's no one here incapable of completing the mission," Banks said. "We've all done our time in the field."

"You were Security, nothing more. You have no idea what *field time* is," John retorted. "This is a different kind of world."

Swallowing hard against the dryness of his throat, the Captain adjusted his collar. The Sweeper's presence was getting to him.

"This isn't what you're thinking, John," the Captain said, with a light glance at Stephen and Maryanne. "There are three targets on that planet. Each one holds a scepter of power. Each one has the same authority to wage war, to destroy absolutely."

"Now, we don't have all the specifics," Banks continued, "But your computer has given us a starting point. By the time we land on Golden, Central will have enough information for us to finish what we need to."

John was listening intently with a discerning eye upon the men when Banks walked down the ramp, pulling him aside. Quietly setting about with a discussion on the few details that they had concerning the Golden planet, the Captain, although unsuccessful in his endeavor, was careful to avoid letting Sofia in on the conversation.

The airships beside them were currently stocked for a reconnoitering of the asteroids, he explained. Central was in the process of sending another ship to Golden that he, Stephen, and Maryanne would need to locate once they arrived. It would contain all the necessary items for them to fit in with the culture. Its onboard computer would also have more details for them regarding the whereabouts of the *Three*.

While Banks was still laying out the details of the basics of their plan, John walked over to Sofia before interrupting him with a request.

"Let me go with you," he asked.

"John," Sofia said with a startle. "No, don't do this," she begged, taking hold of him by the shirt.

"I don't think we could allow that," Stephen interjected.

John moved Sofia's hand away, stepping closer to Stephen. Maryanne slid behind her mate, fearfully peering around his arm at the Sweeper.

"You don't think you can allow it?" John questioned. "So, you three are going to split up when you get there, is that it? Each one of you will take down a single target each?" he continued, shaking his head in disbelief. "Let the woman stay with Stephen as a team. The Captain and I will work separately. There's no way you'd be able to pull it off otherwise."

Facing John's back, Sofia put her hand upon him, but he ignored her touch.

"John, let's go back to Labor, you and me together. We don't need to fight in their war. It's none of ours," she pleaded.

"It is ours, Sofia," he responded.

Stephen looked at the Commander with a shaking of his head. They were not authorized to allow John into the fold. Although he would make an excellent asset, he was too independent, and Central was recognizing him as a potential threat.

"What about this woman here?" the Captain asked, pointing at Sofia.

"Wait," Stephen interjected, "we can't take him."

The Captain held his hand up, silencing the officer.

"She's going back to Blue," John said.

"Going back?" Sofia was aghast. "I'm going to stay with you, John."

"No, you're not," he answered sternly.

"Oh, yes I am. There's no way..."

"Sofia," he yelled at her. "You're not listening to me. This war *is* mine. It's all mine. You need to get on that ship. After I finish this I'll come home. Now go!"

"No, I'm not going back to Labor alone."

"You don't have a choice," John said, taking her firmly by the arm, directing towards the awaiting airship. "You need to go home."

"No! No, John. I'm not going back there without you," she screamed out, tearing her arm away from him and falling to her knees. "Do you think you're the only one suffering? I've lost things, too. I've lost you. Our son is gone... I don't want to be without you ever again. Please, John. Please, don't make me go."

John could do nothing to stop her crying. And he found it impossible to respond to her needs, as he would have liked to. The burning wall of his heart would not allow it. Watching her prostrate at his feet, all he could see were the eyes of the dead staring back at him, hanging on the targets in his death room back on Raw. He was faced with nearly the same choices that originally brought them to the place where they were now standing. Go back to Labor with Sofia, or take her down another path of destruction. The responsibility of his actions, of her well-being, was all on his shoulders. But unlike that day in their home, when he made the decision for the both of them to head north, to seek the answers he desired, it was all about knowledge, to the solving of a mystery. Now, it was about revenge, about righting what had been wronged.

Looking down at the pathetic love of his life, weeping and frail, John chose the only way he knew how to walk. Taking his first step upon the only clear path at the fork in the road, his mind was now set. Looking to Banks, he said, "I guess you'd better notify Central that you're going to require more provisions for the mission. You have another two man team to provide for."

CHAPTER THIRTY-SEVEN

After the briefing with Central, the five passengers of the air
transporter destined for Golden Planet made their way to
the upper deck of the airship. Securing themselves into the flight
seats, they prepared for lift-off.

As Sofia pulled the restraining straps across her chest, she felt the
breeze of adventure blowing upon her once again. Although he was
still at a standoff with her in regards to her insistence in being present
for the mission at hand, she knew that through John's change of mind,
as it pertained to her return home, she was slowly peeling through the
layers of hardship that had covered over his heart for so many years.
Eventually she would reach that core and find her true love waiting.

Buckling himself into the chair, John recognized the frustration building inside of him as he worried about keeping Sofia out of harm's way. Still trying to keep focused on the assignment, especially as they destined themselves once again for an unknown world, he was consumed by a burdening uneasiness of not being fully in control of his own destiny, let alone Sofia's.

Up in the flight control room, Banks and Stephen made their final checks upon the ship's systems. Calling out through the onboard speakers, Stephen turned off the automatic launch sequence, choosing rather to inform his crew manually.

"Engine checks are a go. We have ten seconds to lift off," he said.

With the head pads obscuring her view, the tip of Maryanne's nose was visible to Sofia across from where she was seated. The movement of the ship was steadily growing more erratic under the intensifying vibration of the transporter's engines as it began to rev up, high pitched and whining. Sitting on the other side of her, John's eyes were closed. He appeared to be deep in thought, ignoring the coming flight.

With a burst of flames and thick, black smoke, the pointed, steel machine began to rise above the surface of Red, leaving its charred fingerprint stained upon its sandy crust. The surface of the red planet below was speedily falling away, its hills and valleys shrinking into obscurity. Passing through the greenish-blue expanse, its voyage would take it into the darkness of space.

It had been so many years since the day John first made contact with the red planet. The surreal atmosphere of the moment caused by the events of the past twelve hours seemed almost artificial: a trick of his mind. He was always so certain that he was meant to die there. He found it hard to believe that he would not be stepping foot upon its bloody soil anytime again in the near future.

The unknown is an impossible thing for the mind to grasp: there is just nothing there to conceptualize, to reconcile the thoughts with, nothing to prepare for or against. Golden World was one of those oddities. Each man and woman on the transporter would, eventually, be getting acquainted with its actual existence, but what he or she would find at the end of the journey, no one could tell. There was no point of reference to start from, with the exception of a few items of food and luxury from the crates on Labor. It was all a mystery.

Traversing space to such a distance from the Savior was beginning to physically make its mark, as the coolness was settling into the internal atmosphere of the transporter. With experienced pilots at the helm, who understood the inner workings of the ship, the passengers were able to get a glimpse through the camera system of the distant planets, like tiny balls, encircling a bright sphere of flaming light.

The Savior, from such a far-off view, was an illuminating joy for Sofia to see. Having never witnessed the worlds around them from such a perspective helped her mind to grasp the enormity of His domain with a greater appreciation.

To John, the images on the screen helped him to realize the vastness of his actions. If they were able to achieve what he believed to be their goal, the entire world system would fall into new hands. The idea of turning the tides on the powers-that-be gave him a feeling of moral purpose and empowerment, something he had lacked for so long. It also helped to alleviate his anger, allowing him to periodically peek over the burning wall of rage. Only time would tell whether or not anything would come from their sacrifices, or if they would, like so many brave fools before them, disappear into the obscurity of historical failures.

As the somberness of the mood of the occupants of the transporter seemed to be unanimous, with the exception of Sofia, very little words were exchanged throughout the trip. Meals were consumed in quietness. Sleep was the most common activity. They were, according to the computer's calculations, forty-nine hours until touchdown. The anxiousness for the time to fly away was quite apparent in the short-tempered statements that fell from the mouths of the disquietedly awaiting crew.

Maryanne, Stephen and Banks seemed to be privy to more information than they were letting on to. Ever since descending the ramp on Red, their demeanors seemed more cold and calculating than before their meeting, not too dissimilar to John's. Perhaps, Sofia thought, they were simply making the mental preparations necessary for the task they were embarking on. Whatever the reason, she definitely felt out of place among such an atrabilious crowd. Leaving them to themselves, she lost herself in her own imaginative world, wandering with her and John's son through the warm, thick green of the forests back on Labor.

"Please, Savior, let these days be over quickly. I just want us to go home."

CHAPTER THIRTY-EIGHT

The roar of the reverse thrusters began to kick in as the aircraft entered the atmosphere of Golden Planet. Descending rapidly towards its surface, the tingling of John's gut was nothing new, and he paid little mind to its stimulating effect.

Sofia could see his hand grasped around the armrest beside her. She desired to place her hand upon his arm, but refrained for fear of setting off another one of his frequent outbursts.

Unlike the lift-off a few days earlier, Maryanne was nowhere to be seen, having rather taken a seat above with the two other men in the pilot's room. Throughout the excursion, she seemed more and more to distance herself from Sofia's friendship. With little more than passing glances, communication between them had all but ceased.

The whir of the thrusters began to peak. John and Sofia felt the crushing sensation of their bodies as they sank back into the padding of their seats: the transporter was about to make contact with its landing zone.

Casting a final, brief look at John before they hit the ground, Sofia could see the lights reflecting off the beads of sweat forming about his lip and forehead. His uneasiness about the mission was written on his face.

As they felt the transporter meet the hard surface of the planet, John unhesitatingly unbuckled himself and exited the chair.

"Let's go," he said sharply, moving towards the floor hatch, which led to the ladder below.

Without waiting for the rest of the team, he opened the circular door at his feet. Ordering Sofia to descend to the lower decks, he followed close behind.

In the large bay area at the bottom of the ship, they waited for several minutes while Stephen and the others made the descent. His business on Red was always decorated with a sense of urgency, and he detested the slow and steady movements of his elder commanders.

As they reached the bottom, Stephen dropped a facial expression upon John that said, "This is it." Nothing more was conveyed in his eyes. He and Maryanne walked over to the bay door. Using a handheld computer that was similar to the one John had obtained from Labor, they set the motors of the gate rumbling. Soon after, the door started to rise. It's teeth were a familiar sight to John. Like a leviathan whose mouth they were about to enter, the black, dampness of the rainy environment outside was revealed, dreary and haunting.

Through the trickling drops of water falling from the sky, they could see that the programming engineers at Central had done an incredible job of organizing the mission. The streams of steam rising from the engine of the unmanned air transporter that they were to rendezvous with waited patiently across the way for them, intermittently visible through the dispersion of its exterior flashing lights. It appeared that all the provisions were delivered as promised.

Stepping out into the rainfall, the five-man team descended the ramp, hopping off at the end of its metallic hand and onto the soft, muddy soil. Stephen held his arm around Maryanne, cringing with each step as he grabbed at the wounds of his abdomen. Sofia, on the other hand, pushed herself to conceal the suffering she was experiencing from the mangled tissue caused by John's bullet. He had not wanted her to come along with him as it was, and she was determined not to be a hindrance to him. The strobe of lights, like halos of flashing blue, revealed the fallen trees that surrounded the landing zone, burned and torn, creating a circular perimeter around the two aircraft.

"There's no turning back now, is there, John?" the Captain said, shielding his eyes from the wind.

John ignored him. There was no reason to respond to such meaningless rhetoric.

The door of their former transporter began to close behind them, and with it, the light of the fluorescent glow from its holding cell was slowly taken away. As the one door fell, the bay door to the unmanned craft began to rise. Parked inside they could see three wheeled transporters lined side-by-side, the likes of which neither member of the team had ever seen.

From a distance it was quite obvious that they were different from those of their past experiences. Rounded at the corners, shiny and aerodynamically designed, they were held to a higher standard of craftsmanship than the standard Labor and Raw vehicles. The windows were tinted black, and each of the four rims of the tires was chromed and radiantly bright. Decorated with silvery grills, and headlights that stood out from the bodies of the vehicles, they had a distinct panache that was hard to ignore.

Maryanne accompanied Stephen and Banks to the rear of the vehicles, as if they had held to a pre-knowledge of the presence of what they would find in the trunks. Opening the center transporter's rear quarters, Banks pulled out a hard, gray suitcase that was three times as long as it was wide. Out of the rear of the other vehicles, Maryanne and Stephen performed the same maneuvers. Setting the cases on the floor, they typed their pin numbers into the interfaces under the handles. After a clicked release of the locks, they opened the lids.

Sofia and John moved closer to Stephen, looking over his shoulder to get a better look at the contents inside his case. There were several gadgets embedded within gray, foam slots, a few magazines filled to capacity, and multiple suppressed handguns. John could make out a stash of high explosives tucked away in the corners. The keys to the transporter's ignition system were paper-wrapped inside a clear, labeled container.

Opening the door to the rear seat of one of the vehicles, Banks retrieved the dangling, plastic-draped packages that awaited him. Wrapped about wooden hangers, the teams' suits and dresses, crafted of fine material and tailored specifically to each individual, was readily handed out.

"It's quite apparent that they want us to fit in with the locals," the Captain said as he undressed down to his underwear and began redressing into the attire of Golden's culture.

Following his lead, the rest of the team began to remove their battle dress uniforms and don the fanciful clothing of the wealthiest of the worlds.

Smooth and silky, John felt awkward slipping into the shirt and jacket of the black suit that was assigned to him. Not having knotted a necktie since he was a youth on Labor, he sheepishly asked for the assistance of Stephen who was standing at his side. Once fitted with his new wear, the only comfort of familiarity he could find was when he placed the pistol into his shoulder rig holster.

"Here, hold still," Stephen said, as he strapped a band around John's neck, centering it upon a circular hub just under the lump of his throat. Maryanne, paying no attention to her person, assisted Sofia in the same manner. Just as she worked on Raw, Maryanne moved her hands nimbly and efficiently. Although Sofia tried to make eye contact with her, she continued with her duty, pretending to be completely unaware.

"What are these?" John asked.

"This is how we'll communicate from this point on. Press this button to actuate the mic," Stephen said depressing a flattened nub at the side of the device. Everyone in the party will hear you. "Here," he continued, handing John an electronic earpiece. "Place it as far into your ear as you can get it. We don't want anybody getting suspicious."

John pressed the device into his ear canal. There was an initial blurb of mild static. Banks held his hand to his throat.

"Can everybody hear me?" he asked.

His voice came through loud and clear in John's ear, as if the man were standing directly beside him.

"I need everyone to line up. We need to make this briefing short," Banks ordered.

Gathering at the back wall of the cargo area, the Captain, beginning with Stephen, began handing out the assignments by way of individual handheld computers. As Banks made the rounds, stepping in front of John and Sofia, he placed the apparatus in John's palm, patting him on the shoulder.

Turning on the system as he took it from the Captain's hand, John's face began to glow as the screen immediately lit up. Much to his surprise, his target was merely drawn as a silhouette, with the only description being that it was a male that apparently lived at the address set in the box beside the image.

"We have three individual targets to work with, and three hours before this ship leaves. Central has deemed these to be the highest of priorities," Banks said.

Sitting back upon the rear bumper of the center vehicle, he continued, "Apparently they're considered *weak*. They'll give into any demands we make if we can get to them. Central believes that they alone hold the key to ending this conflict and shutting down Golden's ruling government... and with its demise all of their other installations will fall. If you're not back here before the doors close, you're stuck here," Banks said with a queer expression directed at Stephen.

Maryanne's eyes were cast upon the floor in front of her. To Sofia, it seemed as if she was praying, but she nodded in the affirmative. Perhaps she was merely pondering on their task at hand. To John, it seemed as if the three of them were devising plans of which neither he nor Sofia was to have an involvement with.

"I need all the cases placed into this vehicle," Banks commanded, throwing his thumb over his shoulder at the center transporter behind him.

Walking over to John, he leaned into him, whispering into his ear and pointing at the transporter on his far right, "I'm directing this at you only. I know you don't want Sofia to have involvement with the true nature of this mission. From this point on, you're Team Three, I'm Team One and they're Team Two. What you're carrying is all you'll need. Here are the keys to this vehicle. Find your target. Get all the information you can out of it, no matter what it takes. Get that data to Central… then eliminate the threat. Do you understand, John?"

Looking him in the eye, Banks could see that John thought it a foolish question. The Sweeper was not going to answer him. He also understood that John did not believe that he was truly ready, and that burned his conscience. For deep down inside, Banks knew he was not certain himself if he could make his kill.

The unintentional smile out of the corner of his mouth was all John could give in answer to his superior. Without saying a word, he walked away from the Captain, kneeling down and locking the suitcase before placing it in the center vehicle's trunk.

As he stood up and approached his assigned transporter, he said to Sofia, "Get inside. Let's get this over with."

"Three hours, John," Stephen called out.

"I know. We'll be here," he replied as he opened the door and climbed inside, shutting himself in.

As the motor of the transporter began rumbling, Sofia looked across the room at her friend. Maryanne silently watched her from Stephen's side. There was no expression, no words. Opening the door, Sofia sent her a last smile of goodbye… but with no returning salutation, she looked away uncomfortably and climbed into the vehicle, closing the door behind her.

"Wait," Maryanne, exclaimed, holding up her hand. But it was too late.

As the transporter descended from the airship, disappearing into the foggy darkness outside, Sofia was oblivious to Maryanne as she ran down the ramp to see them off. She never heard the last words falling from her trembling lips as she cried out to her, "Take care, Sofia. Be safe."

The dreariness of the rain falling during the night's drive was undercut by the swirling kaleidoscopic display of colors reflecting off the bottoms of the low-hanging, cloud ceiling hovering over the distant city of Golden. Driving with as high a velocity as seemed safe to him on such a slippery, rural road, John was determined to make it to their destination and finish their part of the business before the first hour had elapsed. Looking down at the glowing hands of his watch, he had no idea what the exact hour of the day was, his timepiece was still synched to the hours on Red. But, a momentary clearing in the thick, blackness of the sky allowed him to capture the dim light of the Savior at its noontime apex: it was mid-day, yet it was as black as the darkest of nights. The Savior appeared as just an extraordinary bright star in the sky.

The hypnotically steady rhythm of the windshield wipers screeching back and forth, silhouetted against the backdrop of the vehicle's headlights made Sofia's eyes heavy. With the dull ache of her leg burning up a great deal of her energy, it wasn't long before she fell into a deep sleep.

John watched her head slump to the side as she breathed heavily under the exhaustion of the emotional trauma she had been through. With the feelings of heartache making their way to the surface of his conscience, the fiery wall began to rise. Before it could build to the full strength of its barrier, John reached over and brushed the hair from her face, and continued driving.

The lights flashing upon Sofia's closed eyelids, coupled with the familiar sound of brass instruments accompanied by a woodwind harmony, brought her mind to that suspended mental state between sleep and wakefulness. As if it were all a dream, she could hear the music so lively and real. The lights of their bedroom were so bright and golden, reflecting off the brass decorations that adorned their home.

As Sofia opened her eyes, she found John by her side.

"Hello, dear," she said, hardly able to comprehend that the whole ordeal of the past had not been one long nightmare.

"We're almost there," he said coldly.

Sitting up to the sound of a blaring horn from a passing vehicle, Sofia was drenched with the neon glow and music of the city: a living, rainbow-fantasy land of vibrant hues and jazzy music that poured through the windshield and bloomed upon the interior of their transporter. Rolling down her window, she allowed the soft drops of rain to enter in. The dull melody of the live bands outside filled her ears, full and rich in their tones, sautéed over with the laughter of the citizens of Golden as they walked under the dryness of their umbrellas, lining the sidewalks at the various fine establishments that decorated their streets. They appeared to be drunk with happiness and over-abundance. Thousands upon thousands of people strolling through a concrete wonderland where no one seemed to exhibit the misery so prevalent on every one of the previous planets they had visited.

With the traffic moving at such a slow and inconsistent pace, Sofia was able to take in the details of the lavishness of the city's architectural beauty. Carved with statues of men and women, children and animals, the layers of brass fixtures and light poles that streamed along the walkways... it was over-stimulating to the brain, and an appropriate superfluous-ness for a citizenry so absorbed and preoccupied with itself that the sufferings of others, and a war that threatened to tear apart the binding threads of their fragile society, appeared non-existent.

Pulling the handheld computer out of his coat pocket and flipping it on, John tapped the screen just below the target's address, bringing up a detailed map that was leading them in real-time to his location. Propping it upon the dashboard, he ignored the present celebratory environment, refusing to let his mind get caught up in the overabundance of the lifestyle of the people of wealth, as it had no bearing upon their mission. Mumbling under his breath at the slowness of the traffic, he squeezed the steering wheel until his knuckles were glowing white.

As the closing of the first hour was nearing, John began to get more impatient. Realizing that they only had a few blocks left to traverse, but that it might take another hour, perhaps more, under the present conditions of the flow, he looked back over his shoulder. Without hesitation he cut their vehicle to the right hand lane, attempting to find a parking spot along the curb of the street.

"We need to get out and walk the rest of the way," he said.

"Walk? Why? It's raining out there," Sofia commented, being cognizant of her tones and the soreness of her leg, trying not to offend his prideful leadership.

"We're not going to make the three-hour time if we don't," he said, slamming his hand on the dash as they came to another stop in the road.

"John, it's alright. We'll make it."

Sofia made the attempt to calm him with her smile, but he was making a conscious effort to ignore her innocent remarks. He understood that she believed that this was a mere recon mission. She was purposefully kept out of the loop regarding the assassination objective. There was no thought in her mind that violence was the end product of their journey on the planet.

With no end in sight to the multitudes of vehicles lining the streets ahead of them, John picked up the handheld and slipped it back into his pocket. Pinching the communications device at his throat he whispered into it, "This is Team Three leader. Abandoning vehicle and moving on foot, how copy, Team One?"

Banks' voice returned immediately, "Do what you have to do. Time's running out and you need to be at that transporter before it takes off. Over."

"Roger that," John whispered, as he unbuckled his seatbelt.

"What are you doing, John?" Sofia asked in concern.

"We're getting out right now."

"But what about the transporter?"

"We're leaving it here. When the time comes, I'll get us another one," he said, slowing the vehicle to a stop in the middle of the busy street.

Opening the door and stepping out to the greetings of horns and cursings from the occupants of the vehicles behind them, John ignored their jeers. Walking around their transporter, he assisted Sofia out the door and onto her feet. Taking her by the hand and pulling her onto the sidewalk, they disappeared into the strolling crowds.

Pretending to be looking over a message on his handheld, John discreetly picked up a folded umbrella that was left hanging from a railing at the front of a restaurant. Opening it up, he blocked the cold drops of the sky from falling upon them.

Directed into a narrow alleyway that crossed to the streets on the other side, Sofia fought against the pain in her leg, refusing to limp in John's sight. Bringing them closer to the target's location faster than would have been possible had they remained with their transporter, John had it firmly planted in his mind that they would not be stranded on Golden once the three hours had expired. With several shortcuts becoming readily available to them by leaving the vehicle, he guessed that they would be losing at least thirty minutes from his former estimation... if everything went smoothly.

As they neared the residential area of the city, the rain began to subside turning, instead, to a light mist that hovered about in the breeze. The street's occupants drastically thinned out. John no longer needed to force his way through the throng, allowing him to pick up the pace. Sofia's ability to maintain the agonizing stride that John was demanding was effectuated only by her will to keep him in the dark about her current condition.

Turning the corner of the final stretch, both John and Sofia could see the target's building from across the intersection: an apartment at the corner where two streets met. Waiting for a clearing in the traffic, they held each other's hands as they crossed the asphalt road. Stepping onto the sidewalk just outside the complex, Sofia took in a breath of relief, discreetly placing the comforting pressure of her hand upon the bandaged wounds of her thigh.

Keeping within the shadows of the alley at the far side of the building, John took extra precautions to be sure that they were not seen. If there was somebody watching them, hidden behind one of the darkened windows, he thought, neither he nor Sofia would be recognizable to any degree of precision.

Pinching his microphone, John spoke into it once again, "This is Team Three leader. How copy Team One?"

Banks once again returned his voice without hesitation.

"Go ahead, Team Three."

"We're outside the target's apartment. We need more details. Over."

"Hold for further instructions."

John sighed and placed his hand on the side of the building.

"It's okay, John. It's almost over," Sofia said, trying to console his anger.

Banks' voice returned, "Team Three leader, this is Team One. How copy?"

Frustrated with their formal radio procedure, John spoke harshly into the mic, "Just give me the room number, Banks!"

There was a moment of silence. Then, in a tone of irritation, Banks returned, "Three-three-one-alpha. Over."

Taking Sofia by the hand, John mumbled, "It's about time."

CHAPTER THIRTY-NINE

Entering the apartment lobby was like entering their home back in Labor's forest. The shininess of the brass, the lights dangling off the ceiling, the rugs decorating the wood flooring, nearly everything, including the smells of flowery perfumes, felt comforting and familiar.

A red rug lined the rich, wooden steps leading to the upper stories. Sofia looked at them with disdain. She foresaw the pain that was in store for her upon scaling such a steep slope.

As they began the ascent cautiously looking about their surroundings, John noticed that the most prominent entity of Labor, the Security, was nonexistent. The governing agency of Golden was more than confident in the security of its distant location in the universe, he thought.

The sleek, dark banister was Sofia's best friend during the climb, allowing her to place the majority of her weight on something other than her own wounded extremity. The muffled laughter and brassy music of the hallways, spilling through the doors of the apartment complex, flooded her ears with the drunken revelry of the structure's occupants.

As they stepped onto the final leg leading to the third floor, they passed by an elderly couple that kindly smiled at them, greeting them as if they were old acquaintances before passing by. Despite her suffering, Sofia seemed quite pleased with their good-natured demeanor, while John had to force a smile in order to avoid looking too out of place.

Upon reaching the target's floor, the ascending numerical order on the doors revealed to them that the room with which they were seeking was only a little further down the hall.

"Which room number are we looking for?" Sofia whispered.

Pulling her behind him, John turned to her and said, "Just walk behind me. I'll take care of everything."

"But isn't there anything that I can do to help?" she asked.

John came to a rest. The racing of his mind made it difficult to concentrate on anything other than the objective at hand. But, despite the fact that he was so near to bringing a closure to the mission, that he was about to make one last revenge-kill upon his true enemy, he opened his mouth and spoke, "Remember when I told you that I wanted you to return to Labor, but you wouldn't listen to me?"

Sofia nodded in affirmation.

"What we're about to do... what I'm about to do, is the exact reason I didn't want you to come along. I'm going to be doing exactly what I was forced into during those years that we were separated. I don't want to tell you what that means. But I'm giving you the option to come with me, or stay here. And, I'm telling you right now, if you choose to go with me, your life, your whole outlook on everything in the world, may change, just as mine has. And in a way that you never meant for it to."

Rubbing the moisture of her palms together, Sofia contemplated her options for a brief moment. She was still so in love with him. And she could see that, hidden under the rough exterior, John was still the same boy that she had known many years ago. She did not understand his cryptic language. Making up her mind on the spot, she answered him, "I love you, John. No matter what happens, I don't ever want to be away from you again."

"Okay," he said, taking her by the hand. "Let's finish this together."

Approaching his target's living quarters, John could see that the brass numbers on the door correlated precisely with Banks' data. He could hear a muffled laughter from within. As he pulled the pistol from his holster, Sofia limped back, wide-eyed and startled.

"What are you...?" she began to ask, but John placed his hand over her mouth.

"I told you, Sofia. You're not going to like what you see. But I still need you to stay quiet, okay?" he said, uncovering her mouth.

As his hand dropped from her face, a sudden, nauseating realization, like black ink spilling over her heart, fell upon her. By going along with John on the mission, she was consenting to enter into his nightmare, to be an active participant of his violent world, and she dreaded the consequences.

The absence of any locked resistance of the doorknob never changed John's expression, even as he found the entrance into the room to be of little concern. He was not surprised in the least to find such a lacking security system in place.

The brass hinges of the door were smooth and silent as he gently moved it aside. A tall lamp that stood at the far end of, what appeared to be, the living room, dimly lit the marvelously decorated walls. Leading Sofia inside, John closed the door behind them. Silently walking across the carpeted floor, he led her to a darkened corner, hidden behind the end table of a long couch.

The laughter and conversation of the people in the next room were now clear and boisterous. Listening intently to their inflections and pitches, John determined that there were two elderly men and their wives having a sit down for a late afternoon lunch. According to his watch they were now past the first hour, heading into the thirty-minute mark of the next.

Pulling back with a slight force on the slide of his pistol, he made sure that there was a cartridge already chambered. Then, with a look of concern, he said to Sofia, "Don't move from this position. If you need to get away from the things you're about to hear, you can close your eyes and cover your ears. It's going to be terrible once I enter that room, but you need to stay here for your safety and mine. Okay?"

Sofia did not like what she was hearing. She was scared, and the feeling of heavy nausea permeated her entire being. But she could see in John's eyes that he was serious, dead serious, and that perhaps there was a greater good that was supposed to come from all this.

Maryanne used to explain to her, with regards to the war they were waging, that the deaths of a few would be the saving grace of the many. Although Sofia never fully understood the rationality behind the concept, she used to let Maryanne continue on as if she was always correct. Sofia never advocated for other options, never gave Maryanne food for thought as to why someone would hold to a differing view... and here she was in the same boat with John, and still, she could get herself to say nothing. She was angered against her own weakness. She had a chance to possibly avert the senseless violence that was about to occur. But something inside of her was preventing it, as if she believed that John would not actually go through with the harm of these strangers.

John waited for a moment. Sofia's silence was enough of an answer for him, and he knew that he had to act fast. Leaving Sofia hidden in the shadows, he sneaked off, drawing closer to the voices, pausing at the threshold of the dining area. Peering around the corner into the adjoining room, he was unnoticeable, essentially invisible for the moment, as the two couples merrily went about their business.

The face of the man sitting at the head of the table had a curious familiarity, as if John had recognized him from an event in his past. To the elderly man's right hand sat his wife, covering her lips as she laughed with a mouthful of food. She carried on with the aged woman sitting in front of her.

Entering the room, John's target stopped mid-laughter, turning pale to the surprise of his wife and their guests.

"Dear. What's the matter?" the old woman asked him.

"Dave, are you alright?" the man sitting beside him, concerned and taking hold of his arm, called out.

Oddly enough, the second man, John thought, was unnervingly familiar in his own rights. Removing the napkin from his lap, the target placed it on his plate.

"May I help you, young man?" he asked with a trembling hesitation.

To the astonished gasps of everyone in the room, they turned to look upon John. Stepping into the dining room, he walked to the far end of the rectangular table.

"What's your name?" John asked bringing the pistol level with the old man's head.

"Arlington. My name's David Arlington," he responded, raising his open hands into the air. "Have we met before?" the elderly target questioned, as if he, too, felt that same sense of déjà vu that John was experiencing.

Unable to immediately place his face, and realizing that he was wasting time, John left off trying to identify the man, returning once again to the mission objective.

"You have some information that I need, and you know what I'm talking about. Where is it?"

"I'm not sure I know what you're referring to, young man," Arlington said with a hesitant, but nervous laugh.

Pointing the pistol at his wife, John said to him, "You don't want to make this harder than it needs to be. You know what I'm after."

Taking her husband by the arm, Arlington's wife cried out to him for protection.

"I'm going to get what I want one way or another," John said, gritting his teeth.

The old man shamefully looked upon his attending guests. He was fearful, probably for the first time in his life, and he was just as weak as Central had believed him to be.

"It's on my computer in the bedroom drawer. It has everything you need," he said.

Arlington's elderly friend grabbed him by the arm, exclaiming, "David, what are you doing?"

"Sofia," John called out. "Go to the bedroom and search the drawers. There's a handheld inside one of them. I need you to bring it here."

Upon his command Sofia obeyed his order, running down the hall that extended away from the living room. Pale and sweating profusely, she entered the sleeping chambers. The shaking of her hands was outside her control as she stopped to look around, attempting to straighten out her thoughts. There were so many drawers and doors, closets full of clothes and more drawers. Randomly choosing a starting point, she began digging frantically through the nearest set, throwing out the contents haphazardly onto the floor.

Arlington and his friend seemed to be at odds with regards to the choices being made. The elderly gentleman seemed crushed by his decision, but he was not going back against it. His companion, on the other hand, was getting more bold and threatening, standing up and pointing at John.

"Are you a leader for the resistance? Or, are you just one of their pawns? How dare you come in here demanding anything of us," he yelled.

The burning in John's eyes was like the consuming fire he felt on the battlefields and in the training room of death.

"You need to sit down, old man," John whispered coldly.

Arlington's companion looked back at him with astonishment, as if he had never been talked down to.

"Are we just going to stand here and take this, Dave? This man's a mere dog, a disgrace to humanity."

Fearfully, Arlington stood up. Taking his friend by the arm, he said, "Corona, please, you need to calm down."

Corona's eyes were deep and menacing, taking John back in time to a day long ago, to a place in the distant, dark past. He was sitting at a sterile table. The General was sitting in front of him.

"John we have some bad news," he said. "Sofia's dead."

Lieutenant Corona chuckled under his breath, figuring John to be unattentive to his surroundings due to the traumatic news he had just received.

A single step in Corona's direction was followed up with a question from John, "Did Sofia die, Lieutenant?"

Corona looked at him with startled curiosity.

"How is it that you know my rank?" he asked suspiciously.

Sofia entered the room shouting, "John I found it!"

Pulling the handheld from his pocket, John kept his eyes on the two officers as he handed his computer to her.

"Go back to the other room," he said. "Plug the two machines together and follow the prompts on the screen."

As Sofia was about to leave the room, she had her first look into the fearful eyes that belonged to the voices she had been hearing. The men and their wives seemed so helpless. Seeing her hesitate, John nudged her through the threshold. Returning back to the living room, she sat down upon the soft cushions of the couch. Plugging the two handhelds together, Sofia began the process of uploading the data to Central.

Corona had not answered his question, and John eyes were searing through him like hot coals.

"So, Lieutenant, is she dead?" John asked once again, slowly inching closer.

The old man began to lose heart, cowering behind his wife.

"You were searching for the One, remember?" John questioned. "You were sent to Raw, and that really put a wrinkle in whatever plans you had for that day."

Corona's image of John was being brought into focus as he suddenly remembered the event... the day when they sent John to the Sweeper training. Realizing that he was standing face to face with one of his own cold-blooded assassins, his legs began to weaken, and he fell back into his chair.

"Sofia, you need to close your ears now, dear," John hollered out.

"John," her voice returned, soft and innocent, he had not called her by that endearing term for, what seemed, an eternity. "Is everything alright?"

"Just stay in the other room and close your ears," he said.

Creeping up to the dining room entrance, taking one last look around the corner, Sofia could see the two couples huddled close together, weeping and begging for their lives. Entering in, she placed her hand upon John's back.

"You don't have to do this. It's not right."

Hardened in face, he turned to her and said, "They did this to themselves. Now go."

Sofia could see that he was not in the mindset to rationalize with. Stepping away from him, she took one last look at the cowering party before hobbling back into the living room, kneeling down beside one of the couches. She wanted to close her ears. She was terrified for the strangers. Lifting the skirt of her dress, she unwound the bandage that John had placed earlier upon her wound. It smelled raw and sickly. The redness and pain around the swelling signified something more pernicious was taking place within her body than she could comprehend. With the pressure of her palm pressed into her leg, Sofia rested her head upon the arm of the couch beside her and wept.

"We did what we had to do, John," Arlington spoke, consoling his wife in his arms. "We were under orders, just like you are now."

It seemed so farcical and humorous to John that these once proud men were being brought so low, begging as they were. He could not help but think of how ridiculous they looked. He wanted to laugh at them. He wanted them to feel his pain.

"Do you know how many wives I've taken from their husbands? Or how many husbands I've taken from their wives?" John asked Corona.

"No, I don't," the old man stuttered.

"Well, how about children?" John continued, directing his attention to Arlington. "How many parents do you think will never see their children again because of my hands?"

"Too many, John, too many. It's a terrible world out there. I wish I could change it for you, take back everything that happened that day," Arlington said.

"You've made me watch my wife suffer in more ways than you'll ever know, Lieutenant," John shouted, pointing the barrel of his pistol at Corona's wife. "Look into her eyes. It's your turn to suffer."

Corona had only a fraction of a second to look upon his wife, to stand up and take hold of her while she still had life in her, before he was forced to watch her become a hollowed corpse with the light snap of John's handgun. The wild screams from Arlington's wife echoed throughout the room as the deceased woman buried her face in her husband's chest. Corona felt her fall away from his arms, dropping face first into the neatly prepared meal set upon her plate. Her neck hyperextended as the weight of her body pushed into her chair, allowing her to slump under the table, falling to his feet.

Aghast with horror, a muffled, feminine scream trickled from Corona's open mouth. In the same manner that the bullet had pierced his wife's temple, leaving its trail of blood and bony matter splattered upon the plush carpet behind him, so too did he succumb to the same fate.

Arlington held up his hand to John, "Don't shoot, sir. Please, spare us."

There was a moment of quietness. And Sofia found the courage to remove her hands from her ears.

"John?" she whispered.

Two snaps, like the crackling of burning wood, echoed off the walls of the living room followed by the sound of dead weight hitting the floor. Rounding the corner of the dining room entryway,

John approached her, picked up the handheld computers from the floor beside her legs, and held his hand out to her.

"We're finished here," he said, "Let's go home, now."

Although those were his words, Sofia could see by the expression of his face that his heart was not ready to allow his old self to come back from the dead. Exiting Arlington's apartment, they closed the door behind them. Working their way in as nonchalant of a manner as they could, they descended the stairwell and headed out the front door of the building.

The street was still as black as night, and the rain continued to drizzle down. Stepping off the entryway stairs, they headed down the shimmering, wet sidewalk, retracing their path back to the airship. Talking into his microphone, John whispered "Team One leader, this is Team Three. How copy?"

With no return answer, John repeated his message, "Team One leader, this is Team Three. How copy?"

The radio was silent. With a sigh of frustration John attempted to make contact with Stephen and Maryanne.

"Team Two, this is Team Three. How Copy?"

Once again, he only received a mute return. Assuming the worst, John began to peer into the windows of the parked transporters that lined the walkway as he dragged Sofia closely behind him.

Too stubborn to mention the infection that had settled into her wounds, Sofia felt like a hindrance to John's progress. She struggled to keep up with him, always feeling the nagging pressure of her body urging her to stop and rest.

After making one last concerted effort to make contact with the other members of their party, John gave up. Continuing with his vehicle-to-vehicle inspections with energetic urgency, he pulled Sofia along the walkway.

It was not long before he found what he was looking for: the dangling keys of the ignition left by a careless soul. Pulling on the door handle, he was not surprised to find it unlocked. Ushering Sophia inside, she quickly climbed over the center console, settling into the passenger's seat and buckling the seatbelt. Sliding in behind the wheel, John closed the door behind them.

Firing up the transporter's engine, John had a sudden feeling of loneliness and desolation well up inside of him, as if he suddenly realized that he had reached the top of a mountain after a hard climb only to find that there was nothing there. He felt no glory in his accomplishment, no satisfaction in achieving what he thought would be the crowning moment that would set him free from all the guilt and hatred.

Closing his eyes, he tried to lower the wall of flame that was growing up within his mind, but it was too resilient. No matter how many times he would fight to bring it down, it always seemed to win in the end. Maybe this was not the mountain, he thought. Perhaps that elusive, crowning achievement was to be found elsewhere.

Expecting at any moment to feel the vehicle accelerating, Sofia noticed that John was motionless. His eyes were closed, as if he were asleep.

"Is everything alright?" she asked.

"Everything's fine," John responded, as his eyes popped open. "I was just thinking."

Pulling the vehicle away from the curb, he drove them out of the residential area and back to the entertainment district, leading them to their escape.

Idling within the city's rain soaked traffic once again, the stolen transporter was aglow under the neon lights of the boulevard. John's fist throbbed from pounding the dashboard with such frequency. His angered outbursts had taken control under the stress of having to worry about Sofia's safety. He feared having to relive the Basket Town incident all over again. If only he had been on this mission alone. Killing everyone that got in his way, carving out a path of destruction leading directly to the escape vehicle, would be too easy. But, with Sofia nearby, her innocence was harping upon his weaker emotions, creating a struggle between, what seemed to be, his two natures: one that feared no consequences of his violent actions, and one that detested the actions themselves.

A sudden pulse of static was brought to his ear followed by the Captain's panting voice, "This is Team One. Do you copy, Team Three?"

Pinching the switch on his mic, John responded, "Team One, this is Team Three, go ahead."

"Team Three, be advised, the LZ has been compromised. Military forces are inbound. Two of three targets neutralized. How copy?"

"Copy all, Team One. What's the plan now."

"Check your handheld for my location. I'm closing in on my man. I need you to have a vehicle waiting and ready at the marked location. I'll explain the rest later. Out."

"Copy that. We're on the move."

Retrieving the computer from his pocket, John flipped on the switch at the side of its casing. A digital map popped up on the display. According to Banks' current position, he was roaming somewhere at the far end of the entertainment district.

"What did he say?" Sofia asked.

John glanced over his shoulder, negligent to the fact that the vehicle in the next lane over was taking up the space he desired.

Steering in front of the transporter beside them, its tires sheered atop the asphalt as the stranger slammed on his brakes. John's erratic action was immediately answered with a blaring horn.

"He said he needs us to be ready for him. He's apparently getting ready to make the hit," he said, mindless to the collision he had nearly initiated.

The sidewalk was within a meter's reach. They were making little progress within the confines of the slow paced traffic. Sofia began to fear that John would make them abandon the transporter, hoofing the rest of the way to the Captain's position. He kept eyeballing the walkway with an expression molded in desperation. He was up to something.

"John, what are you thinking?" Sofia questioned, cringing under the sharp, throbbing pain of her leg.

"Are you buckled in?" he asked, reaching across her lap, feeling for the tension of her restraining belt.

"Buckled in? For what?" Sofia began to say.

An opening between the parked vehicles was currently presenting itself, as a young couple pulled away from the walkway, entering the traffic a little more than two transporter lengths ahead of them. Making a quick scan of the surrounding environment, John was certain he was clear to make the run.

"I need you to hold on tight," he spoke, coldly and calculating

"What are you doing?" she asked.

"Just hold on," he sternly commanded her.

Sofia did not have time to respond to the demand. Bracing herself against the dashboard, she closed her eyes as John accelerated into his targeted area. The tearing and crushing of metal sent the crowds into a panic as the transporter burrowed into the rear end of a parked machine.

Bouncing with a wave-like motion, their front-end slid off the vehicle in front of them, its tires spinning in the muck of the gut-ter. Climbing up the sidewalk, they pinned an elderly man to the entrance of the store John had mercilessly rammed them into. The rumbling of the engine suddenly died, and John and Sofia were left alone under the pitter-patter of the downfall outside. The transporter was stalled.

Slumped across the hood of the engine, the Golden citizen was motionless, the blood draining from his nose and mouth diluted in the puddles of rain. The initial shock of the incident began to subside, the engine was dead and the people were beginning to gather around them. John cranked on the keys.

"Come on," he growled.

The curious onlookers were growing in numbers, some offering them their aid to their fallen mate, while others began banging on the hood and windows, demanding that John and Sofia exit the transporter. Ducking her head down in fear, Sofia could see that John was reaching for his pistol. Making one last attempt at reviving the dead machine, John's mind was prepared for battle. If the transporter did not start this time, he thought to himself, the shooting would commence.

With a final turn of the key, the faint light of the distal Savior pierced through the clouds. Scant particles at the end of their long journey fell upon the stranded couple, swirling through the twisted metal, weaving through the carnage. The transporter suddenly came back to life.

Sofia could not believe her ears. Lifting her head as John threw the transporter into reverse, smashing it into the parked car to their rear, nudging it out into the oncoming traffic where it was met with the front end of another vehicle, she watched as a faintly perceivable ray of light pierced the eyes of the dead man. Under the roaring of their engine, the crowds began to rapidly disperse. Sliding off the hood, the deceased disappeared from view. As John shifted the machine back into its forward gears and began moving into the masses, the wheels skidded onto the sidewalk as the fibrous panels of the vehicle's body tore away as it scraped along the poles and tattered remnants of his destruction. Peering out the rear window, through the smoke-filled haze and sheets of droplets, Sofia, uncertain from the blurry visibility, could make out the silhouetted image of the frail corpse lifting itself to its knees.

"Brace yourself," John yelled.

Sofia turned back, cowering down and covering her ears. With the accelerator to the floor the vehicle was rapidly gaining speed, battering into the droves of onlookers too caught off guard to move out of the way. Blaring his horn, John made no other effort to prevent the injury of Golden's citizenry as several bodies splattered across the windshield and against the grill, crunching underneath the tires, thrown against the walls and into the crawling traffic. Outdoor furniture and other unsecured objects splintered among the shattering glass, annihilated by the impact with their machine. Screaming with panic, Sofia hid her face from the incoming destruction.

Sparks scattered off the undercarriage as their vehicle dropped off the end of the walkway and into a crowded intersection. Forcefully extending his leg, John's foot jammed the brake hard, causing them to spin wildly on the wet asphalt, slamming into the intersection's perpendicularly moving traffic. Hitting the accelerator again, the tires spun in place, creating a cloud of smoke around them. As the rubber finally dug in, the transporter lunged forward, sending them tearing into the oncoming vehicles. The metal of their transporter's frame crinkled and warped as John bullied the other drivers out of the way in an attempt to bring them back onto the sidewalk.

The progression towards their destination was being hindered by their vehicle's inability to fight against such an overwhelming mass. Preparing to bail out with the hopes of securing another machine, John felt the wall of traffic give, as he was finally able to bring them back onto the less resistant walkway.

According to the locator on the screen, they were less than one block away. The wake of death left behind them was exactly what John had hoped to avoid for Sofia's sake, but the circumstances, and the cold-heartedness of his dominant nature, had prevailed. The path of annihilation was progressing with full force.

"We're less than two hundred meters to your location. Whatever you're going to do, you'd better act fast," John yelled into the mic.

Nearing Banks' pick-up point, John could see through the swaying windshield wipers the glowing, neon sign towering ahead of them. The Captain was somewhere inside the main entrance to a large, crystalline structured shopping mall.

"Banks, what's the situation?"

"Get away from the glass building," Banks screamed back, his voice hoarse and panicked.

Steering back into the traffic in order to avoid getting too close to Banks' target, John miscalculated the turn, inadvertently lodging their transporter between two hauler vehicles. Jarred under the strain of the abrupt cessation to their forward motion, he and Sofia sat silent for a moment, gathering their senses. They were locked in the stalled traffic between the towering, rigid bodies of the utility machines, unable to open the side doors and inundated with the shrieking horns and cursing of the drivers outside. Unshackling his restraints, John began kicking at the shattered, filth covered windshield, fighting to create a space from which they could extricate.

As the sheet of glass folded outward, he withdrew his pistol from his holster and unscrewed the suppressor from the barrel. Dropping the metallic tube to the floor, John climbed out the opening into the falling rain, standing upon the hood of the vehicle. Firing sporadically into the air, he sent waves of panic throughout the congested street.

Assisting Sofia out of the window, he hopped down, looking for another vehicle to make their escape in.

"Come on," he demanded, "We need to find Banks."

"Where's he at?" Sofia yelled above the hysteria.

A sudden explosion from the shopping center sent shards of glass and burning debris blasting into the street around them. John forced Sofia to the ground, protecting her with his body.

The environment was heavily polluted with screams and wailing sirens. A black cloud of burning flames of the fire-consumed building was descending upon them. The visibility from their position had devolved to zero among the claustrophobic and chaotic mess. Choking as she inhaled the fumes pouring forth from what was left of the crystalline structure, Sofia gasped for air, covering her mouth with her sleeve.

"John," Banks called out from the drapes of blackness a few meters away.

"We're over here," John shouted back.

Following the sound of John's voice, Banks worked his way through the ensuing turmoil, ignoring John's immediate questioning as he emerged from the din.

"Follow me," he yelled, leading his newly found comrades through the disaster zone and into an alley, a path to another part of the city.

Exiting from between the buildings they found the traffic on the next street gridlocked and frozen. Golden's citizens were attempting to flee the warzone of the local vicinity. Running up to the first idling machine they could find, John forced the driver out of the transporter at gunpoint. Herding Sofia into the back seat, he kept his aim on the innocent civilian as he climbed in behind her.

"You need to drive, Banks. I'll guard the rear," he said.

Jumping behind the wheel and propping his handheld on the dashboard, the Captain accelerated into the traffic, forcing his way across the road and driving them into the nearest alleyway, leading them further away from the city's central hub. With the aid of his device, he busied himself with finding the quickest way out of the metropolis.

"So, where are we going?" John yelled from the backseat.

Removing the pistols from his shoulder holsters, Banks threw them onto the back seat, giving John more firepower in case they were to run into trouble.

"Just make sure no one's following us," he demanded, flipping his eyes back and forth between the road ahead and his handheld computer's map. "I'll figure it out."

"I want to know where we're going, Banks. What's the plan, now?"

Banks continued to ignore John's request for more information. Bringing them nearer to the surrounding forest outside the city limits was his highest priority. He was not about to compromise his attention answering the Sweeper.

Banks secretive behavior was becoming a nuisance, and John wanted to shoot him there on the spot. But he refrained, not just out of concern for Sofia, but because they would have no way of escaping the cursed planet without him. Sofia, meanwhile, huddled on the floor beside John's legs. The enclosed area gave her a more secure feeling than seeing the open world around her.

With his concentration on their path, Banks was oblivious as to how close to death he had come. Pulling out of another alleyway and into the slow moving traffic, it looked as if they were finally leaving the entertainment district behind. Comfortably blended into the flow, the black plumes of smoke expanding into the night sky were visible against the reflected city lights on the underside of the mantel of fog that hung over it. As they watched from their slow crawling position a few miles from the scene, bursts of lightning-like, blue flashes appeared throughout the clouds above, followed closely by the descending airships that began landing around the perimeter of Golden.

"They're here," Banks mumbled.

"Who's here?" John yelled.

"We knew this was going to happen, but I didn't think they had the means to get here so fast," Banks continued.

Leaning over the front seat, John could see through the front windshield that the military's air transporters were raining down heavily into the surrounding forests.

"I hope your friends have that airship ready to take us home," he sneered.

"Central got the data that you sent from the two targets you bagged in the apartment. Our mission isn't over," the Captain said.

"Two? What are you talking about?" John inquired suspiciously.

"Arlington and Corona. They were two of the three targets that we were sent for. Look, John, we don't have time to talk right now. The entire city's going to be crawling with..."

"Wrong answer, Captain. I want to know how Central knew that I eliminated both of them?"

Banks ignored the question, saying, "The new LZ's located off a rural path that leads deep into the forest, just outside of the city. We..."

"You're playing games with me. There's something going on that you're not telling us."

Banks wanted to continue to steer clear of the topic, but getting the Sweeper upset at such a desperate time was not a good idea, and he knew it. They were so close to making their escape, but the Security was just minutes away. After carefully considering his words, he confided to John for the sake of the mission.

"They believe you've supplied them with the data they needed: they've located the *Top Man*."

"*The* Top Man?" John said throwing his hands in the air and sitting back against the seat. "I thought the three targets were the *top* men."

"They never were. They're just pawns taking orders from the guy above them. Our new orders are to..."

"*Our* new orders?" John interrupted. "Who *are* the real pawns in this game?"

Banks had no time to explain. He could see that they were heading towards the flashing lights of the initial stages of a military blockade at the end of their road, perhaps four to five hundred meters ahead. With only moments to react before there were no more options for escape from the city streets, he attempted to swerve into the last visible alleyway, but unwittingly embedded the front end of their vehicle into the transporter beside them. The driver of the transporter, cursing and waiving his fist, immediately laid his hands on his horn, bringing the attention of the military agents upon them.

Banks seemed oblivious to the damage he had caused. Metal twisted and stretched apart as he backed the transporter away from the collision, driving away from the scene and into the early stages of a construction zone situated within a warehouse district. The victim of his reckless actions was screaming for help, and the military agents were quick to answer the call. Weaving through the traffic, they were heading towards their direction.

Ignoring the demands shouting through the bullhorns, small arms fire could be heard as Banks continued the retreat into the construction arena. John immediately returned fire, blowing holes through the back window, littering empty, hot shells upon Sofia. As they continued to make their way between the two large, concrete frames ahead of them, Banks stopped the transporter and cut the engine.

"What are you doing?" John roared out.

"Don't worry about it. It's all part of the plan."

"I'm getting tired of your plans, Banks," John said, pointing the pistol into Banks' face. "If you're not getting us out of here, I will."

He reached across Sofia, grasping the handle to the rear door.

"John," Banks called out. "Just wait. It'll be clear in a moment."

"You're a fool," John said, pinching the microphone on his throat as he kicked open the door and climbed out. "Team Two this is Team Three, how copy?"

"John," the Captain interrupted.

"Shut up, Banks," John yelled at him, pointing his finger in the Captain's face. "Team Two this is Team Three. Do you copy? The LZ is compromised. Repeat: the LZ is compromised. Over."

The rumbling of the military vehicles was growing steadily more aggressive on the street outside. Removing his sights from Banks, John took cover beside their transporter, readying his pistol for the first agent to turn the corner.

"Team Two, do you copy?" he attempted once more.

"They can't hear you," Banks confessed. "Their microphones are off. You need to get inside where it's safer."

"Why are their microphones off?" Sofia spoke up.

John opened the front passenger door and climbed inside while keeping an eye on the street behind them.

"What's going on, old man?" he asked, shoving the barrel of the pistol into Banks' throat. "Why aren't they communicating with us?"

"Didn't Stephen tell you? Don't you remember, kids? The airships are one-way tickets, at least for most of us. Stephen and Maryanne understood that."

"You mean, Maryanne's in danger somewhere in the city?" Sofia cried out. "John, we need to help them!"

"You can't, young lady," the Captain interjected.

"You know where they are, Banks. Take us to them, now," John demanded.

"I can't do that."

John fired the pistol beside Banks' head, shattering the driver's side window, causing the old man to duck his head.

"I can make it so that you'll take us to them, Captain," he whispered, as his commanding officer stared at him under a profusely sweating brow.

"Go ahead, John. Kill me and compromise the entire last leg of the mission. My death won't solve anything. It'll just make things harder everywhere else because we'll have failed to complete the final objective."

"We're going to complete it, but we're doing it with them"

"No we won't... not with Stephen and Maryanne. They volunteered for this. They have a better understanding of sacrifice than you do. Central anticipated almost everything... only we were supposed to be at the airship by now. We all knew that the military would take the city once we made the hits, but things moved a little faster than we had anticipated... and now some of us need to live to finish the job."

To Banks' relief, John removed the pistol's aim and sat back in the seat.

"We have to help them. We need to get to Mary. Please, John," Sofia pleaded.

John leaned his head back. There were so many paths to take.

"They're giving their lives for us, for you. They do not want your help in this matter. Don't let them die in vain, John."

Banks took note of the time, shaking his head.

"I know your pain, young lady," he said to Sofia. "Stephen was my good friend."

"But can't we do something to help them?" she sobbed.

Banks continued to shake his head, his eyes welling up with moisture.

John stepped out of the transporter, taking a steady aim down the alley as the voices of the military agents echoed through their bullhorns, demanding an unconditional surrender.

"There's going to be an explosion that'll dwarf mine in comparison," Banks whispered to Sofia. "But we'll be safe here."

Weeping for her friend, Sofia could not understand why Maryanne would give her life in such a manner.

"Maryanne, why didn't you stay with me?" she cried, burying her face in the palms of her hands.

"John, don't worry about them. In thirty seconds the military will be no threat to us. Come, get inside."

An agent peered around the wall shining the flashlight from his weapon towards their position. John rapidly fired off several rounds, sending him back behind his cover.

"Twenty seconds, John."

A metal canister sailed over the buildings, landing halfway between their transporter and the city street.

"Poison," John yelled, ducking down.

John's words fell upon Sofia's ears like the autumn leaves, dead and insignificant. The pain in her heart was too much for her. The world of darkness that forever seemed to exist on Golden was stifling and suffocating. To think that Maryanne was somewhere out there waiting to die on such a terrible planet was a thought that brought more tears to her eyes.

"Please, Savior, don't let her suffer," Sofia began to pray.

"Ten Seconds," the Captain counted down.

As John lay on the cold, wet asphalt, the wall of burning began to rise in his mind. If he was going to die here, he was not going to give the military the satisfaction of eliminating him with one of their bullets. He would rather the poison do its dirty work for them.

Damp and chilly, he returned to his seat inside the vehicle. He knew he should have chosen a place near Sofia, but he did not want to witness the effects of the gas upon her: the bloody cough, the bloody tears. He certainly did not want her to see any of that falling upon him either. He closed the door as the popping of the canister commenced, bringing with it the thickly rising plume of death.

Within Banks' eyes the continual clicking movement of the hands of his watch were like the beating of a dying heart, the last remaining moments of Golden's glory.

"Four seconds."

"I only wish I could have said to you..." Sofia sobbed.

"Three"

"... how much I cherished our friendship."

"Two"

John closed his eyes, mentally prepared to inhale the deadly fumes that were closing in on them.

"One"

"Good-bye, Mary."

As if the cries of the sufferings of the Savior of the worlds were coming to an end, the rain suddenly ceased. The last drop splashed upon the windshield. An eerie soundlessness fell upon the city as the winds died off. The heavens above were silently anticipating Golden's end.

A blinding cloak of white fell upon the metropolis, preceding the thunderous blast that arose from the fireball that lifted from the heart of Golden, tearing through her streets, burning off the flesh of her inhabitants and scorching the materials of her world.

The poisonous smoke withdrew from of the alley, leaving the transporter nestled alone between the protective walls of concrete. Swirling into the streets, the gaseous cloud met with the burning storm of flames and torment that ripped apart the advancing agents.

There was a change that was taking place in the order of the universe. The iron grip of the old military might was dying. Those that had been suffering under their treacherous conditions were confronting the cold-hearted selfishness of the men of means.

As the burning light of flames died down, flakes of ash fell from the sky. The dimly lit streets were becoming a whitened path of beauty, as if they were covered over with snow. It was an image of grand irony, John thought, as he believed the road outside the alleyway was leading him to the final conclusion of his sordid life. And yet, although he was now a key player in Central's venture, he was still uncertain as to exactly how he fit in to the universal scheme of the ages.

Boarding the airship, John held tightly to Sofia. As the bay door began to close, he was too consumed with his own internal demons to notice the tears falling from her eyes.

The smoldering ruins at the center of the city were visible through the narrowing threshold. It was the pyre of dedication for those that sacrificed everything, even their very lives.

Grateful for the time that she did have with such a spiritually strong woman as Maryanne, Sofia lifted her hand, bidding one final farewell to a wonderful friend.

CHAPTER FORTY

The icy atmosphere was burrowing itself to the bones as the last three survivors neared the planet known to Central as Black Island. The *Top Man* was there somewhere, hidden within its frozen wasteland. Their goal was to flush him out and destroy him. Through the rearward cameras of the airship, the Savior now appeared as just another distant star, one of a million pinholes of light speckled upon the blackness of space.

Central Command was keeping a close eye out for the Captain and his crew, and once again they anticipated their needs with precision. The air transporter had been pre-loaded with all the necessary equipment, even providing the three-man team with the layers of insulated outerwear necessary to their survival and comfort while traversing the frigid lands of the Island.

Floating within the center of the room while pulling the warmth-inducing, hooded shirt over her head, Sofia unfolded it down to her hips, grimacing under the pain of her infected wound. Tugging at the tether cable linked to the floor that held her in place, her body glided back to the table from where she was able to grab her hovering pants.

She had such a strong adoration for the flowing dress that she had received during the mission on Golden. It was a sweet slice of the delicacy of life of which she was not afforded since leaving the crash-site home of Labor so many years past. A nostalgic moment was projecting from the memory reels within her feverish mind as she pulled the cold weather bottoms on, latching them about her waist before throwing the skirt back over her legs. Pants under my skirt, she thought with a pale smile. Although she was now a full-grown woman, her tomboy ways that should have been far behind her were apparently still with her in heart.

John and the Captain had, for some time, been discussing the course of action that they would be taking once the ship landed. Through the opening above her, Sofia listened to them arguing, wiping her hand across her runny, cold nose and sniffling with an occasional sneeze. Unable to discern the actual words that they were using, their tones seemed to her to have descended into frustration. And, more than once, John had floated out of the room, red in the face and with hatred in his eyes. She knew better than to bother him at such a moment.

Pushing off the wall, Sofia left the upper decks of the airship. Still uncontrollably shivering despite the heavy layers of clothes, and cursed with a headache that would not let up, she sought shelter from the raging men above. Sliding through the thresholds of each level of the aircraft, she worked her way to the lowest deck, moving as far away from them as she could.

The nether storage container of the transporter housed a unique set of vehicles used for traversing icy, snow-covered terrain. Secured to the floor with nylon rigging, their two-seated, white painted bodies were covered over with smudges of grayish cloudy shapes, making their actual silhouettes indistinguishable against the gray-white walls of the ship. Unlike the vehicles from the other planets, these lacked the wheels and tires of their otherworldly counterparts. Instead, they were given their motion by way of a tracked mechanism.

Gliding down beside the nearest machine, Sofia opened the passenger door and climbed inside. Consumed by her growing illness and the exhaustion of the past few days' events, compounded with the loss of Maryanne, she was completely emotionally unstable, finding it nearly impossible to hold back her tears during any given moment. Curled up in the seat, she could not escape the constant ringing in her ears. Closing her eyes brought her immediately into the unconscious state of sleep, where the nightmares had been awaiting her arrival.

"When will we return home?" she mumbled.

The fluorescent lights on the panels of the ship's walls passed through the lids of her eyes, unnatural and without the soothing effect of the Savior's warmth. For all the evils that the distant, empty space of the solar system held, the heat of Raw was a little more inviting than the bitter chill of a completely Saviorless world.

The lights of the open bay doors of the airship revealed little to John of the coal blackened atmosphere engulfing the snow-drifted world of the Island outside. According to Central, the base of operation, or as they were calling it, Top Hat's Quarters, was situated somewhere approximately four thousand meters away. With only point *A* and point *B* noted on the handheld's map, the mystery of what they would find at the end of the line was anybody's guess.

Sofia did not need to leave the confines of the snow-transporter. She awoke to John's presence beside her as he reached inside and turned on the ignition. Closing the door and walking back to the Captain, he appeared to be finishing his business with the man.

Through the blurriness of the plastic window, the two soldiers were on much friendlier terms relative to the last time she heard them together. Talking amongst themselves, they smiled and shook hands. The Captain was clearly emotional, wiping his eyes frequently and rubbing them on the sides of his shirt. With one last touch of John's shoulder, Banks, to Sofia's amazement, leaned forward, taking John in his arms in the same manner as a loving father would hug his child, patting him on the back. Releasing him from his hold, the Captain turned away without another word, walking around to the driver's side of his vehicle. In a single motion, the aged officer stepped inside, fired up the engine, peered across the open space between him and her and, after a momentary contact with Sofia's eyes, he drove down the ramp, fading away into nothingness. The lights of his vehicle were consumed by the darkness.

As John took his seat at the wheel, his solemn expression revealed the obvious nature of the conversation: Banks' ride to the Island was his one-way ticket.

At the pace they were traveling, the traversal of the harsh lands would take hours for them to reach their destination. The lights of the vehicle allowed for only a shallow view of the wind blown landscape, as flakes of white drifted across the windshield in endless streams. Although hypnotically similar to the wiping of the rain by the blades of the transporter on Golden, this time Sofia was not in the least desirous for sleep.

Sofia was so frail and weak sitting by his side. Over the past few days John had been witness to the rapidly glossing over of her eyes with a haze of fatigue. Perhaps it was the nearness to the end of their journey that was wearing on her, or maybe it was the fact that they were fighting alone. Whatever it was that was influencing her declining health he could not comprehend, but he could see that she was overwhelmed with fear even though they were together, adventuring like the good, old days. John could never have considered that his own hands were the cause of Sofia's body wasting away. What was happening to her was purely a mystery to him. Sofia was dying. But that was her personal, little secret.

It took a few minutes for him to catch on, but John noticed that he could now look upon his love with adoration, without the burning wall of hate revealing its terrible visage so readily. It was still there, though. He could feel it lying in wait for him, holding out for a drop in his guard. But, it was the fact that it was allowing him to get much further emotionally without restraining, without binding his soul, which caught him by surprise. John now believed that his freedom from the grasp of his murderous training would return. Time would eventually change him back. He knew it had to. But as he looked upon Sofia, her forehead beaded with sweat, her skin pale and moist, he only hoped that there was enough time left in their lives together for the two of them to be happy once again.

Nearing the Top Man's base according to the map, John killed the lights of the transporter and slowed their progress to a near standstill, taking his time with the last few hundred meters that remained before they would need to move on foot. The faint glow of the outer lights of the compound was just ahead of them. Beyond the snowy drapes impeding his vision it was hidden. He was quite aware of the potential dangers that were lying ahead.

Through the murkiness of the unforgiving storm, the perception of a rather formidable mansion, lit up with the brightest of lights, was now coming vaguely into view. A single structure placed in the middle of nowhere, sitting on a desolate planet at the outskirts of their little universe. After a lengthy period of crawling through the snow, it began to reveal itself more clearly.

Gorgeously arrayed with golden statues and white marbled pillars, the lamps of the compound illuminated the local vicinity with a marvelous glow. After moving closer, there appeared several guard towers, but it was quite clear that there were no guards at their posts, no Security personnel on watch. The occupier was either thoroughly comfortable with his safety in such a lonely, and seemingly inaccessible, world, or else Banks had made enough of a distraction to bring to his position every agent on the planet.

"We've reached the Top Man's domain," John whispered into his throat mic.

There was no return answer. Cutting the engine, the eerie rocking of the vehicle's cabin against the wind that whistled along its frame made John aware of just how isolated they were from the rest of humanity. It was a dead planet, and they needed to cross its open waste in order to gain access to their final target.

"We've reached the Top Man's domain. How copy?" John whispered, making one more attempt at communicating.

Radio silence was all that returned. Reaching into the compartment behind them, he retrieved the weapons and goggles that

Central had supplied, along with a backpack of explosive ordinance of unknown yields. Short-barreled and simple, he handed a rifle to Sofia, saying, "I'm not expecting you to use it. Just hold on to it, just in case."

With a pistol already holstered in its shoulder rig, John helped Sofia secure it around her arms while continuing to keep her warm-weather jacket in place.

"Stay close behind me," he said, dropping the goggles over his eyes and pulling the hood of his jacket over his head.

Following suit, Sofia covered herself in the same manner. She was mentally ready to vacate the transporter, but she was not physically prepared to embark through the hoary weather with John.

Opening the doors was like falling into icy waters. The skin of Sofia's face felt like it immediately froze. Had it not been for the protective covering over her eyes, she was certain that they would have iced shut. Pulling the backpack's straps over his shoulders, John approached her from around the front of the transporter.

The mansion was situated on a moderate upgrade that began several meters away. Throwing the rifles over their shoulders, the climb would necessitate that they use both hands and feet to ascend its slippery slope, and they proceeded to move out with caution.

As they neared the final slope leading to the compound, it began to rapidly steepen. The struggle up the snowy face was turning into a strain on the muscles, and Sofia, dizzy and worn, pushed her body to its limit in order to reach its top. As she pulled herself over the upper ledge, she could see John kneeling down beside a stone-fenced path. A flight of stairs on the other side of the walkway terminated at the front door of the compound approximately fifty meters away. Rising to her feet, she was feeling the aches in her joints that accompanied her rising temperature. Hobbling up beside John, Sofia was winded and feeling ill to her stomach. Her condition went unnoticed. And John pressed forward with the mission in spite of her limping attempts to keep up with him.

Leading them down the edge of the walkway, keeping them on the outside of the stony wall, John made certain that they were always hidden in the shadows, out of sight from the lights that decoratively flooded the open grounds.

With the entry to the compound only a few meters away, the two trespassers straddled over the low-lying wall, and stood at the base of the mansion's pillared face. The white-gray, marbled steps leading to their man were coated with a heavy layer of powdery snow that crunched under the weight of their boots.

The stairwell was intricately crafted with statues of animal foundlings and playful children, artificially exuding a meek appearance with regards to the occupier of the house. It was a stark contrast to the personification of evil that they were expecting to find.

A broad doorway made of fine wood, smooth and lacquered, and adorned with brass fixtures, blocked their entry into the compound.

"Breaching the target's HQ. How copy?" John whispered into the mic.

There was no answer from the Captain. Aiming from the hip while turning the handle, to John's surprise the door slid open without any resistance. He and Sofia were immediately greeted by the warmth of the interior air and the brightly illuminating lights that escaped through the slight opening he had created in the threshold. As the expanding entryway revealed the mystery of simplicity behind it, John fully shouldered his rifle, taking aim throughout the room.

Devoid of life, it was curiously quiet once they were inside, and John pulled Sofia closer to his body, but slightly shielding her at his rear. The walls were decorated with a blood red, fabric covering with wooden trim, giving a nightmarish atmosphere of doom. There were several hallways, long, narrow and dimly lit, a virtual crimson colored maze within the madman's house. A staircase built into the side of the opposing wall led to a walkway that extended into another hallway that continued beyond their line of sight.

Unable to assume the time of day, as there were no points of reference to glean that piece of data from, John could not even deduce whether the possibilities for the target to be upstairs sleeping, or downstairs eating, were reasonable.

Relying on chance, he randomly chose the hallway at his right hand, hoping that he was not leading them into a trap.

Proceeding down its path, Sofia held onto the tail end of John's coat, occasionally stumbling over her own feet. The sweat was beginning to drip down John's forehead, saturating his eyebrows before falling across the lashes of his eyes. He wanted desperately to remove the insulated, outer layers of clothing, to release the pent up heat from his body, but he knew that losing the precious articles would make his escape virtually impossible, as he could not survive so tenuously clothed for any extended period of time in such an icy environment.

Despite the multiple layers of covering wrapped around her body, Sofia continued to shiver uncontrollably. Although she was attired in the same material as John, her cold weather outfit felt much too thin to keep her warm.

As they reached the middle of the door-less hallway, John recognized by the varying shades of red reflecting off the walls that their path continued around a corner approximately twenty meters ahead. The stillness of the atmosphere was eerily calm.

As Sofia followed John to the edge of the wall, he peered around the corner, making sure that they were safe to move on.

Their movement was slow and cautious. And with each new turn, and each new threshold to pass through, there were simply more hallways and staircases in abundance for them to follow.

Being led to unknown locales within the monstrous structure, John had become quite disoriented by the lack of variety found within each newly discovered area. It was as if they were going in circles, only to return to the same place from which they had started... and yet, John was not sure if they had returned to any of the same places or not. It all looked the same.

Thirty minutes or more had passed, and they were unsure if they were nearer now to their destination than when they had first begun. Whatever the answer, they were lost within the labyrinth. Was the entire compound designed for the unlikely event that foreigners would find him, John thought. It seemed as if only blind luck would get them to the target now, if they were to get there at all.

The longer they wandered, the more pale and dusky Sofia was becoming. The ruby color of the walls was playing tricks on her mind, and she began to fear that death was stalking her, but she refused to let John in on her fears.

Not ready to give up, John stopped in the middle of the hallway.

"Did you hear something?" he whispered suspiciously.

"No," Sofia replied, listening to the ringing silence.

Knocking the butt end of his rifle upon the floor, John could feel the vibration of the wood planks beneath his feet. Pulling out a bladed weapon he cut into the plush carpet, tearing a hole out and exposing the wooden sub-flooring beneath. As he continued to expand his work area, Sofia moved out his way, sitting back against a wall, blurrily watching him from a short distance away.

With the tang of his knife, John hammered at the ground, creating a crack into which he placed his blade. Prying the floor apart, he tore through several wooden sections until there was nothing visible but a concrete slab.

Dropping the backpack from his shoulders, John rummaged through the varying sizes of explosive bundles that Central had packaged for them. Unsure of their individual, destructive yields, he removed the smallest clay-like block he could find, along with a single, timed detonator. Connecting the two components together, he set its timer to countdown from twenty seconds and placed it upon the exposed surface of the floor.

Grabbing Sofia by the hand, he threw the pack over his shoulder and lifted her up, forcing her to run with him down the hall and back around the last corner from which they had come. Ducking down and covering her under his body, John huddled over Sofia just at the moment that the deafening explosion tore through the house. Plaster and wood fell from the ceiling, cracking off the walls around them. The quaking of the structure had loosened more than just its superficial covering as the echoes of splintering wood and breaking glass resounded everywhere around them.

As John allowed the time for the smoke to clear and the domino effect to cease, Sofia, her skin tactilely ultra-sensitive, bathed in the comfort of John's embrace. It was something she had not felt for so many years.

As the dust began to settle, John stood up brushing off his clothes. He offered his hand to Sofia, but she was too weak to take it. Sickly and frail, she held onto her leg and began cry, sobbing and pitiful.

Up until this very moment John had not taken notice of how dreadfully ill her appearance had become. He had not been observant to Sofia's rapidly deteriorating condition. Neither her pale, moist skin, nor the distress in her laborious breathing had caught his attention to such an emergent degree as now. He had been woefully indifferent to her suffering. Kneeling beside her and placing his hand upon the back of her neck, he could feel her skin burning, as if she were on fire.

"Let's abort this mission and head back to the transporter," he said. "Maybe we can find some medicine at the airship."

Sweating profusely and finding it difficult to swallow due to the cottony, dryness of her mouth, Sofia slid her hand out from under his and placed it upon his cheek. His skin felt so cold and dry.

"You've got to find him," she said. "There are so many people counting on you, John."

"No," he dissented. "We're leaving right now. You need help. You're very sick, girl."

The nickname was so sweet and familiar. She had adored hearing him use the term *girl* since they were children. Perhaps, he was correct. There could be medicine at the airship and she could be saved. But, Maryanne's selflessness was such an inspiration to her. Sofia could not let her own safety stand between the freedom of millions and the destruction of the purveyors of their misery. She struggled against her own selfishness, even upon hearing the soft wind blowing through the grassy fields of Labor, calling out for her return. Taking hold of it, she drowned her self-preservation in the waters of liberty, wiping it out for all eternity.

"I'm going to stay right here," she whispered through a hoarse, fragile voice. "You need to finish this. Maybe this is the answer you were always seeking, John. Don't give up now. I'll still be here waiting for you when you return."

Seeing her in such a pathetic state caused the wall of burning to rise within John's heart and mind. One part of him wanted to hold her, the other part to destroy the ultimate cause of her misery. Standing upon his feet as she closed her eyes, the baser side of John's soul had won again. Without saying a word he walked away from Sofia, disappearing around the corner.

Folding her arms across her chest, Sofia's teeth chattered behind the sunken skin of her cheeks. John would return for her, she thought. He always did.

Approaching the gaping wound of the mansion floor, John aimed his weapon down into the hollowed out room that existed below the hallway that they had been standing in just moments earlier. He flipped the light of the rifle's foregrip on, moving its beam across the shattered remnants of the once hidden compartment. Certain it was clear, he hopped down, landing hard upon the uneven floor. Computer terminals were blown to pieces, and furniture was split and splintered, piled against the walls from the blast of his explosive. As far as he could tell, there were no casualties within the immediate area.

A door on the far end of the wall from which he stood was torn in half, leaving the lower portion intact upon its hinge. Cautiously moving towards the pitch dark unknown awaiting him on the other side, John crept along the wall. His steady aim was only useful within a single meter or less, as the smoke of the smoldering ash wafted through the beam of his light, obscuring his vision.

Pushing the half-door aside, a sudden motion to his left caused his reflexive action to subconsciously take over. He instinctively swiped his rifle towards the moving object with a burst of gunfire.

Sofia awoke with a startle. She was certain John had called out to her, taking her out of her feverish dreamland. Crawling to the corner of the hall, she peered around it. The opening in the floor silently awaited her entrance.

As his body returned back its control to his rational awareness, John could hear a sound as if something heavy was being dragged along the floor. Spotting a splatter of blood upon the wall at the far end of the hall, in an area that had been out of harm's way from the blast, he followed his light to the crimson stain.

Approaching it, he could see that it was shaped like a hand with its fingers spread out. Through the unhindered flood of his light, smeared streams of blood led him up the hall and into a room that was shimmering like the reflections of light off of a pool of bluish-white waters. Rotating his rifle along the sling to his back, John withdrew his pistol and began moving with haste towards the illuminated room.

As he neared the doorway, he could hear the heavy, gurgling breaths of someone suffering under the might of his former weapon. Entering in, John found himself surrounded by a network of computer screens brightly lit. Fallen upon the floor at his feet, lay a man, shot through the chest, bubbling in his throat as he drowned in his own blood.

Dangling by her hands several feet above the blast room floor, Sofia began the arduous search for her love. Releasing her grip, she fell to the ground below with such a force that her knees crashed into her chest, knocking the breath out of her. Scooting back against the wall behind her, she flipped the switch of her flashlight on. The half-door before her was ajar. It had to be the path from which John had called to her.

If this was the *Top Man*, then he was not as old as John expected him to be. And at this point in time there was nothing unique about him, either. He was rather thin and pasty. Perhaps if he were not wounded and bleeding out, John thought, he could possibly be someone that people looked up to, someone with a fair complexion. But as it stood, he was nothing special at all.

John stood over him, waiting to leave until after he had died. He was almost joyous at the thought of seeing the so-called Top

Man so humiliated through his suffering.

"Are you the *Top Man*?" he asked with disdain.

"I... am he," the man sputtered.

John wanted to spit on him, to rub the dying man's face in the fact that his entire, rotten existence was coming to a close.

"You," the man choked, "must take my place... now."

Crawling with anguish and pain to the button-faced console beside him, the agonizing creature reached his blood-soaked hand out, extending his lanky fingers towards a red knob that was encased under a hinged, glass covering. Grabbing the man's finger, John snapped it to the side, deforming it in his rage as the man screamed out in pain.

"You," the man wailed through his raspy, wheeze, "must take my place."

John raised his pistol towards the man's head. He had a burning hatred towards him. Pulling the trigger, the report of the shot echoed throughout the underground bunker, ringing his ears and momentarily blinding him with the blast... but it was just another life ending.

As he stood alone, considering what he had accomplished, John felt hollow and empty. There was no glory once again, just as there had been no glory in the killing of Corona and Arlington. It was just another event, no different than wiping his nose or cleaning the dust off of his weapon. Another mountaintop reached with no prize awaiting him, just a lonely view of a desolate surrounding. What was the point of it all? How could this act have been the saving grace of humanity?

With the report of John's weapon echoing down the hall, Sofia slowly made her way towards the bloody print on the wall at the far end of the trail. She wanted to run, but she was only able to bear a minimum weight upon her wounded extremity.

Reaching his hand to his throat, John called in the victory message as he pinched the mic, "The Top Man is eliminated. I repeat: the Top Man is eliminated."

As he turned to walk out of the room, leaving his handiwork behind him, the computer screens began to flash, decorating the walls with their strobes of white light. The glass-hinged cover of the knob automatically lifted from its position on the console, exposing the red button to John, the lone occupier of the room.

Stopping to look at it, he wondered what its purpose was. Why had the Top Man been so focused on it? Would it set off an alarm, or would it send thousands of missiles of death raining down upon his kingdom, destroying his enemies as a final blow to his rebellious citizens? Would it matter at all if he actuated it, now? Sofia was upstairs, dead, for all he knew. Perhaps this mission was not only Banks' one-way ticket, but his and Sofia's also. Stepping up to the mysterious device, he placed his palm upon its convex surface... and depressed it.

A red light mounted on the wall beside him began to flicker. As the screen above the button began streaming coded messages upon its face, the light of the room turned that same sickly green hue, like that found on the scanners of Labor. The wall beside it began to slide open, revealing a series of elevator booths with a single, belted chair situated within each one.

The computer screen beside him brought up a display, an image of a planet within a planet. Written beneath it were the words, *Black Heart: Access to Nether World Permitted.* Walking up to the booth, John looked it over, searching for actuators or trip devices at the threshold. But it appeared safe to enter in.

Curiously stepping inside, John stood upon its clear, glassy floor. It appeared to hover just above the metallic plate beneath him. The ceiling was a decorative brass network of carved beams, thin and symmetrical. The seat before him was elevated above the glassy surface by a single metal cylinder. The securing buckles of its chest harness dangled from its sides. A series of buttons were overlaying one of the armrests. Before John could touch his fingers to them a thin, brass slider enveloped them under its veil, the door slid shut behind him, pressure sealing him inside, causing his head to momentarily spin and his ears to ring. There were no more buttons to press, no switches to operate: he was trapped.

The base beneath the glassy window of his feet separated at the center seam like the opening of a curtain, revealing a slowly rotating, miniature planet, its surface suspended within the core of Black Island, several hundred meters below. Like the view from a high mountaintop, John could see every tree, every structure that rolled by under the dim glow of the phosphorescent atmosphere that provided the eerie green-yellow hue that the celestial orb was encased in.

Without notice, the elevator booth was released, freefalling towards the planet, bringing John into a state of zero gravity, floating with his feet mere centimeters above the place where he had just been standing. Pulling himself into the chair, he grabbed the harness, locking himself in.

As Sofia entered the control room, the image of the bloodied, disfigured remains of the Top Man caused her to drop her rifle and stumble back through the threshold and onto the floor of the hall. The hollowness of the vacant compartment of a recently released capsule howled through the cracked seals, flashing with a strobe of lights beside the other awaiting booths. The dim, sickly green glow illuminating the empty chairs seemed to be calling to her, as if to tell her they would lead her to John.

The vibratory sensation of the capsule as it became exposed to the friction of the inner planet's atmosphere was brutal on the senses, bouncing John's head against the thinly padded seat. As he leaned forward, attempting to gauge the distance to impact, the vehicle rotated upside down, initiating its reverse boosters, countering the gravitational pull exerted upon it.

Engulfed in blackness, the capsule's hull was secured by mechanical landing machinery of the host planet's docking system. Rotated right side up, the immediate vertigo John was experiencing resolved upon touchdown. The elevator's door opened. Unlatching himself from the restraints, he walked out into a world of glowing haze and silhouetted jungle. Silent and humid, the cool, yellow lights of a building of unobservable detail glimmered from the windows a few meters from the landing port. Bringing his rifle to bear, John advanced toward its location. Shining his light into the shadows of the multi-story structure, he located an entrance just ahead.

CHAPTER FORTY-ONE

The door flung open under the force of John's booted foot, splintering the jam and ripping the knob from its core. An old man, facing away from him, was sitting in the shadows of the room upon an old leather couch, covered over with hose-like formations. It was difficult to discern what exactly surrounded him, but they seemed to move like snakes, slithering about his body.

"I knew you'd come, John," the mysterious stranger said without looking behind him.

Closing the distance between them, the light of John's rifle reflected off the grotesque image of wires and cables protruding from the sides of the humanoids head and spine. They appeared to be fused to his nervous system through the portals of his skin. His face was a pale-green distortion of death. His eyes were cold, lacking any pigmentation. As he turned to look upon John, his mouth began to open.

"Neither Corona nor Arlington could achieve the greatness that each of them desired," he said. "They were weak minded, foolish. I was once a young man like you, full of hatred and hell-bent on destroying everything around me. I stepped on everything in my path to reach the top. And you know what, John?" he continued. "There really is fulfillment there."

As John moved around to the man's front side, the shadows cowering from his face allowed him to see the timid, elderly gentleman, similar in demeanor to Mr. Sanders, sitting plump and helpless in his place. His hollow, gray eyes looked up to him, and John felt a saddened compassion for the disfigured man.

"You don't recognize me do you?" the humanoid asked with a calming smile.

"Why should I?"

"I created you. I also chose you, guided you, sent you to war to fight and learn."

"Are you the Savior?"

"Some say I am. I *am* in control of the Seven Worlds. They are mine, John. I have a connection with them, with all of nature. I supersede all mankind. My ancestors were men of war. Your ancestors were men of technology. Together they created me. Does that not make me the Savior?" the creature asked.

John did not answer. He did not know what to say to him. The light of his rifle blazed into the old man's eyes. It should have been blinding, burning, but the pathetic *thing* just gazed into it without blinking or any appearance of pain.

"Why do you stare at me like that, John."

"How do you know my name?"

"I know everything. With these," he said, lifting his arms into the air, raising the cables off the floor. "I have access into every person's life. Do you not think that I have the power to choose the destinies of man at will? I alone create and destroy. And I alone have chosen you to take the position as my *Top Man*."

Although the creature was a curious item, seemingly brilliant and genuine, John's finger began to bear down on the trigger of his rifle.

"I don't want anything to do with you," he said.

"Oh, but you cannot kill me, my son. I'm the father you always wanted... unlike that *monster* back on Labor."

The pressure of John's finger began to release, as the man's knowledge of him was becoming more revealing.

"And you, you are my heir. The son I've always wanted. Go ahead. See if you can kill me."

John continued to stare at the grotesque being. He found it difficult to take his eyes off of it on account of its bizarre and novel appearance.

"You cannot, can you?" it said to him. "You need me, son. I need you. I need an iron-fisted man to be my prophet, as it were: to bring my message to the world."

Taking aim at the center of the humanoid's face, John intended to end its insanity. This was the final target, the last in line. There would be no more mountains that he would need to conquer. It would be the concluding act of his own story, his raison d'etre. But he could not get himself to depress the trigger, to release the hammer of his weapon. He was burning up inside. His desire was there, but his will to achieve was not. Removing his eye from the rifle's sight, he eventually brought the weapon to a non-threatening posture, leaving the brightness of his flashlight as a shroud upon the god-man.

"I knew you couldn't do it," the creature smiled. "How could you possibly kill yourself? I've created within you everything I could never be, John. You will lead the worlds as I intended. You will be like a king. Sofia will be your queen. I will give you riches and honor among the sons of men. Just think about what all that entails: you will finally have the peace that you desire. Those that ruined your youth can be made to suffer. Come to me, my son. Let us enjoy the fruits of our labor together."

The humanoid held his hand out to John saying, "Through me the worlds will bow down to you."

John's yearning for the peace, the escape from all the hardships that he and Sofia had endured, the authority he was being handed, the power to meet out punishment at will, was urging him to give in.

"The masses will worship you, John."

Taking hold of the cold, pale hand, submitting himself to the caricatured father figure sitting before him, John could not find a reason to refuse as he lowered himself to the knees of the flesh-covered deity.

With his head bowed down, he was unable to see the sinister smile that spread across the pale lips of the face of evil.

"And through you, they will worship *me*."

A crack of gunfire scorched the air as John lifted his head to meet the splattering droplets of blood that splashed across his face: a witness to the exiting bullet boring a hole through the eye socket of his spiritual captor. Crumbling to the floor, the cables and wires that meshed with the cells of the dead man's skin coiled and rolled along the ground. The planet began to rumble with fierceness, quaking violently and rolling like the waves of the sea.

Behind the couch, leaning against the splintered threshold, Sofia was propped up, weak and trembling. A thin stream of smoke streamed from the barrel of her pistol.

As if he had just awaken from a terrible dream, trying to determine which dimension was the true reality, John asked her, "Sofia, what did you do?"

The pistol fell from her fingers as she slid to the floor along the frame of the door, crying and grasping at her thigh.

"I heard you calling. I had to find you. He had you, dear. I know you couldn't see it. But he had you. And I couldn't allow it."

CHAPTER FORTY-TWO

Maneuvering through the softly packed snow while bearing Sofia up in his arms was like running knee deep through mud: John was making little progress while exerting the greatest effort. It had taken him hours to get her back up to the Island's surface and out of the mansion's maze of hallways.

The icy marble staircase, now several hundred meters behind them, had been a welcoming site upon exiting the front door of the compound, as it signaled the nearness of their escape. But the glacial air of the outdoors, at first a respite from the suffocating interior, was now taking its toll upon John's legs, sucking out the much needed heat from them while causing his muscles to cramp and stiffen.

Having made the descent of the steep slope, he knew that the transporter was somewhere nearby, concealed behind the veil of windblown snow. He and Sofia were a single, unified entity moving across the frigid wasteland. The culmination of the mission was just within reach.

"I'm so cold, John," Sofia mumbled, her arms held limply about his neck with her face buried in the heavy padding of the chest of his jacket.

"Just a little further, girl. We're almost there," John panted, the steam of his breath twirling about his face. "I can see it. Almost there."

Under a mound of powdery whiteness, the transporter's deep, gray body was scarcely visible through its veiled covering. John cleared the entryway for Sofia, assisting her inside. Curled up in the fetal position, she was fast asleep the moment he shut the door.

"Banks, this is John, do you copy?" he spoke into the mic.

There was no reply, just the same static return that he had been receiving for the past few hours. As he walked around the vehicle to the driver's side door, John could not help but look back at the mansion's glowing presence upon the distant hill. He wondered, with a hardened heart, what the outcome would have been had Sofia not killed the peculiar man of Black Heart.

Through the haze of swirling flakes, the transporter's headlights reflected off of the airship's hull as John and Sofia made their approach. Behind the static of his earpiece, John could make out the sounds of Banks' voice. The closer that they moved to the air transporter, the clearer it became.

"John, this is Banks, do you copy?" the Captain's voice came through with clarity.

Pinching the tab on his neck, John called out, "Banks! We're inbound to the airship. Target: Top Man, eliminated. Target of unknown person, Black Heart, eliminated. How copy?"

There was a strange cross-chatter between Banks and an agent from Central, but John was unable to discern the specifics of their verbal exchange. After a moment Banks returned to him, "John, we need to make a run for it ASAP. Military is en route. You need to move fast. As soon as you're onboard we're lifting off, so make sure you two are secure for the ride."

"Roger that," John shot back.

Moaning under the pain that racked her nervous system, John could not understand why Sofia was so ill. The infection had been advancing rapidly, and John still had no knowledge of its destructive presence.

The bay doors were opening, bringing with it the fluorescent brightness of the interior lamps that haloed within the snowdrift, filtering through the windshield. The mechanical extension of the ship's cargo ramp was in full swing. John could feel the anxiousness in his gut from being so close to freedom, so close to leaving the frozen world of the Island behind.

As he made the ascension, the lights flooding the interior of the airship felt welcoming and warm, even if they were not actually dispensing any heat. Skidding to a halt in the cargo bay, he hopped out of the vehicle, securing the tie-down straps to the tracks.

"Banks, we're in," he shouted into the mic. "Get us out of here!"

The odd, incomprehensible cross-chatter between Banks and Central initiated once again, followed by the clear voice of the Captain sounding off in John's ear.

"Ten seconds, John! Stay clear of the door," he said with eerie calmness.

Climbing back inside their vehicle, John put his hand over Sofia's ear as the rising drum of the firing engines, igniting with their brilliant flames outside, began their roaring escalation. Under the violent upheaval of the airship struggling to break free from the gravitational pull of the planet, Banks returned to the mic, "Mission complete. Are you ready to go home?"

Depressing the actuator of his microphone, John relaxed his head back in the chair, saying, "I'm ready to be done, Captain."

With the airship reaching the outer atmosphere, the engines died down. The ride immediately became smooth and stable. Feeling the sensation of weightlessness slowly taking hold, John felt a sense of relief knowing that they had reached the emptiness of outer space.

"Banks," he said. "When's the debriefing?"

After another cross chatter session, the Captain returned, "We'll worry about that later. Try to get some sleep, friend. Fighting for freedom can be exhausting work."

Sleep. That was something John had not had a good dose of in a long time. He brushed his hand through Sofia's wet hair. She was burning up, sweating profusely. He figured that a good rest would help to heal whatever it was that she had caught.

Watching the snow float in cakes of melting ice and spheres of liquid off the top of the engine's hood, John could not help but think about how their little corner of the universe was on a path of change, hopefully for the better. But for now, philosophical inquiry was of no interest. Sleep sounded like the only good proposition.

Settling himself into the seat, he was able to relax for the first time in years. To close his eyes without the images of death filling his mind was true freedom indeed.

CHAPTER FORTY-THREE

Sofia had not moved in the slightest since John had last looked upon her before dozing off himself. He had no idea how long he had been sleeping, but he felt quite rested. Brushing aside the long bangs of hair that draped across her face, Sofia was much paler than she was earlier, almost a greenish-white, and her breathing was more rapid. He was not about to disturb her now, though. Central would have the medicines she needed, he thought. The more she rested, the better off she would be. Leaving the tracked vehicle behind, John floated to the upper decks, maintaining his coordination using the ladder's rungs.

"How are we doing, Banks? Are we almost home?" John spoke into the mic, his voice hoarse from fatigue.

Unlike the previous exchanges, there was no cross-chatter this time, no words returned from the Captain. John understood that the stresses of war were energy depleting. Banks was probably asleep at the wheel with the autopilot engaged.

Passing through the many holding cells of the airship, he straddled the final ladder leading to the flight deck. Although he did not care for Banks during his first encounter with the man on Red, the finality of the mission seemed to have altered his view of the world in general, and he was becoming rather fond of the Captain in particular.

Through the windowed portal of the door leading to the control room, John could see what appeared to be sparks flashing around the compartment. His first thought was that something was damaged during the escape, and Banks was probably in the process of making the repairs.

The steel door was tightly sealed, John muscled it with all his strength to get the locking mechanism to give. After fighting with it for several minutes, he was able to rotate it around, gaining access to the Captain's quarters.

"Banks! What's going on in...?" John said stepping inside, but cutting his question short... as there was nobody there to inquire of.

The entire flight console was a bludgeoned mess of wires and spark-sputtering smoke. The computer terminal ports had been pried from their panels and left dangling from damaged wires. Through the pilot's window it appeared that they were set on a course, destined to a place they did not want to get near to: the Great Star. It was still quite a distance from them, but considering how small it had appeared while en route to Black Island, it was much larger now. At the rate in which they were traveling, it would not be long before they were to meet its fiery essence face-to-face.

John was beside himself. He had been duped, and there was no denying it. Banks had tricked them into doing the dirty work for him on Black Island: an action the Captain himself was incapable of performing. The *Top Man* was obviously a front, a handsome mask for the masses to look upon without actually seeing the true demon controlling him from behind.

The homicidal virulence building up inside was too much for John to control. Grasping the mic that collared his throat, John screamed into it, "Banks! Banks, you filthy dog, where are you? Talk to me?"

The cross-chatter with Central filled his ears. It was the Captain speaking with an unknown agent.

"Central, all cold assets are inbound to the final destination. Black Island and Black Heart are secured. They're all ours, now. Prepare for full initiation."

"Copy that, Captain. Marvelous work. On your mark, begin the uplink."

"Central, be advised of a momentary delay. I've got two teams working to get the organic module to full operation. Medical standby is still preparing for my implantation. The deity-system is fully intact. I'll give you a head's up before we make the intro."

"Copy that, Captain," returned the unknown agent, "Welcome to the top of the world."

"I never thought we'd see this day," Banks laughed in reply.

Although not fully versed in every aspect of their conversation, John could deduce what was taking place: the Captain was about to take over where John had left off. He was being primed for full control, and there was nothing to stop him.

The Great Star was burning less than twenty-four hours from their current position in space. The airship had no internal controls, and John was at a loss for how to get them to safety. Sofia was too convalescent to provide any helpful input. John had made several wellness checks on her during the course of his search of the airship. She had hardly budged from her original position curled up on the seat in the tracked transporter.

Frustrated by his inability to find a solution to their problem, it seemed as if Banks' plan to kill them off was moving exactly as the Captain had hoped it would. John was beginning to feel the full brunt of guilt for the insolence of his youth. Unable to hide behind the blood shed from his hands, or the cries of pain from the nameless faces that he witnessed suffering under his will, he could no longer place the blame of his actions on the *enemy*. The reason for all his and Sofia's troubles lay completely at his feet.

Perplexed by his overwhelming desires for that spiritual and intellectual fulfillment that he had yearned for back in their home on Labor, John was finally brought to a point in his life where his mortality was on full display. He could see that every action he had initiated, and every choice he had made for them, it all seemed, in retrospect, to have been the wrong ones. His end and Sofia's end was now so near, too near. He wanted nothing more than to be by her side when it came.

Floating through the threshold and down the ladder that had brought him to the flight control room, John pulled the bag of explosives from his shoulder. He could easily prevent the suffering that they would soon be experiencing slowly burning up in the flames. A simple setting of the detonator would solve the problem. But taking his own life, for all the misery his birth had brought to the worlds, was of no moral consequence to him. It was the idea of Sofia's life that was the cause of his concerns. It was the burden with which he struggled most heavily. The most difficult aspect of the plan was not that he did not have the strength or courage to perform the task, but that he would, essentially, become the murderer of his own love... and that was the most profound charge against the entire case. It was the only act of violence that he knew he could never endure.

Passing through the next threshold, taking him closer to where he had left Sofia, John was startled to find her climbing through the circular opening in the floor below.

"Sofia," he called out. "What are you doing down there?"

Even in the weightlessness of space she could barely bend the joints of her extremities, as if they were becoming rigid and too resistant to her command.

"Is everything alright, dear? Where are Mary and Stephen? Are they with the Captain?" she asked in her state of confusion.

Pushing off with his legs, John descended from his lofty position on the ceiling, slowly falling beside her.

"Don't worry about them, girl. They're fine," he whispered into her ear as he took her up in his arms.

Carrying her back down to the transporter, he buckled her in, covered her up with his jacket and assisted her with light sips of water. Like thin glass, she seemed so frail in his arms, as if the slightest pressure would cause her to break. Running his fingers through her hair, John eased her back to sleep, kissing her on the forehead. If death was at their backdoor, there was no need for her to know about it. If nothing else, he could at least protect her from the suffering of knowing it was so near. Buckling himself in beside her, he closed his eyes, although he knew there would be no rest for him.

The heat of the cabin was growing steadily more uncomfortable as they neared the burning star. Removing his jacket from her, Sofia moved about restlessly, shivering despite the uncomfortably high temperature that was engulfing them.

John had not gone up to check where they were in their relative location in space. It did not matter in any way. He was helpless in the matter knowing he could no longer change the fate of his own course, let alone Sofia's.

Hours were passing by like the clouds that drifted through the skies over the forests of Labor. They could neither be captured nor restrained. The ticking of the hands of John's watch echoed in his ears, as if they were voices shouting out to him that their time had come.

As he slid his hands over his ears, drowning out the metronome-like beat of the gears of his timepiece, a violent turbulence rattled the airship.

The brilliance of the Savior's light was wandering through the windows of the control deck, illuminating the cabin and spilling through the small window upon the door. Trickling through the glass, it flowed through the hollow of the room, bouncing off the walls and raining through the threshold on the floor. Pouring into the deck below, like a creature following a trail, the particles swirled about like a whirlwind, followed by a tail of golden dust. Passing through threshold after threshold, winding through the rungs of the ladders that were bolted to the walls of the towering transporter, its mist of radiance entered the lowest bay, where a single tracked transporter was secured to the landing. Enshrouding it like a tomb, the light passed through the windshield, watering John and Sofia with its warmth.

With a gasp of her breath John sat up, his eyes filled with a whiteness so pure it was blinding.

CHAPTER FORTY-FOUR

The rolling dunes of golden sands covered over with scales of waving ripples, reached out to the edge of another windswept world of which, until now, John had not been privy to. The thick blackness of the burning airship, lying on its side, buried halfway into the crust of the planet upon impact, swelled and swirled into the yellow-orange sky of flaming tongues above.

He was dressed in his thin, battle uniform from Red. At his feet, Sofia was asleep, lying upon a makeshift cot fashioned from his insulated coat and pant. John had apparently dragged her from the ship, a few hundred meters below, if the concave trail formed in the sand behind them was any indication, although he did not recall doing it.

As far as he could see, there were no rocky outcroppings, no watering holes or places of refuge. Were it not for the wasted air transporter behind them, the fiery sky above and the soft golden sand beneath his feet, stretching for endless kilometers in every direction, were all that would appear to exist.

Shaking his head and rubbing his eyes, he was unsure if he was alive or if he was in the afterlife. The last thing he could recall was the warmth of a bright light, and perhaps, a voice, as of a child, but even that was vague and full of discontinuity. Taking up the leggings of the "cot" as if they were handles, John proceeded to pull Sofia behind him, hoping, with some luck, to find the help she needed.

With his lips parched and dry, his tongue pale and sticky, John thirsted for water, but there appeared to be no end to the desert. The planet was so warm and overwhelming. And by the flaming tongues that swirled endlessly in the cloudless atmosphere, he was certain that rainfall was not a feature of the world, either. Wherever he looked: above him was a fiery sky, below him stretched the rolling hills of fine grain sand creating beautiful patterns under the hand of the invisible wind.

After a lengthy period of wandering, John could not force himself to push on any further. He had reached the peak of the highest hill he could locate. Looking behind him, he could see the rising, black funnel of smoke, an oddity and a foreign object to such a golden desert.

Taking a seat beside Sofia, he laid his head down upon a soft, sandy mound to rest his mind. Gazing at the flames dancing upon the horizon, the breeze whistled through his ears as he closed his burning eyes. He intended for only a moment to leave the world behind, soothed by the light-filtering shades of his eyelids.

As John awoke several hours later, he sat up in a startle, as he caught a glimpse of a young boy disappearing over the edge of a hill in the distance.

"Sofia," he said. "I saw someone."

She did not answer. Pulling himself to his feet, he looked about his surroundings. The smoky rise from the airship was gone along with the carcass of the destroyed transporter. Even the wounded land upon which it crashed had been healed over. Faint with thirst, he picked up the "handles" once again, heading in the direction of what he thought might have been an apparition, a game his mind was playing under the influences of a dehydrated body.

The dunes were much more difficult to traverse now than they had been in the hours past. The deep cramping of the muscles of John's legs were hindering his progression up the steep sand banks. Leaving Sofia behind, he covered her up, protecting her from getting any particles blown into her mouth and lungs.

Crawling up the sand dune, John finally reached the place in which the young boy had disappeared. He was not expecting to see anyone, as he had been through a similar mental duress in the past while going through the Sweeper training. Hallucinations were not uncommon for someone in his condition, he thought. But the image of a young child, perhaps ten to twelve years of age, sitting upon a lone, black rock beside a crystal clear pond of water was the last thing he expected to find.

The boy smiled at him, and then cast his eyes skyward. "Who are you?" John asked, his voice was coarse and his throat sore with dryness.

There was no verbal response from the child. Hopping down from his seat, the boy dipped his hands into the water, forming a cup with his palms. Scooping up the precious liquid as if he were carrying a bowl, he walked up the embankment and poured it upon John's head.

As the water filtered through his hair, rolling onto his back and down his forehead, John felt the refreshment of his lost youth flowering inside of him. Tugging at his shirt, the young child, distressed in expression, pointed to Sofia at the bottom of the dune.

Sliding down its face, John trampled through the sand, renewed in strength, allowing him to pull Sofia effortlessly to the top of the hill. Reaching its apex, he dragged her down the slope, bringing her to the edge of the pool of soothing waters.

The child was waiting there for them, his hands cupped at his waist. John dropped the sleeves of the cot to the ground. Sofia's shallow breathing was quite apparent, and each breath passed by with a long, distinct pause. John recognized the detrimental state in which she was. He had seen it before, countless times in his training and on the battlefields: she was near death. Her body was gasping at its final taste of the air.

He was too exhausted and focused on the mission to realize her condition before. But now John's renewed alertness gave him the provisions he needed to allow his heart to burn with anger against Banks and the new government of men that had taken possession of the worlds. He wanted his mind back the way it was before the terrible turn of events on Raw. He wanted to wipe it clean of all that he had seen, all that he had heard, all the horrific acts he had performed. He hated the thought that he had been used. He was a pawn sent to its death in order to assist the planetary order out of one evil dress and into another, equally sinister outfit. And through all of this, Sofia had been dying, but he was oblivious to her suffering.

The young boy, as if aware of John's feelings and motives, cast his eyes down in despair before approaching the sickly woman.

Releasing the waters from his hands, the liquid came into contact with her skin. Sofia gasped aloud, sucking in the fresh atmosphere of the newly found planet. Her eyes opened and she grimaced in pain as she grabbed her leg.

Pulling the knife from his pocket, John flipped open its blade, jabbing it into her pant leg and ripping a hole in it, tearing through it to get at her wound. Horrified at the smell of her rotting flesh and the red-streaked, creamy liquid draining from the inflamed site of his bullet's impact, he was taken back, astonished. He looked to the child.

"Is there someone here that can help her?" he cried out.

The child stared at him, tilting his head in confusion.

"Little boy, where are your parents? She needs help," John screamed at him, expressing with his hands, motioning the child's attention to her infected leg.

Kneeling down by the water's edge, the young boy retrieved another handful of water. After looking to the sky as he had done before, he walked over to Sofia and poured it onto her traumatized flesh. The skin immediately began to foam upon contact, releasing a soothing sound, like the sounds of receding waves on the sands of a beach.

After performing the same operation on the exit wound, he strode through the shallow of the pool. Climbing back to the top of his rock, he sat down.

From the position on her back, Sofia stared into the flaming sky above. She was suddenly painless and free from the assault of the spreading infection and burning fever. As if the poisoned fluid of life that flowed through her veins was cleansed, she had the same renewed vigor of adolescence that John was experiencing, a feeling of true liberty. As she sat up, John knelt at her side, placing his arms around her.

"Where are we?" she asked.

"I'm not sure," he said.

Over John's shoulder, the young boy behind him sat, patient and quiet.

"John, who's that on the rock over there?"

"He's the one that saved us," Sofia heard him say.

The child was reminiscent of her and John's lost son. He was equal in bodily stature and shape. He had a confidence about him that was sure, yet humble. Although he was obviously someone else's little boy, she had an overwhelming sense of oneness with his being, as if he were her own. Her smile towards him was warm, like the ambience that surrounded them, and the young child, a strange curiosity in such a desolate land, smiled in return.

The journey from the pool into the rolling, orange sands of the desert seemed like a foolhardy excursion, but John consented to Sofia's wishes after much pleading from her to follow the child wherever he led them. She had argued with him regarding the native nature of the boy, and that he was obviously quite able to survive without anyone else's assistance. John could say little to counter her words.

Pulling her by the hand, the young child led Sofia deeper into the beautiful, yet barren land, with John in tow. He seemed to know exactly where he was taking them. Sofia was quite content with the trek, as it felt as though she and John were with their own son on a pilgrimage through their own personal planet.

Perplexed at their situation, John could not shake the nudging irritation that urged his temper. The more he stewed on the recent events of the past, the more he lost the vigor of life he received from the pool, and the more he began to thirst.

"If we could only find a way out of here," he murmured indignantly, as he scanned his eyes around, looking at the endless hills of sand. "I could probably get to Banks."

"The Captain?" Sofia asked with surprise. "Is he alive?"

Irked by her tone of glee, he responded with out hesitation, "Unfortunately. He tried to kill us."

"He what?" Sofia said with astonishment. "Why?"

"That mission we did on Black Island. It was all part of their plan. I killed the men at the highest level," he said, unaware of the saddened expression the young boy was bearing as he listened to John from over his shoulder. "That allowed Banks and Central to take control of the worlds."

Bewildered by the news, Sofia was brought back to the reality of their present circumstances. As she thought about Maryanne and Stephen, the fantasy world she was enjoying so much had suddenly vanished. Her innocent mindset lost out to the cares of the cold, hard worlds she had wanted so much to leave behind. Gone was her dream. And a deep, unforgiving thirst began to set in.

Under the blackness of her demeanor, the child released Sofia's hand, listening to her and John converse. There was very little expression from him... until John said, "Maybe we could find our ship. If we could somehow get it working again we could probably return back to the Island and I could kill him, putting an end to their plans."

Hanging his head down in grief, the child despondently led them over one last sandy hill where they were presented with another pool of water, less clear and mildly bitter in aroma. Holding his hand out, as if to offer them a drink from its glassy waters, he seemed disappointed, but neither John nor Sofia noticed as the desire of thirst burned within them.

Scooping up the water in their hands and taking their sips, they noticed in the reflection on the pond's surface, the airship was standing erect behind them, reaching up to the flames of the sky. As they turned back to look upon it, the particles of the Savior fell over its silhouette and into their eyes, blindingly white and arrayed in softness.

With her bare feet strolling through the cool, green grass of a world without death, Sofia looked upon the ball of light that radiated from her hands. Turning her palms over, the light fell to the ground, disappearing into the pores of the soil, like water poured upon dry sand.

John watched as Sofia's feet playfully trampled through the crimson waters of the Red Sea. He had somehow returned to the planet of war, but, while he instinctively knew that the great battle was playing out in the distant valley, he also knew that he had to run to Sofia, she had something of great importance to tell him.

Strapped inside the tracked transporter in the loading bay of the airship, Sofia awoke beside John, who was yawning and stretching as if he, too, had just risen from a deep slumber. The rumbling of the reverse thrusters was wailing outside. The sudden sensation of slowing down from a rapid descent began to bear down upon their sense of orientation. Before they could question each other as to the strange events that had befallen them, the air transporter touched down and the bay doors immediately began to rise.

The familiar breeze of red dust blowing in was indicative of the fact that they had somehow managed to return to planet Red. Its choking air and distant booming battle sounds were characteristic features of the ruby painted world John had come to know so intimately.

Exiting the tracked vehicle, John walked around to meet Sofia. Taking her by the hand, they proceeded to the ramp outside.

Surprised to find the young child already standing at the bottom edge of the downslope, they approached him from behind as he curiously bowed his head. Nearing him, they could see that he had been weeping for, what appeared to be, an impossibly extended duration of time, as the crystalline pool of water resting at his feet seemed to have formed from the tears he had been shedding.

"Why are you crying, little boy?" Sofia asked as she knelt beside him and placed a loving arm over his shoulder.

Lifting his hand he pointed to the world below. The explosive nature of the planet had intensified ten fold since the last time they had experienced its deadly display. The overview of the land from their mountainous outlook allowed them to see that the carnage of the Valley of Death had spread like a cancer to the surrounding regions, reaching even to the heart of the ruins. Hundreds upon hundreds of columns of smoke arose from the burning heaps that littered the battlegrounds upon the layers of corpses, the blistering explosions and the constant chatter of small arms fire. It was all an accompaniment to the blackness of the heavy air that polluted and poisoned the planet.

As John looked upon the war weary scene, he could not help but feel the burning wall of hatred naturally building up inside of him. As if the young child had, once again, been given access to the thoughts going through John's mind, he cast his tearfully youthful gaze upon him and, pushing Sofia's arm away, he held his hand out to them, as if to offer a drink from his waters.

The sudden thirst that overcame John was oddly familiar, and he could feel the skin of his lips suddenly drying up and withering. His tongue became strangely sticky, as if someone had opened the tap to his body and drained him of all of his fluids. The crystal waters of the pool looked so inviting. Giving into his desire to quench his craving, he fell at the boy's feet gulping the salty liquid.

Heartbroken at the child's insistence of removing her arm from him, Sofia's mouth began to dry, and the appetite for liquid refreshment caught her unaware. Seeing John partaking of the bitter waters made her hunger for it as well, forcing her to bow down beside him. Dunking her hand into the spring, she brought the cool, refreshing waters to her mouth and drank.

The special particles of light from the Savior traveled along the rays of golden bars that broke through the clouds. Scorching a path across the land, the flames of its wrath devoured everything in its course. As the lights reached the young boy, with Sofia and John at his feet, the brightness poured into their eyes, filling them with the whiteness of its purity.

Searching through the rich dirt of the fertile valley, Sofia dug passionately for the light that she had lost. She knew it illuminated John's body, giving it life. The palms and fingers of her hands were covered over with soil, but that meant John was nearby. She only needed to find the light.

The warmth of water was up to John's knees as he approached his love while she bathed in the Sea of Red. Its waters dripped from Sofia's hair, forming circular ripples upon the glassy surface into which she was submerged.

"Come closer, dear," she said, holding out her arms.

The water was up to his chest by the time he reached her. As he held his arms out, Sofia fell into them, dipping her head back and looking into his eyes.

"What did you want to tell me?" he asked.

"John, my dear, this is the day that you will find all the answers that you have been seeking."

He wanted to inquire more deeply, but the brightness of a blinding light was consuming the world.

The cargo bay doors of the transporter began to open and Sofia and John found themselves overlooking the scorched flatlands of Raw. Basket Town was in chaos. Like the warzones of Red, the blackened funnels of smoke lifted to the heavens from the buildings and vehicles that fell victim to the rebellious battles. Screams and wailing filled the air in an accompaniment of small arms fire reminiscent of the Valley of Death.

Running down the ramp, Sofia stopped at the edge of the cliff beside which the transporter had landed. Horrified by the visions of violence, she covered her eyes and fell to her knees. As John walked up beside her, the burning wall of hatred filled his heart. Seeing the destruction of the people brought back the corruption of his mind. The first thoughts to enter in were flooded with vengeance.

The young boy, teary eyed and mournful, took him by the hand and looked to the sky. Certain he had seen the child before,

John noted mentally every detail of his actions: the movement of his arm, the upward gaze, the short stepped gait. The light of the Savior hid behind the rapidly forming clouds, and then, without any hint of its approach, the rains began to fall.

Pooling around their feet, the waters filled the land, muddied and murky to behold. But the puddle of liquid around which the child stood was as clear as a diamond, sparkling and pure.

Under the coolness of the storm, Sofia pushed back her yellowy-white bangs and began to thirst. The battles of the valley had become obscured and muffled, too difficult to sense through the torrential rains. Seeing John and the young boy a few meters away, fogged by the mist that was forming over the warm land of Raw, it appeared that her mate was bowing down to the child. Running through the soft, wet soil, she found him lapping up the bitter waters in which the young boy stood. Kneeling beside him she joined him in the pool.

The cloudy skies began to abate, and the Savior's lights filled the air. Blanketed with the warmth, the clean brightness of its purity once again entered their eyes and filled their souls.

The light of John sprung forth from the grassy soil at Sofia's feet, like the flowering plants in the newness of the springtime. The message that she had delivered to him at the Sea of Red had become his awareness: he was rising up like the stars of the night.

John held Sofia in his arms. The waters of the Sea dripped warmly across his hands.

"Where will the answers come from, Sofia? Please, answer me," he pleaded.

She opened her eyes. His image was reflecting off the blackness of her pupils. Like strings of time, they played a melody of beauty that only he could hear.

The sky filled with the brilliance of the reverse thrusters of millions of transporters descending upon Red's surface around the sea, shaking the planet to its very foundation. The light of the Savior burned with fury, blinding John from witnessing the continuance of its power.

The bay doors opened once again. Sofia and John were standing on the ramp leading to the overgrown, ivy patches of the ruins of Labor's launch facility at the base of the mountains: a place they had once thought to be named the Red Plant. Devoid of human life, the vegetation had concealed its once ash-laden soil, hiding it beneath layers of grass, bushes and youthful trees. The warehouses that used to extend for kilometers were now covered over, appearing like mounds of natural formations, rolling away in the distance. The brightly lit fencing was long torn down with nary a hint of their ever having existed. A thick strip of grass, like a pathway, meandered away from the burnt out umbrage that fell under the devouring heat of their transporter.

Descending the ramp, neither John nor Sofia could believe the changes that had taken place in their former planet. As far as they were able to see, the Highway's tunnel had fallen in upon itself, leaving heaps of overgrown concrete in a trail of moss and ivy covered rubble that twisted through the valleys and hills, into the world beyond. The young boy was somehow already taken to walking upon its path when they passed through remains of the ivy-coated pylons standing erect at what had once been the entrance to the compound. Waving his hands, the child waited for them to catch up.

Climbing along the Highway's remains, the spaces in the concrete slabs and boulder-shaped rubble revealed the skeletal remains of the dead, trapped within their transporters or crushed under the fallen roof and walls. By the bleached bones that lightly protruded from the soil outside of the ruins, it appeared that some of the people had tried to flee from the terror, but died en route to the forest while attempting to make their escape.

The damage was concise and thorough, leaving nothing alive within its walls, and leaving nothing intact as to its structure. Whatever happened, Sofia thought, it must have been a terrible sight to behold.

Following the course of destruction, both she and John knew that they would be eventually reaching the boundaries of Labor City. Fearing what they would find at the end of the line, Sofia intuitively walked closely beside the young boy with maternal protection, subconsciously vigilant and prepared to do everything in her power to keep him safe.

After several hours of traversal, it became quite apparent to John that the Savior had not so much as moved a single centimeter across the open expanse above. It had remained static upon its skyward resting place, hanging as it were, like a glowing ornament upon a wall of ocean blue. Had the planet come to a standstill? Had it stopped rotating on its axis, he wondered. With the bizarre nature of their journey, he kept the observation to himself and pressed onward.

Sofia could not help but look to the West, hoping to see the place that they had once called *home*. The thick green of the forest, and the distance that would need to be covered to reach it, were much greater than their view allowed, and she knew it. But still, the yearning for the peace that she had while it lasted was something she believed would never leave her. Holding tightly to Sofia's hand, the child looked contently upon her, as if he were in a state of emotive unity with her, enjoying the peacefulness of life as she did.

As the Savior still had not changed from its position for an unimaginative number of hours, John understood that they were actually going to make the entire trip to Labor before the Great Star had set over the westerly horizon. It seemed remotely impossible to traverse such a long distance in a single day, as he remembered several nights transpiring before he and Sofia had made the full journey. But an unmoving light source had not been available to them before. The impossible was seemingly possible, now.

Highly aware of his surroundings, John had an incredible sense of well-being. The thirstless strength that carried him onward allowed him to effortlessly move through the ruinous heaps of concrete without so much as breaking a sweat.

Fully healed of her wounds, Sofia could hardly remember what the suffering felt like. She was able to traverse the land with as much ease as John, hopping from structure to structure. Physically, she seemed as fit as she had been years ago, on that day when they left the City through the wound in the Highway's wall.

The young boy provided their pace without ever tiring. He was peculiar in his own right, so quiet and secure. His aura was a living entity all its own. Sofia wondered why it was that he was leading them in the direction of Labor, but she did not have the desire to ask him.

The hike across the Highway's ruins, slithering through the valleys and across the forest-lined fields, was time consuming, but enjoyable. Sofia and John felt at home, as if they had never left the forests of Labor in the first place. Were it not for the burning wall of John's mind that would creep in during their discussions of sensitive topics, the thoughts of other planets existing in the farthest reaches of their little portion of the universe, the wars and disputes between the varying factions vying for power, could have easily been forgotten, concealed under a perspective of deliberate ignorance.

Although there were many hours to waste away, time had finally made an allowance for the two of them to get reacquainted. But neither John nor Sofia considered for a single moment about bringing up what had transpired during their time apart. It was much too painful. Instead, they kept close to each other. That was comfort enough.

Having only traveled once near the Highway, the world around them was unfamiliar in particulars. Generally speaking, it was still home. But with each passing minute the city drew closer, and the anxious feeling bubbling in John's stomach grew more intense. There was no way to tell what it was that awaited them at the end of the day's journey, but they continued to put their faith in the child, following him wherever he led.

CHAPTER FORTY-FIVE

Labor had finally come into view. It was nothing like John and Sofia had remembered. From the distance that they were observing it, and after their experiences with the other worlds, the breadth and depth of the once thriving metropolis seemed so minute in comparison, especially when considering the ravaged state in which it presented itself to them.

The overlapping rooftops had collapsed long ago, decaying in the streets under thick layers of moss and green brush, allowing the light of the Savior to saturate its once hidden face. The walls of the city, the Corral, had also fallen into disrepair and waste, leaving only hints of its past existence visible under the free roaming grass.

As they advanced nearer to the City, John's fire began to kindle. The memories of its claustrophobic, controlled environment had jumped to the forefront of his mind. Although the landscape had changed, and the Great Light from the sky was leading the way, it was still Labor, no matter how much he tried to rationalize upon it.

From the street level view, just outside what had once been the original border of the Corral, the City appeared to be a ghost town. Its streets were deserted and barren. The peoples were scarce, perhaps hidden in their apartments waiting for the Savior to return to his home on the other side of the planet, and the night skies to present them anew. Or, perhaps, John thought, they were all dead, destroyed by the ravages of a violent uprising, like that of Raw.

Holding Sofia and the young boy back, John insisted that he lead the way in. Following close behind him, Sofia gripped the child's hand firmly as they passed through, what had once been, the red brick structure that coupled the City to the Highway.

The eerie feeling of returning to their place of origin, but under differing circumstances and environmental conditions, was somewhat overwhelming to Sofia. Although the memories of her youth were not so wonderful, it was the place from which she and John had made their vows to each other that they would always be one. It still held that special place in her heart.

With the rooftops destroyed, the buildings seemed to John to be so short and unimpressive. The dull, blue-gray dreariness that once pervaded the culture was now green and vibrant, allowing only scant glimpses of its morbid past to peek through the unfettered growth of the natural world. The inhabitants, if there were any left, and if they still shunned the Light above, would now merely exist as nocturnal beasts.

Walking beside Sofia, the young boy grasped the reins of her heart with maternal care, giving her the sense that he was her own. His fingers were about the same size that her son's had been on the day that he disappeared from her life. His hair was similarly shaded. His eyes were as equally bright. Sofia wanted to kneel down and hug him, but she refrained, for she knew deep inside, somewhere out there, perhaps hidden in the City, his mother was waiting. She would do whatever she could to reunite the woman with her little boy. But if she could not be found, then Sofia would keep him for her own, providing the love he lost, just as she hoped someone, somewhere, was providing the same for her child.

Passing through the emptiness of the decayed metropolis, John found very little difficulty remembering it the way it had been. Gone for the good were the orange lights above, the Security agents, the congested streets. Walking among the destruction, he was feeling rather envious of those that laid the once proud City to waste, wishing he had been a partaker of its demise. As if John's appetite for violence was being projected into the child's mind, the young boy bowed his head in shame.

"John," Sofia whispered from behind.

Turning back towards her, John was quite surprised at how far he had unwittingly led them into the City, as the red, brick entrance visible over Sofia's shoulder was now several blocks away.

"Let's let him lead the way now, okay?" she asked with a tone of concern. "I think he's looking for somebody."

The deteriorated, windowless buildings prevented that *being watched* feeling from ever making its presence known, and John did not have that insecure intuition that he usually experienced when a threat was nearby. Agreeing to her request, he said, "Alright, but just for a little while."

With the young boy situated between them holding their hands, he began to guide them back down the street they had come. The Savior was still hovering directly overhead, floating in the same fixed position for the past several hours. His beams of light pierced through the fractured frames of the city's edifices, creating an ambience of reassurance.

Directing John and Sofia down several more streets, the child guided them with an apparent confidence of mind. Crossing through multiple alleyways before taking one final path between the skeletal remains of two fallen apartment complexes, he, to Sofia and John's amazement, had escorted them directly to Labor Apartment: Building 1A, the birthplace of their wearisome journey.

CHAPTER FORTY-SIX

The scanner to access the elevator was lying on the floor beside the cracked and jagged threshold leading to the empty shaft. With the sliding doors having been removed, John peered upward into the emptiness through which the lift had once run its course. The blueness of the sky gazed back at him. The roof of that section of the building was no longer there.

Bringing his head back inside the crumbling, dreary lobby, with its stained walls and morbid past, John stepped aside as Sofia took his place. She curiously took in a peek to see for herself what had become of their old ride. Several of the floors above appeared to be missing the elevator's doors, as well. Feeling a tug upon her arm, the child was desirous of her attention. Pulling her towards the stairwell, he urged her and John to follow him further up into the structure's remains.

The entrance scanner to the stairway was, as the previous one, a mess of rusted metal and tangled wires torn from the wall. Glass from its lens and screen scattered across the dirt of the floor. With the electrical generators of the city appearing to be non-functional, John expected to find the stairway hidden in the blackness of its enclosed design, but the holes of the walls provided enough room for the Savior to find them, allowing His light to reflect off of the high volume of dust floating in the air, illuminating their steps.

Walking into the hall of the top floor brought back a mix of emotions. The roof over their heads in this portion of the building still existed to some extent, but the apartment in which John had grown up was no longer there. Along with that entire side of the building it had been torn away and thrown into the streets below. Looking out at the city from, what used to be, a blackened hallway, but now existed as an open view, was in his mind, a much more comfortable image, as he truly did not want, in his heart, to return to the Monster's lair ever again.

Passing by Mr. Sander's old home, the frame of the door appeared to have been blown open, perhaps by explosive force, or some other destructive means. The floor of his living room had collapsed into the apartment below it, making it too dangerous for them to consider going inside.

Leading them further down the hall, the child pulled on their arms, as if to hasten them to their destination. The hallway leading to the Forbidden Room was dark and damp, its walls dripping with moisture. Lit up at the other end by the Savior's light, the red hue that they remembered so vividly was no longer present. Although much of the roof above them was missing, the door leading up to their paradise, to their once secret place above the city, was still intact.

As the child continued to lead them up the steps, he released Sofia's hand and pushed the door aside. She could feel the deep and heavy thumping of her heart beneath the bony plate of her chest, as if she was experiencing the discovery of the rooftop for the first time.

The brightness of the Savior was blinding as they passed through the doorway and ascended the final steps leading to the platform-like structure above: a portion of their hidden world, a few meters across, that had not fallen into corruption.

The highest structure of the City overlooking the distant hills, unhindered by the ugliness of the Corral or the bustling noise of the peoples below, held them aloft once again, as it had done so many times in the past. Their journey seemed to have taken a full three hundred sixty degree turn, bringing them back to where they had first begun. Only this time around the circumstances were altered to suit them better.

Releasing John's hand, the child allowed them to walk together without his interference. Holding each other, the first thing Sofia did was to instinctively look to the sky for a wishing star, but there were none.

John could not believe the view. With the city in such decay and overgrown with the vegetation of the wilderness, the metropolis itself was no longer a point of contention. He wanted to ask Sofia to renew their vows, to return with him to their home in the forest. But vengeance was still on his mind, pushing him to find a means to fulfilling its devious end. It was holding him captive, just as the desire for knowledge had once held him many years ago, when it forced him to take Sofia far from their home, far from each other.

He tried to fight against it, but the burning anger of the wall of fire struck back. Why could he not control it, he thought. Why would it not leave him alone?

From their location above him, neither John nor Sofia could see the child waiting at the bottom of the stairs, alone and saddened by John's inability for self-control. Sitting down and closing his eyes, a teardrop, as if it were pure light, rolled down his cheek, falling into his open palm. A rumbling in the sky, like an approaching storm, proceeded to shake the City's foundations. The shadows of the hills, the blackened bars of the shades of the trees, began to stretch and accumulate. The Savior flew across the sky from its eastward perch, fluttering to the west, where it suddenly set behind the mountains, bringing an immediate blackness upon the land.

In the streets below, the movement, the voices, the sounds of the City coming to life were everywhere. Generators across Labor were turning over, allowing the orange lights that littered the walkways to flicker and shine. The darkness of the skies above filled with the bluish glow of hundreds of wishing stars returning home, descending upon Labor.

As the ground beneath them quaked with an increasing energy, their rooftop platform began to crumble and fall into disarray. Pulling Sofia behind him, John led her back down the stairs and hoisted the child up into his arm. Leaving the Forbidden Room behind, they ran through the darkened hallway, stumbling and reeling as the building swayed and convulsed. Turning the corner and heading towards the stairwell, they could hear voices blaring throughout the metropolis through strategically positioned loudspeakers, repeating over and over, "The terror and his army have returned. Prepare yourselves to fight in the war to end all wars. The child among you must be destroyed. Only then will his army fall."

The stairwell was once again lit up with the dim, pumpkin orange of the terrible lights of the old days, allowing John and Sofia to descend it with minimal interference. Entering into the lobby, they could see through the threshold leading to the streets that the City was still equally as populated as it had been long ago, perhaps more so, now. But the peoples of Labor had changed. Although equally hateful and full of rage, they were now armed with weapons of war. They seemed to be eagerly awaiting the arrival of the airships, as each person's face was reflecting the bluish-white light that emitted from the transporters as they looked to the skies.

"Destroy the child, destroy his army," the voice of the speaker proclaimed. "Long lives the Savior of the Island!"

Destroy the child, John thought as his eyes met the young boy's.

"Who are you?" he asked him, but the child did not answer.

"John," Sofia whispered, motioning to the boy. "Are they talking about him?"

"I think they are."

"Why would they want to...?"

"I don't know, girl," John interrupted, as she broke through his chain of thought. He had to think fast. He had to make a plan, a way to sneak them out of the compound.

Pulling Sofia by the hand, he carried the boy into the shadows of the orange lights, taking them out of the apartment building and edging them along the ruinous piles of concrete debris. The forest was just a few hundred meters away. As long as they were not spotted, they could easily escape without harm.

Crossing along the unlit, blackened paths in the middle of the street, they quietly headed towards an alleyway that ran alongside a gathering of the Labor's citizenry. Entering between the two buildings, they scurried along the walls, eventually reaching the exit on the other side.

John held Sofia and the young boy back while he continued ahead, peering around the corner. It appeared that the way was clear. But as he proceeded to take the first step onto the open sidewalk, two burly men, mumbling to each under the excess of alcohol of which they both reeked, exited the building through a doorway beside him, startling at the sight of the child. One of them, rather heavy-set and covered over with filth, appeared to recognize the boy, and in a fearful rage, he lifted the pistol from his waist belt, aiming it towards him.

John lunged at the man, dropping him to the floor with a crushing slam of his fist against the man's stubbly face. Grabbing at the barrel of the weapon, he forced the firearm's line of sight away from the child in an attempt to disarm him. Pulling the trigger, the stranger blindly fired into the wall of the building, the bullet burrowing deep into it in a puff of dust and falling concrete particulate. Under the intense recoil, the firearm slipped from the man's hand, falling to the ground.

As the attacker groaned on the pavement, dazed by the blow to his head, John pulled the wounded savage up, shielding himself with the man's body. Taking up the handgun, he turned it on the other crazed citizen. The confused drunkard was fumbling about for the rifle he had slung over his shoulder.

"Stop," Sofia yelled to the man of Labor, but it was too late. John's bullet tore into the man's head, dropping him to the ground.

Instinctively placing the barrel at the back of the head, John fired again, killing his captive, sending his life's fluid bursting into the air. As the drops hit the wall, the child screamed out, seemingly bringing to pass another, more intense quaking of the ground.

In a sudden chaotic uproar, voices began to rise from the masses down the street, "It's him, the child! Kill it!"

Several mobs began to run at them. John, taking up the boy once again, yelled out, "Sofia, run!"

Dark and confused, it was difficult to discern from which direction the hordes were closing in. The rumbling of the skies was beginning to drown out the noise of the streets, as the transporters of the air were now visible in their fullness.

Setting the child down, it appeared that they were surrounded. Taking Sofia by the hand John said, "I don't know what else to do. There's no where to run to."

John covered the boy's face and squinted as the dust kicked up wildly around them. The flaming blue teardrops of the heavens were getting acquainted with streets of the City and the forested lands upon its perimeter. The shadows of the mobs bearing down upon them through the smoke and haze were like the beasts of the forest, stalking and evil. Protecting their eyes, they huddled close together and waited.

Too difficult to see anything under an arm's length, Sofia uncovered her face as she heard the distant screams of the young boy.

"John," She yelled looking about. "Where is he? What happened to him?"

Drowned out in the roaring of the engines, John pulled Sofia towards the direction from which they last heard him. He dragged her into the swarms of faceless men and women standing in the gloom.

As the rumblings eased down to idling hums, the haze began to reconcile with the stillness of the air, settling out and allowing for the return to visible normalcy. The bay doors of the airships drew their mouths open, releasing their lights, and extending their ramps to the masses.

"The war to end all wars has come. Enter in to fight the fight," the speakers wailed.

The City's populace began to gather inside the transporters, roaring with emotion and energy for the battle, leaving the world of Labor forever behind. A group of men and women shouted to the approval of those within earshot, "We have drawn first blood! Their king is dead! Their king is dead!"

The rise of the city's energetic life resounded with the chant, "The king is dead!" as Sofia and John pushed their way through the ocean of people and into the area from which the chant began. The concentration of the masses was beginning to dilute as the airships were being filled to capacity. Through the thinning remnants, laughing and spitting upon a bloodied pool in their midst, the crowds dispersed. Entering into the heart of the tumult, Sofia found the shoe of the young boy smeared and disturbed among the gruesome puddles of his lost life. There was nothing else left of him.

With her legs weakened under the strain of the moment, she fell to her knees, covering her face and weeping, for it was like losing her own child all over again. John stood beside her, his mouth agape with horror: it was as if he was back in his Room of Death on Raw, and had been partaker in the boy's murder. He should have done more, he thought.

Turning his pistol upon those last few men and women that had spit upon the child's blood, he pulled the trigger. But the magazine was empty, and the hammer fell to no effect.

Unaware of his volatile environment, too focused on his immediate concerns, John did not see that the Security agents were pulling up the rear of the crowds, forcing the stragglers to move into the awaiting ships.

A baton knocked the empty pistol out of his hand, while a gruff voice yelled at him from behind, "Get moving, the war's waiting."

Two men lifted Sofia to her feet and shoved her into John's arms. Urging them to move with haste to an awaiting air transporter, the line of agents forcing the peoples into the airships stretched throughout the streets, disappearing around the corners and into the forests.

John assisted Sofia on the path that they were being directed, jostled about by the hordes of men and women surrounding them. He wanted to avoid all negative contact with the Security personnel, if possible.

"He's gone, John. They killed him," Sofia cried. "I can't believe it. I couldn't do anything to help him."

John did not have any words of consoling for her, as he was as equally bewildered by the event as she. Finally reaching the top of the ramp of the rumbling machine, he could find no room for escape.

Once inside, John could see that the interior of the bay was packed with Labor's citizenry. With men and women in a consistent stream ascending the ladder at the opposite side of the bay, he was certain that the upper levels were equally filled.

Stepping over the orifices of the bay door's teeth, he pressed into the crowds, forcing enough room for him and Sofia to avoid being crushed under the lowering door of the ship's hull. Outside in the City, the generators were powering down. The orange lights of the streets were flickering off in large sections throughout the dead metropolis until it became, as it actually existed in its heart, one with the darkness.

With the transporter sealed shut, the engines began to rev up. If war were to be their destination, it would not be long before they would be stepping back onto the bloody soil of planet Red.

CHAPTER FORTY-SEVEN

A s the airship touched down, the mouth of its hull opened to
the ravages of Red's plains. Overlooking the surface of the dev-
astated planet, its sky black with smoke, its land shimmering under
the layers of coagulated liquid, the smell of death heavy in the air,
John and Sofia were pressed with the crowds to exit the transporter.

One phase of the battle before them was coming to an end. The
last few hundred soldiers remaining on the death fields struggled
to make their final kills before the next drove of awaiting forces
were called in to the fight.

Stepping down the ship's ramp, followed by the howling and
cursing hordes of Labor ready for the war, Sofia and John appeared

as merely two of the millions of faces that lined their side of the battlefield. Transporters as far as the eye could see, had landed in a single file line, emptying their contents of warriors and war machines out from their bellies. Formations of soldiers, wearing various dresses of civilian and military apparel, were already set in battle array before them. Consisting of tens of thousands of individuals per unit, they stretched along the red desert's rolling hills, awaiting their calling to enter into the fray. Surrounding them, wheeled transporters carrying mounted weaponry, prepared for their calling, as well.

The Valley of Death was far to John's right, its polluted hills still receiving the dead that were falling upon it. Too small to contain the war-to-end-all-wars, the overflow from its veins had spread into the hilly desert in which he and Sofia were now standing.

To his left, he could see what had become of the ruins. Structures no higher than those found on Labor were all that remained, the smoke of its torment rising to the heavens in continual funnels of blackened clouds.

Directly across from their camp, the *enemy* of the people of this side of the wasteland was set in their formations. Equal in size, waiting their turn to enter the killing fields, the offspring of the murderous pit of the Valley, the opposing forces were a mirrored image of one another.

But John knew the game now: every man and women on the planet was merely following orders. Nobody was acting with a certainty that they were shooting in self-defense. How could anyone know that those that they were trying to kill actually wanted to do him or her harm prior to the command to do so? Banks and his new government were starting over. They were wiping out every last remnant of humanity that they could not directly control with ease and simplicity.

As the final deathblow was given to the opposing side, the few individuals that remained were limping, kneeling and crawling through the battlefield, ignored by the agents in charge. The command was given, echoing through the choking air, for the awaiting formations of soldiers and vehicles to make the charge.

Both sides initiated with the cries of hatred. Like an avalanche of human madness, millions of men and women rushed upon each other, savagely firing their weapons before them, dropping the survivors of the previous engagement, or else swallowing them up in their rolling waves of destruction. With the front lines of both sides fallen, the masses behind trampled their corpses into the ground, burying them deep within the blood soaked soil.

As John and Sofia, and the other peoples of the recently arrived airships, reached the end of the ramps, they were handed their weapons, a rifle and a sword. By threat of a slow, painful death, they were coerced into joining their assigned units, if they were not so inclined already to do so.

The bullets of the battle below were buzzing around freely, ricocheting off the airships, burying into the sand with puffs of dust, slamming into the awaiting men and women, killing some, wounding others.

John kept Sofia's head low as they were led into an organized structure of soldiers. Stepping over the corpses and pieces of the dead, they took their positions among the rank and file. Several wheeled transporters, scattered throughout the airship landing zones, pulled up alongside them. John saw an opportunity waiting. Blending in with the masses, he pulled Sofia to the rear of their unit.

"We're going to try to make a break for one of those vehicles," he said, looking around for a clear opening, hoping the agents in charge would be too busy to notice.

Sofia's eyes were awash with redness, swollen and glossy. Seemingly unable to give a verbal exchange, she just stared and nodded her head in the affirmative.

"If we can make it," John continued. "I'll try to get us through the warzone. We might be able to find a place to hide in the mountainous region beyond the Red Sea."

A soldier to his side fell to his knees in the sand, holding his bleeding gut, screaming in pain. John tried to ignore him, but with the bullets flying by and the screams of agony from those being wounded by the stray projectiles increasing beyond comfort, he pulled Sofia closer to him, providing his body as her shield.

His girl was no soldier. She was fearful, even now refusing to hold her rifle, covering her ears instead. She had thrown her sword down moments earlier when the agents were out of sight. She was refusing to partake in being a murderer.

The battle below had reached its peak as the two sides had absorbed each other into one organic whole of annihilation. The smoke of the destroyed vehicles, like black pillars holding the sky in place, arose from the sands. As the explosions rocked the hills, John knew that within a few minutes time their turn would come to make the charge of death.

Blocked from the view of any of the commanding agents by the offroad vehicle idling next to them, John directed Sofia to crouch down with him beside the passenger door. Reaching for the door handle, he slid a knife from his pocket, unfolding its blade. Just as he was about to make his move, a knock, like a fist pounding on a wooden table, resounded from behind him. From over his shoulder John could see Sofia lying down, her arms spread out and the back of her head pressed into the red sand. Her skin was pale, as it had been on the Island, but there no rise and fall to her chest this time. She just lay there, peaceful and still.

"Sofia, are you alright?" he asked, leaving off with his plan and crawling over to her.

As he placed his hand under her head, he noticed the small puncture wound in her temple. Trickling the red fluid of life into her ear and onto the soil beneath her, the dust receiving her blood began to take on a deep burgundy hue. John could only stare in disbelief.

"No, this can't be happening," he whispered.

His hands were trembling as he began taking her body gently into his arms. Brushing her hair from her face, tears trickled down his cheeks.

"It's alright, Sofia," he said. "I'm going to get us out of here. I promise. Just give me a little more time, girl. Just a little more time."

As his fingers continued to stream through the strands of her hair, the yellow-whiteness of Sofia's locks began to conform to the ruby red of the sand beneath them.

"Don't go, Sofia. Not here. Not now," he cried.

The roar of the battle sounds was thrown upon him with the likes of an audience cheering for her death. Brought back to the planet of war, to die in such a lonely world forsaken by any hint of beauty, Sophia's lifeless shell was all that remained of everything John had the purpose of living for.

"Let me take you home, girl," he wept. "Let's go home, now. I just want to go home."

Her eyes were still open, staring into nothingness. The sky blue beauty of her youth was draining out of her with the streams of her blood, turning them into the ashen gray color of an overcast morning. The warmth of her skin was fleeing, taking with it the blush-pinkness of her once rosy cheeks.

With his hand supporting her head, he took one last look into the blackness of her pupils. She had no tears left. Her pain was gone. All he could see was a reflection of his own face. It was youthful and innocent.

A passing courier on the sidewalk of Labor bumped into him, and John suddenly came to his senses, as if he had been asleep. From the edge of the sidewalk he could see the falling shoe of Mr. Sanders, tumbling to the rooftop below.

"Let's go see what that was, John." Sofia said with a twinkle in her eye.

It was a feeling of relief to see her so alive, to be by her side as he was sitting beside her upon the rooftop of Labor Apartment 1A, watching the rising of the Savior. Pointing her finger at the star that streaked through the morning sky, she had a smile that was nearly as bright. As the light of the rising Savior fell upon him, it spoke to him, telling him to take Sofia, to leave the world of Labor behind.

"Let's leave this place," John said to her.

Holding her hand out to him, he grasped it firmly, lifting Sofia up the edge of the steep hill from which they could overlook the valley of trees and rolling hills. The adventure of their lifetime awaited them.

The setting Savior was closing the show of the day with a drapery of pinkish clouds set into an orange mood.

"John," she said. "I'll follow you wherever you go. Always."

Her eyes were so sincere, so watery blue. They were like the ripples of the cold lake that were a bitter relief, as they kept away the pursuing creatures, howling within the fog-coated lands surrounding them. Sofia's lips were trembling, but she fought to keep up with his demands as they waded across the shallow pool, for she loved him so.

"If we find the answers you're looking for, will we return to our home in the woods?" she asked.

"Of course we will," John said, as he thought of the compass sinking to the bottom of the lake. "I promise."

The sloshing of the water diminished behind him. Sofia was standing a ways off, her complexion downcast.

"Where are you going, girl?" John asked.

She looked at him in silence as the doors of the Security transporter closed her in, leaving him alone on the dusty streets of Basket Town.

Through the darkened, back window she continued to stare. Her eyes were so gray, like storm clouds covering the softness of the heavens as they rumbled over the Red Sea.

Sofia was so tranquil in his arms, her head dripping with the crimson waters.

"What did you want to tell me?" he asked.

"This is the day you will find all the answers that you have been seeking, my love," she whispered, as the sheets of death drew over her.

Sofia was lifelessly staring at the Savior as John looked upon his reflection in the blackness of her pupils. Why, he wondered in sorrow, had it taken so much toil for him to realize how much she sacrificed for their relationship, how much she truly meant to him? But he never gave as much in return, although his love for her was equally as strong.

Leaning his forehead into Sofia's, John's tears rolled onto her cold cheeks, dripping into the deep red sea that warmly pooled in the sand beneath them. Closing his eyes he held her tightly. He could not let her go.

"Sofia, my love. I'm so sorry. I'm so terribly sorry."

The battle below was waning fast. The preparatory call for his unit's turn to join in the fray was wailing in his ears. Caressing Sofia's face, John realized that he had lost all awareness of the here and now.

"She's gone, boy," came a familiar voice, monotone and cruel, from the shadow that fell upon him. "And here we are, together again."

John lifted up his swollen eyes to the man he hated more than any other human, living or dead. The Monster stood before him, as wicked as the devil himself.

He had aged quite well. His gray hair was still thick upon his head, and his brow was now creased and wrinkled, a permanence of his evil demeanor. The rifle on his shoulder, the air of courage, the lack of respect for the hot lead randomly tearing through the breeze around him, all of it reeked of that haughty disposition John hated so much about the man.

"You're not going to bring her back," the Monster mumbled, spitting in the sand. "Get up."

Closing his eyes, John could feel the burning redness of his face and the taste of Sofia's salty, tear-diluted blood drying upon his lips.

"Those men out there killed her, John," he said, pointing at the massive formations on the other side of the warzone. "Our people have been fighting them for ages. And today we're going to end it all. Get up. Avenge Sofia's death."

John's eyes opened, and his countenance changed. The feet of the men in his formation were standing among the dead. The moaning of the wounded followed the last crack of a weapon in the distance. Setting Sofia down softly upon the warm sand, John pulled the rifle out from under the back of her arm.

"That's right, boy," his father said as he watched his son rising to his feet.

John's face was like flint, hard and set. His mind was burning, enflamed by the desire to destroy. With everything worth living for consumed in the pages of time, he walked into his formation, pushing his way to the front lines, followed closely behind by the grimacing face of the Monster.

Pulling Sofia's sword from the mound on which she dropped it, John dragged the tip of its blade through the crimson soil, leaving its trail as a wake upon which the Monster was being led. His feet crunched through the dried layers of blood with each progressing step. Like exiting the trees of the forest and entering into the open plains, John and his father stepped out of the formation of war-hungry masses and into the front of the battle line, staring across the corpse-filled field of death. The few remaining wounded were limping and crawling, ankle deep in the coagulated pool that filled the land. They could do nothing but await the commencement of the waves of their own demise.

The Monster was at John's side, but he was no longer accounted as one of the enemy. To his left stood millions of men and women, mostly hungering for the fight. To his right were millions more, anxious to get it on. Across the desert, their reflected image waited in the same preparatory anticipation. Were it not for the agonizing shrill of the dying, silence would be the law.

Sofia was gone. She would never return to John again. There would be no more thoughts of happiness sneaking by, no more feelings of his past to guide him, with the one exception: Sofia's death. The worlds were going to burn today. Men were going to die. And the burning wall of anger reached the apex of its purpose.

The descending airships fell by the thousands to the surface of the planet, touching down behind the awaiting forces of both sides. Delivering the next wave to the warzone, the arriving transporters were the final piece of the machinery needed to bring about the commencement of the call to battle.

In the final moment of silence, the wind fluttered through John's hair, flapping the loose layers of his clothing.

"Vengeance is mine," John shouted.

The roar of the masses resounded upon the surface of the planet as the essence of humanities treacherous ways rushed upon one another, sprinting through the open expanse between ruins and valley, between brother and brother, between flesh and blood. Within his left hand John held Sofia's sword confidently gleaming behind him. With his right hand he raised her rifle at arms length, preparing to pull the trigger with purposeful rage. Soldiers dropped under foot around him, falling to the oncoming clouds of vapor-trailing lead. Squeezing his trigger, heads broke apart, limbs fell, bodies crumbled.

With clouds of dust on their tails, the two armies collided. John thrust his blade into the side of a head, tearing it back out with a crimson bow decorating the air. A burning jolt grabbed his side, sending him into an agonizing spin. Pulling the trigger, he sprayed wildly around him. Thrusting, killing, shouting, killing, tearing, killing, it was the day of violence. It was the end of the era of men without a moral compass.

CHAPTER FORTY-EIGHT

The land was flooded, but not by water. The broken sword supported John as he, like the thousands of other wandering survivors, limped and struggled in the battle's aftermath. His clothes were tattered, appearing as shreds of flesh dangling from his blood-soaked body.

The suction of the warm congelation sifting though the toes of his one bare foot was nauseatingly morose, and he began to vomit as it slid through the loose bones of the dead hidden beneath the collecting thickness. Exasperated and drained of all hydrated substance, he fell splashing to his knees, leaning upon the hilt of his weapon. The suffering screams of the air were too much to bear, and John placed a sticky hand upon his ear attempting to drown out the moans and cries of the dying.

In the glassy red sea flooding about his thighs, the Monster's face stared up from its surface, peering into John's soul. Thrusting his arm towards the man's face, he wanted nothing more, whether the old man was dead or alive, than to tear his eyes out of his skull. As his fist made contact with the ghastly figure, the splattering ripples that grew about his buried hand destroyed the image entirely. And he realized it was not his father he was seeing, but his own reflection.

As he drew his dripping palm back out of the muck, he dropped his head to his chest. Covering his face, he began to cry, "Savior, my Savior. What have I become?"

The roar of the oncoming wave of humanity was rolling in like a storm from before and behind. The bullets were, once again, beginning to fly. The bodies were already starting to fall.

A beam of light from the heavens dropped upon a kneeling soldier, wounded in the battle from which John had also emerged. His hands were lifting to the sky, as if he were pleading for help from an unseen being. Beyond him, towards the ruins, another ray fell upon a distant fighter, then another, then another.

Each stream of light from the Savior was destined for someone. Like roots from the heavens, the branching bars of illumination fell upon the battlefield's crimson lake causing a disturbance in the calm liquid, but no *living* man or woman appeared to be present to receive them. As the two masses of warriors began to converge upon the center of the warzone, the clouds above John parted, and the glowing particles began to settle around him.

The light of the Savior entering into his heart was warm and healing. As if it had taken hold of his soul, rending it from his body, it lifted him up, suspending him between heaven and red soil.

The liberation with which he was feeling was nothing short of absolute serenity. His state of mind was pure. The burning madness of his corporeal time seemed to have been left behind in the transformation. Although he was able to continue to visualize the material world, oddly enough, there was nothing visible in his own person. He had not the hands to rub his eyes, or the feet below to dangle. He was nothing more than *mind*.

The body that once draped over him, corrupted and evil, continued in its prostrate position below until the masses met in the violent collision, and it was trampled under foot in the war of the flesh.

Rising higher into the air, the ruins stood erect to his one side in a concentrated gathering of concrete towers engulfed in flames and smoke. The Valley of Death, shimmering against the reflection of the parting skies, stood to the other side, complete in all its wretchedness. The rows of airships on the outskirts of the warzone had ceased with their transportational activities, as the greatest battle the planet had ever seen was about to come to its end. The lives of the fighters destroying one another, destroying themselves, destroying the worlds, were a lamentable display of the power of greed, and the love of authority.

Reaching a height from which the entire warzone was visible with one glance, John shouted with jubilation as the Land of Blood began to collapse from within. The planet was swallowing itself up, as if to destroy its own murderous face.

From the highest levels of its atmosphere, John was witness to the engulfing of the entire Red Sea and the mountainous regions around it. Floating further away from him, Planet Red became deformed and mutilated, twisting and contorting, like dough in a baker's hands, until it fragmented, drifting within the emptiness of space towards the Savior, its fiery end.

The light of the Great Star was intensifying, but it was not so bright that John could not look into it. The worlds that encircled it fell from their orbits, dropping as leaves drop to the dead grass in the autumn air. Planet Raw rolled by, seemingly an arms length away, allowing John to pass above the surface of its fracturing flatlands, to lay his eyes upon the shattered remnants of its military installation, to glimpse the end of the misery of Basket Town. Its trajectory was on course with Red: a place in the burning pyre at the center of life.

The velocity at which the other planets were traveling towards him was too wonderful for words, yet terrifying in the glory of the power of the Savior. Planet Blue exploded into an immeasurable display of dust and glittering particles before being lit up with the brightness of its destruction in the Savior's awaiting arms.

The screams of the selfish men and women of Golden could be heard for a final, brief moment of time, before being suddenly cut off as it fell into the ocean of fire.

Like the splitting shell of an egg, a circumferential fracture line sent Black Island's shroud of mystery to its death, leaving Black Heart exposed for the first time. Gliding ever so slowly to its scorching finality, it melted like a candle and evaporated into fine mist.

Having consumed the seven worlds, the Savior had become the sole body of the heavens, a mass of purity at the heart of the universe. No more would mankind be allowed to destroy itself. Those days were gone forever.

A new planet, fashioned after His essence, clean and bright, emerged from the blaze of glory, stretching out from the Savior's surface, full of the lands of green and plenty, filled with abundance. It is a world fit for His dominion.

As if the invisible chords holding John in place had suddenly been cut, releasing him from his stationary point floating in space, he began to freefall towards the newly created sphere. The rushing sensation of falling was exhilarating, liberating and eternally satisfying to his being.

As if all his sensations of the material world were being granted a return, like dipping into a warm bath, John entered the atmosphere of planet Rest. Falling gently towards the surface several kilometers below, his heart was lost to his terrible past, and created anew.

A wonder of sights and sounds came into his mind as he was renewed in spirit. The land began to take on a sudden energy of life as the trees of the forests individualized, and the beauty of the City of Light came into view. Living among its marvelous structure of golden glass, the masses of those granted with life became more distinct with each passing moment. The beasts of the fields were living harmoniously with the peace of the age. The wars were nonexistent, the hatred gone and the love of man prevailed under the veil of the Light of the World.

A grassy knoll, hidden within a valley of lush green, surrounded by towering mountains of inviting soul, was the setting in which a mother and her child had been guided, brought here to await John's arrival.

Sofia was alive, youthful and innocent, as in the days of their Savior gazing. The brightness of life was falling upon her as she cast her blue eyes to the skies above. Behind her, among a grove of trees, the child, so full and energetic, climbed and played.

Calling to him, Sofia pointed towards John, directing her child to look upon the formations of cottony clouds above. He immediately ran to her side, gazing into the vastness of the heavens. His smile was like hers: joyful and content. John wondered if they were able, somehow, to see him, as he had no material substance of which to speak.

As he neared the surface of the planet, Sofia and the child drew near, and the grass began to part, exposing the deep, rich soil beneath.

At a distance from which his toes should have been able to reach it, the dirt arose in twisting spirals, like a rising plume of smoke, forming the bones and the cartilage, the muscles and the skin, of his legs. His spinal column began to take shape, wrapping about his organs with his ribs, his arms and his chest plate. Covering over by the guidance of the light, the flesh was renewed, unscarred, regenerated in purity.

As his skull took form and his eyes welled up in his sockets, his external features were newly refashioned. He was as he had been so long ago: innocent.

John's eyes opened and he drew in his first breath. Sofia was there, waiting for him as she had always said she would be. She and the child ran to him, wrapping her arms around his neck, holding him tightly. Embracing his son for the first time, John finally looked into his little boy's eyes. They were like looking into tiny windows, and seeing the sky beyond.

The New World was eternal, its marvels and wonders so vast and expansive. Citizens of a new age, John and Sofia were now free to wander where death and darkness were no longer permitted. They were strangers and foreigners no more. Mr. Sanders was there with his wife. John would one day meet her, but not today. As with Stephen and Maryanne, he and Sofia had an eternity to converse with them. But, this day was meant for each other... and their child.

A streak of light, like that of a wishing star, fell from the heavens, disappearing beyond the cordillera in the distance, a glancing blow at the side of Sofia's eye. She turned to John with an inquisitive expression, a twinkling of curiosity.

"Did you see something?" she said, with a hint of adventure.

Placing his hand gently upon her cheek, John turned her face away from the mountains and back to him.

"No," he said, shaking his head, "I didn't see anything."

Taking her by the hand, they turned their backs to the path of the mysterious light, content with the love that their life's adventure had finally brought them.

They were home. Home forever.

.

The End

www.ingramcontent.com/pod-product-compliance
Lightning Source LLC
Chambersburg PA
CBHW030236030726
47493CB00022B/79